THE BARKERVILLE MURDERS

JOHN GRANVILLE AND EMILY TURNER HISTORICAL MYSTERIES

MYSTERIES

BOOK EIGHT

SHARON ROWSE

THREE CEDARS PRESS

THE BARKERVILLE MURDERS

A John Granville & Emily Turner Historical Mystery

By Sharon Rowse

ISBN: 978-1988037-479

ALSO BY SHARON ROWSE

The John Granville & Emily Turner Historical Mystery Series: (in order)

The Silk Train Murder

The Lost Mine Murders

The Missing Heir Murders

The Terminal City Murders

The Cannery Row Murders

The Hidden City Murders

The Dockside Murders

The Barbara O'Grady Series: (in order)

Death of a Secret

Death of a Threat

Death of a Promise

Death of a Shadow

Death of a Lie

Death of a Dream

Death of a Chance

Want to know out more? Or be the first to find out when Sharon's next book is coming out?

Check out her website at: www.sharonrowse.com

CHAPTER 1

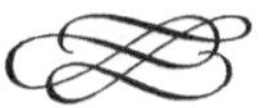

John Granville was just finishing up for the day when there was a rattle at the outer office door followed by a firm rapping on the frosted glass. He glanced at his desk calendar and frowned. He wasn't expecting anyone.

Miss Kent, their typewriter and receptionist, must have locked up as she left, following her usual custom. She'd turned off the overhead lights as well, leaving only a desk lamp on the reception desk to cut the gloom of an October evening. She would not have done either if Granville and Scott Investigations had any further appointments booked.

That forceful knock came again. Whoever it was, he was determined. And must have noticed the light still on in Granville's office.

Curious now, Granville put his pen back in the penholder and dusted fine sand over his notes to set them. Striding down the hall and into the main office, he flipped on the electric overhead lights as he did so. It was colder in the main room, he noted, and wondered in passing if the boilers that heated the offices had gone down again. But since the mercury was predicted to remain well above freezing overnight, that was a problem that would wait for the morning.

He flung open the door, and eyed the well-dressed man standing in the hallway on the other side, hand raised to knock again. Dark-haired, mid-forties, confident and wearing a suit every bit as expensive as Granville's own. And carrying a sleek leather briefcase. Not their usual after hours client.

"Can I help you?" Granville asked, his tone deceptively smooth.

"I hope so," the other man said, giving him an assessing look. "John Granville?"

"Yes. And you are…?"

"Stephen Robertson," the other man said, holding out a hand. "Of San Francisco. William Foster of Pinkerton's gave me your name, said you're the man to talk to."

Granville shook hands, approving of the firm grip that didn't turn a greeting into a contest.

"Come in," he said, stepping back. "I'd offer you coffee, but as you can see I'm the only one here."

"I apologize for the late hour," Robertson said. "Normally I'd have made an appointment, but I've been putting this off for too long now. I have to head back home tonight, and I had a few hours free. So when I saw your lights, I took a chance."

Intrigued now, Granville waved off the apology. "Come into my office and you can tell me what the problem is."

Robertson held up a hand. "Let me make up for the late hour by buying you dinner. We can talk there."

"There's no need for that," Granville said.

"You'd be doing me a favor. I have a ticket for the ten o'clock train, and I'd appreciate a hearty meal first. Know any good steakhouses nearby?"

"I know a few of them," Granville said. "Some of them are grander than others."

"Don't let this suit fool you," Robertson said with a grin. "As long as I make that train, the only thing I care about is the quality of the steak. And the bloodier, the better."

"I know just the place," Granville said, returning the grin.

"And bring a blank contract," his would-be client said.

GRANVILLE and his potential client walked in comfortable silence the few blocks to Garrity's Steakhouse. He could smell wood smoke, chrysanthemums and fallen leaves on the breeze. The scent of autumn.

It was the last week of October and already the aspen leaves were sticking wetly to the board sidewalks. Despite the rainstorm that afternoon, that first hint of frost teased the air. Winter would come early this year.

Walking into the restaurant, he welcomed the sudden warmth and the rich aromas of grilling steak and frying bacon. The place itself was plain enough, with raw plank walls and floors, but they'd recently added upholstered benches, it was spotlessly clean and they made the best steaks in town.

Robertson paused in the doorway, and drew in a deep breath. Then shot Granville a wide smile

"My kinda place," he said. "I'm hoping that bacon I smell means they know how to do a proper baked potato."

"They do indeed," Granville said, catching the cook's eye and holding up two fingers. He glanced around the half-full room, then led the way to a booth in the back. "Steak's not bad, either."

Robertson followed him, and Granville felt his would-be client's eyes on his back, taking in every move he made.

The contradictions in the fellow puzzled him. Robertson's suit and his language said he was well-off, but walking into the cafe, he had the wary eyes and alert look of someone who had fought hard to reach the place he was now.

"I'll have to thank my contact at Pinkerton's for the recommendation," Robertson said as they slid into opposite sides of the booth Granville had chosen.

"Oh?" Granville said, well aware the fellow wasn't talking about the food. Robertson had been evaluating Granville every bit as much as Granville had been evaluating him. And he evidently hadn't missed the fact that the booth Granville had chosen was isolated enough to talk privately, while commanding a clear view of the room.

Before Robertson could respond, a lanky lad slapped two whiskeys and a small ice bucket in front of them. "Evening, sirs," he said. "Cook says your steaks will be right up."

"Cheers," Robertson said once the boy was gone. He took a deep swallow of whiskey, then placed the glass carefully in front of him before looking up.

"I want you to find a missing person," he said. "Or find out what happened to him. And it isn't going to be easy."

Granville had an odd feeling that nothing about Robertson's case was going to be easy. "Does this fellow have a name?" he asked.

"Thomas Robertson," was the answer. "My father."

"How long has your father been missing?"

"Thirty-two years," Robertson said. The words came out hard, Robertson's expression set. "We last heard from him in 1868. I was fourteen that year."

"Thirty-two years," Granville said slowly. And the fellow was just looking for him now?

It was going to be one of those cases. After that much time, the odds were stacked against finding anything, never mind the fellow's missing father.

"Yes," Robertson said, as if he'd been asked a question. And he took another swig of his whiskey.

The look on his face told Granville the fellow knew exactly what he was thinking. "And where was your father thirty-two years ago?"

"Barkerville," Robertson said. "Chasing gold."

Granville had heard of Barkerville. Founded during the Cariboo Gold Rush, the town had sprung up almost overnight in 1862, when Billy Barker struck gold at forty feet down. At the time it was the single richest gold strike in the province, and miners flocked to William's Creek.

At least the town was still standing, if not exactly thriving. That was something. A lot of the boomtowns that had sprung up when gold was found had vanished into dust and ruins not even ten years later.

"Tell me," he said.

Robertson swallowed more whiskey. "I was ten when he left. Old enough to help my mother take care of our small ranch outside Seattle, while my father signed on to drive cattle north to the Cariboo. It was good money in those days. Gold miners ate a lot of beef, it seems. And we needed the money to see us through the winter."

Granville did a quick calculation. "This was 1863?"

"Yes. He left in the early summer of that year," Robertson said.

Granville could guess where this was heading. "Your father caught gold fever."

"Yes. He was lucky at first, if you can call it that," Robertson said with a bitter laugh. "He found some small nuggets right off. There were a few letters. He even managed to send money. We got the last letter in late 1868, though it was postmarked that spring. Then, nothing."

"Fourteen is a hard age to lose your father. You grow up in a hurry."

"At first I was worried. Then I got angry." Robertson drained his whiskey, signaled for another. "It was the not knowing that was the worst."

"What did his last letter say?"

"His latest venture had come to nothing, but he had hopes of a new strike. He sounded delusional, frankly. Promising riches beyond our wildest dreams."

"Was your father a dreamer?"

Robertson shook his head. "No. He was hard-headed, practical. That's why I've never understood how he could have abandoned us like that."

Their food was delivered then, perfectly cooked steak, potatoes brimming with sour cream and bacon chunks, and two more whiskies. There was silence for a moment as both of them dug in.

Granville was the one to break it.

"Gold fever's a funny thing," he said. "I've seen down-to-earth, practical men who are sane in every other sense, utterly consumed by the lust for gold. And certain that their fortune is about to be made with the next claim, the next shovel of dirt or pan of gravel."

Robertson stared at him. "I've known gamblers like that," he said after a moment. "Never thought of gold mining that way."

"You wouldn't expect it," Granville said. "The work's too hard, you're fighting cold and starvation every day. Some give up right away. But the ones who don't, well, the harder they fight for that perfect strike, the more convinced they are that it's out there for them."

He gave a rueful laugh. "I should know. It took me long enough to quit chasing that dream."

Robertson gave him a surprised look. "You were a gold miner?"

"Klondike," Granville said with a grin. "Eighteen months of the coldest, dirtiest job in the world. Never found enough gold to make it worthwhile, but it took me that long to finally admit defeat. Sometimes I still miss it."

"Why?"

Granville nearly didn't answer, but something in Robertson's expression, maybe a hint of the young boy whose father had never come home, made him do so.

"It's not just the lure of gold, or the chance for more money than you know what to do with," he said softly. "It's pitting yourself against something so much stronger and older than you are. Looking for gold, you're going places no-one's gone before. It's beautiful out there—and cold. And deadly."

Robertson just shook his head. "Ranching was hard. And cold. And dirty. There was beauty in the land, but you fought the elements every single day. And I got out of there first chance I got."

"You don't look like someone who would enjoy ranching," Granville said. Robertson had the sharp eyes and uncalloused hands of a businessman. And ranching had likely been the father's dream, not the son's.

"No. While Pa—my father—was away, it was hard, but we just had to keep holding on. For him. We had just enough money, with the bit he sent us, to see us through until he got back. Then the letters stopped. We didn't know what had happened to him."

Robertson raised his glass, draining half of it. "My mother never recovered, especially after we lost the ranch."

And now the son was a successful businessman, one who looked as if he'd never even seen a ranch. There was a story there.

"Why search for him now?" Granville asked. Was he hoping to find his father alive? After thirty-two years?

"There was no money before. And after my mother died, it didn't seem to matter," Robertson said. "But I have my own family now, and enough money to indulge what is probably a wasted search. And my own son is turning fourteen just before Christmas. Watching him…"

He paused, shook his head. "I find I need to know what happened to my own father. Did he die? Or did he abandon us for some other reason?"

"After this long, there may be nothing to find," Granville said. "Gold-rush towns appear and disappear like the gold seams themselves. And the miners, and any information they may have had, vanish with them."

"I'm prepared to take that risk," Robertson said. He flipped open his gold pocket watch, glanced at it. "But now, I'm afraid I have a train to catch. Will you take the case?"

There wasn't much to go on, and the odds of finding anything after all this time were slim. But something in Robertson's story had touched him. And since it was a Pinkerton's referral, taking the case could only help his business.

Besides, Granville had heard the stories about the golden dream that was Barkerville. He was curious. Both about the town itself, and about what might have enticed a rancher and a father away from his family for so long. Had it been dreams of gold? Or had there been something else?

"I'll need all the details you have," Granville said. "But the search will be costly. We have little to go on. And I can't guarantee results. We may find nothing at all. Or nothing but bad news."

"I appreciate that, but I need to know," Robertson said. He opened his briefcase and drew out a slim file and an embossed leather check book.

"Everything I know is here," he said, tapping the file. "I've written out a timeline, and everything I can remember. I've also included his letters, just as we received them. I'd like those back, no matter what you find."

Robertson opened his check book. "Name your price."

CHAPTER 2

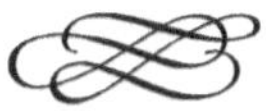

Friday, October 26, 1900

On Friday morning, Emily glanced at the heavy clouds and the rain sliding down her bedroom window and grimaced. It was going to be one of those days, chilly and damp, where you started the day wet and never quite felt dry. The sooner she got to the office and immersed herself in her current case the better.

Dressing quickly in her favorite navy suit, she quietly made her way down the stairs to their cozy breakfast parlor. Mama and her eldest sister Jane sat at the end of the table nearest the fire, chatting as they ate the pancakes with homemade blackberry compote that were one of Cook's specialties.

Smiling a greeting at both of them, Emily limited herself to a quick breakfast of tea and toast, along with a poached egg from the warming plate kept ready on the sideboard. She didn't want to be trapped in the small parlor for too long, not when she'd recognized that glint in Mama's eyes. The one that said she wanted to discuss wedding plans.

Emily's wedding plans, to be precise.

A month ago, Emily would have been all too pleased to discuss them. When it had seemed that Jane's wedding plans would mean a three or even four year delay in her own wedding, she'd begun to realize that she didn't want to wait even another year to be married to Granville. And she'd given a lot of thought to how best to raise that subject with Mama.

Then Jane's plans had vanished—along with her fiancé—an outcome Emily had helped along, encouraged by Mama. Once Mr. Bray had been exposed for the charlatan he was, even Jane had been relieved he was gone from her life.

Emily had breathed a sigh of relief, and things had got back to normal. Except for one small problem.

It seemed that all the energy Mama had built up in pretending to plan Jane's elaborate wedding had been transferred to planning Emily's very real wedding to Granville. An event that grew more elaborate by the minute, with a timeline that stretched further and further into the future. Mama seemed determined to stage an event that was going to make society forget all about Mr. Bray.

The thought of having to participate in something so elaborate set Emily's teeth on edge. And the idea of waiting for what seemed forever to finally marry her own fiancé? It made no sense. But any attempt to talk sense to Mama had failed.

Emily had even tried to bring up the possibility of a spring wedding, which her mother had happily embraced. But unfortunately Mama had completely ignored the idea of changing the wedding to *this* spring. Instead she'd added yet another six months to her own timeframe.

Emily was still trying to work out if that meant she'd be marrying Granville in two and a half years, or did that make it three and a half? Either was much too long.

And there was no reasoning with Mama. She didn't even seem to hear anything Emily said. So Emily was reduced to avoiding any situation where she'd be forced to have a wedding discussion with Mama. At least until she came up with another strategy.

She hadn't even told Granville about Mama's latest wedding delays. Not when they'd both thought the cancellation of her sister's wedding had solved that problem. And not when she'd half-promised him they'd be married next spring.

She needed to work out another solution first.

She'd been too discouraged by it all to even tell her best friend, Clara Miles, of the latest developments. And Clara could well have some ideas that might help. Other than eloping, which had been her previous—and impractical—suggestion.

As Mama and Jane sipped their tea and discussed every detail of a recent wedding, Emily made polite "I'm listening" noises while finishing her breakfast as quickly as possible. Then she'd made her excuses and fled to the hallway.

Buttoning up the fine wool coat she'd bought a few weeks before, Emily pulled on the galoshes that fit over her half-boots. Adjusting the navy hat Clara had insisted matched her coat perfectly, Emily put up her umbrella and stepped out to face the heavy downpour.

It was far too wet to walk, but at least it wasn't windy, she thought as she waited for the tram to take her the few blocks to the office. She absolutely hated those gusty days when the wind blew the rain right in under her umbrella, no matter how she held it. Or worse, just blew her umbrella inside out. Either way, she'd arrive at the office dripping and spitting like a wet cat.

Today she'd just be damp and chilled to the bone. Which was an improvement, if you looked at it right.

DESCENDING from the crowded interior of the tram, Emily dashed through the double doors so she wouldn't have to put her umbrella up again. Then she walked carefully across the marble of the lobby. It was so easy to slip on the wet stone. She nodded a greeting to the small group waiting for the elevator to descend, and chose to take the stairs. It was only two flights, and the slow ascent in an elevator crammed with dripping people was not going to improve her mood.

With a feeling of relief, Emily turned the brass door handle and pushed open the heavy outer door of their office. Stepping inside, she stopped short, and drew in a quick breath. Something felt different.

Yesterday had been a perfectly normal day, with several minor cases wrapping up. This morning, though, it felt like there was electricity buzzing in the air. She could almost taste that sharp scent that comes just after a lightning bolt.

Yet everything looked quiet. Aside from Marie Rizzo, their receptionist, the front office was deserted. Emily smiled at Marie and glanced around. Granville's door was closed, which was unusual at this hour, and there was no sign of Scott. Or Trent.

"Is there a meeting?" Emily asked casually as she dropped her dripping umbrella into the stand and removed her boot covers.

Marie smiled. "Not an official meeting, at least," she said with a significant glance.

Emily nodded back. That confirmed her own feeling that something was up.

"A new case, then?" she asked, feeling a little zing of excitement at the thought.

With the Puppet Master out of the way, they had been enjoying nearly a month of uncomplicated cases. The period of relative calm had been welcome after the strain of that case, but Emily had to admit to herself it had begun to feel a tad…boring.

Not a word she'd ever thought to apply to her work with Granville and the others, but those complex, difficult cases were exciting. It felt good to challenge their skills against whatever bad guys lurked out there.

Emily hid a grin. Granville would say that she'd read too many penny dreadfuls and that the detective business was not really like that most of the time. While Clara would simply roll her eyes and drag her off to a milliner's shop or some such nonsense. Which admittedly would make their current cases seem more exciting by contrast. Clara knew her too well.

And increasingly, so did Granville. Which both pleased and worried her, so she put the thought aside.

"Nothing has been announced," Marie said, leaning forward.

Then with a rare slip of her professional demeanor, she added with a half-smile, "And you would probably hear about a new case before the rest of us, anyway."

That was generally true. Most evenings Granville would telephone her, especially if something interesting came up. They'd developed a kind of code for talking about cases over a party line where anyone might be listening in.

Yet last night he hadn't called. So perhaps it wasn't a new case. But what else could it be?

Before she could analyze that thought, Granville's office door opened and Trent Davis bounced into the reception area. "I'll be out for the day," he told Marie grandly. "Errands."

Suddenly noticing Emily standing near the door, he gave her a brief, slightly panicked nod.

She knew that look. Something was definitely up. "I have several errands too," Emily told him cheerily. "Why don't I accompany you, at least partway?"

"Sorry. No time," he said, grabbing his jacket and cap from the walnut coat rack, and dashing for the door before she could answer.

Frowning slightly, Emily watched the door close behind him, then turned to survey the office again. "Where are the others this morning?"

"In the back room," Marie said. "There's tea made. Would you like a cup?"

Emily looked at Granville's door, now slightly ajar. If a closed door sent one message, that partly open door could be considered an invitation, couldn't it?

"Thank you, but not just yet," she told her. Hanging up her coat and hat, she shook out her long skirts so that they fell smoothly over her elegant half-boots, and headed straight for Granville's office.

CHAPTER 3

GRANVILLE AND SCOTT WERE STANDING ON THE FAR SIDE OF HIS office, where several large maps were pinned to the wall. Emily couldn't quite tell which map they were looking at, but it likely wasn't the Vancouver map, given the direction of their gazes. It had to be the large map of the province, with its contour lines, scattered towns, and few roads.

"A new case?" she asked as she pushed the door wider and stepped into the room. "And out of town?"

Granville turned and smiled at her. "Good morning," he said. "Not exactly. We were just talking about gold rushes."

"Gold rushes?" It wasn't what she had expected to hear.

He smiled, and traced a finger along the line on the map that represented the Fraser River. "Gold. All up and down this river, for nearly fifty years, from what Scott tells me."

She nodded, and moved to stand beside him. "The Fraser River rush. Hill's Bar. Boston Bar. Kanaka Bar," she said, and touched her finger to each spot along the Fraser Canyon. "Then the Cariboo." Sliding her finger north. "Quesnel Forks. Richfield. Barkerville. Each find richer than the last."

"I didn't expect you'd know about them," Scott said in surprise. "These mines were finished long before you were born."

"People still tell stories of the gold rush days in British Columbia," Emily said. "And every summer there are those who stock up and go searching for gold that still lies undiscovered. Like all those who looked for the Lost Mine you were hired to find last winter."

Granville gave her a sharp look. "You won't convince me you're one of them. So who is it tells those stories now?"

Emily smiled at him. "Papa."

She'd grown up on them, the stories of the mad rush to those gold creeks and the men who'd followed that lure.

Granville frowned. "Really? Your father does?"

"He does indeed."

"Was he part of this?" Granville asked, waving his hand towards the map on the wall.

Emily laughed at the look on his face. "No. Papa was fifteen and living in Toronto with his family when they found gold on the Fraser. From the way he talks about it, he was mad for the adventure of it all, but too young to join the gold seekers. By the later rushes, he was already working for the CPR and focused on his career. He followed every newspaper report on the goldfields, though, and kept most of them. Get him to show you, some day."

Granville was nodding, as if that made sense to him. There seemed to be something about the lure of gold that those who had felt it never quite got over, Emily thought, watching her fiancé's face in fascination.

"Did he ever go gold hunting?" Granville asked.

"No. Once he was working for the CPR, I don't think Papa even considered seeking gold himself. They don't have the proper hotels in a gold field, after all," Emily said with a wry smile. "But it still holds a fascination for him, you can see it in his eyes when he talks about it.

And there are old-timers around who, for the price of a beer, are happy to re-live every step of their search for gold. Now and again, Papa will seek them out. He can tell you the story of each site, and locate every single strike on each of them. On a map."

Scott was staring at her, as if trying to reconcile the stout railway manager who had been his and Granville's boss for a short time last year with what she was saying.

"Why hasn't he, then?" Scott said. "He's never even mentioned it."

"You're just lucky he's never asked you about your time in the Klondike," Emily said.

"He did mention the Klondike rush to me, just the once," Granville said. "Something about he'd never understood what all the fuss was about, when there were perfectly good mines here." He gave Emily a wry smile. "I suppose I should have guessed."

She nodded, gave him a wicked grin. "You should indeed."

He winked at her.

Scott rolled his eyes. "Enough, you two. This is a place of business."

Emily looked from one to the other. "So it is. And speaking of business, why are you looking at gold rush sites?"

She nearly asked again if there was a new case, but managed to hold back her curiosity. Better to let them tell her in their own way.

Unless for some reason Granville didn't want her involved this time? She pushed back the unwelcome thought. He wouldn't do that.

It was just this air of suppressed excitement that seemed to hang in the air around them. They were excited about something, and it felt as if they were trying to keep it from showing.

Scott tapped a fingernail at a small dot about halfway up and nearly in the center of the map. "Barkerville," he said.

Emily took in a sharp breath. Barkerville? Really?

When she'd been very small, her father used to sometimes sit for a time after dinner, and tell them stories of those gold rushes. Of all those tales, the ones of Billy Barker and his unlikely claim had fascinated her the most.

And now they had a case there?

"Home of the single richest claim in the Cariboo," Granville was saying.

"And the biggest gold town," Scott added.

As if she didn't know that. "So Papa has told me," Emily said. "But that was in its heyday, back in the 1860's."

She paused, and looked from one man the other. "Does that mean we have a case there?"

And a chance to visit Barkerville?

The two men exchanged glances, and Emily suddenly wondered if her earlier fear was so irrational after all.

"We do have a possible case," Granville said.

"Oh?" Emily said. And waited.

"A missing person," Scott said. "Last heard of in Barkerville."

She looked from one to the other. Neither man's face showed any expression. Which wasn't like either of them. "When was this missing person last seen?" she asked suspiciously.

Granville shot a grin at Scott. "Told you she wouldn't miss that."

Scott rolled his eyes. Again.

"Well?" Emily asked, hiding a smile of her own. This was more like them.

"1868," Granville told her.

More than thirty years ago. What was he thinking? "You don't really expect to find someone who has been missing that long, do you?"

"No. But that's the thing. Our client doesn't expect us to find him—not alive, anyway. He simply wants to know what happened to him."

Well, at least that made a little more sense. "Still, it may not even be possible after so long. And it certainly won't be easy. I don't understand why you would take this on?"

But after he'd explained about Stephen Robertson and his missing father, she did understand.

Until Granville and Scott exchanged glances again.

She glared at her fiancé. "What aren't you telling me?" Emily asked.

But it was Scott who answered. "Our client is hoping for answers before Christmas, if at all possible," he said.

Emily stared at him for a moment. "What? He wants you to go north in the middle of winter? And to that area? Why?"

But when Granville explained about the son's birthday, she could only nod. There was really nothing to say to that. "When would you leave?"

"As soon as we can assemble the information and the supplies we need," Granville said. "It is the only way to be sure we will return in time for Christmas."

It would be their first Christmas as an engaged couple, Emily thought. She hadn't expected to spend the months leading up to it apart from him. She cringed at the thought of Mama's reaction to Granville's absence from the most 'important' balls of the winter season. But she could deal with Mama.

The hard part would be worrying about what Granville might be facing—what all three of them might face. Because of course, he'd take Scott and Trent with him on this adventure.

And she'd give anything to be able to go with them.

She looked from him to Scott and back again. "What would it take to change your minds?" she asked them both.

"If we learn the journey is impossible at this time of year," Granville said.

"As it would have been in the early days of the gold rush," Scott added. "Before the Cariboo Wagon Road went through, and made the stagecoach route possible."

"And is the route passable now?" Emily asked. She realized as she asked that she knew far too much about the hazards of the 1860's route to Barkerville and very little about what it might be like now. It was an odd feeling.

Again that exchange of glances. "According to the information we have so far, travel to the area should be safe enough this time of year," Granville said. "We've sent Trent to confirm what he can about the route."

He was holding something back, she could tell. And that air of suppressed excitement still lay over both of them. It seemed she was not the only one growing a little tired of mundane cases. Like it or not, their detective agency had become one that specialized in challenging cases. And once the relief of successfully completing a particularly difficult case wore off, they all grew just a little bored.

She frowned at Granville. "This trip you're planning? It will be just the three of you?"

Knowing exactly what she was asking, he nodded. "I'm afraid so. From what I know so far, the hardships of this particular journey at this time of year are still too much for any woman. Even you. I'm sorry."

She could tell he meant it, too. He would take her if he could.

But Emily didn't quite believe the journey would be too hard for her. Not when it was Barkerville. A chance to see that legendary place was worth a little hardship.

There were all those fascinating stories of the women mountaineers who had been conquering higher and higher peaks in the Rocky Mountains over the past few years. Many of the climbs were done in summer, but a few had been in the depth of winter. If they could do it, she could certainly face a winter journey in a stagecoach. Or a sleigh, if the snow was deep enough.

And she'd always been intrigued by the notion of traveling the wilder lands in winter. Granville's own tales of surviving the goldfields in winter—despite the hardships—had rung with the beauty of the land and the exhilaration of surviving against whatever the elements could throw at him. She couldn't help comparing that to the restrictions of her own life. It had been a fight just to be allowed to ride a bicycle in Stanley Park.

And she had never been truly challenged, not like that. For once, she'd like to face that kind of situation. Perhaps this would be her opportunity?

A glance at Granville's set expression told her it wouldn't be that easy. And in any case, as an unmarried lady, she couldn't travel unchaperoned—not even with her fiancé. And she had to hide a grin at the thought of trying to persuade Clara to accompany her north in November. Flying poodles would be more likely.

No, Granville would get to go off on his adventure, while she was left home, bored and cut off from any word of him. Which sounded awful.

She cast a glance at Granville from under her lashes. There had to be a way. She just needed to think on it a bit.

CHAPTER 4

On Monday morning Granville got to the office early. Shaking the rain off his damp overcoat, he turned up the heat a little, grateful for the warmth on a cold and blustery day. He grinned a little at the thought.

He'd become soft. It was a good thing this case was taking him north again. From what he'd learned so far about winter in the Cariboo, the trip was likely to freeze the softness right out of him.

If Scott didn't tease it out of him first.

The idea of a case taking them to Barkerville intrigued him. But a thirty-two year old case? He had never heard of anyone working a case that old. If they were going to succeed, they needed to think like the missing man.

Whom they knew almost nothing about. Only the words in the few letters he'd managed to send home, all of which were postmarked Barkerville. He'd mentioned very few people, most of them only by nicknames or initials, and made a few cryptic comments about where he was and what he was doing.

It was clear he was searching for gold, but he was cagey about location. The last letter, though? That one said he had hopes of a new strike, and "riches beyond his wildest dreams". With not even a hint of where that might be.

No, to find Thomas Robertson, they'd need to learn more about Barkerville and the Cariboo in general in the 1860's; about the gold rush itself, and about the miners and the communities they'd built along the gold bearing rivers and streams. Without that knowledge, they wouldn't begin to know where to look for a man who had vanished so long ago.

He was looking forward to the challenge.

But first they had to get to Barkerville, where Thomas Robertson's very cold trail began. And there wasn't a lot of time, not with over-night temperatures already below freezing in the region. If they were going to do this at all, the sooner they began their journey north, the better.

Granville frowned at the stack of papers collecting on his desk. He, Scott and Trent had been busy during the weekend researching their trip. Tickets, maps, the beginning of lists for everything from provisions to train and stage coach schedules to information from the Cariboo old timers who now lived in Vancouver.

Those early miners had happily shared information on the temperatures they could expect, the best routes to take and the schedules for those routes, as well as stories of killer frosts, rain swollen streams and raging rivers. It wasn't easy country, and they'd been warned that they ignored that fact at their peril. The Cariboo might not be as obviously hostile as the Klondike had been, but it could be just as dangerous.

Between the old timers' tales and the newspaper archives, they'd begun to learn what they could about Barkerville as it had been more than thirty years ago, as well as how it was now. But not one of the men they'd talked to remembered meeting or even hearing of a Thomas Robertson.

Which probably wasn't surprising, given the number of would-be miners who had descended on what quickly became the town of Barkerville, from every corner of the world. But it wasn't encouraging, either. This was not going to be an easy case.

It didn't help that nick-names were common along the creeks, just as they had been in the Klondike. Miners nicknamed "Big Jim" and "Little Jim" might not even be named Jim or even James. And their fellow miners often knew them only by their nickname.

He glared at the stack of papers they'd collected. He had a feeling they'd be chasing a lot of dead ends before they found the answers their client needed. They would need a plan. So he'd best begin one.

An hour later, Granville sat back, glancing from the departure plan he'd put together to the neatly stacked piles on his desktop, each with a note for one of his team, directing him or her on the next step needed.

The three of them would take the train to Ashcroft on Monday next, the fourth of November. The BX Express Stage-coach route that connected with Barkerville departed from Ashcroft on Tuesdays.

For a mad moment on Saturday, he'd considered trying to leave earlier, perhaps hire a private coach, just to get ahead of the weather. But there was still too much they didn't know about what they'd be facing. Even if they'd been ready, he quickly learned that the drivers of the BX, as it was known, were considered the experts in the area.

"Even if you could find someone crazy enough to take you, they don't have the knowledge or the resources the BX does," he heard over and over. "It'd take longer, if you got there at all."

Remembering the bitter winter weather he'd faced in the Klondike, and the men who'd died because they were unprepared, he fought back the urge to take the risk and get underway. If they were taking this case, they would do it right.

And as he'd reviewed the information they'd been given about the weather they could expect in the Cariboo in November, December and January, he made himself another promise. If the three of them hadn't found the answers they needed by the fifteenth of December, they would turn back. No matter what.

The last thing they needed was to face the unforgiving January weather. And he couldn't bear the thought of being the one responsible for Trent's death. Or Scott's. All because they were chasing a client's need for answers.

He didn't want to let Emily down, either, by missing his first Christmas with her as an engaged couple. But if something happened and he had to do so, she would understand. As long as he made sure all three of them came back alive and well.

With his plan firmly in mind, Granville intended to spend this next week making very sure they'd gathered everything they'd need, including supplies and more detailed maps of the area. And more stories of Barkerville in its heyday. It was a little daunting, but exhilarating at the same time. He'd missed that feeling of pitting himself against the worst of the weather.

He hated the idea of leaving Emily for so long—he was going to miss her. But it couldn't be helped. And she'd likely be busy with Christmas plans, as well as getting dragged into her mother's plans for their too-often delayed wedding, in any case.

She wouldn't be happy about the schedule he had in mind, but she'd understand.

He hoped.

Granville heard the outer door opening and glanced at his pocket watch. Still early. The voices in the lobby, raised in what sounded like a heated argument, had him grinning. Scott and Trent. Good. There was a lot to discuss yet, including the risks they might face. It wasn't too late to contact Robertson and turn down the case.

He stood up and grabbed his hat and overcoat. If those two were arguing already, they were probably hungry. And he had a hankering for one of Mary's big breakfasts, since he hadn't eaten this morning, having yet to hire a cook. He'd have to do something about that, one of these days.

CHAPTER 5

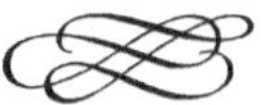

Mary's Cafe was warm and steamy, with condensation running down the big windows that faced the street. It smelled of bacon frying and good coffee, and was as busy and as raucous as ever. Granville was pleased to see a group of dockworkers just leaving the big booth in the far corner that was their usual favorite, and he sent Trent ahead to stake their claim before anyone else did so.

As they passed the counter, he waved at Mary behind the till, and she yelled something to the cook. Their regular order of eggs, bacon, flapjacks and coffee was on its way.

Granville slid into the booth opposite Scott and Trent, and began filling them in on the planning he'd done that morning, and the questions it had raised for him. Before he'd even finished, steaming plates of food were placed in front of each of them. He nodded his thanks to the waitress as she rapidly poured the coffee.

"Well, I don't see why you'd even consider turning this case down," Trent said, his fork already halfway to his mouth. He was scowling at Granville and seemed oblivious to the egg yolk dripping onto the table.

Granville bit back a grin, which would only annoy the lad further. It was a good thing he hadn't decided to eat somewhere fancier. At Mary's, none of the diners were interested in anything other than their own meals.

"Remind me never to take you to Stroh's," he said. The idea of Trent waving his food around on a fork at Emily's favorite tea shop amused him.

"What?" Trent asked. But at least he looked puzzled, instead of furious. "Is Emily there?"

So he did know about Stroh's. Interesting, Granville thought, wondering how that had come about.

"No, I expect she'll be in the office shortly," Granville said. "And I'd prefer it if we could finalize our plans before we return there."

And before he had to tell Emily he'd be leaving next week, and that he might be gone for more than a month.

Trent suddenly sat back, putting his fork down carefully. "So what's the problem with this case?" he asked, not a scowl in sight.

For a moment, Granville wondered what his own expression had been, to trigger this reaction. No matter. "Before we board that train next Monday, we need to be prepared for anything we might face," he said. "And we aren't going to know all of the dangers."

"We know a bunch of 'em now," Scott said. "And it can't be worse than what we faced in the Klondike."

"We'd both had time to prepare for that, and a long list of provisions we had to have with us in order to be allowed to enter the Yukon," Granville said

"Fat lot of good that did us," Scott muttered. "I lost most of my provisions when our poorly built boat overturned in the first set of rapids we had to run, remember?"

He grinned. "Only too well."

Trent stared at them. "How did you survive?" he asked. "Is that when you partnered up?"

"It wasn't easy," Granville said. "And yes."

"I wish I could have gone," Trent said, all of his earlier frustration apparently forgotten. "But we didn't have any money for provisions, and Pa said I was too young anyway."

"So why are you so worried about this little adventure?" Scott asked Granville, ignoring Trent.

"It's tough country. And you know as well as I do that this is the wrong time of year to be heading north. From everything we heard this weekend, winter in the Cariboo country is just as unpredictable—and as deadly—as it was in the Klondike."

Scott looked thoughtful. "True. But we're not actually digging into the ground. We just need to find out what happened to Robertson, Sr."

"A man no-one has heard from in thirty-two years."

Scott shrugged. "We probably just need to check the head-boards in the Barkerville cemetery for names. Easiest case we'll ever see."

Granville shook his head. "You wish. The only thing that is clear from his letters is that he didn't stay in Barkerville, but headed off in search of his own gold mine. And he could have gone in practically any direction, since the letters don't talk about more than "by the big crooked tree" or "on a small creek flowing off a tributary of one of the big strikes"."

"Why wouldn't he be clearer?" Trent asked.

"He likely didn't want to take the risk someone would get hold of his letters and get a jump on his claim," Scott said. "That is, if he hadn't registered it yet."

"Probably," Granville said. "We'll need to check if he ever registered a claim anywhere."

"He may not have had the chance," Scott said slowly. "That's if he really did find a big strike. Maybe he didn't make it back to register it."

"You think someone killed him for his claim?" Trent asked.

Scott shrugged. "It's possible. But there are a lot of other reasons for a man to stop writing home."

"Like what?" Trent demanded. "If he found gold…"

"Maybe he got caught in a flash flood," Scott said. "Or got

sick. If he was keeping his claim secret, maybe there was no-one close enough to help him if he needed it."

"Oh," Trent said.

"Or perhaps he didn't find much gold, and couldn't face telling his family that his 'big strike' was yet another failure," Granville said. "Sometimes a miner won't head home without the gold they came for. It's as if they can't stop."

He glanced at Scott, who nodded at him. They'd seen that before.

"Or they spent everything they had looking for gold, found barely enough to feed themselves, and don't have the money to get home," Scott added. "There's lots of reasons."

"When was the last time our client heard from his father, d'you know?" Trent asked.

"In the spring of 1868, the year the town burned down," Granville said. "It's hard to tell from the letters if he returned to Barkerville from time to time, or just entrusted his mail to anyone returning to Barkerville."

"His secrecy suggest the second," Scott said.

"I agree," Granville said. "In any case, I think it unlikely Robertson spent much time in Barkerville itself, since none of the old timers we've talked to so far have even so much as recognized his name."

"Maybe he changed it," Trent said.

Granville's coffee cup stopped halfway to his lips as he considered that. "Maybe he did at that," he said after a moment, and swallowed some of the rich dark brew that this place seemed to make better than anywhere else in town.

"Doesn't make it easier, though," Scott added. "If he changed his name, we don't even have a starting point for finding him."

"No, but it would give us another explanation of why all the letters were mailed from Barkerville, yet he doesn't seem to have lived there long enough to be remembered," Granville said.

"Not much help," Trent muttered.

"No, it isn't," Granville said. "Which is why we're talking

about it. Now is the time to be realistic about what we're up against. By the time we get to Barkerville, it'll be too late."

Scott gave him a considering look. "You can't tell me you won't be glad to be getting out of town. Even if we end up facing a few blizzards. After the ugliness of our last case, we could both use some fresh air, and a good challenge."

"True enough," Granville said. "But that's big country up there, and from what the old timers told us, in the 1860's, there wasn't a creek out there that wasn't being dug by someone searching for gold. The weather this time of year isn't going to make it easy to explore even one creek, never mind the number that are actually in the region."

Unexpectedly, it was Trent who answered him. "So we have to be smart about this. We've all three of us dealt with treacherous winter storms. We know what we're up against. We need to find us some good maps. And talk to everyone who's been near the place in the last thirty-two years. We have a week before we leave. Someone must have heard of Robertson."

Granville raised his cup in a silent toast. "And there we have our tasks for the week. We'll meet again on Saturday, and have this discussion one last time."

Scott just shook his head and Trent rolled his eyes. Granville ignored them. When he'd headed for the Klondike, risk hadn't mattered. He'd had nothing to lose, his only goal to strike it rich and go home with money of his own. A lot of it.

Things were different now. He had his own business. A house. And he had Emily. They'd be married soon.

This case promised to be a meaty one, the lapsed time creating a challenge he'd never faced before. But for the first time in his life, he had something he didn't want to lose. Something more important than challenging himself again and again.

To his own surprise, he wouldn't risk that for any case. And he'd be sticking to his December 15th timeline, and bringing all three of them home safely, no matter what happened.

The one thing he hadn't counted on was Emily.

CHAPTER 6

DESPITE THE RAIN, EMILY ARRIVED AT THE OFFICE EARLY ON Monday morning. She hadn't slept well, and she'd wanted to avoid another argument with Mama. Marie was just unlocking the door as Emily stepped off the elevator, so they entered the office together.

Emily was disappointed to find the office deserted—she couldn't see any lights, and it had that echoey feeling empty offices sometimes got. Granville often came in early, and she'd hoped to have a quiet chat with him before the others arrived.

While Marie turned on the lights, Emily removed her boot covers, deposited her wet umbrella in the stand, and brushed the rain off her coat sleeves before hanging it up. She then stepped down the short hallway and glanced into Granville's office just to be sure he wasn't there.

His normally clear desktop was covered with neat stacks of paper, and there was fresh ink in the inkwell. It felt as if he'd just left. Perhaps he had been in early, and then he and Scott had gone out for breakfast, as she knew they often did.

"Marie, I'm just about to put on the kettle for tea," she said as she walked back into reception. "Would you like a cup?"

"Very much. But I can brew it, if you'd like?" Marie said.

"It's no trouble," Emily said. "I'm hoping to talk to Mr. Granville before I start anything else, in any case. Can you let me know when he arrives?"

But Emily and Marie had time to enjoy a quiet chat over their tea, and then Emily had finished the paperwork on an open case before Granville and Scott returned. Emily gave Granville a few minutes to settle in, then she tapped at his half-open door. His head was bent over one of the formerly neat stacks of paper, which was now spread out in front of him.

When he looked up with a welcoming smile, she stepped into the office. Her eyes drank him in, noting the slightly disheveled hair and the shadows under his eyes. He must have been working hard. She'd barely seen him this weekend.

Oh, he had joined her and her family for church on Sunday, and then for a meal afterwards. But there had been no opportunity for a private talk then. Quite the contrary. Her father, on hearing that Granville was intending to make a trip to Barkerville, had completely monopolized the conversation.

Granville had been an amazingly good sport about it, and had asked a number of questions that drew Papa out further. She just hoped that he'd actually learned something of value for his journey. And wasn't just avoiding talking about his own plans.

Which she was dying to hear more about.

Usually, Granville would have found time for just the two of them and told her more about the case. But yesterday he'd made his excuses to all of them, and vanished right after luncheon, leaving her feeling frustrated and just a little worried.

Could he be avoiding telling her what he was planning? Surely not.

It's just wedding nerves, she scolded herself. And the fact that she was avoiding telling Granville that Mama had delayed their wedding plans. Yet again.

"Good morning, Emily," he said with the smile he kept just for her. "How are you this morning?"

"A little damp," she said, smiling back at him. "And I am also a bit worried about how the plans for Barkerville are coming along. I hope Papa's tales were of some help, at least?"

"Actually, they were quite helpful," he said. "To find Thomas Robertson, we will need to know as much as possible about what was happening in and around the area when he disappeared. And your father paid quite an amazing amount of attention to that."

"I'm glad," Emily said. "Do you know yet when you will be leaving?

He nodded, and showed her the plan. "This is the draft version that the three of us are working with," he said.

As she read it, Emily's heart sank. It was obvious that he still wasn't planning for her to come with them. And he was talking to Trent about it, but not her?

"So you are leaving next Monday, then?" she said carefully. "For certain?"

Granville nodded. "We are."

"How long will you be gone?"

"It could be as little as two or three weeks. Though we won't really know until we get up there and start looking for Robertson's trail. Thirty-two years is a long time, especially in a gold town."

Momentarily distracted, she nodded. "I know. Gold towns by their nature are transient, aren't they? From everything Papa has told me over the years, they spring up as soon as gold is found, and then begin to die or vanish altogether when the strike plays out."

He'd given her an odd look, and laughed. "You sound like an old timer yourself. How did you come to know the lingo so well?"

She grinned back at him. "From the time I was small, I loved to hear Papa tell the stories of the gold miners and the rivers and streams where they dug."

For a moment she could almost smell the scent of cheap cigars and whiskey that Papa had always brought with him whenever he'd been out talking to the men who'd once left everything behind to follow the call of gold. And the stories he'd tell…

"I always used to fantasize that one day I'd get to see some of those places I heard so much about. Especially Barkerville," Emily said. "I don't know why that one caught my attention so, but it did."

She frowned at him. "And now you're going there, on a case, and you're not including me?"

Granville looked surprised. "I've never heard you talk of this. When we went looking for the Lost Mine in the mountains behind New Westminster, you never mentioned wanting to join us."

"Because that mine was a more recent discovery. And not part of the Fraser River gold rush, or the one to the Cariboo," Emily said. And realized as she spoke that her answer didn't actually make a lot of sense.

Granville gave her an odd look, but to his credit, didn't point out her lack of logic.

So she explained a little. "I suppose those were the stories I heard in childhood, and the daydreams I wove from them. There's still a little magic for me whenever those places are mentioned."

"When we are married, I'll take you there one summer," Granville promised.

"Why not now?" Emily said. "If you're only going for a few weeks. The weather shouldn't be so bad, yet. And now that the railroad runs to Ashcroft, we would only have to be, what? Two days on the stagecoach."

"Four, actually," Granville said. "Two days only gets us as far as 150 Mile House."

"Four days, then," Emily said, mentally doing the math. One day each way by train, then four each way by stagecoach. Or sleigh. Ten days just traveling. She frowned at him.

"You couldn't possibly be gone for only two weeks, not if you're spending ten days traveling," she said. "That would leave you only four days in Barkerville to solve a thirty-two year-old case and find out what happened to your client's father. And that's assuming everything goes well. Which it probably won't."

Granville gave her a pleased look and she glared at him. "Are you going to tell me you can somehow pull it off?"

"Not at all," he said smoothly, still looking pleased about something. "My own estimation is that we'll be lucky to get it done in a month."

Emily just looked at him. Now what was he up to? "And?" she said, equally smoothly.

"And you saw that immediately," he said. "I was just thinking what an impressive detective you are turning into. And what a waste your being a typewriter, and cooped up in an office all day, would have been."

Oh.

"Thank you," Emily said, smiling at him. She'd often thought the same thing, but not many men would have. Or admitted it to her, if they did.

He wasn't getting off that easily, however.

"If the journey is going to be a long one, then that is all the more reason for me to come too," she said.

"If I were sure we could find the answers we needed in Barkerville itself, I would agree," he surprised her by saying.

"Well then," Emily began.

Granville held up a hand. "Like you, I believe it will take more than four days to find the answers our client needs. However, given what little he told his family in his letters, it is likely that the elder Robertson did not stay in Barkerville, but left on ventures of his own. If he thought to make his fortune looking for gold, he could have headed up any number of creeks in the area and beyond."

Emily knew he was right. "And the rumors were flying thickly back then, about new finds on this creek or that."

"We'd need to search some very rough country, in the depth of winter—and in November, the weather is likely to be unpredictable. We'd be traveling hard and sleeping rough. It's no place for a lady."

"I could come with you as far as Barkerville," Emily said,

thinking fast. "I believe they have several hotels there. I could keep investigating there while you and Scott and Trent go up the creeks. Just as I did when we traveled to Ketchikan in search of the missing heir."

Granville gave her a shrewd look. "That was in the spring. And you had Clara with you. Is your friend willing to go with you to Barkerville in November?"

Trust Granville to pick up on the one flaw in her plan. He might be proud that she was so quick, but he was equally sharp, and right now, she wished him a little less so.

"Actually, I have someone else in mind," she said airily. Surely Laura Kent would come with her, since she was a friend as well as being one of Granville's investigators. Although she usually searched out her answers in documents. Or even Marie Rizzo?

He gave her a skeptical look. "Miss Kent needs to stay in town and finish off the case she and Mac are working on," he said dryly. "And we need Miss Rizzo in the office, since she greets visitors as well as keeping track of cases, clients and potential clients.

Darn it. He knew her too well.

KNOWING A LOSING argument when she heard one, Emily offered to help with the research into Barkerville and Thomas Robertson. Which Granville agreed to. Then she quickly brought the discussion to a close, and hurried back down the hall to ensconce herself in her small, neat office and come up with a new plan.

But first, she still had work she should be doing. She frowned at the two short stacks of files on the desktop in front of her. One was closed cases, the other cases they had nearly closed. There wasn't a single interesting case in the lot. And while Granville, Scott and Trent were off to the Cariboo looking for Mr. Robertson, there would be more boring cases just like these for her to work on.

She felt like kicking the desk in frustration. Not that she would ever do such a thing. That would be unprofessional. Gritting her teeth, she drew in a deep breath, then another.

Glancing across the hall, she could see Laura's office, with Mac MacKenzie's beside that. Mac and Laura were both in Laura's office, deep in discussion over a thick file with dozens of paper markers sticking out of it. Which looked even more boring than what she was faced with.

None of it compared to a trip to Barkerville. Even in November.

Despite being tempted to keep arguing with Granville, Emily recognized the need for a strategic retreat when she saw one. She'd watched her friend Clara deftly execute them in social situations often enough, and, occasionally, Mama doing the same in a 'discussion' with Papa. Somehow those were never called arguments—at least not in front of 'the children'. Even though none of them were still legally children any longer. It didn't seem to matter.

Emily preferred a more straightforward approach. Still, she knew strategic retreats, when called for, could be effective. For both Clara and Mama, they always seemed to result in them getting their way.

When it came to the case in Barkerville, though, it wasn't so much about getting her own way. It was what would benefit the case. Emily knew she was a good investigator, bringing a perspective that otherwise would be missing, and she had no urgent cases.

If she were male, Granville wouldn't hesitate to include her.

He was usually reasonable, when he could see her point. She just needed to find something that would help him see it this time.

And another female to go with her, just for appearances sake. It was all so ridiculous. And it wasn't going to stop her working on this case.

At least digging into the history of Barkerville and Mr. Robertson's place in it was a decent place to begin. For the next few days, she'd spend her time reading old newspaper stories about Barkerville and the miners who had ended up there. Starting with her Papa's collection.

CHAPTER 7

Granville watched the door close behind Emily and wondered just how difficult he would be making life for her by leaving her behind on this case. They were newly engaged, and leading up to Christmas was the height of the local social scene.

A quick rap on the door followed by Scott's concerned face gave him little warning to get his own poker face in place.

"Is something wrong?" his partner asked, stepping through the doorway and closing the door behind him.

"Not really," Granville said carefully. "Why do you ask?"

"I just saw your fiancée leaving your office. She didn't seem too happy," Scott said, settling into the chair opposite him.

"She's concerned we're leaving on Monday," Granville said. "And that despite our planning we won't be taking everything we need with us."

Which was a portion of the truth, if not the most important part. He didn't want to drag Scott into what should be settled between him and Emily.

He should have known better. Scott gave him a shrewd look. "Everything? You mean like her?"

Granville nodded, not really surprised Scott had figured it out so quickly, and waved his partner to a seat. "Yes, that's it."

"I'm not surprised that she wants to go," Scott said. "She seemed pretty intrigued with all the stories her father evidently told her about the Cariboo and the gold rush days. And it's an interesting case."

"It is. And she'll never be one to pass up an adventure."

"She does know we're going into some pretty nasty weather up there?"

"I think that's part of the attraction. She's read some of the recent exploits of lady mountaineers, and the feats they have achieved appeal to her."

"I can see that," Scott said. "She's pretty fearless. And she's good at investigating."

"If I were in her shoes, I'd want to go," Granville admitted. That was the problem.

Scott stared at him. "You aren't thinking of taking her along with us? In November? Tell me you've told her she can't join us"

"I'm hoping I won't have to. Thus far, Emily hasn't found another woman willing to travel with her."

Scott nodded. "And she can't join the three of us on her own. It would be social suicide."

Granville bit back a laugh. He doubted that such a thought would even have crossed Scott's mind, before he'd met Emily. It was a testament to his fiancée's strength of character, that Scott even knew the phrase—and cared about what it could mean for her—even if Emily didn't.

"For now, let's hope that's enough to solve the problem," Granville said. Though he suspected it wouldn't stop Emily for long. "Meanwhile, we need to go over these lists, and make sure we haven't forgotten anything that might prove to be essential on this trip."

"Why don't we take a look at these maps, first," Scott said, dumping the bundle he'd been carrying on Granville's desk. "After we met this morning, I talked to a few people. These seem to be the best maps available for the journey we'll need to take, as well as for the Cariboo region and the Barkerville area."

"You were able to buy these?" Granville asked, unrolling the first map, which showed the area from Quesnel to Barkerville in some detail, including elevation as well as roads, rivers, and lakes. And there were at least four rivers feeding into the area within a twenty mile radius of Barkerville.

"Some of them," Scott said. "The one you're looking at, yes. And the route maps, of course. But the Barkerville one…" He paused as Granville looked quickly through the maps, unrolling each one and scanning it quickly.

"That one," Scott said, as Granville picked up the smallest map of the lot. "That one is borrowed. But we have permission to have it copied, if we need to. And I think we'll need it."

Granville carefully considered the map he now held open. It was carefully hand drawn and lettered, and lacked the elevation markings. Some of the names seem to have been added in another hand, and the map was grubby around the edges with much handling. But unlike any of the other maps, it showed streams, as well as rivers. A lot of streams.

"It isn't going to be easy, finding out where Robertson might have been digging, given this many places where he could have been testing a claim," he said.

"I know," Scott said. "But if we keep looking, I'm hoping we'll find someone or something that can narrow down the terri-tory we'll have to look in."

"We can only hope," Granville said, his gaze still on the map. "The level of detail here is amazing. And I agree that we need copies of this one. Possibly several copies, just in case."

"Good idea," Scott said. "I know a mapmaker can get the copies made for us before we leave. And perhaps we might also have copies made of the letters our client loaned us, too. We'll need them with us, and it'd be bad if the originals fell in a creek or something."

"Agreed," Granville said. "Miss Kent may be able to copy the letters for us. She writes a fair hand, and she can likely do a reasonable copy of the little scribbles he made in the margins.

He glanced at the map again. "Given the names of some of these streams, those doodles might prove extremely useful, once we're there."

"If she's doing all that, do you think she'll have time to make a copy of that photograph—the one our client left? She could probably sketch it so it only shows our missing miner," Scott said. "The way she did on our last case. That worked out pretty well."

"It did indeed. I'll ask her," Granville said.

CHAPTER 8

Emily retrieved her still-damp umbrella and braved the downpour again to start her search in Papa's very masculine study, reading through his catalogue of clippings. And she discovered with some shock that Papa had whitewashed many of the stories she'd loved as a child.

Yes, there were heroic stories, and fortunes in gold uncovered. But stories of hardship and starvation and men too broke to afford passage home threaded through those yellowed pages too.

And a few very ugly conflicts between the local tribes and the tens of thousands of miners arriving from all over the globe. Some of whom thought they should be entitled to behave as conquerors while seeking gold anywhere they could find it. One of the local Chiefs had brokered a peace that saw the gangs of vigilantes driven out, and a peaceful end to what could have been a brutal war.

But she was here for a purpose. Emily settled in, making notes and jotting down questions as she read the familiar stories. By the time she'd worked through the last of the scrapbooks, it was nearly lunch time. Perfect.

She made a quick call from the telephone in the hallway, then bundled into her still damp coat, unfurled her umbrella and set off for Stroh's Tea Shoppe.

SHAKING OUT HER DRIPPING UMBRELLA, Emily furled it and hurried through the glass door into the welcoming warmth of the teashop. Dropping her umbrella into the stand by the door, she scanned the crowded room. And was pleased to see Clara was already seated at an inside table off to the side.

Stroh's was a cosy place on a wet day, smelling of tea and vanilla, and that particular table was nicely screened by luxurious palm fronds. That comforting contrast to the cold rain sheeting down outside was part of what made Stroh's a favorite place for both of them.

"Clara. Thank you for meeting me," Emily said as she freed herself from her damp coat and draped it over a chair, sinking into the other chair opposite her friend.

"I suspect you wanted to meet for more than lunch," Clara said. "Since as far as I know you're working today. You know I hate it when you don't tell me what you really want from me."

"Then why did you agree to meet me?" Emily asked.

Clara looked down at the menu she held open in front of her. "I have my reasons," she said with a sideways glance.

Well, that was fair. But what was she up to? Emily wondered.

They chatted about nothing much while they both enjoyed the butternut squash soup and a deliciously creamy chicken pot pie. Once the plates were cleared, and a pot of tea and a plate of custard pastries sat in front of them, Clara leaned forward a little.

"So," she said. "What is this new case that you are so interested in?"

"What makes you think there is a new case?" Emily asked.

Clara poured tea for both of them, then slowly and deliberately stirred sugar and milk into her cup. She was doing this on purpose, Emily thought with amusement.

Putting down the teaspoon equally slowly, Clara finally met

Emily's eyes. "I know that tone in your voice," she said. "You're excited about something. And you are determined, too. So what is the case?"

"Why does it have to be a case? Couldn't I be excited about something else?"

"Such as?" Clara said. "The decorating plan for Granville's house is well underway. Your wedding, perhaps? The last thing I heard, it was moved to three years from now."

"Well, it's now three and a half years," Emily said bitterly. "And you should see the gowns Mama likes for the bridesmaids. And for the maid of honor."

Emily knew her friend well. Any mention of fashion should be sufficient to distract her entirely from the case Emily didn't want to be interrogated on. Especially since, as maid of honor, Clara would have to wear Mama's latest bad idea.

"Your Mama usually has impeccable taste," Clara said immediately, her eyes narrowing. "What can be so awful?"

Emily was almost distracted herself watching her friend's face as she described the yellow satin gowns with huge puffed sleeves.

"Yellow? Who wears yellow in a wedding party?" Clara said.

"It's a pale yellow, what Mama calls a delicate color," Emily said.

"As if that made it better," Clara said. "Yellow is my absolute worst color. And a pale yellow? I'll look as if I'm sickening for something."

"I know," Emily said gloomily. "But it's like arguing with a fence post. I swear Mama doesn't hear a word I say."

"Emily, you have to make a stand here."

"I know. And I *am* trying," Emily said, reaching for her teacup and adding a little milk.

"And you are not succeeding," Clara said tartly.

"You know Mama when she's focused on something. I can't even get her to listen to me about moving the wedding date forward.'

"You'll just have to find a way to get her to listen," Clara said.

"I know. And I will," Emily said. "I'm hoping that if I am out of town for a bit, Mama will switch her focus to Jane or Miriam, and be more reasonable when I get back."

Which was true, if not her only reason for wanting to go. It was the reason Clara would understand best, though. Her friend was more interested in what was in style now than in what she called "old things". She had never understood Emily's fascination with the gold rush days.

"Out of town?" Clara said. "Now we come to it. Your new case."

"Well, yes," Emily said. "Or at least I hope so."

"Tell me."

After Emily explained about Barkerville and the missing man who had gone searching for gold thirty-two years before, Clara stared at her in disbelief. "And you've convinced your fiancé to take you north with them? Unaccompanied?"

"I haven't exactly convinced him yet. But I know he'll end up agreeing," Emily said, with a confidence she didn't feel.

Her friend looked as if she knew exactly what Emily really meant. "Oh, no," Clara said. "I am not going to Barkerville with you."

Emily laughed. "Don't worry, I would never expect you to. I just need a little help looking for our client's father in old newspapers."

"Well, it's not my favorite thing, but that much I can do," Clara said. "As long as you help me find a new hat afterwards."

It was Emily's turn to roll her eyes, but she hastily agreed, knowing she was getting off easily. That settled, they finished off the pastries and headed for the nearby offices of the *World*.

CHAPTER 9

WHEN THEY REACHED THE NEWSPAPER OFFICES, ONE OF THE clerks kindly showed them to the dusty, rather chilly room in the basement that held the newspaper archives. He switched on the overhead light and a rather brighter reading lamp on the large table in the center of the room. Then he retrieved the large bound volumes dating from 1863 to 1885 that Emily had asked for, and left them to it.

Clara surveyed the room, and shook her head. "I had forgotten how depressing this place is. I think after this I may need two hats."

Emily smiled at her, then carefully draped her wet coat over a spare chair, and wrapped her shawl closely around her against the slightly damp air. Gathering her long skirts out of the worst of the dust, she settled herself in front of the lamp. With a martyred sigh, Clara did the same on the other side of the table.

Emily looked at the three stacks of bound volumes weighing down one end of the sturdy table. Each volume held full-sized copies of every newspaper the *World* had published in that particular year. And each stack held ten volumes. At first glance it was overwhelming. They needed to be smart about this.

"Why don't I take the first ten years, and you start with the second ten," Emily suggested.

"Fine," Clara agreed. "What are we looking for?"

Emily thought about it for a moment. This was different from her father's clippings, which had only been about the gold rush.

"We'll only need to look at stories from the Cariboo region," she said. "Particularly anything about gold strikes there, or about Barkerville or areas near it. And there may be nothing at all in most issues of the paper."

"The most useful information would be any mention of Thomas Robertson, especially after his disappearance in 1868," she added, passing Clara the volume from 1871. "Though I'm not hopeful we'll find that."

"Why not?" Clara asked as she opened the big volume carefully and grimaced at the dense page of type.

"Because he was only one of hundreds who had headed into the Cariboo looking for gold. And he was neither famous nor rich."

"Not worth reporting on," Clara said. "There would be no story there."

Emily smiled inwardly at Clara's easy familiarity with what made a good news story. They had both learned quite a bit about how newspapers worked during previous cases, most especially from Tim O'Hearn, who wrote for the *World*. He had become a friend, and he was sweet on Clara. Who hadn't mentioned him yet today. What was going on there, Emily wondered, but she kept the thought to herself.

"Exactly," was all she said. "Unless Mr. Robertson struck it rich. Or something happened to him. Which is why you're also looking for disasters in the region—accidents, deaths, murders. Anything that might keep a man from writing home."

"But isn't that the same thing as looking for any mention of his name?"

"Not necessarily," Emily said. "They might not have known who he was. Or if he was worried about someone finding his claim, he might have been using a false name. Or..."

Laughing, Clara held up a hand. "Enough. I get it. I'll need something to take notes, though."

Emily reached into her bag, pulling out her own notebook, and a second one for Clara. "Here," she said, and passed her a sharpened pencil too.

Shaking her head, Clara lowered her head and began to read. Emily opened the heavy volume for 1863 and did the same, carefully turning the brittle, yellowing pages as she searched for relevant stories.

She slowly worked through the volume spread in front of her, stopping frequently to rest her gritty eyes, and wishing she had a cup of tea. Across from her, Clara seemed to be doing the same, though she wasn't turning pages as quickly. Emily hid a smile.

Unless the Cariboo was mentioned more often in 1870, which wasn't likely given that 1863 was the height of the gold rush, she suspected her friend was spending more time looking at advertisements and articles that had nothing to do with their search. No matter. She was grateful for Clara's company, and whatever help she could give.

Several hours later, Emily put down her pencil, rubbed at the red indent it had left on her finger, and stretched out her aching back. She had found no mention of the missing Mr. Robertson. Which was a relief, in one way. At least he hadn't fallen from a cliff to his death, or been horribly murdered. Those events would have been recorded. If anyone had known about them, that is.

She did find stories about the cattle drives north from Washington and Oregon into British Columbia. Not all of them went to the Cariboo, but Mr. Robertson would have been part of one that had made that long journey.

After making the border crossing at Osoyoos Lake, they'd still had to travel up the rough track bordering Lake Okanagan to the grasslands of Grande Prairie. Then they'd headed west to Fort Kamloops, riding across semi-desert country in the heat of summer, driving hundreds of head of cattle ahead of them. From there, they had the long journey north to the Cariboo to face.

After she'd finished reading that story, Emily had sat quietly for a moment, trying to imagine what that journey had been like.

The Cariboo Wagon Road hadn't been completed until two years later, so they must have spent hour after tedious hour on narrow, dusty roads. Hats pulled low against the unrelenting heat and glare, eyes gritty and throats dry from the dust that billowed up behind the cattle's hooves. In constant motion, always alert for a straying cow, or the beginnings of a stampede. Day after day after day.

It must have been a kind of hell for them. Emily swallowed hard and loosened the shawl she wore over her crisp blouse. She was suddenly thirsty, and too hot, despite the chill of the room.

If just thinking about that cattle drive had such an effect on her, how must Mr. Robertson have felt, crawling out of his blanket every morning, limbs stiff from the hard ground. Knowing what the day ahead would bring.

And Granville was worried about taking her north now, when they could take the train part of the way, and had good roads the rest of it? And hotels or roadhouses to stay in. Granted, they might be facing freezing weather and deep snow, but personally, she'd take that over drought and dust and hundred and ten degree heat any day.

She'd tell him that, next time they talked about Barkerville, she vowed. Let's see him keep arguing after that!

Emily smiled to herself at the thought, then realized Clara was watching her. "Are you finding anything?" she asked.

"A few mentions of the Cariboo here and there. Nothing about Mr. Robertson. You?"

"The same."

"And yet you're smiling?"

Emily explained about the cattle drive, and what she'd been thinking.

"And you're smiling because you would prefer sleeping in a tent in freezing weather to baking on a desert plain? Emily, you can't be serious."

"Why not? I like the cold."

"It isn't about hot or cold. It's the hardships. I don't under-stand why you even think you want to leave the city for these hardships," Clara said.

Emily looked at her. "I don't think I can explain it," she said after a moment. "I just do."

"I know," Clara said. "But Emily, you've never really been out of the city."

"We went to Hazelton."

"Yes. And we spent most of our time in what passes for a town there."

"And then I went on to Kispiox with the Reverend and his wife."

"Which was wilder than Hazelton, but still a settlement. You were sleeping in a building there, not a tent. That's my point. Neither of us ventured into the real wilderness on that trip. And that was adventure enough for me."

"Not for me," Emily said. "I want to do more. See more."

"I know. That is what worries me," Clara said. "I'm afraid you don't know what you're getting into. And that you'll manage to convince your Granville to take you with him, and that you'll both regret it."

Emily hoped she could convince Granville. If there was regret, it would come if he chose to leave her behind. No matter how difficult a trip to Barkerville—and beyond—might prove to be, she would find a way to deal with it. She wasn't sure she could deal with a marriage in which she was always the one left behind.

"I need to try," Emily said quietly.

Clara looked at her for a moment, then nodded. "Tell me how I can help," she said.

"You're helping now," Emily said. "Just keep reading." And she turned back to her own quest for even the slightest hint of Mr. Robertson.

By quarter-past four, her eyes were burning and her back felt knotted from poring over the huge pages of tiny print. Worse, she'd found nothing more. And she'd only reached to the end of 1867. They'd have to come back the next day.

"Clara, shall we stop for tea?"

"I thought you would never ask," Clara said in heartfelt tones.

CHAPTER 10

Tuesday morning found Emily and Clara back in the chilly basement of the *World*, working their way through the last decade and a half of newspapers. Emily quickly realized that she'd been right the previous day in her assessment that these volumes would go quickly. Once she'd worked her way through the coverage of the fire that had destroyed the town of Barkerville in 1868, only to see it rebuilt almost overnight—there was little coverage of the Cariboo region from one month to the next. She found herself skimming whole weeks of stories without stopping once to read anything more than the headlines. Glancing across at her friend, she could tell that Clara was working her way through 1879 just as quickly as Emily was doing 1869.

Clara noticed her glance and looked up. "I'm finding surprisingly few accidents and deaths being reported from the Cariboo. Is it possible there were none? Or am I missing them?"

"I'm not finding many, either," Emily said. "I'm not sure if that means there were none, or if they simply weren't covered here. One of the things I need to do when I reach Barkerville is to read through the archives of the *Cariboo Sentinel*. They will have all of the coverage for the region."

"Are they still in business?"

"No, they only published from 1865 to 1875. But I'm hoping those are the years that matter." And they both went back to their reading.

As they left the 1860's and 70's behind and began to read the stories from the 1880's and 90's, they were finding even less coverage of Barkerville. The easy gold was long gone, and it took a large company to unearth the gold that remained. Emily and Clara practically raced through the remaining volumes and by eleven they had reached their goal.

Clearly it was time for an early luncheon. And a pot of hot, strong tea. Clara, of course, happily agreed when Emily suggested a retreat to Stroh's.

THE AFTERNOON FOUND the two of them across town in the second floor home of the Vancouver Free Library. Since the alternative was spending hours in the basement archives of the *News Advertiser*, which was just as cold, just as dusty, and likely just as tedious as the search through the *World's* archives, Clara had happily agreed to their change of plans.

"But what are we doing here? And why the change?" she asked while they waited for the librarian to bring the volumes Emily had requested.

"When I was reading through the notices from 1870, I saw an obituary for Mr. Chartres Brew," Emily began.

"I've never heard of him," Clara said. "Why does he matter?"

"Well, it seems that at the time of his death, he was the Assistant Gold Commissioner for Barkerville, and in fact, he's buried there. But prior to that he had been the Chief of Police for all of British Columbia, for decades."

"Then why was he in Barkerville?"

"I'm not quite sure, though it appears he may have been doing both jobs in 1868."

"The year your Mr. Thompson vanished? Might that matter, though, when this Mr. Brew passed on so long ago?"

"Perhaps not. But it did make me wonder who is in charge in Barkerville now. And whether any of them might have lived there when our missing miner was there."

"Thirty-two years? I don't think that's very likely, do you?"

"Maybe not. But you never know when a piece of knowledge is going to be useful."

"And how is the library going to help us find that out?"

"They have copies of most of the provincial directories going all the way back to 1860."

"Do you mean Henderson's BC Gazetteer?" Clara asked. "I know my father uses it often. Which probably means it's as dry as dust."

"I think directories have been produced by different companies over the years, but the premise is the same. And you'd be amazed how much information is available inside."

"So what are we looking for?"

"We need to make a list of the Government officials based in Barkerville, Richfield or Camerontown for each year, and then we see if we can find any overlaps."

"Starting when?"

The helpful librarian reappeared at that moment and carefully placed a stack of books on the long wooden table in front of them before disappearing into the stacks again.

Clara watched him go with a dismayed look. "He isn't done filling your request, is he?"

Emily smiled. "I'm afraid not. But if you begin with 1867, the year before Mr. Robertson disappeared, I'll take 1868. And we work forward."

Clara sighed a little, but accepted her assignment, bending her head over the hard-bound volume Emily handed her from the top of the stack of blue books. Fairly quickly she looked up again. "Is Barkerville in Cariboo East or Cariboo West?"

"Cariboo West."

"Oh," Clara said, and made a careful note, then flipped forward a few pages and made another note.

Emily watched her work with some amusement. Her friend was more interested in puzzle-solving than she'd ever admit. And she was good at it, too. When she wanted to be.

Just at that moment Clara looked up to catch her amused look. "What is so funny?"

"How quickly you seem to be finding the answers we need."

"Well, it turns out this might be easier than I thought. Most of these officials are either based in Victoria or New Westminster. I found only an Assistant Gold Commissioner for Cariboo West in Barkerville. And he's also the Justice of the Peace for the area."

"Chartres Brew?"

"No, this is one is Henry Ball. Chartres Brew is listed as Chief of Police, and based in New Westminster. What did you find?"

"By 1868, Chartres Brew is listed as chief of police for the whole province as well as gold commissioner for all of the Cariboo, and he's living in Barkerville."

"Just him?"

"No, the listing now also shows a clerk and a chief constable, with two constables in Barkerville, and one in Quesnel. And I also found a Mr. D. Cranston who is the postmaster for the Cariboo, based in Richfield."

"I'm ready to check 1870 now, if you'd like."

"It seems we don't have the 1870 directory. See if the 1871 one tells you anything," Emily said, hiding her grin. Clara had the bit between her teeth now.

More silence, except for the turning of pages, and the nearly silent tread of the librarian returning with a second stack of directories. Emily glanced up to thank him just in time to catch the brilliant smile Clara was throwing his way, and the pinkening of the tips of his ears. She hid a grin, and turned back to her research.

～

OVER LUNCH, they chatted easily about this and that, but Emily had been careful not to mentioned the proposed trip to Barkerville. Yet in the back of her mind, she was always aware that she was no closer to convincing Granville to take her with him.

She had tried again when Granville had telephoned her the previous evening.

"But there were women who traveled to the Klondike gold fields," she'd told him. "Including a reporter from New York who was famous for her stories. And some couples ventured to the gold fields together, too, and even families with children."

"This journey is different," he had said.

Emily could hear the concern in his voice, but she wasn't letting it stop her.

"Different how?" she had asked him. "You knew little about the weather conditions before you embarked for the Klondike gold fields. And conditions were far worse in the Klondike then, than they are in Barkerville now, from what I understand."

"This is an investigation," Granville said. "We could be uncovering any kind of violence and criminal behavior."

"It's an investigation of events that took place thirty-two years ago. It's perfectly safe. It isn't like a murder that just happened."

"It's unsettled country. The weather alone is a threat."

"So was the Klondike," Emily had reminded him. But he wasn't budging. And even she could tell that she needed a new approach.

She'd tried again this morning, but nothing she said helped. Granville couldn't get past the hardships and danger of winter travel, or of leaving her on her own in Barkerville. And she couldn't accept that she'd be left behind in Vancouver.

Emily stared at the yellowed directory page in front of her until the words blurred and danced. She sighed softly, remembering how discouraged she'd felt after that conversation. She wasn't even sure what a new approach would look like.

Clara started and looked up. "Emily, are you all right?"

Emily blinked, realizing her friend must have heard her sigh.

"This is just discouraging, finding so little," she said.

Clara shook her head slowly, her gaze fixed on Emily's face. "Emily, I know you. When things get difficult, you get more determined. You don't sigh over them."

How could she argue with truth?

"Is it still the wedding?" Clara asked before she could answer. "Has your mother done something? Or did you finally tell your poor fiancé about the wedding delays?"

"I suppose it's all of it," Emily said carefully, very aware of her friend's sharp gaze.

Clara wasn't having it. "Hogwash," she said inelegantly. "Emily, this is me. The only thing I've seen you that upset over lately is…" she paused, and narrowed her eyes. "Mr. Granville. You still want to go north with him, don't you? And he won't agree because of the danger."

Emily swallowed, a little stunned by Clara's accuracy. "That isn't it."

"No?" Clara said. "Then what is so upsetting that you're sitting and sighing like that?"

"Well, I do want to go with them to Barkerville," Emily said. "It's part of the reason for all this research."

"I thought we were doing it to help the case?" Clara said.

"Of course we are. But if we can find some hint of where Mr. Robertson went, it would make it easier to find out what happened to him."

"And safer?" Clara asked.

"Well, yes," Emily said.

"And if it was safer, he might agree to your joining them?"

Emily nodded. "I don't want to be left behind, like some baggage that isn't fit for the journey. And it isn't how I want to start a marriage. I've never wanted that."

Clara shook her head. "Emily, you know that's how most marriages work."

"But Granville isn't like that," she said. "He's included me. We discuss things. It's one of the things I love about him. He doesn't put women in small boxes and expect them to stay there. Like Papa does.

The only reason Papa isn't still trying to stop me from detecting is because I'm engaged, and he sees me as Granville's problem now."

"And now you're afraid Mr. Granville might change once you're wed?" Clara asked shrewdly.

Emily considered her friend's question for a moment. It was quiet in the little library, and fairly dim outside the circle of light shed by the table lamp. It felt oddly easy to talk here.

She nodded slowly.

"I suppose I am," Emily said. Admitting it to herself as well as to Clara. "Especially now, because he doesn't seem to be hearing me. I even said I'd only go as far as Barkerville, like we did in Hazelton. But I don't really want to stay in Barkerville while they go off adventuring either."

"And?" Clara said.

"He said no," Emily said unhappily. "Even to me staying in Barkerville."

Clara gave her a thoughtful look. Is there another woman going on this trip?" she asked. "Or is it just Mr. Granville and Mr. Scott?"

"Just them," Emily said, not caring about her grammar. "And Trent. Which isn't fair at all. I'm older than he is."

"And female," Clara said. "Which is the real issue, is it not?"

Emily nodded, her throat suddenly too tight to for words. And not quite sure what she'd say, in any case. She seemed to have run out of arguments. She stared down at the volume in front of her, not meeting Clara's too-seeing gaze.

"It isn't just the danger then, is it?" Clara asked shrewdly. "There's also the matter of what society would say about you going to Barkerville with three men. Even if one of them is your fiancé."

"Trent's just a boy," Emily protested weakly. Knowing it was irrelevant even as she said it.

Clara ignored her, and focused on the real issue. "Look, I'm sorry, but I cannot see my way to going north with you. Not in winter. And so close to Christmas."

She paused, but Emily didn't look up.

"Emily, can you see your way to not caring, just this once?" Clara said. "I could come with you in the spring, and I'm sure Mr. Granville will take you then."

"He's already offered," Emily said, still not looking up.

"Then?"

"I can't," Emily said in a rush. "I love the idea of winter travel, and if Granville leaves me behind this time, why should the next time be any different?"

She looked up and met Clara's eyes. "You know better than I do how our world works. From what little I know of marriages, they need to work through the difficult times, not just the easy ones. And what I want—well, it's different from what society says I should want. Which will always create difficult times for us if Granville is always trying to protect me."

"But he hasn't in the past, has he?" Clara asked.

"No. Quite the opposite."

"So why is this different?"

It was a good question. Emily thought for a moment. "I can only guess, but I think it might be because of his experience in the Klondike gold fields. He doesn't talk about it a lot, but I think he and Scott saw it break strong men."

"Hmmmf. Women are stronger," Clara said.

Emily was startled into a grin. "Clara? Is that you?"

"Very funny. You know it's true."

"I do. I wasn't sure you did."

"Well, now you know," Clara said. "So what are you going to do about this?"

Emily straightened her shoulders and lifted her chin. "I have no idea. But I will find a way."

"See that you do," Clara said, and turned back to the newspaper she'd been reading.

Leaving Emily feeling oddly better. And resolving yet again never to underestimate her friend.

❧

SEVERAL HOURS LATER, Emily put her pencil down. "In 1869, I have Chartres Brew as gold commissioner again," she said. "Along with a clerk, a chief constable, two constables in Barkerville and one in Quesnel."

"Well, this is interesting," Clara said after some time.

"Why? What did you find?"

"In 1871 the assistant gold commissioner for the entire Cariboo region is Henry Ball again. "

"Wasn't he the one from 1867?"

"He is," Clara agreed. "And now he has a clerk and two constables in Barkerville. I wonder what happened to Mr. Brew?"

As Emily hid a smile at her interest, Clara turned a page. "Oh, this is sad," she said. "Chartres Brew fell ill in Barkerville in 1870 and passed away there in 1871. He was only 55."

"Those are big districts, with very poor roads. The poor man must have spent a lot of time on horseback. And in all weathers," Emily said with a shudder.

"I wonder how much time a gold commissioner actually spent in Barkerville? And how much time they spent visiting the various mining sites?" Clara said. "I can certainly see why. Listen to this. They shipped just over a million dollars in mined gold from the province in 1871.

Which sounds an amazing amount of money, until you compare it to the more than two million dollars worth of gold shipped in 1867."

As they worked their way through the directories over the next several hours, comparing notes in a hushed voice as they went, Emily formed a clearer picture of the evolution of the gold towns, and particularly Barkerville. By the time they were done, they had identified two key players in Barkerville.

To her surprise, the Gold Commissioner for the Cariboo was now David Cranston, the same man who had been postmaster the year Thomas Robertson left Barkerville and vanished. He'd be the one to ask about the missing man.

Working with Commissioner Cranston was a constable in Barkerville, with two more constables in Quesnel. The post office was now in the charge of a Mrs. Darrow, who also served as the telegraph agent.

Clearly their search for the missing man needed to go north to Barkerville. Emily's pulse sped up at the thought. She could already imagine how good it would feel to participate in those interviews. Now all she had to do was convince Granville that she needed to be part of this case.

Which included accompanying him all the way to Barkerville.

CHAPTER 11

WEDNESDAY, OCTOBER 31, 1900

Early Wednesday morning found Granville sitting behind his heavily laden desk, running through yet another list. Putting the last checkmark in place, he sat back and contemplated it. It was beginning to feel like he had everything under control for their trip. But did he?

He needed a sounding board.

At times like this he missed the partners desk he and Scott used to share. Much as he appreciated the occasional privacy of his own office, he valued tossing around ideas with his partner even more. Since no-one else was in the office yet, he called out Scott's name.

When Scott appeared in the doorway, he was holding yet another list and frowning.

"You hollered?" Scott said with an edge in his voice.

"I can't look at another list," Granville said, slapping his finished list on top of a teetering pile as he stood up. "And I think we might be ready to go. I could do with coffee, a lot of it. How about you?"

"We're done with the lists? Now you're talking," Scott said, clapping him on the back. "Bacon for me, at least a double order. Let's get out of here."

As one, the two men clattered down the back stairs and strode out into the blustery wind and rain.

Less than half an hour later they were sitting in the back booth at Mary's Diner, with full cups of fresh coffee in front of them and the rich smell of frying bacon in their nostrils, it was time to get down to business. "It looks to me like we'll be ready to depart by Monday," Granville said. "What do you think?"

"It's lookin' good," Scott said, downing half of his coffee and signalling for more. "I think we can take on anything the Cariboo can throw at us. Except we don't seem to be finding much on our quarry."

"Perhaps we shouldn't call him that," Granville said.

"He's missing, isn't he? And we're going after him. Sounds like a quarry to me," Scott said. Though the twinkle in his brown eyes gave him away.

"I'm sure our client will be thrilled to hear his father referred to in those terms," Granville said, equally dryly.

Scott cocked his head to one side. "From what you've said, I thought our client wasn't that fond of his missing father. He did desert them, after all."

"I think that's the problem. My read on the man is that he's spent years resenting his father for not coming home, but at the same time, he's still hoping that there was a good reason for it. That the fellow hadn't simply abandoned them."

"Could make for a difficult report to write at the end of this," Scott said, then sat back as heavy plates heaped with eggs, toast, and rashers of thick, curling bacon were slid in front of them. "Odds are, the man did just that."

That was only the thin edge of the problem, Granville thought as he thanked the waitress. "We still have too little to go on," he told Scott.

"Isn't that why we're heading north?" Scott said.

THAT AFTERNOON, there was a quick rap at his door, and Granville looked up from reviewing the final list of supplies Scott and Trent had put together. He was relieved to see Emily. Something about the brief telephone conversation they'd had the previous day had worried him, and it hadn't helped that he hadn't been able to see her face. She had seemed more upset about not accompanying them on this trip than he'd anticipated.

And this was the first he'd seen of her today, though Miss Rizzo had told him she was in the office.

"Emily. Come in," he said. "How can I help?"

"I wanted to talk about the Barkerville case," she said as she slid into the chair across from his desk, carefully arranging her long skirts around her.

Was she trying to avoid looking at him, Granville wondered? She didn't meet his eyes when she looked up, either, which wasn't like her.

"Clara and I spent the last few days working in the newspaper archives, looking for any mention of Mr. Robertson," she began. "We haven't found a single one. And when I talked to Trent, he still hasn't found any of the old miners who'd even heard of him."

"Scott and I were just discussing how thin this case is, just this morning," he told her.

"Doesn't that worry you?"

He grinned. "I never could resist a challenge. And looking for a man no one has heard from in thirty-two years? Now that is a challenge."

"It is. But Clara and I were able to unearth at least some information that might be helpful," she said. And then she told him about the government agents who had worked in Barkerville in the years they thought Mr. Robertson had lived there. And the ones who worked there now."

"But that's excellent," he said when she'd done. "The current Gold Commissioner—Cranston, is it?"

She nodded. "Yes, David Cranston. He's the only one we

found who was in Barkerville from the time Thomas Robertson vanished until now."

"I'm amazed there was anyone to find, quite frankly," he told her. "After thirty-two years."

"I know. I wish we had been able to track down one of the earlier Gold Commissioners, but the one from 1868 passed on in 1870, and we couldn't find any trace of the other without going to Victoria to look further."

"And since we don't even know what questions we might need to ask the fellow, there's no point in making that trip. Not yet," he said.

"We seem to have so little information, though. Compared to our usual cases."

"We've never had a case this old before."

"I suppose that's true."

He grinned at her serious look. "Our client knows we're facing long odds against finding answers here. As long as he's happy with the risk, I'm intrigued by this one. Especially since our odds of failing on this case are far higher than on any previous one."

She tilted her head a little to one side and gave him a look he couldn't quite read. Then she smiled. "Really? Even when you were looking for the missing heir? Or trying to uncover the puppet master? Or..."

"Well, we started those cases with more information, at least."

"True. I still wish I could have found more this time..."

"I am impressed by how much you did find, after so many years," he said. "Besides, trying to track the senior Mr. Robertson from Barkerville with few clues is also part of what makes this case so challenging."

"As is trying to find him in the ghost towns of the Cariboo," Emily added, returning his grin. "I know why you want to go. It's what intrigues me too."

"I can understand that," he said.

"And it's why I want to go with you," she said, leaning

towards him across the desk. "I can help, Granville. Really, I can."

"I know you can," he said, finding her determination as appealing as ever. But this case was different. She had to know that, surely? "But while the lack of information on Robertson doesn't worry me, I am worried about what the winter weather and the landscape might throw at us. That's where the real danger lies, not in our missing man."

"But…" Emily began.

He held up a hand. "Emily, you've spent your life in town. Have you ever slept out in a tent? Or on the ground?"

"Well, no, but…"

"And you have never faced weather so cold. Have you ever ridden in a stagecoach?"

She set her jaw, but shook her head.

Granville hated to do this, but he hated the idea of her badly hurt under winter conditions even worse.

"The motion of a stagecoach over a trail is enough to make every passenger nauseous, if not outright unwell. And you'd be riding in a cramped coach with only canvas walls and a canvas roof between you and the cold and the snow. Hour after hour, for four days. Disembarking only for meals."

"I'd be with you," she said. "And I can dress warmly, and bring blankets. Besides, didn't you mention we'd likely be riding in a sleigh part of the way? Surely that would be smooth."

He couldn't help himself. He had to smile at her determined optimism. "Smoother, anyway. If colder. But this is four straight days of travel."

She smiled back, not daunted in the least. "If you can do it, so can I."

"Have you ever spent an entire day outside in winter?" he asked.

"Well, no. But I've skated or walked in bad weather, and of course we go out in the carriage…"

"I'm afraid that isn't anywhere near the same thing," he said bluntly. Hating to watch her face fall at his words.

She blinked at him. "But…"

"You need to stay in Vancouver this time, Emily. I'll take you and Clara to Barkerville next summer. I promise."

"It isn't the same, Granville. You know it isn't."

"I do know." he said. "But Emily, I won't put you at risk. And that is final."

Every word came hard.

She stared at him for a moment, her eyes wide. Then she stood up, shook out her skirts, and left his office.

Leaving him staring after her, wondering just how he was going to fix this one.

CHAPTER 12

After her demoralizing discussion with Granville, Emily arranged to meet Clara in the basement archives of the *News Advertiser*, following the same process they'd used at the *World*. It was just as cold, just as dusty, and just as tedious as the search through the *World's* archives. At least they had a few new names to focus on, thanks to their work the day before with the provincial directories.

Several hours later Emily had had enough. The one thing their mountain of research confirmed for her was how little information was available to help them find Mr. Robertson. This case was going to be even more difficult than she had feared.

On top of her conversation with Granville, it was too much.

At least there was always Stroh's.

Over several pots of tea and an astounding selection of delicate sandwiches and pastries, Emily and Clara discussed their limited findings. Which hadn't impressed either of them.

"Are you going to let that stop you from going to the Cariboo?" Clara asked.

"Of course not."

"Then how do you plan to get Granville to agree?"

Since she still didn't have an answer, Emily tried for a little distraction. It had worked last time, after all. "I did talk to Mama about my wedding to Granville. Which she's continuing to plan."

"And is that a good thing?" Clara asked cautiously.

Emily had to smile. With Mama, you never knew. "Well, it might be. It doesn't seem quite so far in the future, this time. But you should see the gown Mama intends me to wear."

"Is it worse than the yellow bridesmaid dresses?"

"Yes, indeed." Emily said. And was almost distracted herself, watching her friend's face as she described the puffy sleeves, the lace overlays and the short lace-trimmed train embroidered with doves.

"Puffed sleeves? Embroidered with doves! And a train?"

"Just a short one."

"No such thing," Clara said firmly. "You should never wear a train. What is she thinking? That dress won't show you to advantage at all."

"I think she's thinking about upstaging Mrs. Smythe," Emily said. "I believe one of her daughters is getting married, also."

"Yes, the oldest. In the spring," Clara said absently. "But you can't let your Mama have her way with this. This time, you have to put your foot down."

"I'm trying," Emily said, reaching for her teacup and adding a little milk.

"And you are not succeeding," Clara said tartly.

"You know Mama. I can't even get her to talk to me about a proper date for the wedding. Which is far more important than a train."

"Nothing is more important than how ridiculous you'd look in that train," Clara said.

Emily had a brief mental picture of herself staggering down the aisle under the weight of all that fabric, and bit back a laugh. "You might be right," she said.

"Of course I'm right," Clara said. "This is your wedding. Yours and Granville's. You can't give up. Not when it matters to you."

～

THAT EVENING, Emily was heading back to her own room after a quiet family dinner when Mama beckoned her into the morning parlor. Emily was still feeling queasy after her discussion with Granville—and his ultimatum. The last thing she wanted was yet another discussion with Mama. But she couldn't think of anything she could say to get herself out of it. Dutifully, she followed Mama into the cozy room.

"I believe I have found something you will love," Mama said as they entered, and gestured Emily towards the small writing table under the window.

With a sense of occasion, she unrolled a large sheet of paper covered with colored sketches, and held it up for Emily to see.

Emily stared. "What is it?" she asked, trying to make sense of what seemed to be a fashion designer gone crazy, when all she could think of was the Barkerville case.

Mama smiled, her eyes gleaming. "Your wedding party," she said. "I've rethought everything. These are the newest, most daring of styles, fresh from Paris. Aren't they exquisite?"

Emily swallowed hard. Her wedding? To Granville? Oh no.

But there was nothing she could say, so she squinted at the drawings. The bridesmaids no longer wore yellow, but a deep sapphire blue. At least Clara would be happy, though they were so ornate, it looked like the dress would be wearing Clara. Then she looked a little closer.

"And that will be me? In the center, in white?" Well, at least the pouffy sleeves were gone, she thought. And the lace. Then she looked a little closer. "Only one sleeve? And... is that satin? Won't it be too shiny?"

"Not at all. It makes the perfect background for all of the beading."

"Beading? And why is the neckline so low?"

"Of course, beading. With rhinestones," Mama said with a smile. "And as I said a minute ago, it is the absolute latest in French style."

Emily just stared at her mother.

"Why, with this one design, you will outdo every bride of the last three years," Mama said, beaming at the thought. "Just look at that train. It's every inch of twelve feet long."

"I am looking," Emily said faintly. The train was also heavily beaded, and embroidered with doves holding rhinestones. All twelve feet of it.

When she finally managed to escape from Mama's latest visions of her wedding, Emily climbed the three flights of stairs to her bedroom and locked herself in.

"I can't do it," she said to her reflection in the mirror. "I can't be the person behind all that lace. I can't have such an elaborate wedding. It's just not me.

And I can't keep trying to reason with Mama about this. Not when she doesn't hear half of what I say and ignores the rest."

It was all too much. The frustration of arguing with Granville about their newest case for the last three days. The heartache of his ultimatum. The months long attempts to deal with Mama over her much-delayed wedding plans. And now these horrific dresses?

Emily flung herself onto the quilted coverlet on her narrow bed in a storm of tears.

When the worst of it was over, she lay on her back staring at the ceiling, feeling utterly exhausted.

"I can't," she said to the empty room as she wiped her eyes with a handkerchief. "I can't keep on like this. Something has to change."

And she felt a moment of complete despair. She'd been trying, and nothing had worked. Nothing at all.

Emily glanced around her comfortable bedroom. She'd loved this room for years. It had always been her retreat when Papa's restrictions or being the youngest daughter had frustrated her. So why did it feel like a prison now? Her eyes landed on her favorite green dress, freshly pressed and hanging on the closet door.

She'd been wearing that very dress last month when she'd confided in Clara about her problems with the delay in her wedding to Granville. "You'll have to elope," Clara had said then, with just a hint of laughter in her eyes.

And then today, Clara had challenged her not to give up.

Emily's lips started to curl up as she remembered both moments. Clara might not have been absolutely serious about her eloping with Granville, but that didn't mean the idea wasn't a good one. Or at least, it was a good idea now.

If they eloped, she and Granville could go to the Cariboo together as man and wife. He wouldn't have to leave her behind in Vancouver, or even in Barkerville with some ridiculous chaperone. She could travel with them.

And Mama? There would be no wedding to plan, no hideous gown, no social niceties to be met.

Emily smiled. An elopement would solve all of her problems, just like that. And she and Granville would be married. Would finally get to live together in the house they'd chosen together.

Now she just had to convince him.

CHAPTER 13

On Thursday morning, Granville was in his office early, and trying to concentrate on the preparations for their departure on Monday. It wasn't easy. He hadn't slept well, worrying about his last conversation with Emily, and her reaction to it.

Her face had gone so white, and she hadn't said another word. The minute she turned and left, he felt terrible. He was afraid he'd hurt her, and it was the last thing he'd ever wanted to do.

But seeing Emily sick or injured from the elements, would be worse. And if she were to die, on a trip he'd taken her on? That would be unbearable. He couldn't imagine how he'd be able to live with himself, afterward.

For the last hour he'd been debating what he'd say to her, when she came into the office this morning. He'd asked Miss Rizzo to let him know the minute Emily showed up, and then tried and discarded three different approaches.

It wasn't like him, but he'd never faced a situation where someone he cared for like this wanted to rush headlong into danger. And he had to be the one to stop her.

~

EMILY DIDN'T MAKE it to the office until after ten.

Miss Rizzo must have said something, because Emily tapped on his door just after he'd heard her arrive. And she strode into his office without waiting for his acknowledgement. Tiny raindrops caught in her hair like spangles told him she'd just come in from outside.

"You wanted to see me?" she asked, sitting straight-backed in the chair across from his desk. She fidgeted a bit, then leaned back, as if putting a little distance between them.

He watched her with concern. This wasn't like her. "Yes, I did," he began.

Before he could say more, she held up a hand. "I'm glad you did, because I have something to I need to tell you. Please, may I start?"

He nodded.

"Thank you," Emily said. She looked down at her hands, twisting in her lap. She stilled them, then took a deep breath, looked up, and met his eyes. "I'm afraid I have some difficult news."

He studied her for a moment, wondering if he'd ever seen her face so serious. She hadn't looked this worried after she'd been knifed in one of their earlier cases. Granted, it had been a shallow cut on her arm, but any injury is a shock. And especially to someone who has been gently reared, as she had.

He braced himself, not certain what was coming next. But sure it couldn't be good.

"Ever since Jane's fiancée left town so suddenly…"

"With a great deal of help from you," he quipped, hoping for a smile.

It didn't work. She ignored the comment and plunged on. "Mama has been focusing on our upcoming wedding."

Surely that was a good thing? And if Emily was still calling it their upcoming wedding, he couldn't have blundered too seriously yesterday.

"Mama's plans for our wedding grow more elaborate by the day. And the date of our wedding moves further and further into the future," she said, all in a rush, as if desperate to get the words out.

Oh. Now he understood her serious expression. Surely she hadn't been worrying about this for the last month, had she?

"It can't be that bad," he said with a grin. "How far in the future is she planning?"

"It's at three and a half years now," Emily said, not meeting his eyes."

"Our wedding is being planned for 1904?" he asked, appalled at the notion. "Surely she is not serious?"

"I'm afraid she is. And the more Mama works on the plans, the more elaborate they become. And the further our wedding date recedes into the future."

"I'd thought you were planning to talk to your Mama about moving our wedding to this coming spring?" Granville said carefully.

Emily looked up and leaned forward, planting her hands on the edge of his desk. "I did talk to her. And she agreed that a spring wedding would be much better than the fall one she had planned. That was when the date moved from three years away to three and a half years away."

"I see," Granville said. Emily's mother was a formidable lady, for all her short stature. It might not be easy to change her mind. But she had never struck him as unreasonable.

"Surely your Mama can be brought to see reason? It makes no sense for us to wait so long. Unless she is deliberately delaying our marriage for some reason?"

"I have been trying to talk to her. To no avail," Emily said, sounding aggravated and disappointed all at once. He put a hand out to cover hers where it lay on his desk. "And I am beginning to suspect what the problem is."

"Tell me," he said.

"I thought at first it might be about her role in Vancouver society, and her rivalry with Mrs. Smythe," Emily said. "But the more she changes the proposed date, the more I am beginning to suspect she is doing it for Jane and Miriam."

Granville nodded at that. "You are the youngest daughter," he said. "The eldest is supposed to marry first."

Emily heaved what sounded like a sigh of relief. "I knew you would understand. Since you have sisters."

Unfortunately, he understood the rules of the social world all too well. What he found difficult was the realization that those strictures applied even more firmly here, in colonial British Columbia, than they did in the whirl of London's social scene.

"I hadn't heard that either of your sisters was engaged," he said.

"No, because they aren't," Emily said. "That's the ridiculous part. But after Jane's heroic actions in regard to her scoundrel of a fiancé…

"You mean your heroic actions, that you attributed to your sister," he put in, and received a grin in return.

"Well, yes," Emily said. "Which may have been a mistake, as Jane now has several prospective suitors. And even Miriam has formed a possible connection with a fellow stamp collector."

"Which gives your Mama reason to hope she may settle all three of her daughters," he said, seeing the implications at once.

"And in the 'proper' order," she agreed, putting a weight of sarcasm into her words that had Granville hiding a smile.

That was his Emily. Nothing was going to keep her down for long.

"So your Mama is trying to delay our wedding long enough to allow for your sisters' romances to play out, and for both of them to marry before you do."

Emily nodded. "I think so. And she won't admit it, because it isn't fair, and she knows it. So she simply doesn't listen to anything I say on the subject of our marriage. It is beyond frustrating."

"And you've been worrying about this on your own? Why didn't you tell me this before?"

"Because I thought I could bring Mama to see sense. It was

only last night that I realized it had more to do with Jane and Miriam than with me."

He nodded. Unfortunately, her logic made sense, and her reading of the situation was likely accurate. Which gave them little room to maneuver.

There had to be a way, though. 1904 seemed impossibly distant. Anything could happen between then and now.

"But I think I might have a solution," Emily said softly.

Something in her tone alerted him, and he focused again on her face, trying to read her expression. What was she up to now?

"As it stands, this is a decidedly tricky situation," he said. "A solution would be welcome."

"I hoped you'd think so. Because I see only one way to avoid waiting three or four years to wed," Emily said, leaning towards him. "We have to elope."

"Elope," he repeated, staring at her. He hadn't anticipated that, though probably he should have. "Eloping would be social suicide for you. And your parents would be devastated."

"They will understand our situation," she said. "Especially Mama."

"Emily…" he began. Only to be waved off.

"I've been thinking about this," she said, her face alight. "We don't want to wait. And Mama doesn't want to prevent our marriage. Only to let my sisters have their weddings first. Our elopement would solve both those problems. If we elope now, we can put on a big reception at Christmas and invite all of society then, to celebrate our marriage."

Granville stared at her. He had a feeling he was missing something. "And how would you explain our need to elope?"

"That's the best part," she said with glee. "The Robertson case gives us the perfect excuse. If we're married, I can go north with you, and you can keep me safe. You said it yourself, it's the only way I can go."

Granville just shook his head at her logic, but he couldn't help grinning back at the twinkle in her eye. "I suppose you've worked out the logistics of this elopement?" he asked.

"We'll need a special license," she said. "Any judge or magistrate can provide that. And I thought perhaps we could marry in Ashcroft, before we head north. Clara and her cousin Claudia are willing to take the train with us that far, for propriety's sake, and then come back again that same day. If you can find a judge willing to grant the license, I can find someone to marry us in Ashcroft."

He had to laugh at how neatly she'd cornered him into taking her to Barkerville with him. And the thought of waiting nearly four years to marry her was intolerable. "You've thought out everything, haven't you? I'm surprised you don't have the name of a judge I might ask.

"Well," she said slowly. "I believe Judge Harrison is in town tomorrow. Perhaps you could ask him?"

He laughed even harder. "Of course I could. He'd probably be supportive of your desire to visit the Cariboo goldfields, as well, given that he was a magistrate in that area for several years."

She cast her eyes down demurely, as if the thought had never occurred to her, then gave him a mischievous look from under her lashes. "And he might even know something about our missing Mr. Robertson."

He shook his head at her, his grin widening. Then he sobered.

"Emily, are you sure this is what you really want? Marriage, and starting a life together can be a huge adjustment. To start out by eloping and facing the hardships and dangers of this case all at once is a lot. And a highly uncomfortable journey by stagecoach hardly makes for a pleasant honeymoon."

She smiled at him. "But it would be memorable."

"Nightmares are memorable," he retorted. "Emily, be reasonable. We don't need to do this, you know. Between us, I am certain we can find a way to change your Mama's mind, and move our marriage to this spring."

"I think we've waited long enough, don't you?" Emily said, moving around the desk and perching on the arm of his chair. She gave him a mischievous look. "For one thing, if I don't marry you quickly, you might die of malnourishment. I know you're still putting off hiring a cook, and have been eating all your meals at the diner."

"You are offering to cook for me?" he asked innocently.

She shot him a horrified look, then smiled as she realized what he was up to. "Hardly. I'm planning to steal Bertie from Mama's household. If we hire him, he'd take care of finding any other staff we need. We would come back to an efficiently run household."

"I see," he said. "And exactly how would would we pay for all of this?"

"Mama did teach me household management, you know," Emily said. "Even if I didn't like it. I know how a household is run. And I know how much money you're making from your business, as well. Don't worry. You can afford it."

It was the least of his concerns, but he was impressed with her very efficient solution to a problem he'd been avoiding.

"And we'll come back from the Cariboo to a home, instead of a half-empty house," she added.

As if she'd needed anything to seal the deal.

But Granville was taken with the picture she'd painted, of the two of them starting their lives as man and wife in a warm, well-run little house. One they'd chosen together.

Somehow the reality of the trip to Barkerville, with its hazards and trials—which was their immediate future—had faded in importance. Faced the with idea of waiting nearly four years for her, he realized how much he wanted the life they'd build here, in the house they'd chosen together. Surely that was all that mattered?

Even if it didn't quite work out that way.

WEDNESDAY EVENING FOUND Granville and Scott holding down the bar in some back alley watering hole Scott had decided to introduce him to. Why, Granville wasn't quite sure. Nor did he much care. The whiskey might be second-rate—or maybe third

—but it was plentiful, and at least they hadn't watered it. For this conversation, that was all he cared about.

They stood at the far end of the bar. Granville was leaning against a dingy wall, keeping an eye on the door, while Scott was facing him, with one foot braced on the tarnished bar rail. The place was crowded, dim with smoke, and noisy—all of which were to be expected at most of the bars in town. At least it was fairly clean, and they had this small corner to themselves.

"So what went wrong?" Scott asked, signalling the bartender for two more whiskies as Granville tossed his back.

"What do you mean?" Granville said.

"This morning you were in pretty good spirits. Now you're lower than I've seen you since you and Miss Emily got engaged. So what's up?"

Granville shrugged, and deftly catching the two shots of whiskey the bartender slid down the bar to them, passed one to Scott and tossed back the other.

With a shake of his head, Scott did the same. "You know we can keep at this all day," he said. "I'm not giving up until you tell me. Is it the client?"

Granville considered keeping silent, just to see how far Scott would take this. But he was thinking in circles, and he needed to hear his friend's take.

"I think I may have misstepped with Emily," he said quietly.

Scott stared. "Impossible," he said. "I've seen the two of you together, remember?"

Granville signaled for another round. "None the less," he said.

"This is about the case and the trip to Barkerville?"

"I'm afraid so."

"You mean she found a friend to accompany her? To Barkerville? In November?"

"Keep your voice down," Granville said. "And no. She wasn't able to find anyone."

"I guess she won't let that stop her."

"No. This trip seems really important to her."

"Well, damn," Scott said, and downed the whiskey the bartender had just sent their way. "So what did you say?"

"That she had no idea how dangerous winter weather can be. And that I wouldn't take her with me. And that was final," Granville said.

It sounded awful to his own ears. He could only imagine how it had sounded to Emily.

Scott winced. "What did she say to that?"

"Not a word. She just looked at me for a moment, and walked out."

"I think you're right," Scott said.

"To tell her I wouldn't take her?"

Scott shook his head. "That you really blew it."

"I know."

"So what are you going to do about it?"

"I wish I knew."

CHAPTER 14

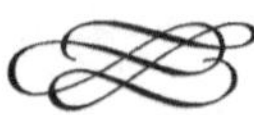

Monday, November 5, 1900

Suddenly, or so it seemed to Emily, it was Monday. Her wedding day. The start of her life with Granville.

And also the beginning of their journey to Barkerville.

Standing with the others on the railway platform in the chilly darkness of early morning, Emily could see puffs of her breath rising then vanishing in the damp air. As she watched the train chugging towards them through the mist of rain, she pinched herself, and yelped at the sharp pain. Then laughed at herself. She felt positively gleeful.

It had all worked. Somehow, it had come together. The elopement, the marriage license, the traveling minister who would meet them in Ashcroft and marry them there. Even a wedding dress, thanks to Clara's modiste, who had been brought into the secret.

And between Clara and Granville, somehow she'd assembled the clothing and equipment she would need for a winter journey into the Cariboo. Several times during the last few days, she'd had to stop and remind herself to breathe. She couldn't quite decide if she was more excited about her upcoming marriage, or the trip to Barkerville.

Clara had given her a horrified look when she'd made the mistake of mentioning that a few days ago. "Emily, you can't mean that," she'd said. "We've been talking about our weddings forever."

"That's because they fascinate you."

"And you don't feel the same? Even after you met Mr. Granville?"

"I feel that way about marrying him. I don't care where or how."

Clara had given her a disbelieving look, but dropped the subject and turned her attention to finding what she called "the perfect wedding dress for the circumstances."

"No lace. Or rhinestones," Emily had said, and left her friend to it. She did want to look her best, but she was more concerned about the clothes she'd need for the journey ahead. A frisson of excitement ran through her and she smiled. Clara, seeing it, just shook her head.

Emily grinned. At least Granville understood. There was more than one reason she was marrying him.

She'd somehow even managed to get Mama agree to her 'excursion' to Ashcroft with Clara and Clara's cousin, to see Granville off on his months long journey. All without giving herself away, or alerting anyone to the planned elopement.

She'd left a carefully worded letter for Mama with Bertie, who was Cook's assistant, and made him promise he wouldn't deliver it until mid-morning on Tuesday. Long after she and Granville would be safely married, but before Mama could realize Emily wasn't on the return train from Ashcroft. She trusted Bertie to keep his word about the timing of their elopement in any case.

Especially after Bertie had hinted, strongly, that he'd prefer to work for her and Granville at their new home once they were wed. And she'd agreed he could start when they returned. She'd even told him he could make what arrangements were required to ensure the house was ready on their return. She felt a little guilty that she hadn't been more specific about that detail to Granville yet. But not so guilty that she'd say anything that might jeopardize this trip.

Emily looked around her. Granville, and Scott, and Trent stood ready to board, surrounded by piles of luggage. Including her new set, though it was labelled as belonging to Granville.

She stood with Clara and Clara's cousin Claudia, a diehard romantic who was in on the secret and thought it too romantic for words. All three of them traveled with only a small overnight bag. Emily's hadn't even had enough room for her camera, which she'd had to pack in her trunk.

As the train blew in with a loud whistle and a cloud of soot, she and Granville exchanged a look and a smile. They were really doing this!

AN HOUR LATER, they were well underway, steaming through Vancouver and then New Westminster, and crossing the railway bridge over the Fraser River. Looking out through the rain streaked window as the sun rose, Emily could see the muddy, churning waters of the river below them. It felt unreal, seeing the river from this height and this angle. The water was high, bloated with rain and debris washed down, perhaps from hundreds of miles upstream. She wondered if it would flood this year, or whether the sandbags kept ready along the banks would be enough to hold it back.

Sitting beside her, Granville touched her shoulder and pointed out a tug, small against the breadth of the river, steaming its slow, steady progress downstream with a corralled boom of water-dark logs in tow. They exchanged smiles at the sight. In the seat ahead of her, Clara was ignoring the rain-smeared view, chatting with Claudia over the ladies fashion magazines they'd brought with them.

The train racketed over the rails through a constant drizzle instead of the sunshine she'd hoped for—today of all days. Still, after the last few weeks of constant rain, even an overcast day with scattered showers was welcome. At least it wasn't snowing.

And she and Granville were getting married! She almost pinched herself, just to check. Except that he would notice. And she'd feel embarrassed, for some reason. Even though she knew he wouldn't care.

Instead she focused on the scenery unrolling below her, and thought about their case. Only that reminded her that she was actually headed for Barkerville. And she wanted to pinch herself all over again.

Instead she smiled at her fiancé—nearly her husband, now— and tucked her hand around his arm. No more doubting that any of this was real for her!

What seemed like hours later, their train was making its way through the Fraser Canyon, on tracks that had been blasted out of sheer rock faces. The rain had let up and a bit of sun fought through the thick clouds. Far, far below them the river had shrunk to a foaming ribbon, punctured here and there by sandbars. Clara had taken one look, closed her eyes and refused to look again, but Emily couldn't look away.

She was watching every sandbar, trying to put a name to each of the gold sites she'd heard so much about. Yale was easy; the train stopped there. Sailor Bar. Alexandra. She had to guess those, but she could see the rapids at Hell's Gate, roiling the dark water. Ferrabee and China Bar were also guesses. Boston Bar, another train station.

After all the stories she'd heard from her father, there was magic in those names. Despite the harsh realities she'd uncovered in her research, it still felt amazing to see the actual route of the gold rushes.

During the Fraser River rush, they'd found gold, thousands of ounces of it, on those sandbars and along those banks. Right below her, men had struggled and died of injury, accident and disease, made and lost fortunes. Those rapids had killed countless would-be gold seekers.

And, unforgivably, these shores saw conflicts between the local tribes, who had made their home here long before the gold-seekers ever came, and some of those miners who didn't recognize any authority here other than the lure of gold. Which had resulted in at least one village slaughtered, and attacks up and down this shoreline, with fatalities on both sides. She shivered at the thought.

Eventually Chief Cxpentlum, the Peacemaker, with the backing of his fellow chiefs, had succeeded in negotiating a treaty between the miners and the tribes, and the fighting had ended.

Looking down from the comfort of their railcar, it seemed impossible to believe that she was traveling so easily above the harsh lands that were once the richest goldfields in the world. She shivered at the thought.

She tried to point them out to Clara, who still refused to look. Granville was made of sterner stuff, and told her a bit about his own gold rush days in the Klondike. She could hear Scott's chuckle from the seat behind them at his words.

Emily kept her eyes glued to the landscape passing by. Despite the damp, she would have kept the window beside her open if she could, but the occasional burning spark from the engines was enough to deter even her enthusiasm.

Only when the clouds closed in again and it became impossible to see anything did she agree to Granville's suggestion of lunch in the café car. It turned out to be a good idea, though. She'd had no idea how hungry she was.

CHAPTER 15

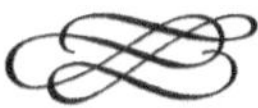

AFTER THEY'D EATEN AND THE TABLE WAS CLEARED, THE STEWARD brought pots of tea and chocolate biscuits. Emily turned to Granville. "I'd meant to ask you. When you got the special license from Judge Harrison, was he able to contribute anything to our search for Mr. Robertson?"

"Not a great deal, I'm afraid. He suggested the current Gold Commissioner, David Cranston, has been working for the government there for more than thirty years. Making him our best resource, because he's been in the area so long. Which you'd already worked out from the directory entries."

"That's all?"

"I'm afraid so."

"He didn't know anything about Thomas Robertson himself, then?"

"No-one seems to," Trent muttered.

"Which isn't surprising," Granville said. "There were thousands upon thousands of men passing through the area at the time. And Robertson himself may not have been particularly memorable."

"That's a point," Scott said. "Did Miss Kent get a chance to

finish those sketches she made from the photograph our client left
with you? Those might work better than just the name. Especially
if our missing miner had a nickname."

Granville nodded. "She did indeed, along with additional
copies for us. I have them here," and he pulled out another folder,
passed the copies around."

"These are very good," Emily said. "Did you have them
before—when you were talking to the old-timers, I mean?"

"We showed them the original photo," Scott said. "Didn't
help much."

Granville retrieved it from the folder and passed it to her. "It's
a group shot, which seemed to confuse them."

Emily looked more closely. "Yes, I can see why. The lighting
isn't very good, either." She held it up against the sketch. "Somehow, Miss Kent has fixed all of that. She's made everything
bigger, too, and much clearer. And if some of the older miners
have failing eyesight, this would really help them to identify him."

"I suspect our Miss Kent is something of an artist," Granville
said.

"Huh," Trent said, peering over Emily's shoulder. "She's
really made it better. If she's going to be doing this a lot, you
should pay for lessons for her."

"You want us to pay for art lessons?" Scott said.

"Drawing lessons," Trent said. "And why not? It helps us do
our job, right?"

"That's actually not a bad idea," Granville said. "If it's something that she'd be interested in, that is. We can look into it in the
new year."

Trent smirked, and Emily grinned as Scott rolled his eyes at
both of them. She suspected Laura would be thrilled at the
opportunity. And that they'd all benefit from it. Though Trent
being the one to recognize that surprised her.

He was changing on this trip, testing his limits. She couldn't
tell if he was deliberately trying to irritate Scott or not, though.
Was something wrong there?

"Something else that might be useful when we reach Barkerville," Granville said, apparently deciding to ignore the byplay. He passed a map tube to Scott, who spread out maps of the area around Barkerville, while Granville put the copies of Thomas Robertson's letters in the middle of the table. Emily leaned closer to see better.

She was enthralled by the very detailed map of the Cariboo area, which she hadn't seen before. Clara and even her cousin Claudia seemed intrigued by the letters. Sipping their tea, and being careful to keep the crumbs off of the documents, they read in silence for a bit.

"These doodles," Clara said suddenly, looking up from one letter. "The ones in the margin. How accurate are they?"

"Very," Granville said. "Miss Kent copied them for us, too, and she has an eye for these things. She not only drew these little scribbles in every detail, she's even caught the look of his handwriting, and that is not an easy thing to do."

"Why do you ask?" Emily asked, looking up from her own study of the map. An intent note in her friend's tone had caught her attention.

"Look at the creek names," Clara said. "The letters never mention exactly where he is when he mentions the "opportunities" or talks about "hopeful prospects". But in the first letter, he talks about a "lost chance" creek, and goes into a bit of detail about the nature of the diggings there. I looked, and there's no creek of that name on this map. But the doodle in the margin of that first letter. Doesn't that look like a lightning bolt? What if that refers to the real name of the creek?"

Emily sat up straight. "What? Where?" she said.

Clara pointed it out.

"I think you might be right, Clara," Emily said. "Lightning Creek was a fair distance from Barkerville, and was one of the richest areas in the region. Maybe he decided to try digging there?"

She noted Granville and Scott exchange glances. "You knew?" she asked.

"No," Granville said. "We just got the copies of the map back from the stationer's on Saturday and Miss Kent finished copying the letters the same day. So there was no time to study them in detail. I just had a feeling those scribbles of Robertson's might be important. He took the time to send them to his family, after all."

They spent the next several hours comparing the letters to the detailed map, and speculating about what Robertson had been trying to tell his wife and son.

"Our client didn't see much significance in the scribbles in the margin," Granville said. "Though we didn't have this map at the time, and I would assume he had never seen a detailed map of the area."

"So he's never been to Barkerville?" Emily asked. "Our client, I mean."

"No. His travel is usually for business, mostly in the United States, from what I understand," Granville said.

"Some of these scribbles are more like tiny sketches," Claudia said, looking up from a letter she'd been examining closely. "He even has cross-hatching and shadow details on some of them. Look at this one."

And she passed the letter across the table to Emily and Granville. "It's a detail of a tree," Emily said. "And you're right, I can practically feel the roughness of the bark, just from this."

She passed the page down the table to Scott and Trent.

"But what does it mean?" Clara asked. "Too many of these creeks have people's names, and I can't see anything that this drawing would relate to."

"Maybe he just liked the challenge of drawing it so clearly," Claudia suggested.

"What if he's showing us the fork of the tree?" Scott said, squinting at the letter. "There's lots of forks in these rivers and streams."

"Depending on where he was, he could'a been talking about Quesnel Forks," Trent said. "I heard that name from some of the old timers, but I think it's a long way from Barkerville."

"It is," Granville said, tracing his finger along the route on the map. "I suspect some of these squiggles might mean more once we get to Barkerville, and begin to retrace his footsteps. For now, let's see how far we can get with just the letters in combination with this map."

They spent several hours, which included more tea and biscuits, with the letters and the maps, chatting about how what they knew about the gold rush fit with the map and what the letters revealed about their client's father. From there the talk turned to the journey to Barkerville, and what might lie ahead for the four of them there.

"So you don't necessarily expect to find anything at all," Clara said eventually. "Is it worth it?"

Trent glared at her. "'Course it is," he said. "We've got a client, don't we? A paying client. And a chance to follow the gold trail, even if it was so long ago."

"This is no weather to be chasing gold," Clara retorted. "And I suspect Mr. Granville would agree with that."

He nodded. "I would."

"Then why are you all going?" Clara asked. "And taking Emily with you."

Emily watched the interaction with interest. Granville had been so focused on talking her out of coming with him on this trip, they hadn't really talked about why he was taking all those risks that he didn't want her to take. Why had he accepted the case, really?

He grinned. "I suspect you know very why Emily has joined us," was all he said. "As for myself, why do we take on any case? We have a client that needs our help, a test of our collective abilities and a challenging puzzle—made more difficult by the passage of time—all tied into one. How could I refuse?"

"My thoughts exactly," Emily said firmly.

Clara just shook her head, and Granville winked at her. Emily sat back, satisfied. This was going to be so much fun.

Shortly after that, they all returned to their seats for the remaining hours of the journey. The skies had cleared a little, so Emily watched the landscape roll by, trying to work out where they were. They followed the river most of the way, though after they left Lytton the steep cliffs and thick trees gave way to a flatter more open landscape.

Several hours later the train's whistle jolted Emily awake and she discovered with some embarrassment that she'd been sleeping against Granville's shoulder.

"I hope I didn't put your shoulder to sleep," she whispered.

"You didn't even drool on me," he whispered back.

She couldn't help but grin back in the dim lighting of their car. Around her, everyone seemed asleep. "Are we there?"

"This is Spence's Bridge. We have one more stop before Ashcroft, according to my schedule."

"It must be nearly four, then."

"It lacks ten of the hour."

"I need to freshen up," she said, desperate to splash water on her face and shake this foggy feeling. It would never do to arrive for her wedding feeling like this.

CHAPTER 16

Her heart in her throat, Emily stepped down from the train at Ashcroft Station. She was relieved to feel the solid unmoving planks of the platform beneath her feet. She'd loved the train and found it an exciting way to travel, but still, it had been a long nine hours. Especially after their early start.

Looking around her, she noted that while tiny compared to Vancouver, Ashcroft was a busy town. Carriages and wagons were lined up along the platform, waiting to greet the train and its passengers and goods. From where she stood, she could see several good sized buildings as well as smaller stores, with houses in the distance.

The sun was already low on the horizon, and it would be dusk soon. Before she had time to even wonder where they were meeting the minister who would marry them, Granville was hailing several porters for their baggage, and, offering her his arm, began directing their party through the station and out onto a sidewalk bordering the main street.

Emily just hoped there would be somewhere for her to change into her wedding dress, since he had been unusually cagey about the arrangements. Before she could ask, Granville looked down at her and seemed to read her mind. He gestured across the street from where they now stood.

As he did so, a delivery wagon pulled away in a cloud of dust, and she had a clear view of an imposing two story, L-shaped building. Painted a bright white, with a peaked roofline and broad verandahs running along the second story, an ornate sign read "Ashcroft Hotel". The hotel looked particularly inviting in contrast to the bare brown hills surrounding the town.

"We're staying there?" she asked.

He nodded. "It seemed convenient," he said with a sideways grin. "Especially when we'd been traveling all day."

"Oh, I do love you," she said in heartfelt tones.

"So do I," said Scott from the other side of Granville. "And I'll love you even more when I have a whiskey in front of me."

Granville placed his hand atop hers where it lay on his arm, and ignored Scott.

Who grinned and winked at Emily, leaving her biting back a giddy laugh.

It seemed that Granville had booked the entire dining room for their wedding. And Reverend White, the minister Judge Harrison had found for them, was meeting them there. Granville had also booked rooms for all of them.

Everything seemed in place. Emily drew in a shivery breath, and crossed her fingers.

She was shown to a large bedroom at the end of the hall with a verandah and a view of a quiet side street. The clouds had lifted when the train turned inland, away from the Fraser River but it was too dark now to see much other than the town's lights glittering in the clear air. And in the distance the shimmer of moonlight on a wide stretch of the Thompson River.

Turning away from the window, Emily glanced at the double bed, and realized Granville's cases as well as her own were neatly lined up in front of the closet. She swallowed hard when she realized this was the room they would share once they were married.

Behind her, Clara and Claudia entered noisily, exclaiming over her room, and how elegantly appointed the hotel was.

"We're just down the hall a bit," Clara said, "With Scott and Trent on the far side of us. After the wedding, they will serve us all a wedding dinner. And in the morning the carriage will take Claudia and I to the train for our journey home, then come back in time to take you and your new husband to the stagecoach for your journey north."

Emily blushed. It seemed so intimate, hearing the words "your new husband" when she was standing a foot from the bed she would share with him.

Clara gave her a knowing look. "No cold feet, now, you hear me? No matter how odd this might feel…"

"She is eloping, after all," Claudia put in. "But it's romantic. Not odd."

Both Clara and Emily ignored the comment.

"You know Granville is the man you were meant to marry. He's perfect for you. You chose this," Clara finished.

Emily nodded, oddly comforted by her friend's brusque tone. And it was true, all of it.

"I know," she said.

Clara suddenly stopped and stared at Emily for a moment. "Wait. You are eloping. I hope… that is… did your Mama ever have 'The Talk' with you? About a wedding night, and what that entails?"

Emily shook her head, and watched Clara's face turn pale. Then she took pity on her. "No, but she did have 'The Talk' with Jane…"

"And Jane told you," Clara said, her relief evident.

"Not exactly," Emily said with a sly sideways look.

"You eavesdropped!" Clara said.

"Of course," Emily said.

Claudia looked shocked, but not Clara.

"Good for you. Now hurry up, before Mr. Granville changes his mind," Clara said with a teasing smile. "Go and have your bath. You smell like soot from the engine."

While Emily soaked in rose scented water, Clara and Claudia unpacked her new dress of white silk brocade for her, shaking out the wrinkles as they did so. Less than thirty minutes later, Emily was ready.

"Emily, you look gorgeous. You make the perfect bride. It only needs this," Clara said, and lowered the fragile veil she'd borrowed from her sister.

For Emily, the marriage ceremony passed in a blur. Afterwards, all she remembered was the minister's resonant voice, the look in Granville's eyes as he spoke his vows, and the utter certainty with which she said her own.

The wedding dinner was a happy affair. The inn had outdone themselves with eight courses, each more elaborate than the last. The food itself was delicious, and plentiful. After a long day of traveling, all of them were hungry—Emily couldn't remember having eaten so much before—and the champagne Granville had also arranged for flowed steadily. She looked at the familiar faces of her friends, and tried to freeze the moment in her memory.

No matter how good the photographer was, he couldn't capture the warmth of Granville's hand holding hers, the scent of candles and flowers.

CHAPTER 17

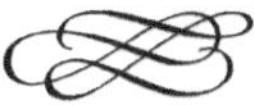

TUESDAY, NOVEMBER 6, 1900

The following morning, the dining room at the hotel lacked the starched linen tablecloths and sparkling silver settings from the night before, but the mouthwatering smell of frying steak and bacon beckoned them down from their rooms to join the rest of the party. Despite the early hour, Granville had made sure that they were served a hearty breakfast of steak, bacon and eggs, with toast and sweet rolls to tempt the ladies. Plus champagne and orange juice to toast the happy couple. Something their friends were more than happy to do, with ever zestier comments and not a few winks.

Granville was relieved when they had to cut these festivities short in order to see Clara and her cousin off to the station in time to catch the early train. Though Emily beamed throughout breakfast, laughing at the toasts, and grew a little teary saying goodbye to her friend. Granville played the polite host, but his eyes kept seeking out hers. And every smile touched his heart.

Then the train was gone, and everyone's attention turned to the case. The four of them gathered over cups of coffee to discuss and plan for the next stage of their journey. Granville looked across the table at Emily—his new wife—and couldn't quite believe it.

They were married. And on their way to Barkerville.

It was as if he'd been caught up in a whirlwind that had deposited them here, together. He didn't regret any of it, though. Marrying Emily, the night they'd spent together. Then waking beside her this morning—he could never regret a moment of it.

And he'd keep her safe, he vowed to himself. Even on this journey. And any other journeys their life together might throw at them.

As a lad, his father had often told him that once he was a man, it would be his privilege to provide a home and care for his wife and any family they might have together. At the time, he hadn't really understood, except when he looked at the life his father had built for his own wife and six children. He couldn't then imagine having that life for himself.

Even when he'd been in love with Julia—or thought he was— the life they might have together had never seemed real.

But this did. Looking across the table at Emily, he saw very clearly what he wanted. What he'd build. For her. And for both of them, together.

She looked up at that moment, as if sensing his regard, and smiled at him. In that moment, he thought he'd never seen anyone so beautiful. Her eyes shone, and every inch of her was so alive. If they hadn't had a stagecoach to board, he'd have taken her straight back upstairs. And not come down for a week.

At least he'd promised her a honeymoon in the spring. Perhaps they'd visit his family, in England. Aboard an ocean liner, they would have plenty of time alone together when the ship was at sea. From their journey to Ketchican last spring, he already knew she didn't suffer from seasickness.

"Hey, Granville. You with us?" Scott asked.

He smiled at Emily, then turned to his partner. "Unfortunately. Can't a man enjoy his coffee in peace?"

"Not when we have less than three hours before our stage-coach leaves. We need to check that everything gets delivered and loaded. Anything we have to replace will cost an arm and a leg in Barkerville. If we can find it at all."

"Fine," Granville said. "You and Trent are in charge of the baggage for the rest of the trip. And for making sure our provisions get to where we're going along with us."

"Don't we need to spend some more time looking at these maps?" Trent asked.

"Baggage first. Maps later," Granville said. "We have several days to discuss the maps. If we leave something behind here, we will likely have to manage without it."

Trent looked mutinous, but made no comment.

"And what will you be responsible for?" Scott asked with a sly look.

"My lady wife," Granville said, with a smile at Emily. He saw no need to mention that he'd made arrangements for a hot bath to be prepared for Emily in their room. After a leisurely soak, she could nap for an hour or so before they'd need to get ready to leave.

Trent rolled his eyes.

"It is our first day as a married couple, you know," Emily informed the lad.

Trent seemed about to blurt something out, but after a glance at Granville, changed his mind and sat back.

Granville hid a smile. This promised to be an interesting journey, in more ways than one.

JUST BEFORE TEN the stagecoach they would be traveling in was hauled to the front of the hotel. Several men began to load the bulk of the baggage into the boot at the back of the coach, and then the rest was tied down on the roof. The driver, easily identified by the long, curled up bullwhip he carried over one shoulder, was issuing orders in a quiet voice that was instantly obeyed.

Granville watched the process with interest. He'd taken any number of stagecoaches in England, and they came in all shapes and sizes. But the BX stagecoach was a narrower style, designed just for these roads.

The stagecoach in front of him was a large, very solid wooden vehicle, with heavy canvas drapes providing protection at the open windows. The body of the coach was red, with the wagon wheels, the running gear and the company name picked out in bright yellow. He understood from their various informants that the suspension on these stagecoaches was different from the ones he was used to.

English coaches traveling on macadam roads used steel spring suspension. These coaches used wide straps of heavy, stiffened leather, running from front to back and supporting the entire body of the coach, which apparently gave greater maneuverability on the uneven and often rocky or muddy roads they would face. The result for the passengers was a swaying motion from side to side, which some old-timers equated to the motion of a ship in a rough sea.

Curious though he was, Granville wasn't looking forward to four days of such travel. It was a small relief, knowing that Emily was resistant to seasickness. But it was going to be a long journey, in crowded quarters. It wasn't likely to be a comfortable trip, not for any of them. Even if the weather held.

Then, to Granville's surprise, came the call to load the passengers. He'd expected the horses to be hitched in place first, but apparently things were done differently here.

This particular coach held room for nine passengers, in three rows of three. Two of the rows of seats had a forwards view, while the one directly behind the driver looked backwards. The old timers had told him that the advantage of the backwards seats was that the motion of the coach was reduced slightly in that position. Even that little would make a difference over the distance they were planning to travel.

CHAPTER 18

THE FOUR OF THEM SHARED THE STAGECOACH WITH ONLY TWO
other passengers. Granville was glad to see they'd have the extra
space. Spending the next few hours in the coach was likely to by
trying enough for Emily, without being hemmed in on all sides as
well.

Emily, Scott and Trent settled themselves on the padded
leather bench seats, stowing their hand luggage under the seats
where it wouldn't be flung around. Granville stood by the coach
door, ready to leap into his seat when needed. But he wanted to
see the horses harnessed first.

And it was worth waiting for. Six magnificent horses were
brought out, their heads tossing proudly and their coats gleaming
with health. Each one had clearly been bred for strength and
stamina. Granville considered the intelligent eyes and well shaped
heads of the lead pair, and approved.

They were harnessed one pair at a time, in three sets of
matched pairs. As impressed as he was by the quality of the
horses, Granville was equally taken by the complexity of the
harnessing, which presumably would give them a great deal of
maneuverability over poor roads. If he wasn't mistaken, the

harnessing was also designed to allow the coach to be backed out in case of difficulties.

However dangerous the upcoming trip might prove, the BX stagecoach was clearly designed to handle anything that was thrown at it. He hoped for Emily's sake those safeguards wouldn't be needed on this trip.

And then they were off.

THEIR FIRST STOP was to be the roadhouse in Hat Creek, several hours away. When their planned trip had turned into an elopement on Thursday, he'd been horrified to realize that the best accommodation he could offer Emily on their honeymoon was in roadhouses along the way. Once they left Ashcroft, there was not a hotel to be found along the route.

He hadn't been exactly backwards in expressing himself, either. Scott had listened for a bit, then held up a meaty hand.

"You have stagecoaches in England, right?"

Granville had just stared at him. "Of course. Obviously."

"And where do their passengers spend the night? In the coach?"

"Not these days. There are staging stops. Inns, mostly."

"Then think of a roadhouse as being like an inn."

"I've heard the stories, too, you know. Rough and tumble accommodation, too many men to a room. Rats and lice." He shook his head. "I can't—and won't—subject Emily to that."

"That was more than thirty years ago, at the height of the gold rush. These days, the roadhouses that have survived have similar standards to one of your English inns."

"And how do I ensure that the rooms I'm booking are decent ones?"

"Ask Trent. He'll know."

And he had. Between them, they'd worked through the stagecoach line to arrange the accommodations, even for last night's hotel.

As they disembarked in Hat Creek, Granville looked at the well built structure in front of them and had to laugh at himself. This roadhouse looked nothing like those he'd first imagined.

And he teased Emily for her enjoyment of "penny dreadfuls." Apparently he had also paid too much attention to Cariboo gold rush tales that were equally exaggerated.

Or too many years had gone by.

Shaking his head at himself, he drew in a deep breath of fresh, pine scented air. It was chilly here, but not yet truly cold. Just cold enough to keep the interior of the stagecoach from growing over-warm, which was helpful.

And not cold enough that Emily would find it challenging. Not yet.

As the others filed into the roadhouse for a cup of tea, Granville stopped to chat with the driver. Jay Powers was a long-time driver on this route, and considered a 'crack whip'. His reputation for handling his team in the most difficult situations was the first thing he'd heard when he asked about travel conditions for this journey.

"With Powers in the driver's seat, you'll have a safe journey. And a fast one," he'd been told. And certainly what he'd seen so far had borne that out. But they'd only begun.

"The road seems good so far?" he commented.

"No problems yet," Powers replied cheerfully.

"How far have we come this morning?"

"A good sixteen miles," Powers said. "At this rate we'll lunch in Clinton, and make 83 Mile House in time for a late dinner, easy."

"Well, my thanks for your efforts. They are appreciated, especially when I have my wife along," Granville said and held out his hand to the other man. He wondered if he'd ever get used to calling Emily his wife, and the little frisson of pride he felt in saying the words.

∽

INSIDE, he joined the others in a dining room that was far rougher than the refinement of the Ashcroft Inn the previous evening. This had uneven pine walls and benches rather than chairs, but the room smelled of fresh baked bread and sweet rolls. Emily sat with Scott and Trent on one end of the large communal table with a pot of tea and a plate of what looked to be fresh biscuits, served with several kinds of preserves. As he slid into the space she'd left open beside her, he noted that Emily looked happy and at ease as she chatted with one of their seat mates about the area they were passing through.

When the conversation moved on, she turned to him with a smile. "May I pour you some tea while it's still hot? And the biscuits are hot, too and delicious. Or there is bread, if you'd rather. All with fresh butter and homemade preserves."

He laughed. "You won't lack for food on our journey, don't worry. After all, I can hardly let my wife starve, now can I?"

She got an odd expression on her face for a second, and he wondered what she was thinking. Was it being called his wife? Then she laughed back. "You know me too well to make the mistake of letting me go hungry," she teased.

She glanced around the table, and seeing everyone involved in their own conversations, turned back to him. "I'm glad we have a moment to talk. I'd hoped there would be time to discuss our case while we traveled, but it seems there isn't enough privacy to discuss it, is there?"

"Not really, I'm afraid," Granville said. "These men are too young to know anything useful. We can talk about the general area, though, and the history of the gold rush. We can even show Miss Kent's sketch of Thomas Robertson, see if he looks familiar to them."

"You mean they might recognize the man he became, years later?" she said. "What about asking for him by name?"

"I'd rather try with just the sketch," he said.

"A name can be too easy," she said after a moment's thought. "Without one, they'll have to look harder at the sketch, try to envision the man he'd be now."

She really did think like an investigator. It amazed him more the longer they worked together. "That's what I'm hoping. And if Robertson had a nickname, he might be known only by that nickname on the creeks. Using the sketch instead of his real name might still get us an answer."

"So we have the sketch to discuss. But we really can't talk about the maps, or the letters. Not in front of the others, anyway," she said, sounding disappointed. "Oh well, I suppose there will be plenty to see, and plenty to talk about, too."

"How are you finding it so far? The stagecoach, that is."

"Not bad at all," she said cheerily. "It isn't the most comfortable ride, as you warned me. But if we're stopping regularly for food like this, I don't mind at all."

Riding in a stagecoach tended to get more uncomfortable with time, unfortunately. Emily would undoubtedly find herself stiff and rather sore by evening, despite the cushions they'd brought. But they'd had that conversation before now, and there was no point bringing it up.

He couldn't send her back to town on her own. Not that there was any possibility she'd agree to go back, in any case.

CHAPTER 19

As they waited to re-board the coach in Hat Creek, Emily was happy to see that the sun was well up. The air was still crisp, but it smelled so fresh after spending a few hours in the closed coach. She was hoping that it would be warm enough that they could lift the heavy canvas curtains for at least part of the day, so she could see something of the land and the towns they were passing through.

She even had her camera ready, hoping for a chance to take a few photos. She'd brought it along in case they needed it for the investigation. Then Clara's cousin Claudia—who enjoyed photography as much as Emily did—had offered to take photos of the wedding.

Emily hadn't even been aware of Claudia during the wedding, but she had taken twelve photographs—an entire roll of film. Which she'd pressed into Emily's hand just before she and Clara took the train back to Vancouver.

Emily had mailed the completed roll off that very morning, and found herself eagerly looking forward to seeing the resulting photos once they returned home.

Now she couldn't resist the urge to document the journey

north as well. It was a good thing she'd packed several extra rolls of film.

On Clara's urging, come to think of it. In fact, it was a few seemingly offhand remarks her friend had made that got Emily thinking about wedding pictures in the first place.

Emily smiled and shook her head, reminding herself yet again never to underestimate her friend. In anything.

To her surprise, just as she and Granville were about to climb into the coach Mr. Powers stopped them.

"I was wondering if your wife would like to ride up beside me for a bit," he said to Granville. "The weather has warmed some. It'll be chilly, but there's blankets should keep her warm enough."

Emily blinked at him. She'd heard that sometimes one lucky passenger got to ride up beside the driver, in the most comfortable seat of them all. The one with fresh air, and the view.

And a perfect opportunity to take photos.

She smiled at him, then at Granville. "Oh, I would love to," she said. She had so many questions she wanted to ask.

Granville nodded, just as she'd known he would, and put a hand under her elbow to assist her up to her new perch.

Emily looked around her, seeing the stretch of empty land beyond the small town, all low hills with bleached grass and stark leafless trees against a washed out blue sky. The crisp air smelled so good, of sagebrush and pine.

"Thank you, Mr. Powers," she said, turning towards him as he took his post. "I really appreciate this."

"And I appreciate the company," he said gallantly. As soon as Granville had disappeared inside the coach to take his own seat, the driver unwound his long whip.

"Let 'em go," he said to the lad holding the reins of the lead horses. And cracked the whip so that it flicked just beside the one on the near side. It never touched him, she noted with relief.

"Do you use the whip often?" she asked.

"All the time," he said. "It's one of the ways I communicate with the horses. But if you watch, you'll see that the whip seldom actually touches the horse, and only lightly then. Pain is no way to control an animal, especially not beauties like these. They know the roads even better than I do."

"How intriguing," Emily said, and settled back to enjoy herself. "How are they trained?"

The next few hours passed swiftly as the landscape around them shifted from low grass and sagebrush plains to sparsely treed rocky ground rising into steeper foothills. The scenery was austere, even bleak in parts, all grays and browns and the dark green of stunted pines. Mostly following the Fraser River, the wagon road was steep in places, narrow in others, and very uneven. After carefully observing the driver's competence and the confidence of the horses, Emily felt perfectly safe.

And she lined up several potential photographs as they rolled past, finally snapping a shot that she thought would work well.

"Won't that just be a blur?" Mr. Powers asked.

Emily jumped a little. She hadn't realized he'd noticed her looking down through the viewfinder and finally choosing to snap a picture.

"I hope not," she told him. "We are moving slower than the train does, and I focused on the trees and hills in the distance, rather than anything in the foreground."

"Hmmm," was his only response.

Which was enough to decide her to save her film for pictures she was sure would be clear. At least until she'd seen how a photo taken from a moving coach turned out.

When the road wasn't demanding all his attention, she plied Mr. Powers with questions about the trip, about Barkerville, and what he knew of the gold mining days. He seemed impressed by her knowledge and interest in the gold rush, and the hours flew as they exchanged stories.

To her disappointment, he didn't recognize the sketch. But he told her stories of other would-be miners who had joined the rush north, and the amazingly diverse lives some of them had gone on to lead.

Emily felt as if she could listen to his stories for the entire journey.

"What of those who didn't leave at all?" she asked, keeping their case in mind. "In those days, it would have been a hard life. And a dangerous one?"

"Indeed it would," he agreed. "Some of those who didn't leave chose to stay in Barkerville, make a life and raise a family there. But you're right about the danger. Too many ended up in one of the cemeteries in the area.

Mostly from accidents, some of which were pretty odd. I heard of one miner who died of what they called congestion of the brain, three years after falling on an axe. He'd been cutting trees for timber near Mosquito Creek in pretty rough terrain, and I guess he lost his footing."

"And it killed him three years later? How very odd. That poor man."

"That's what I heard. Another miner was working over on Jack of Clubs Creek. There had been a heavy snowfall overnight, and the snow was packed deep everywhere. And those shaft houses were all built with a steep roof, like an inverted "V", so that the snow slides right off. And that poor man was working right underneath.

The buildup of snow slid right off that slanted roof and killed him dead. They say 250 miners attended his funeral."

Emily could only shake her head.

"It's dangerous work. Mines caved in, or flooded. Dynamite didn't go where you wanted it. And miners died," Mr. Powers said. While skillfully handling the reins of his team as they bowled along a narrow road with steep hundred foot drop-offs on either side.

Emily wondered that he could be so oblivious to the dangers he faced every day.

"But it wasn't just the miners. There were wounds that went septic, cholera from bad water, frozen toes turning gangrenous, a few bar fights that turned lethal. Even holdups that ended in death. And more than a few unsolved murders."

"Really? Were the bodies always identified?" Emily asked.

"As far's I know, they were. The worst were a couple killings attributed to Boone Helm, a notorious killer and bank robber who worked mostly on the American side. But he was up here for a bit in the '60's.

No-one ever proved it was Helm, but a couple of miners were headed back to Vancouver with their bags of gold. Worth upwards of $20,000 then. Those poor miner's bodies were found a few days later, lying in some bushes just a few hundred yards off the trail. They'd been shot right through the head.

That was Helm's signature, that precise shot to the head. There were rumors of other killings, too, but I never heard those were confirmed. And no arrests were made.

"And no-one ever proved any of the killings were Helm?" Emily asked.

"Couldn't even prove he was in the area on the days in question. Though in every case he'd been seen locally a few weeks before."

"If I was looking for all the names of those who died over Cariboo gold…" Emily began.

Mr. Powers laughed, his hand light on the reins. "Your best bet would be to search every graveyard. Though some of them are so overgrown you'd likely not find them."

He glanced across at her. "Of course, for a scholar who was serious about finding them all, the graveyards wouldn't be enough."

"What should I do instead?"

"I'm afraid it would be in addition to. You need to hear the stories passed on from the Argonauts. Like the ones I'm telling you. Taken together, that would give you a much better understanding of the life of a Cariboo miner. Of who was here. And who wasn't."

"Thank you," Emily said, fascinated by his perspective. She thought she could listen to Mr. Powers talk about the goldfields as long as he was willing to talk to her about them.

By the time they reached Clinton, where they would change horses again and gain a new driver, she was more than ready to stop and stretch her legs. She was hungry, too, and just a little cold. The mercury had dropped into the forties and a wind had sprung up.

As he turned off the road and into the small town, Mr. Powers told her that luncheon would be waiting for them here.

"Oh, good," Emily said, drawing the blanket a little closer around herself. She had never felt so hungry in her life.

And she couldn't wait to tell Granville everything she'd learned.

CHAPTER 20

WHEN THEY DREW IN AT THE CLINTON HOTEL, GRANVILLE WAS standing below waiting to help her down almost as soon as the stage came to a halt. She turned to thank Mr. Powers, then took Granville's waiting hand as she returned his smile. It was nice to be a recent bride, and have Granville so attentive. Even if it wasn't necessary at all.

The next moment her chilled limbs nearly crumpled under her, and she was very glad for his assistance. She had underestimated the effect of sitting unmoving for so long. And in the cold, too.

Her muscles quickly recovered, but Granville hustled her indoors. Before she'd taken in more than a glimpse of the two story hotel with its log walls, steep shake roof and a second floor verandah made of peeled branches. She promised herself to stop and take a photo of Granville, Scott and Trent in front of the hotel before they left again.

As they'd driven into town, Mr. Powers had pointed out the steeply peaked roofs on most of the buildings. "They get a lot of snow here, too," he said. "A steep roof lets the snow slide off, instead of collapsing under the weight."

Which had made Emily think of the story he'd told about that poor miner. As she looked up at the overhang, she realized it was the same design that worked so well in Vancouver's heavy rainfalls.

Just with an additional danger if the snowfall was heavy enough.

The proprietress, all smiles, met them at the door. Emily had no further chance to talk to Granville before that lady quickly ushered Emily into the cozy ladies parlor—which Emily suspected was their hostess's own parlor—to "rest and refresh yourself before luncheon". Following a quick trip to the outhouse out back, Emily was actually glad to have a quiet moment to herself in the nicely decorated room.

After she removed her hat, washed her hands and face, and tidied her hair, she felt immensely better. She curled up on the settee in front of the fire and closed her eyes for a moment. She wasn't at all tired, not when there was so much happening. It was just that the heat of the fire and the soft, unmoving comfort of the settee felt so wonderful.

The next thing she knew was a tap on the door, and Granville's voice calling her name. Emily's eyes flew open and she jumped up.

"Just a minute," she called out as she rushed to tidy her hair and make sure there were no sleep creases in her face.

She probably could have invited him in, she realized. There were no other ladies present to be offended. And now that he was her husband, Granville would often see her when she'd first woken. But the notion was too new to be comfortable, quite yet.

It was only moments later that she opened the door and took his arm.

"Luncheon is ready?" she asked. At his nod, she smiled. "Good, because I'm even more hungry now than when we arrived. And I was starving then."

"Then it's a good thing they are planning to feed us well," he said. "I gather they are particularly known for their steak. Did you get a chance to rest at all?"

"I fell asleep," she confessed. "I didn't think I would."

"I'm glad you did. traveling by stage is more tiring than you might expect. It is not exactly an ideal honeymoon for you."

Emily grinned up at him. "I think it's perfect," she said with emphasis.

As they stepped through the doorway into a spacious dining room, four sets of eyes focused on them and their private conversation was at an end.

During the luncheon , Emily entertained the others by sharing some of Mr. Powers' stories, and they all contributed travel tales of other journeys. Mr. Jameson had traveled this route often, and was happy to talk about the next leg of the trip.

"We'll make a stop at the 70 mile post to change horses before we stop for the night at 83 Mile House. That's where the north and southbound stagecoaches connect, and change drivers," he said. "So that is where we'll get our dinner and spend the night."

Emily blinked at the information. Clinton was at the 47 mile post, though only thirty-two miles from Ashcroft, Mr. Powers had told her. And they had to go all the way to the 83 mile post—which was as far again—before stopping for the day? The reality of the journey they were on seemed much more daunting now.

They'd only been traveling by coach for four hours, and already she found it a relief to lie down for a moment. What would the next four hours be like?

To say nothing of three more days of this kind of travel?

Granville bent over to whisper in her ear. "I've booked a very private room for us at 83 Mile House," he said.

Emily had seen some of the large shared rooms, where bunkbeds lined the walls and cots filled the center of the room. After a day of stage travel, the thought of getting any kind of restful sleep in such accommodations didn't appeal. She flashed him a relieved smile, and squeezed his arm in thanks.

After the short nap she'd just had, she felt a little more rested. Surely tomorrow, she'd feel like a seasoned traveler, fresh and ready for the day's journey.

She was with Granville, on their honeymoon, after all. No matter what anyone else thought.

Sitting at the table across from them, Scott grinned broadly. "What are you two lovebirds cooing about now?"

Emily blushed a little at where her thoughts had taken her, but met his twinkling eyes. "None of your business," she said firmly. If not exactly elegantly. Mama would be horrified.

But then, this was hardly an elegant situation. They were traveling by stagecoach, in November, along the trail of gold. She grinned at the realization that it was all real. It was happening, here. Now.

She and Granville were married. And they were on their way to Barkerville. On a case.

It was too perfect.

"You've got that look on your face again," Trent accused her, from his seat beside Scott.

"Eat your steak before it goes cold," she told him. "And quit worrying about what I'm thinking."

Trent never needed telling twice when it came to food. But he gave her half-full plate a speaking look before turning his attention back to his own food.

Emily glanced sideways at Granville, and found him watching her with a little light in his eyes. She fought back another blush as she smiled at him. "I guess I'd best pay attention to my meal," she said.

"I guess you had," he quipped. "Especially since the food is indeed quite good. I think they grow much of it locally. And it sounds as if we'll be eating a late dinner."

She nodded, and dug into her own steak. Which was just as good as he had promised.

CHAPTER 21

Wednesday, November 7, 1900

The second day of their journey to Barkerville began very much as the first had, Granville thought with a quiet grin. He woke beside his new wife, had an excellent breakfast at a decent roadhouse, and after Emily had taken her photograph, joined her in the stagecoach for the next leg of their journey. He could only count his blessings that Emily saw it all as a great adventure and had woken in as sunny a mood this morning as she had the previous day.

Perhaps it had something to do with the fact they were newly married, with all the privileges that state entailed. Even if they only shared a bed in a roadhouse, they had a private room. His grin widened at the memory.

Before they left the 83 Mile House, Granville took the opportunity to have a quick word with Powers, and thank him for making their first day's journey an easy one.

"Happy to do so, and especially since your wife told me that the two of you are newlyweds," Powers said. "Though some might find traveling to Barkerville in November an odd way to spend a honeymoon."

"It was the bride's choice," Granville told him.

"And it seems to suit her," Powers said. "She pays attention to everything. Knows a lot about the gold days, too."

"That she does," Granville said. "And thank you for taking such good care of her, and giving her the opportunity to travel in style. She values being able to see the country we pass through."

"I'd hardly call it style," Powers said with a wink. "And she's good company, the way she enjoys everything. You're a lucky man."

"And I know it," Granville said.

Emily planned to spend most of today inside the stagecoach, despite the crowded conditions—another three passengers had joined them at 83 Mile, so all the inside seats were full. She found the weather a bit too cold to ride outside for more than one sixteen mile segment, much as she enjoyed the view and the easier ride of that higher perch.

Powers must have said something to their new driver Ed Owens, because Owens had offered Emily the choice seat up beside him whenever and for as long as she chose. Which was a relief, since it meant Emily didn't have to spend the entire day inside the crowded coach.

For the segments of the route Emily chose to travel inside the coach, Owens then offered the opportunity to ride beside him to whichever other passenger he favored for that segment. Granville had politely declined his own invitation—he found himself unwilling to spend time away from Emily. "We are recently wed," he told the driver.

"So I understand," Owens had said with a nod.

So he and Powers had spoken, then. Granville spared a moment to wonder what information the drivers shared on their passengers. And promptly showed Owens the sketch of Robertson. "He originally came to the area in 1863, then his family lost touch with him," Granville said.

Owens didn't recognize the sketch. Which was hardly surprising. The fellow had been too young to be driving back then, and it was a long shot to imagine Robertson still taking the stage from Barkerville to the coast some thirty years later.

He hoped they would have better luck in Barkerville, or this case could prove a complete waste of time. But either way, he'd never forget this trip. Or the wedding that had preceded it.

The day was cool but clear, and once the sun was well up, they periodically raised the heavy canvas curtains on one of the windows for fresh air and a glimpse of the country they were passing through. Despite their wraps and cramped quarters, it was too cold to leave the curtains up for too long.

They made good time through the Cariboo country, the wagon road mostly following the Fraser River north. They didn't stop for luncheon. Instead, they had individual packets of thick roast beef sandwiches, slices of pound cake and crisp apples packed for them by the cook at the 83 Mile Ranch. By early afternoon, they changed horses on a large ranch just past the 134 mile post near Horsefly. Passengers were offered hot drinks, or fresh milk from the dairy herd.

It made for a long day.

Granville worried about Emily, but she seemed to be adapting well to the pace of their travel, and the motion of the stage. Between the heavy woolen layers she wore and the traveling blankets they'd brought, she seemed to stay warm enough. One advantage of the cramped conditions was that the inside of the coach stayed much warmer than the air outside.

It also helped that their traveling companions were polite and used to this mode of travel. And that none showed any sign of motion sickness. Except perhaps Trent, who looked a little green at times. Luckily Owens invited the lad to take a turn up beside him, which seemed to have solved it.

Afterwards, Trent was too busy talking about his experience to notice the motion of the stage. He and Emily compared notes for nearly an hour, leaving Granville amused and Scott rolling his eyes. After a time, talk turned to mining, and the gold rushes.

Since the other passengers were all miners, returning to their jobs at one of the big mining companies that now mined the creeks around Barkerville, they had some interesting discussions about what things were like now compared to how they had been at the height of the gold rush.

He and Scott threw in a few stories from their Klondike days.

"I've always wondered," Emily said after listening for a bit. "How dangerous is mining now compared to how it was in the height of the Cariboo Gold Rush?"

"You mean back in the 1860's?" one of the miners, almost as tall as Scott and heavy with muscle, asked.

She nodded.

"It's still risky," he told her. "But mining technology has improved. Accidents that would have been killers back then, miners can survive these days."

The oldest of the men, whose wiry build and gray hair suggested he might have been around for at least the latter years of the Cariboo rush, was nodding.

"Some of the stories from those early days make that clear," he said. "They didn't have much in the way of machinery, and only wood supports for their tunnels. In '67, an experienced Welsh miner drowned in a mineshaft.

Then, a year later, another Welsh miner—a decade younger —died in a cave-in. It was his last shift at the mine, too. He was planning on heading out the next day."

"Unlucky Welshmen?" Trent asked with a grin.

The older man shrugged. "Probably no more so than anyone else. There were a lot of experienced Welsh miners came to Barkerville to try their luck. Times were hard in Wales, then."

"Couple years later, a Scottish miner and a Chinese one drowned in a mine shaft at midnight," the third miner, a young fellow with a competent look about him, said. "Water broke into the shaft.

"Then there's the story of young Franklin, Julius his name was. Came to Barkerville when he was just 17," the older miner said. "Did pretty well, for the first six months, then he fell down a mineshaft, and died."

"That's so young. And so sad," Emily said.

Her attention was riveted on the tales the men were telling, Granville noted with a private grin. And her interest was inspiring them.

"It was," the youngest miner replied. "They all were. The accidents."

"The one as got me was the miner that went to the store at Richfield one winter night," the tall miner said. "Storm got so bad, he got turned around. Froze to death less than a quarter mile from his front door."

"That was Lynch, wasn't it? The Irishman? Up on Lowhee Creek?" asked the oldest miner.

"That's the one."

"1874 was a bad year for weather."

Nods all around.

"It's not easy country, the Cariboo," the oldest miner told Emily. "And mining? Well, striking it rich might be worth everything. But you pay a pretty high price."

"You'd know," he added, looking at Granville.

Who nodded. He did indeed. And he knew how low their odds were of finding Robertson alive.

That's if they could find him at all.

THEIR NEXT STOP was the 150 Mile House, where they were offered afternoon tea. Emily beamed at the invitation, and Granville was quietly amused to note that everyone else was equally appreciative.

"Clara would have approved of this, at least," Emily said quietly to Granville as she picked up a flaky pastry with some kind of sweet filling. "Though I think she would have been horrified by most of the journey."

"And here I'd been wondering if I had married the right woman," Granville said, straight faced.

She poked him in the rib. "It would have served you right, if you had married her," she told him. "Clara is a wonderful person, but you and she together?" She shook her head sadly. "She would have made you miserable."

"I don't doubt it for a moment," he said. "And I'm very glad indeed that you are here with me."

"You mean that?" she asked. "You had a lot of doubts before. About my coming to Barkerville, I mean."

"I still think investigating at this time of year could prove treacherous, once we get to the creeks. And there is no knowing what Robertson might have become involved in," he said. "But I'm beginning to believe my new wife can handle anything."

"You mean you didn't believe that before?" Emily said, giving him a sideways look.

"It's a flaw, I admit it," he said dryly. "But one I hope you'll overlook."

"I married you, didn't I?" she said, matching his tone. Then she grinned at him. "And so far, I'm not regretting it. Not a moment of it."

After tea, they drove another eight miles further, stopping for the night at Carpenter's House. Dinner was spectacular. The best steak he'd ever tasted, baked potatoes with lashings of butter and cream and some kind of winter vegetable stew. Whatever it was, it was perfectly cooked and very tasty.

After dinner they were served tea or coffee and apple pie, and they sat chatting with the other passengers for a time, enjoying the camaraderie. The pie was seasoned with cinnamon and served with a generous amount of thick cream. As he demolished every mouthful, he noted Emily was doing the same.

She was chatting with the youngest miner, who was sitting across the table from them. The fellow had traveled on the box up beside Owens after Emily had spent a few hours there, and they were exchanging impressions of the experience. The fellow commented

"Found myself amazingly hungry after spending a couple hours in that brisk air," he said.

Emily smiled and nodded. And ate another mouthful of pie and cream.

The fellow seemed impressed with Emily, which showed good judgement. But he was a little too interested in her. Which didn't, Granville thought. But it was good to see her so relaxed and happy.

He couldn't think of another woman of his acquaintance—except perhaps his oldest sister Louisa, in her younger days—who would have adapted so well to this form of travel. Or enjoyed it so much. Especially when they were newlyweds.

As soon as everyone had finished eating, Granville made their excuses and he and Emily went upstairs to their room, followed by knowing glances. Neither of them cared in the least.

CHAPTER 22

Thursday, November 8, 1900

The following day Emily awoke to Granville gently shaking her shoulder. She stretched a little in the luxurious warmth of the feather bed and smiled sleepily at him. "It's still dark," she said. "Surely it can't be morning yet?"

"It's always dark these days," he said. "It isn't really morning yet, but we are required downstairs for an early breakfast. Today is going to be a long one."

"We reach Quesnel tonight, don't we?" she said, sitting bolt up right. "Is it snowing?"

"You sound entirely too excited at the prospect of snow," he told her.

"I'm hoping we get to ride in one of their sleighs," she said. "It's a grand way to travel."

"You might not think so after a long day riding in one," he said.

"But I've always loved sleighing."

"You do know that the sleighs have no roof or walls?"

Emily grinned at him. "I have been in sleighs before," she said. "Stop trying to ruin my fun."

He got out of bed and went to the window, twitching the curtain just enough to see out. "You'll be disappointed to hear that it's clear out and the stars are twinkling, meaning it's quite cold. Too cold to snow."

Emily was too busy appreciating the view to reply for a moment. It had surprised her, that first night, to discover he slept without a nightshirt. And at first, she kept looking away. But now she was getting used to being married, and to him.

Though she still looked away as soon as he began to turn around. It embarrassed her to be caught staring. "Maybe as the day warms up it will snow," she said quickly.

"Perhaps. But we'll be starting out in the stagecoach, at least."

"Then we should dress and go down for breakfast," she said. "You'll have to play ladies maid again."

"I look forward to it," he said, with a sideways glance at her.

"I'm very glad to hear it," she said. And then spoiled it by blushing. She still wasn't quite used to this marriage thing.

They were served in the dining room, which was chilly this morning, though the fire in the hearth was beginning to take the cold off the room. Emily was pleased to see that breakfast was another feast. The staff at Carpenter House had laid out huge platters of scrambled eggs, bacon and pan-fried potatoes. Plus there were hot soda biscuits served with homemade berry jam and fresh-churned butter. Big pots of tea steamed on the long dining table. She couldn't believe how hungry she was, despite the early hour.

She tried to remember if she had ever eaten breakfast this early, and couldn't think of a time. Even that felt exciting.

She could feel Granville watching her, and smiled up at him. He seemed to be waiting for the moment she realized this wasn't a proper honeymoon, whatever that might be, and be disappointed. She just hoped it wasn't her he would be disappointed with. Then she thought about the night they had just spent, and smiled quietly to herself.

Perhaps not, as he might say.

After they'd eaten, they just had time to wash up after breakfast and gather their things before the stage left at five.

She chose to ride inside for a bit, because Granville had been right. It was cold out. And still too dark to see anything. She preferred the warmer, brighter parts of the day.

Apparently she wasn't the only one, because Mr. Owens had no company on the box for that stretch of road. The sun was well up by the time they stopped at Soda Creek several hours later for a change of horses and to collect the mail. Despite their very early breakfast, Emily was surprised to learn that a second breakfast was waiting for them. And even more surprised to realize she was hungry.

After that first breakfast, she'd felt too full to even think about food before lunch. But when a plate of steak and eggs was put in front of her, she dug in with a will. And didn't even consider refusing the toasted sourdough bread that was served along with it. For a moment she wondered if something was wrong with her, eating so much.

She was relieved to see Granville, Scott and Trent eating equally heartily, and all three of them asked for seconds. And said yes to a large slice of apple pie. She was too full to even consider seconds. Or pie. Though the food was so good, she almost regretted that she didn't have room.

When Mr. Owens asked her if she wanted to ride on the box until they reached Alexandria, she was very happy to accept. Though she made sure she took her photograph of her companions and the inn before they left.

"Try not to miss me too much," she told Granville as he assisted her up onto high seat.

"Of course," he said. "Scott, Trent and I will use the time to plan our strategy for Barkerville."

"Without me?" she said, feeling hurt.

Then she realized he was joking, and shook her head at him. "If you do that, I'll develop my own strategy. And execute it on my own, too," she told him with a straight face.

"Then I suppose we'll have to wait for you before we plan,

won't we?" he said with a wink. And he made sure she was well wrapped in blankets before rejoining Scott and Trent in the stagecoach for the next leg.

As the day warmed, the sun burned off the frost from the long, flattened golden grasses that covered the plains that rolled into low, bluish-purple hills in the distance. Emily was caught up in the fresh scent of crisp, dry air, so very different from the damp, heavy feel of the air on the coast.

The altitude was higher here, too, so the air felt thinner as well as lighter. Much as she loved living beside the ocean, she found this exhilarating.

They weren't too far from the river, and she caught glimpses of the water glittering in the sun when the road curved closer. When she asked, Owens explained that they were still following the Fraser River inland. "And we'll do so until we reach Quesnel. Did you know it used to be called Quesnellemouth?"

"I'd never heard that. What an odd name. Why call it that?"

"It's a mouthful, isn't it? Because it's located at the mouth of the Quesnel River, where it meets the Fraser. They shortened it in 1864, when the town became the commercial center for the Cariboo gold rush," he added with a grin.

"That was smart," she said, smiling back at him.

As they drove north, Emily started to notice stands of leafless aspen, their papery white trunks stark against the deep green of the firs behind them. Then it was back to the grasslands, though here and there gray-green mounds of sagebrush took over from the long grass.

"You'd want to watch for rattlesnakes, if you were walking through this area in the warmer weather," Owens pointed out. "You don't see 'em much this time of year, though. Too cold."

"Do you think it will snow?" she asked.

He shrugged. "Might. We'll be fine until we reach Quesnel, though. And if the weather changed suddenly, we have sleighs available at Alexandria as well as Quesnel. Have to get the mail through, after all."

The comment caught Emily's interest. "You're carrying mail on this trip?"

He grinned. "We carry Express Mail on every trip," he said. "That's letters in special envelopes, that get priority over everything."

"Where are the letters going?"

"A lot of it goes on to Barkerville, but usually we have at least a few to pickup or deliver for every stop. Letters are important out here."

She nodded, imagining what it must feel like to get a letter when most of the roads are closed for snow. "You carry mail even in winter?"

"Of course. Express mail isn't heavy, and doesn't take up much room, so if we can get through, those letters get through. But we also have a government contract for mail delivery in the Cariboo, so there's a schedule where one of the stages carries packages and bags—whatever people will pay to transport—as well as letters."

Emily thought about that. "So we could have mailed some of our supplies ahead of us, instead of bringing them ourselves?"

"Could. But it gets expensive. And all freight except the Express Mail only runs once a month this time of year."

Too bad. She still felt a bit uneasy about whether she'd packed everything she'd need once this case really got underway. Another thought struck her.

"If I wanted to mail a letter from Barkerville, I could send it Express Mail, and it would be back in Vancouver four days later?" she asked.

"Yes. And delivered on the fifth day," he said.

Emily thought about the note she'd left Mama telling her about her elopement with Granville, and felt badly. It might help if she sent a letter by Express Mail once they reached Barkerville. Just to let Mama and everyone else know she was all right. And properly married.

In case Mama hadn't already pried that information out of Clara.

Then another thought struck her. "Have stagecoaches always carried the mail? I mean, when gold was first found near Barkerville, how did the miners send letters?"

"Mostly miners leaving the area and heading to the coast agreed to take whatever letters people wanted to send," he said. "Once the stagecoach line was set up, we took on that service. There were no formal Express letters then, but the mail got delivered every week. Course, it took longer to make the trip. Usually seven days, longer if the weather was bad, instead of the four days it takes now."

Emily wondered what that had meant for Mr. Robertson. "Did the letters always get delivered?"

"Mostly. Back then, before the wagon road went through, the stages crossed the river on a steamboat. Occasionally boats overturned, and the mail was lost. Or if a miner had been charged with delivering a letter, and something happened to him, that letter would be lost, too."

Could that be why Mr. Robertson's family had only received six letters? Had there been other letters, that had gone missing?

What if he'd written to ask them to join him in Barkerville, or somewhere in the Cariboo, and his wife and son had never received that letter?

Or maybe he'd been injured or taken ill, and had written a deathbed letter that was never delivered?

She didn't see how that could help them solve the case, but the possibilities were interesting. And she'd learned that you never knew what might be important on a case. She mentally filed these new facts away.

And turned back to her earlier thought, unable to shake the thought of how Mama must have felt, after reading the note she'd left. The one that said she was eloping with Granville, and going with him to Barkerville. Leaving Mama with only what little Clara could tell her about Emily's sudden marriage and journey into the unknown.

"If I wrote a letter today, could it go out from Quesnel?" she asked. "Or even from the next stop?"

"From Alexandria? No reason it couldn't. But I don't recommend trying to write anything when you're riding in the coach," he said. "Even if you had enough time before we get there, writing a letter while we're in motion might make you feel a bit sick. And anything you wrote while the coach was swaying back and forth might be pretty hard for its recipient to read."

"Quesnel, then."

"That would work better. We'll be there before dark. Write your letter tonight, and it could go out on the return stagecoach."

"Or sleigh," she said with a smile.

"Or sleigh, indeed. We have heavy leather pouches with waxed seams to make sure the mail is kept safe and dry, no matter the conditions."

"Good," she said and changed the subject to the history of the area, hoping he might know something more about the cattle drives or the gold rush that would provide some link to the Robertson case. But she found no link in the stories he told, fascinating thought they were.

As the wind rose, blowing harder out of the north, Emily started to feel tiny ice crystals being driven against her exposed nose and cheeks. She was very glad to learn that they were only a few miles outside Alexandria, and that the Moffat Ranch was just ahead.

In what seemed like moments the stagecoach drew into the hard-packed dirt of the driveway, and made its way up to the front entrance of a sprawling ranch house. Several ranch hands came quickly forward to unharness the horses and lead them away.

"The stables are out back," Mr. Owens told Emily. "While the horses are changed, they'll serve us luncheon here," he added as he assisted her down from the box. "You might want to get inside out of the cold. You're looking a mite wind burned."

"She is indeed," Granville said, stepping out from inside the coach and offering her his arm. "I suspect you'll be glad for a break?"

Emily thanked Mr. Owens and turned to take Granville's arm. "Very glad," she said. "I'd give anything for a cup of tea. And I'm hungry again. How is that even possible?"

"I suspect the cold and the fresh air are the culprits," Granville said with a laugh as they went inside. "And by all appearances, this is a productive and well-run ranch. I suspect they'll feed us very well indeed."

"Good," Emily said with feeling.

CHAPTER 23

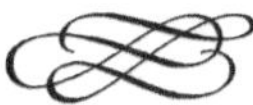

FRIDAY, NOVEMBER 9, 1900

The following morning Granville awoke well before dawn. They'd had an early night the day before, having arrived at Quesnel well before darkness fell. There had been just enough time before the dinner hour to retreat to their room and rest for a bit. Emily had taken the time to write a quick letter to her mother.

"I'm concerned that Mama will worry," she'd said, looking up from the small writing desk in their room. "And I didn't really explain much in my last note. So I've told her I'm fine, and promised we'll be back before Christmas.

I know it sounds silly, but I feel as if I've cheated her out of the society wedding she wanted for me, and then run off with no word since Monday."

"It isn't silly at all," he had told her. "Merely thoughtful. And from what you told me before we left, your sister Jane will soon be giving your Mama a chance to organize a full society wedding to her heart's content."

His new bride had laughed at that, which he'd been relieved to see.

"You're quite right. About both of them," she'd said. "And if Miriam's fellow is as interested as I think he is, Mama will probably have enough weddings to plan over the next two years to make her entirely sick of them."

"Meanwhile, we will be enjoying our wedded bliss," he said, stealing a quick kiss. "With none of that wedding nonsense to worry about."

"You're lucky you did such a good job taking care of the pieces of "wedding nonsense" I actually care about," she said. "Or I'd likely be quite annoyed with you for saying that. And possibly even feel the need to get even."

He'd grinned, and kissed her again. It was some time before she managed to finish her letter.

But they'd still had time to wash up and brush the road dust from their clothes before going down for dinner.

The meal had been of the high standard they'd come to expect, and their long day of traveling had left them all hungry enough to fully enjoy it. After dinner, though, none of them were feeling particularly social. Knowing they'd be up again before dawn for a five a.m. start, everyone had turned in early.

Turning his head, Granville smiled to see Emily still deeply asleep, her face turned into the pillow. He reached for his robe, shrugged into it and moved quietly to the window to check on their travel conditions.

Twitching the curtain aside, he had to breathe on the glass to melt away the frost so he could see out. It was immediately clear that the mercury had fallen well below freezing overnight. Despite the early hour, Granville could see only thick clouds obscuring the stars, and a light snow had begun to fall. They were likely to get more snow today. Possibly a lot more snow.

Which might mean they'd need to ready the sleighs.

Taking another glance at his wife's sleeping face, Granville hurriedly dressed and tiptoed out the door, taking Emily's completed letter to her mother with him. He didn't want to wake Emily if the weather was going to delay their departure. After three days of early mornings and travel, she needed all the sleep she could get.

Twenty minutes later, he was back carrying a laden tray. Setting it down outside their door, he quietly turned the handle and pushed the door open just wide enough to get himself and the tray inside. Carefully placing the heavy tray on the small desk, he turned to see Emily watching him, a look in her eyes he couldn't read.

Her gaze went from him to the tray he'd put down. "Is that tea?" she asked, with a beaming smile.

"It is."

"I thought we had an early morning departure."

"We did. But it's snowing."

With a little squeal she leapt out of bed and rushed to the window, nearly tripping as her long, sheer cotton nightgown with its delicate lace trim wrapped itself around her legs. He smiled as she righted herself.

Discovering the frost on the window panes, Emily stood on tiptoe so she could look through the patch he'd cleared off earlier, placing her palm against the narrowing circle to melt it again.

"It's snowing!" she said. "I love the snow."

She whirled to face him, then seemed to remember she wore only her rather transparent nightgown, blushed, and hastily reached for her robe. "Does this mean we get to take a sleigh?"

He smiled at her. "If the snow gets worse, yes. It also means we will depart a little later. They are waiting to see if the snow piles up deep enough on the road for the sleigh runners. Which is why I brought the tray up."

Emily's eyes went to the tray, taking in fresh scones, butter and preserves, and she looked delighted. "You brought me breakfast in bed."

"Not quite," he said. "There will be a full breakfast in an hour or so. But you deserve a little pampering…"

"Since this is our honeymoon," she finished for him. "You won't catch me arguing. Not this time. Thank you. It's a lovely thought," she said. And promptly dived back under the covers.

"The room is a little chilly," she emerged enough to tell him. "And everything smells wonderful."

With a grin, he poured her a cup of black tea, adding milk and a little sugar as she liked it, then handed her the delicate china cup and saucer.

"Thank you," Emily said, accepting it. "But what if the snow doesn't fall fast enough for the sleigh? We can't stay here all day waiting for it to get deeper."

"True," he said. "In that case, we'll take the coach to Cottonwood, and then the sleigh from there. Either way, we'll get to enjoy the first leisurely morning that we've had since we married. Just the two of us."

Emily beamed at him.

❧

By six a.m. it was clear the snow was going to stick to the roads, and likely deepen. Granville and Emily finished dressing, packed their bags and went downstairs to meet Scott, Trent and their fellow travelers for breakfast. The various platters of steak, eggs, bacon, flapjacks and biscuits they'd come to expect were laid out on a sideboard for them to help themselves. Pots of coffee and tea were set out on the table, along with fresh milk and cream, honey and sugar.

During the journey, the coach travelers had become used to taking particular places at the table. The driver of the day sat at the head, to ensure that the passengers were well taken care of, and any problems were quickly resolved. As the only woman on the stage, Emily was given the place of honor on his right, with Granville beside her. Scott and Trent sat across the table from them. Then the various other travelers ranged themselves down the table.

This morning they had a new driver, one Sandy Locke, who would see them through to Barkerville. Granville had met him earlier when he'd made arrangements to have Emily's letter go out on the next stage back to Vancouver, and had been impressed by the fellow's competence.

There was no sign of him now, though. Given the weather, the driver was probably still sorting out whatever changes would be required to travel by sleigh instead of by coach.

To Granville's amusement, despite the driver's absence, all of them arranged themselves around the table in their usual places, just as if the fellow were there. They had barely finished their meals when Locke joined them, and quickly introduced himself to those he hadn't met. Then, rather than sitting down with his own breakfast, he asked them all to finish their meals as quickly as possible.

"The snowfall is thick and getting thicker. Therefore, we will be traveling by sleigh today, rather than by coach. Everything is now ready for our departure, and we should easily reach Barkerville before nightfall.

But I'd like to get underway as quickly as possible, in case the weather changes. Too much snow may slow us down, because we'd be forced to clear our path. On the other hand, if it unexpectedly warms up, we need to be in Cottonwood so we can switch back to a coach before everything melts.

So as soon as you're done, please gather your things and get them out to us so we can finish loading. Thank you."

He looked across the table at Emily. "Mrs. Granville, if you'd like to ride beside me this morning, I'd be pleased to have you."

Emily smiled at the fellow and gave a quick nod. "I'd like that very much, Mr. Locke, thank you."

He nodded back. Looking back at the others, he said "For any of those who haven't traveled with us by sleigh before, the cold shouldn't be a concern. In fact, you'll be warmer in the sleigh than you would have been in the coach. We have blankets and furs to tuck around you, and large stones have been heated that will keep your feet toasty."

And so it proved.

It was a well bundled group that drove away from Quesnel that morning. Granville appreciated the efficiency of the arrangements, and he was particularly pleased to see Emily's excited face as she sat up beside the driver, well wrapped up against the cold and snow.

It had amused him that snow or not, she'd had them all line up for her to take a photo in front of the inn, and then another in front of the sleigh, before they departed.

CHAPTER 24

As the sleigh pulled away from the Occidental Hotel, leaving Quesnel behind, Emily sat slightly above the others on the seat beside the driver. She couldn't quite believe this was real. It was the last day of their trip to Barkerville, and while they breakfasted, the snow had fallen thickly enough to completely cover the ground.

And it was still snowing!

Under cover of her warm wraps, Emily pinched herself, just to be sure. But it was all real. She was here, she and Granville were married, and by the end of the day, they'd be arriving at the end of their journey in a snow-covered Barkerville. In a sleigh!

She hadn't dared to dream of anything so wonderful.

Now if only she could find some bit of information that would give them a direction on this case.

The driver clicked to the horses, and they were off, the sleigh runners gliding over the coating of snow with a shushing sound. As soon as they were out of town and on the open road, Emily took the opportunity to show Mr. Locke the sketch.

"I don't recognize him," he said glancing at the sketch and shaking his head. "When was he last heard from?"

"In the late 1860's," she said.

"That's more than thirty years," he said. "How is it you're looking for him now?"

"He's related to someone my husband knows," she said, aware that the others in the sleigh might be able to hear them. "He asked us to see if anyone remembered him."

"Huh. When did he come north, do you know?"

"1863, I believe."

So he was one of the original Argonauts, then?" Mr. Locke asked.

"He was."

"He ever find gold?"

"Not that we know of."

"And he hasn't been heard from in more than thirty years?" He cast her a doubtful look. "Good luck, then," was all he said.

Emily smiled a little. "I suspect we'll need it," she said, and turned her attention to the landscape they were traveling through.

The coating of snow on the dark branches of the aspen along the riverbank made the trees seem to vanish against the white of land and sky. The pines were thicker here, still shorter and narrower than the pines of the coastal forests, and thickly covered with snow. It was still snowing, but more lightly now, the flakes drifting lazily downwards.

Emily drew in a breath. The air was cold, scented with pine and fir, and so fresh it was almost painful. But it wasn't the hard cold she'd smelled from her window early this morning. The day was still warming. Did that mean it would keep snowing?

She turned to ask Mr. Locke, and realized his gaze was fixed on one of the two pairs of horses pulling the sleigh. "Is there a problem?" she asked him instead.

"I hope not," he said. "The horses were fine this morning, but one of the rear pair—the one on the left, see?—might be favoring his front foot."

Emily looked closely, trying to see what he saw. "I can't see anything," she said. "But I'm not familiar enough with horses and what their gaits should look like to be sure."

As she spoke, she continued to watch the brown mare with the coat that gleamed like silk. Even she could tell that these animals were very well cared for.

She said as much, and Mr. Locke laughed. "Of course they are," he said. "The BX would have no business at all if it weren't for these beauties. They aren't broken for anything except pulling the stage, you know."

"So they've never been ridden?" Emily asked, surprised.

"No," was the answer. "Their only role is to pull the stages. In fact, most of them are bred and raised on one of the BX farms, and trained there, too."

Suddenly Emily thought she saw something. There was the smallest hitch in the brown mare's gait. Or was there? It was so slight, it almost wasn't there. She started to say something, stopped. It was gone.

And then she saw it again. "There is something," she said quickly. "Exactly as you said. It's a tiny change in how she steps, and it stops and starts. What is it?"

"Possibly something in her hoof," he said. "A bit of rock, even part of a small pine cone. We'll need to stop and check. It's flat and safe enough here. Does your man have any experience with horses?"

He meant Granville. Emily hid a smile, happy to think of Granville as hers, now. "He does," she said. "His family raises them."

Though Emily suspected it was a much bigger operation than those words suggested. She suddenly realized that she now had a brother-in-law who was a Baron and owned an estate in England. And she had several other titled brothers and sisters-in-law, too. How odd.

Mr. Locke gradually slowed the horses, and drew the sleigh off to one side. "I'll need you to ask your husband to come and help me," he said. "Can you get him while I hold them?"

Of course she could. Emily just nodded, and half-turned in

her seat to call out the request to Granville and Scott. Then she began to unwind herself from the coverings, taking a bit of extra time to be sure she didn't get caught in something and trip. It would be humiliating, to sprain her ankle on her honeymoon by falling out of a sleigh. Or worse, to break something, so far from a doctor.

But she made it down just fine, and hurried towards the small group gathered at the front of the sleigh. Granville and Scott were there, along with Trent, who'd tagged along, as did several of the miners, who professed familiarity with horses. Between them all, it was quickly determined that the skittish brown mare had picked up a small stone, and with her harness firmly held by Mr. Locke, Granville was able to dislodge it.

"She's a beautiful animal," he told the driver. "You'll want to have a blacksmith check her hoof when we get to Cottonwood, just in case. I'd hate to see any lasting harm occur from this."

"We should be there in a couple of hours," Mr. Locke told him. "Just in time for luncheon. And we'll be changing horses there, so the mare will get a rest in any case. My thanks to all of you for this assistance."

And then they were underway again. Once the mare settled back into what the driver said was her normal pace, the sleigh seemed to glide effortlessly through the fresh snow.

It seemed to Emily no time later that she spotted what Mr. Locke said was the Cottonwood River, winding towards them from the north. She had been so busy taking in the changing scenery through the little flurries of snow while keeping an eye on the brown mare, the time had flown. As the river grew closer, she could see the narrow wooden bridge that crossed it. It didn't look wide enough or sturdy enough for their sleigh to cross. There was a cluster of buildings on the other side.

"Is that Cottonwood?" she asked Mr. Locke, pointing.

"Part of it, anyway," the driver said, glancing down at her. "That's the inn."

Something in her expression must have told him what she was

thinking. "Don't worry," he was quick to say. "I've driven over that bridge hundreds of times without incident."

Emily nodded. She didn't doubt him, exactly. But her stomach tied in knots, and remained that way until they had glided smoothly across the bridge. She kept her hands clenched tightly together under the blankets.

They passed so close to the rails on either side, she felt she could reach out and touch the one beside her. Then they were pulling up in front of Cottonwood House, and Granville was helping her down from the sleigh. Emily stepped down, happily taking in the beauty of the place, snow clad under a clearing sky.

The giant cottonwood tree in front of the inn was the first thing she noticed. With its graceful branches laden with snow, it was impossible to ignore. She wondered how long the tree had stood there, to have grown to that majestic size.

The inn itself was the largest building. Two stories high, it had a steep roof and the now-familiar board front with wide caulking. Here the wide boards had been stained dark, creating a pleasing look against the white caulking.

The passengers disembarked in the wide, snow-covered driveway, where the big double doors of the inn welcomed them. From where she stood, Emily could see a variety of wooden buildings spread out beyond the inn. This was clearly a working farm, though she couldn't see the livestock that must have been driven inside by the snow.

The doors were flung open and the rich scent of cooking wafted out. Emily's nose twitched, and her stomach growled. She was hungry again. Which was better than being afraid.

As Granville smiled down at her, Scott and Trent caught up with them, and the four made their way inside the well-laid out inn.

CHAPTER 25

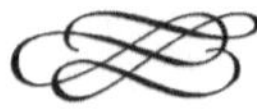

AFTER LUNCHEON, THE SLEIGH SET OFF AGAIN, RE-CROSSING THE Cottonwood River back to the wagon road that dated back to the gold rush days. The weather was slightly colder but the snow was still light and the fresh team of horses had no trouble breaking trail along the wagon road.

Emily had chosen to keep her seat beside the driver. She was determined not to miss a moment of this magical ride through the snow to Barkerville. How many women got to do this? The thought made her happy all over again that she'd managed to convince Granville to include her in this trip.

Pleasantly warm and full after a luncheon of chicken stew with dumplings, dried apple and currant pie, and two cups of tea, Emily burrowed deep into the slightly chilly coverings. They'd warm soon enough, she thought, placing her feet on the heated rock at her feet.

A snowflake landed on the tip of her nose, and she laughed.

The driver gave her a sideways look. "I've been thinking about the questions you asked this morning about that fellow you're looking for. One thing I can tell you, though I'm not sure if it will help," he said. "Things have changed almost beyond recognition from the time the man you were asking about earlier was here."

Emily had been feeling a little defeated by her lack of progress on learning anything more about Mr. Robertson, and at Mr. Locke's words she straightened and turned to him with enthusiasm. "How have they changed?" she asked.

"Probably in every way," he said with a wry smile, obviously not having expected the bright smile she was giving him. "I can't speak to all of it, but I can tell you how much easier it is to make the trip you're making now, than it was then."

"I've heard that it became much faster, after the wagon road was built. And then the railroad was built through the Fraser Canyon and the journey got faster yet."

"All true," he said. "The old route through the Canyon from Vancouver to Yale was slow and treacherous at the best of times. You'll have seen the steep falls from the railroad to the rapids below."

Emily nodded, picturing some of the cliffs she'd seen on Monday's journey with a shiver.

"They used to lose pack trains over some of those cliffs regularly. It's how Jackass Pass got its name, you know. In honor of the poor beasts that lost their lives in just that one area," he said.

She'd read as much, though she didn't tell him that. It was different, anyway, having seen the actual twists and turns through the mountain, instead of just reading newspaper reports about it. Now she could almost taste the fear the early travelers must have felt when the weather was bad and the trail turned treacherous.

"At least once the wagon road went through, the stages followed," Mr. Locke said. "But the trail we're on now was the worst. This section of road wasn't finished until the late 1860's. Up until then, neither wagons nor sleighs could get through. It was only accessible on horseback. And the minute it rained or snowed, the path became a horror of mud, fallen trees and washouts."

Emily looked at the vista unfurling in front of her; the pristine white of the snow covered road, bracketed on either side by deep green of pine and fir trees frosted with snow. Every now and again the gap between the trees widened and she could see the river, running wide and muddy here. She blinked, and tried to imagine what it must have looked like to the early miners. To Mr. Robertson, if he'd come this way.

"I can't even imagine it," she said.

"The road is too smooth here," Mr. Locke said. "It's hard to picture what it must once have looked like. But as we head further east, the land grows steeper. We've been paralleling Lightning Creek since we left Cottonwood. When the trees open out, there are views that still give a sense of what the whole area once looked like. I'll show you, if you like?"

"I'd like that very much," Emily said, and settled back to watch the passing landscape. Mr. Locke had given her a lot to think about.

Now she was questioning some of the assumptions she'd made when doing her research in the newspaper archives. That lapse of thirty-two years struck her as a much bigger problem out here than it had seemed in Vancouver. Likely because she'd had no real sense of how much those years had changed the Cariboo, and Barkerville in particular.

Which was silly, really, because thirty-two years was so much longer than she'd been alive. And if she stopped to think about it, she knew so many things in Vancouver that had changed enormously, just in the last ten years.

She couldn't quite get her thinking around the reality of thirty-two years of change.

So how were they supposed to figure out what had happened to a would-be miner in an area none of them knew at all, thirty-two years before?

"You can see Lightning Creek below us now," Mr. Locke said, jolting Emily out of her reverie.

She looked to her right to see the famous creek, still unfrozen, rushing between snow covered banks. "This is where some of the first gold strikes in this area were found," she said, her eyes wide.

"That's right," Locke said. "Back in the day, there were

dozens of claims all up and down this whole creek. Though most of the claims clustered around Richfield and Barkerville on William's Creek."

"Because that's where the richest claims were," Emily said, her eyes fixed on the creek. "And looking at it now, you would never know. It looks like any stream. It could be anywhere."

"Well, maybe not. You see how close the stream is to the road in places?" the driver asked.

She nodded.

"That stream tended to flood every spring. It overran the road, and before there was a road, it overran the trails. Just like it did the main streets in Barkerville."

"Barkerville used to flood?" she asked. It wasn't something her research had turned up.

"Still does, most every spring," was the answer. "When you get to town, you'll see many of the buildings are built on stilts, so they can be jacked higher above the street if a major flood is imminent. Then the wooden sidewalks in front of a store are raised to match. Some of the sidewalks are raised up nearly ten feet off the street."

"Ten feet?" Emily said, fascinated by this tidbit. "The stream floods that high?"

"Some years it does," he said. "Now, just imagine what that kind of water would do to a road. Or worse, a mud track."

Emily painted a mental picture of the scene before her, with the stream overrunning its banks, and the rain still pouring down. "There would be mud, everywhere. Maybe sinkholes in the path. If the storms were bad, trees would be down across the path. Or the path washed out entirely."

She shuddered, and looked at the peaceful snow scene in front of her. "It would take days to cover the distance that we're covering in one day."

Mr. Locke nodded. "If you could cover it at all. In bad years, the storms sometimes meant that even the mail couldn't get through."

"And the miners, digging on the creeks in the cold and the

wet and the wind? Their life must have been miserable," Emily said, shivering a little at the cold in her imagination.

As the life Mr. Robertson might have led here in the 1860's came alive for her, another thought struck her. Just how bad had Granville's time in the Klondike been, anyway? Was this why he seldom talked about it?

And she'd thought life became impossible when the streetcars weren't running. She'd have to get him to tell her about it.

She looked up from her contemplation of the creek, and caught a glimpse of snow-capped mountains, blue in the distance at the end of the road.

Or what seemed from here to be the end of the road. She noted that the drifts of snow along the banks seemed deeper than before. And it was snowing harder, too.

"It seems colder here, she said. "Are we traveling higher?"

"You've a good sense of the land," Mr. Locke said approvingly as they crested a small rise. "Yes, we're climbing now, moving into the foothills. That's the Cariboo Mountains you see in the far distance, up behind Barkerville a way. There's more snow, the higher we go, and it stays longer."

Emily watched the horses, moving through unbroken snow. "It must be more tiring for the horses," she said.

"Not too bad now," he said. "The snow is fresh, so it's lighter than the stuff that's been packed down. It isn't icy, either, which helps. And they're still fresh. We change teams again in a bit, and they'll be glad of a rest by then."

"And we're on a wagon road," Emily said, still watching the horses, their legs flashing in and out of the snow. "During the gold rush, there would only have been trails."

"Barely that, in some places," he told her. "Travel then was much harder on man and beast, no matter the season."

Breathing deeply of the frosty, pine-scented air, Emily tried to imagine what it must have felt like thirty years before. Part of her wished she'd been alive then. Not that they'd have let women prospect for gold, of course. But surely some must have accompanied their husbands?

Much as she was doing, she thought proudly. And Mrs. Harrison, whom she'd met on another case, had traveled in these parts with her husband thirty years ago. Even in winter. So she could certainly do so now.

In the meantime, she wanted to hear about the 1860's on these creeks. "Tell me more," she said to Mr. Locke.

THEY STOPPED to change horses in Van Winkle, which seemed to be no more than a few buildings. As they departed Mr. Locke pointed out that they were leaving the original route of the Cariboo Wagon Road, and taking the shorter route that had been built in the mid-1870's.

"Does that mean we're leaving Lightning Creek?"

"It does. The original route followed that creek all the way, then entered Barkerville from the south via the town of Richfield. We're going north, and that road leads straight to Barkerville.

Not quite an hour later, they stopped for a quick cup of tea and to change horses again at the Beaver Pass roadhouse on William's Creek itself. Emily thanked Mr. Locke profusely for the opportunity to ride up beside him, and for the information he'd given her. Then she joined Granville in the sleigh.

Their next stop would be Barkerville.

She wanted to be sitting beside Granville as they drove those last miles into town.

WELL WRAPPED in furs and heavy blankets, Emily's hand was in Granville's and her heart beating fast as they drove into that small town. It was still a few hours before sunset, and it had stopped snowing, so she could see everything clearly, which made her smile.

The whole town was thickly coated in snow. At the far end of the street, the snow capped mountains loomed against a white-gray sky, seeming much closer than the glimpses she'd caught from the sleigh. They reminded her of the mountains behind Vancouver, which sometimes seemed distant and at others, almost close enough to touch.

Barkerville itself was a town of steeply roofed wooden houses, very like many of the others she'd seen on this journey. Except for the sidewalks Mr. Locke had told her about, which were indeed raised well above street level, with steep stairs leading up from the street. It was one thing to hear about it, but to actually see it was something of a shock. The huge discrepancy in heights looked much odder than she'd expected.

Mr. Locke drove the sleigh along the wagon road, which turned into Main Street, to pull up in front of the stairs leading up to the Barkerville Hotel, perched several feet above them. Emily looked up to note with some delight that their hotel was another two story building with a peaked roof and a second story balcony. Though the white-painted front and cantilevered balcony gave it an air of elegance that she hadn't seen since the Ashcroft Hotel, where they had married.

Which seemed much longer than four days ago. She felt as if she'd lived a year since then. How could she ever have felt the least doubt about marrying Granville?

"We're here," she said to Granville. "We're actually here."

He smiled at her, and gave her a hand down from the sleigh. "Welcome to Barkerville," he said, giving her hand a warm squeeze. Which she returned with interest.

Then turned to reach for her camera case. "I'll just be a moment," Emily said.

CHAPTER 26

On Saturday morning, Granville got his first real chance in days to discuss the Robertson case with Emily, Scott and Trent. Despite all the time they'd spent together over the last five days, there had been few moments when there were not listening ears all around them. Except for the times he and Emily had spent alone together, but neither of them had been much interested in talking about the case then.

Now they were in Barkerville, and the real work of finding out what happened to Thomas Robertson all those years ago could begin.

Both he and Emily had woken early—it seemed they had become accustomed to stagecoach hours. He hadn't had much sleep, and nor had Emily, but she looked radiant. It seemed marriage suited her.

Or maybe it was the adventure.

By six-thirty, they were seated at a table for four in the breakfast parlor, waiting for Scott and Trent to join them. He glanced around the room with satisfaction. Instead of the large communal table that was common at the roadhouses where they had stayed, the Barkerville hotel had both a spacious dining room and this cozy parlor, both of which offered a number of smaller tables.

It was still pitch black outside, the few street lanterns barely touching the thick darkness. Kerosene lanterns lit up the warm pine of the tables scattered around the parlor. A pot of tea steamed gently on the table in front of them, and their hostess was quick to bustle around the tables with a coffee pot for those who needed a refill.

The smell of bacon, eggs and fresh biscuits reminded him he was hungry. He glanced at Emily, sitting beside him, and she smiled back.

"Yes, I'm hungry," she said, reading his look. "It smells wonderful, doesn't it? I just hope Mr. Scott and Trent won't be too long in joining us. Now that we're finally here, I want to start really looking for Mr. Robertson."

"And what do you call what we've been doing?" he asked dryly.

"Background research," she said promptly, with a mischievous look.

She wasn't far wrong, at that. "You never know…" he began.

"Which bit of information will end up solving the case," she finished for him.

"I say that a lot, do I?" he said.

"I'll say," Trent said from behind him. "At least once a day in the midst of a case. Sometimes more."

Granville glanced over his shoulder to see Scott and Trent, both looking like they'd slept hard and weren't quite awake yet. "Then why haven't you learned it yet?" he retorted.

Trent shrugged and half-fell into the seat opposite Emily. "I did. But you seem to like repeating it, so I stopped listening."

Scott took the chair opposite Granville and sat down, a broad grin splitting his heavy beard. "The lad has a point. This time, anyway."

Granville gave Emily a sideways glance, waiting for her to say something diplomatic, as his mother would have done. He should have known better.

"You're outnumbered," she told him, with a nod to Scott and grin at Trent. "It's officially annoying."

Granville laughed, and threw up his hands in surrender. She might be his wife now, but she was still the Emily he'd fallen in love with. She'd never do what the world expected of her.

And he wouldn't want her to.

"Well, we're here now," he said, pulling his notepad from his pocket. "And we have a missing man to find. It's time to take all of our research and start digging in. This is where it gets challenging."

He was looking at Scott and Trent as he spoke. He already knew Emily was ready. Emily had been born ready.

"About time," Trent said. "And as long as we don't have to get back in another stagecoach, I don't care what I have to do."

Granville laughed. "I suspect you'll eat those words before we're done," he said. "But I'm in no hurry to get back in a coach myself. We'll probably go on horseback anytime we leave Barkerville over the next few weeks."

"Good," Trent said.

Emily looked a little worried.

Granville suddenly wondered just how much experience she had on horseback. He'd never seen her ride. And they hadn't actually discussed her riding ability before they left Vancouver. Not after she brought up the possibility of having to wait four years to marry if they didn't elope.

He'd made the elopement work, and this odd honeymoon of theirs, too. He'd find a way to make the rest of this journey work. He wasn't about to see that joy wiped off his new bride's face.

Then their breakfasts were served, and the moment was lost.

But his determination was not.

∾

"Where do we want to start?" Emily asked once they'd all finished breakfast.

Their plates had been cleared and they were sitting with refilled cups of tea or coffee in front of them. "When we looked at the letters and the maps on the train, we decided that some of Mr. Robertson's references would make more sense once we were here. Well, we're here. So do we start with the maps?"

"We talk to people," Trent said firmly before Granville could answer. "Ask questions."

Granville hid his grin. The lad was gaining confidence, even if it was sometimes misplaced. He was young. He'd learn.

"Usually Clara and I start at a teahouse," Emily was saying. "But here, we might do better at the Post Office? Or one of the stores?"

"A bar is better. That's where we do our best planning, too," Trent said, then faltered, looking to Granville for help.

Granville exchanged glances with Scott. Trent was right. They did often get the most useful information in a bar. And strategize there, too.

But women, at least gently raised women like Emily, were not a usual sight in most bars. Having her join them in a bar might create an awkward situation, one unlikely to encourage potential informants to talk.

Emily looked around the table, then met Granville's eyes. "It doesn't matter that we're married," she said slowly. "The fact that I'm a woman is enough to make it difficult to bring me into some parts of your investigation, isn't it? No wonder you wanted to leave me behind in Vancouver."

"That wasn't the reason," he told her, hoping she'd hear the truth behind his words as clearly as he heard the hurt behind hers. "And you have proved, again and again, that you bring an invaluable perspective to our investigations. This particular trip will simply require us to re-think how we approach some parts of the case, that's all."

"It's all right," she said. "Go ahead and begin the investigation in your normal manner. I can stay and re-read the letters, take another look at the maps. Then when you all return, we can compare notes."

Granville couldn't stand the look on her face.

"We have a strategy to follow," he said. "One all of us developed on the train on Monday. We start by learning everything we can of Thomas Robertson and his time here in Barkerville, thirty years ago."

"How?" Emily said.

"The Post Office is a logical place to start, since it is often the heart of a community. Especially one as small as Barkerville is now. You and I can start there. Then we'll see if we can track down the Gold Commissioner that Harrison mentioned as a possible resource."

"Mr. Cranston? I agree. And even if he's traveling, someone will be in the Gold Commissioners office, and might know something."

"Excellent point. Scott, can you and Trent check out the local bars, and anywhere else the old-timers congregate?"

"No complaints here," Scott said with a broad smile.

"If any of them are still alive," Trent said dubiously. "The old duffers we talked to in Vancouver all said they'd moved south 'cause they didn't think they'd survive another winter up here."

Scott gave him a light cuff to the back of the head. "And you believed them? Come along, youngling. Let's go meet some real old sourdoughs."

"I thought that was a Klondike word," Trent muttered, but followed Scott out the door.

Leaving Emily and Granville staring at each other.

"I wonder what got into him?" she said. "Maybe spending the morning in the bars will improve Trent's outlook."

"We can only hope so. Are you ready to go?"

She grinned. "Unlike Trent, I can't wait. Let me just get my coat and handbag."

GRANVILLE FINISHED the last of his tea, giving Emily time. Then he followed his new wife up the stairs, the heavy carpet muffling the sound of his footsteps. Reaching their door, he gave a quick tap on the door so he didn't startle her.

Closing the door behind him, he leaned back against it. Giving her space in the small room, in case she needed it. He wasn't quite certain what she did need, only that he'd do everything he could to give it to her. And that he'd somehow let her down.

Emily was standing at the window, her back to the room, watching the snow falling on the town still wrapped in darkness. "It's beautiful, isn't it?" she said without turning her head.

"It is."

"I'm sorry if having me here is going to be a burden," she said, still not looking at him.

"How could it be?" he said in quiet tones. He didn't move either.

"All I considered was the romance of it all. Barkerville, the missing man, a trip along the gold trails in winter," she said, gaze still fixed on the falling snow. "I didn't think about how we usually handled investigations, or where I could or couldn't go."

"You've never let that stop you before."

"No, I haven't, have I?" Emily said with a laugh that cracked a little. "And look where it's got me."

He came quietly up behind her and enveloped her in his arms. "You're in Barkerville, with a husband who loves you, in the middle of an investigation," he said. "Where else would you be?"

She turned in his embrace, looked up. "You mean that," she said, her eyes searching his face.

"Of course I do."

"And you think I can help on this case? Here? Without Clara?"

Before he could answer, Emily gave him a wry smile. "Clara would be very pleased to hear me say those words," she said.

"Though she'd give me no end of grief for even suggesting I should bring her along on my honeymoon."

"I have to believe that you and I will prove at least as competent an investigative team as you and Clara have been," he said, returning her smile.

She poked him in the ribs, but leant into his embrace. "You know what I meant. In my investigations, I've always gone where women go, with Clara along for propriety. You and Scott have always investigated those places where men go."

He held her closer. "I'm a little concerned that I actually understood that explanation," he said. "And that you could so doubt my respect for your abilities."

"No, it isn't that," she said, throwing her arms around his neck. "Don't you see? This is different."

"I should hope so," he said, dropping a kiss on the tip of her nose. "We're married now. And we have yet to explore what a husband and wife team can accomplish."

She looked up at him from under her lashes. "I think we've been exploring that quite nicely," she said with a little grin. "Weren't you paying attention?"

"Minx," he said, holding her closer still. "You know what I meant."

"You mean it?" she asked, suddenly serious. Searching his face, her green eyes intent. "You really think we can work in a new way on this case?"

"I really do," he said. "We've always worked well together. Why would that stop now?"

"Then I think this case might just be the most fun we've ever had," she said.

"The most fun?" he said. "Then I must be doing something wrong." And he tumbled them both onto the featherbed behind them.

CHAPTER 27

As she and Granville stepped out of the hotel some time later, Emily drew in an excited breath. It was light enough that she could see it had snowed heavily overnight, though only a few flakes of snow drifted down now. She reached for her camera, and used the flash to take a photo of Granville, posed in front of the snow-covered hotel. Then she took another of the flood-proofed shops rising on stilts, with the street ten feet below them and the mountains faint in the distance.

As they walked briskly toward the Post Office, she noted all the windows were thick with frost. Their breath hung like tumbles of frost on the air in front of them, the sharply cold scent telling her that the blanket of snow covering the town wasn't likely to melt anytime soon.

Glancing around her, she was pleased to notice at least one coffeehouse. Perhaps Granville was right about the ways in which they could expand their partnership, after all. She began to smile as she came up with a few ideas that might work.

Before she had time to share her thoughts with Granville, they reached the Post Office. Located at the north end of Main Street, it was yet another steep roofed building—now capped with snow—with board siding of weathered fir. But it was perched high above the road.

Luckily it was on the same side of the street as their hotel, so they didn't have to walk down the block to the pedestrian bridge that crossed over the road, then double back again. Though they still had to climb down one set of stairs and up another, since the Post Office building had been raised to a higher level above the street than than the shops beside it.

However did people manage to run their daily errands here? Emily wondered. Maybe they visited one side of the street one day, and the other side the next?

She was smiling to herself as Granville opened the door into the Post Office for her. As the bell over the door jangled a greeting, he gave her a questioning look, but she just shook her head. Then they were being welcomed by the woman behind the counter.

Mrs. Darrow, as she introduced herself, obviously took that role to heart. And embellished it, too, with a flirtatious look at Granville which Emily might have found irritating had the woman been several decades younger. Was there a Mr. Darrow somewhere, or was the Mrs. just a courtesy title?

"You'll have come in on the stage last night," Mrs. Darrow said as she watched them enter. "I hope the journey wasn't too exhausting? What with you two just married, and having spent four days on that stage, and all. What can I do for you?"

Her information was excellent. Emily wondered if she'd been talking to someone at the BX, or someone at their hotel. Probably both.

"I'm Miss—I mean Mrs.—Granville," Emily hastily corrected herself. "This is my husband, and yes, we are newlyweds."

She blushed a little at Mrs. Darrow's overwhelming congratulations and sly looks.

"I'm wondering if you have any letters waiting for either of us," Emily persevered.

"Nothing's come in for you today," the postmistress said. "I gather you left Ashcroft on Tuesday?"

At Emily's nod, Mrs. Darrow continued, "Then tomorrow or the next day is the earliest you could expect a letter, depending on how bad the snow gets. I can imagine you must be impatient for news from home."

Not at all sure she wanted to hear Mama's reaction to their elopement, even in written form, Emily simply thanked her and changed the subject.

"This is my first trip here. I've always been fascinated by the tales of the gold rush days and especially by this town and everything that went on here," she said. "I'm sure that in your role you hear most of the stories."

If she'd read her correctly, Mrs. Darrow was a committed gossip. Which wasn't a surprise. Even in Vancouver, the Post Office was gossip central. Postmasters knew everything that was going on, important or unimportant.

"You don't know the half of it," Mrs. Darrow said, leaning forward and lowering her voice. "The shenanigans in this town you wouldn't believe. The newspaper stories, even the worst of them, were tame in comparison."

"Surely you couldn't have been here then," Emily exclaimed, understating Mrs. Darrow's age by a dozen years or so.

That lady beamed. "Oh, I was the merest child, of course. But the town was settled early, and people stayed, even after the easy gold was gone. Some of the early miners, even, are still here. And I heard all the stories. First hand!"

Emily tried to look suitably impressed. And tried even harder not to look at Granville, who had taken a step back once Mrs. Darrow had stopped fluttering her lashes at him and focused on her. If she met his gaze, Emily suspected she'd dissolve into a fit of giggles, which would hardly get the information they needed out of Mrs. Darrow.

"What kind of stories?" she asked.

"They'd curl your hair. But these lips are sealed," Mrs. Darrow said, gesturing towards heavily painted lips.

"Oh, what a shame," she said. "Perhaps I can persuade you?"

A decided shake of Mrs. Darrow's golden curls. Which Emily

was pretty sure had come out of a bottle. And the postmistress cast another look across the counter at Granville.

Surely she wasn't trying to draw him in? She fought back a laugh at the thought of Granville's likely reaction. Knowing him, he'd probably flirt back. But just enough to get the lady talking.

Not while she was standing here! She leaned a little towards Mrs. Darrow, and lowered her own voice. "But… do you mean some of the miners are still alive? And in town?" Emily asked, trying to sound as young and uninformed as possible.

"Of course they are. It was thirty years ago, not a lifetime," the postmistress said, bristling a little in defense of what were probably her contemporaries, or close to it. "That's hardly any time, these days."

Emily hid her grin. "I suppose not," she said dubiously. "But… well, would they still remember? I mean, after so long."

"Sharp as tacks, most of them," was the response. "And why shouldn't they be?"

Emily was starting to like Mrs. Darrow. And to wonder how she'd ended up here. She hoped she had as much fire in her when she was that age. But perhaps with a lighter hand on the cosmetics.

"It would be so wonderful to hear those stories first hand, from those who were here then," Emily said, playing it up. "Since of course I'd never ask you to betray a confidence. Is there somewhere I could talk to them?"

"Well, they come in here, obviously," Mrs. Darrow said. "But you and your husband would hardly want to be hanging around here all day, waiting. The next best place is Delaney's Saloon, down the street away. It's a gathering place for those who came north looking for gold."

She glanced at Granville and then back at Emily. "Of course, women are not exactly welcome at Delaney's. So it would have to be your husband who talked to them," she finished with a sideways glance at Granville.

"Of course," Emily said. "And we thank you for the information. Can you recommend a tea shop in town, where I could wait for him?"

"I'm afraid there isn't one," Mrs. Darrow answered with a sharp look. "Tea isn't much favored here. There are two coffee-houses, though. And Kelly's bakery is good, and may serve you tea if you insist on it."

Emily hid a grin. "I'll remember that," she said. "But before we go, and since you heard all the stories…"

The postmistress leaned a little closer. "Go on."

"Did you ever hear of a miner named Thomas Robertson? This would have been in the late 1860's."

Mrs. Darrow looked disappointed. "No, him I've never heard of. You're sure he was in Barkerville?"

"He sent letters home, postmarked from here," Emily said."

"Well, I never heard of him," she said in a tone that conveyed clearly that Emily must be wrong.

"Thank you for the information," Granville said diplomatically. He stepped forward and put a supportive hand under Emily's elbow, while she firmed her lips to keep from laughing out loud. "I do have one further request. I noticed the telegraph lines outside. Would you be able to telegraph a message to Seattle for me?"

Which earned him a tiny frown. "Normally I'd be happy to send your message," Mrs. Darrow said. "But with all this snow, the wires to the south are down. I can't tell you when they'll be repaired."

He smiled at her. "Thank you anyway. We'll look forward to seeing you again during our visit. When the telegraph lines are back up."

And as Mrs. Darrow nodded to him, they left the Post Office together.

~

Half a block away, Emily turned to Granville. "Did you ever?" she asked with a small laugh. She was proud of herself it wasn't an actual giggle.

"I'm afraid so," he said. "Nicely played."

"Thank you. I suspect Mrs. Darrow would have been more forth-coming with you."

"Except if I want to send a telegram," he said, straight-faced.

Emily grinned at that. "Who were you intending to telegraph?"

"The Pinkerton's in Seattle."

"But why? I thought they were the ones who recommended us to Stephen Robertson?"

"They were. And I assumed they did so because they had no information on his missing father."

Which made sense. "What changed your mind?"

"Nothing has done so."

Was he setting her a puzzle? "So then why the telegram?"

He grinned and lightly squeezed her elbow. "Even here in Barkerville, I suspect Robertson Senior will prove elusive, after three decades. As insurance, I thought I'd send a wire to find out if Pinkerton's has any information different than what our client knows. Or chose to share."

"You mean did Thomas Robertson really join the cattle drive to Barkerville in 1863?"

"That's it."

"But since the wires are down…?"

"It's unlikely our client lied. He's paying us too much money to get an answer."

"Which leaves information he didn't know about, though."

"True. I still think it unlikely, but I'll check back about the telegraph lines."

"Well, maybe the Gold Commissioner will have heard of Thomas Robertson. And if not, at least we have some of the information we need," she said. "Mrs. Darrow was helpful that far, anyway. And I'm sure she'd gladly tell you anything you needed to know about her own experiences in the 1860's. If you went back without me."

"Which may be a very good strategy. But it's one I hope to avoid," he said with a straight face. "Where to next? The Gold Commissioner, or the coffeehouse?

"Why don't we see if Mr. Cranston or his constable is available? Maybe they have information that will be helpful. The coffeeshops will wait for us, after all."

The Gold Commissioner's office was a narrow building a few doors from the Post Office. There were three desks sharing the small space, but only one was occupied. His brown uniform and unlined face suggested he was the constable.

Identifying himself as Constable George McCall, he stood to an impressive height and gave them a welcoming smile. Probably he was every bit as well informed as Mrs. Darrow on who they were and why they were in town, but far more circumspect about it.

Unfortunately there was little he could tell them. He was too young to have known Thomas Robertson, and he'd never heard the name before.

"Gold Commissioner Cranston is really the best person for you to speak with, since he knows the area well. In fact, he was the postmaster for the region at the time in question."

"Yes, so we understand," Granville said. "Is he available?"

"Unfortunately, Commissioner Cranston is away for several days. He should be back early next week, if you'd like to meet with him then?"

They agreed that would be helpful, thanked him and left.

"So, the coffeehouses and the bakery next?" Granville asked as they left the building. "I assume you're not really intending to sit in a coffeehouse while I go and ask questions in the saloon?"

"No, not really," she said with a sideways glance. "Mrs. Darrow strongly recommended Delaney's, but it's likely that Mr. Scott and Trent will be visiting there today, isn't it?"

"Very likely indeed," Granville said, his breath emerging in misty clouds with every word.

"It's a particularly chilly day," she said, giving him a significant glance. "And it's been quite a while since breakfast."

"A hot cup of coffee would be welcome," he agreed.

"And I'd enjoy a cup of tea. Or chocolate. If I can insist strongly enough to get anyone to serve it," she said, grinning up at him.

At which he laughed, and gently tightened his hold on her elbow.

CHAPTER 28

By mid-morning, they had talked to at least four prospectors, the oldest man—weathered and wiry—proudly in his eighties. It seemed the coffeehouse was a popular spot for them in the mornings, especially this time of year.

They heard story after story of Barkerville in the early days. The hurdy gurdy girls. The raucous saloons. The fortunes lost and won.

And then fire destroyed the town. Oh, it was rebuilt quickly enough, and better than before. But the streak of blue clay where they'd been finding gold disappeared below sixty feet, and it became increasingly costly to bring up the gold.

And Barkerville slowly changed.

"It's a company town, now," seventy-seven year old Silas Dunham told them. "There's still mining done here, but most everyone works for a few companies. Except for some of the tribes, who know this land well, including all of the gold streams. And the Chinese, who seem able to wring gold out of the most played-out claim. Plus a few of the old-timers who are less successful but have never given up."

He looked so sad that Emily quickly changed the topic back

to the early days. "I've heard that in the early years, after those first claims on William's Creek, food was so expensive they used to drive herds of cattle north from the States all the way here, and sell the meat."

"Sure did," Mr. Dunham said with a reminiscent smile. "And got a pretty penny for it, too."

Emily smiled. "So it is true. I'm glad. I've always wondered what happened to the men who drove the cattle north, though. Did they go home? Or did they stay, and look for their own fortune?"

He gave her a thoughtful look. "You know, there's not many would think to ask that. A few went home. But most stayed. The gold you know. It's hard to resist that lure."

Mr. Dunham looked over Emily's head at Granville. "You look like a man who's known the call of gold."

Granville nodded. "I do indeed. The Klondike."

"Find much?"

"Enough to eat. Not enough to pay my way home,"

Mr. Dunham nodded, seemingly unsurprised. "That's always the way. Even for those who strike it rich. A few years in this country, and then it all tends to vanish, somehow."

He looked back at her. "I never knew what happened to most of the miners, after the fire. But I can't remember hearing about a single one of them striking it really rich. And if a claim's big enough, you always hear. It's those early stories of sudden riches that kept some of us here, all these years."

He grinned, and winked at Granville. "Or at least, that's what I tell myself. I still spend most of the summers out on the creeks myself, looking for my next strike. It's pretty country, up here. Mean, at times. But pretty."

Granville inclined his head. "It it weren't for the interminable winters, and the isolation, I might have stayed in the Klondike and done the same. It's pretty country up there, too."

"With so many people flooding up here to look for gold, was there a sense of camaraderie?" Emily asked. "Or were you all too focused on finding your own strike?"

Mr. Dunham shook his head. "We worked together. Helped each other out. You had to, up here. It was too primitive. Most of us had nothing but what we carried on our backs, and what goods were available were too dear to buy. Without a helping hand now and again—given or received, most of us would have starved our first winter.

And then there was the way the gold lay. There were a few areas where you could pan out nuggets, but mostly it was too deep for one man, or even two or three, to dig out. We formed collectives, and worked together."

"An experience like that must build unbreakable bonds," Emily said. Which explained a lot about Granville's friendship with Scott.

"That it does," Mr. Dunham said.

"Did you keep in touch with them?" she asked. "Once they left Barkerville, I mean?"

"Not usually. The mails were too uncertain, and digging for gold didn't leave a lot of energy for things like letter writing," Mr. Dunham said. He gave her a sharp look. "You ask some pretty interesting questions, for a visitor. You looking for someone?"

Emily flushed a little, feeling caught out. She'd thought she was being subtle.

"We're looking for one of the cattle drovers in particular," Granville said. "A fellow named Robertson. Thomas Robertson. Came up in '63."

"He stayed up here?"

"We think so," Granville said. "Did some digging in the area, though he never told his family exactly where."

"How long'd he last?"

"He was last heard from in '68."

"Huh," Mr. Dunham said, swallowing the last of his coffee. "The name doesn't ring a bell. He wouldn't have been someone I worked with. But then, a lot of men went through here in those years. He never made it home?"

"No, he didn't," Granville said.

"A shame, that."

The two men shared a look, and Emily felt left out of something they'd experienced that she never would.

But at the same time, she was learning more about Granville, and what had made him into the man she'd married.

Emily quietly drank some of her hard won tea, then, judging the moment to be right, brought out the sketch of their client's father. "This is the man we're looking for, as he was then," she said, and handed it to Mr. Dunham.

Who studied it carefully for a long moment.

"I can't say I recognize him," he said at last, handing it back. "Though there is a half-sense I've seen him before. Or someone like him. But it isn't strong enough to be helpful."

Emily accepted the sketch with a smile, and tucked it away again. "Thank you. Can you suggest anywhere we might look for him?"

Mr. Dunham picked up his coffee cup and seemed to contemplate it for a moment before he took a sip. "Have you tried the graveyard?"

"Not yet," she said.

"It's at the far end of town, on the road your sleigh came in on," he said. "Quite a few of the miners and early settlers are buried there."

"Is there any kind of plan for who is buried where?" Emily asked.

"No. The cemetery isn't really that big," he said. "You'll find people easily enough. Most of 'em, anyway."

"Thank you," Emily said. "I look forward to spending some time there. I imagine it is fascinating to read what people have chosen to put on their grave markers."

"Yes, if they have a proper grave marker. Some folks are buried with a simple wooden cross giving their name and dates, which haven't survived the seasons very well. Or with nothing at all, if they had no money."

"How sad," she said quietly.

"It is," he said. "It was the reality of the time. Even for those who paid for a proper marker, it would be wood rather than stone. And heavily carved epitaphs weather poorly up here."

He paused, scratched his chin. "In fact, you might be best to visit on a day when there's a little sun. Some of the letters are worn and you'll need the light. Also, it's a flat area that catches the wind. On a cold day, it's easy to freeze before you know it, especially if you're busy reading grave markers."

"Oh, that's very helpful. If unfortunate," Emily said. "We had hoped to start with the graveyard today, because if Mr. Robertson is there, that ends our search."

"But it's not worth freezing over," Mr. Dunham said.

"No, indeed it isn't," Emily said, smiling at him.

"One thing you might want to try, even on a dull cold day, is the dead letters at the Post Office. Unlike some communities, they are kept here rather than being sent back. Even after more than thirty years, it might be worth asking there, at least."

Emily and Granville exchanged glances. They wouldn't have expected that after so long.

"Thanks. It's worth a try," Granville said.

"Other than that, I'm stumped, I'm afraid," Mr. Dunham said. "If I think of anything, though, I'll let you know. You're staying in town?"

"Yes, at the Barkerville Inn," Granville said. "And we'd appreciate that."

CHAPTER 29

When he and Emily left the bakery, it was nearly noon.
The ring of their footprints on the icy wood of the sidewalks
echoed the pattern of Granville's thoughts as they returned to the
inn after a morning of questioning that had gone nowhere.

Still, they had at least one possible lead out of it all.

He glanced up, noting the brightening sky overhead. The air
was still cold, but without the bite it had earlier this morning.
With a little sun, it would warm quickly enough. They might be
able to spend some time in the graveyard this afternoon, after all.

He didn't expect they'd actually find Robertson there—that
would be too easy. But it was a possibility, if a remote one. And a
reasonable next step.

Especially since not a single one of the miners they'd talked to
had recognized Robertson's name. Or the sketch of him. Though
Dunham and two others had taken a second look at the sketch,
recognizing something about the fellow that seemed familiar. But
none of them could identify just what that was.

Perhaps Scott and Trent had had better luck. They'd
arranged to meet the two of them for lunch back at the hotel.

They were starting with so little information, even a small lead could turn their case around.

He was beginning to wonder if they'd come on a fool's errand, though. Thirty years was turning out to be a very long time in a place like Barkerville.

Built by those who'd come for gold—and left when it was gone—any physical evidence of the past had nearly eroded away. Only fading memories were left.

This case was beyond cold.

"What are you thinking?" Emily asked, her hand tightening on his arm.

"That you may have been right in your estimate of how long we'd be away on this case," he said. "Given our recent lack of results on finding anyone who remembers Robertson."

"You don't think Mr. Dunham will remember where he's seen whoever it is the sketch half-reminds him of?"

"Anything is possible. But I doubt it," Granville said. "Thirty-two years seems a longer period here than it does in either London or Vancouver."

Emily looked up and down the street, seemingly taking in the shops and services with their brave signs, the irregular heights of the sidewalk and the stairs leading to the street far below. He knew that considering look of her face, had seen it on other cases. What was she seeing?

"Everything here is built of wood, instead of brick or stone," she said. "But that isn't what you meant, is it? It's pretty, all covered with snow, and I love the sound of the creek burbling along nearby. It feels quaint—like it's still a frontier town. Which I suppose it is."

"Except that the frontier has moved on with the gold rush," he said. "And left Barkerville behind."

Emily nodded. "Yes, that's it. I felt it too," she said. "As if, when the gold-seekers moved on, following the next gold rush, the life of this town went with them."

"Was there another gold rush in the area?" he asked.

"Yes, to the Omenica. We met some of those miners when we

were in Kispiox this spring, looking for the lost heir. It's odd, in a way. We went there to search for a lost heir, and now we're searching for another missing man. Both ended up in the goldfields."

"Though for different reasons," he said. "But it raises a good point. Robertson's son is assuming—or perhaps hoping is the better description—that something happened to his father while he was here."

"Something that would justify his failure to return to them?" Emily said.

"Exactly that. And despite trying to prepare our client for the worst, I'm afraid I've been making the same assumption," Granville said. "But gold rushes draw people for different reasons. Some are leaving the home of their parents to find their own life, others are looking to recover from a financial crisis, while still others are running away from the responsibilities of a wife and family."

"You think Thomas Robertson might have been running?" she asked.

He shrugged. "It's certainly possible. Goldfields, with so many people finding themselves a stranger amongst strangers, all having left their homes and connections behind, are a good place for a man to get lost. Or to exchange his old life for a new one."

"And yet he kept writing letters back home. If he wanted a new life, he could have simply stopped writing."

"Sometimes letters home just keep loved ones from searching. Or asking questions."

"That's sad."

"Certainly for the families left behind, it was."

"You left England behind. First for the Klondike, and now for your life in Vancouver. Leaving behind your family, your parents and siblings," she said, glancing over at him. Her face was serious. "Will you regret it?"

"No," he said. "The circumstances are very different. I was the fourth son, with no hope of inheriting the title, and no role for me to play. Traditionally, the second son joined the church, the third son the army. There was no place for me as a fourth son in the Britain of this new century.

"That must have been hard," she said.

He smiled. "It took the challenge of the Klondike goldfields and surviving the frigid winters of the far north for me to find a sense of purpose. And when my father died, leaving my oldest brother the new Baron Granville, going home became impossible. His values are too different from my own. Then in Vancouver I found friends, a job and finally a home. With you."

"Are you sure?" she asked.

She sounded sincere. And determined. Was she regretting their hasty elopement and marriage? Or afraid he was?

"Very sure," he said. "You are my future, you and any children we might be blessed with. Which doesn't mean my mother and siblings don't matter to me. I hope in the spring to take you on a real honeymoon, to England. And to introduce my bride to my family."

"Oh," she said. "Oh my." And she squeezed his arm tightly.

They walked in silence for a moment, then Emily circled back to an earlier part of their conversation. "Barkerville does seem to be stuck in time," she said in a determined tone. "Yet the Omenica area didn't feel that way to me. Have they other industries than gold mining?"

Granville wondered what Emily thought about his plan to take her to England. She hadn't said a word, and it was unlike his new bride not to have strong opinions. And express them.

Now she was clearly changing the subject. He probably should have waited until they were back in Vancouver to broach the subject of meeting his family. No matter. They had time.

And if Emily really hated the idea, there was a simple solution. They wouldn't go.

"The Omenica is very different region than the Cariboo," he said. "Fur trapping still brings in a lot of money, more than most of the miners do these days. In fact, the entire region was still growing."

"Unlike this one? I wonder what would happen here, if the big mining companies closed down?" she asked.

"I think Barkerville would fade away," he said. "It's glory days seem behind it."

"They need a new industry here," Emily said decidedly. "None of which will help us find Mr. Robertson, though."

"The clouds are clearing," he said "We may have sunshine this afternoon. Which would give us a chance to visit the graveyard."

"The graveyard?" she said. "Really?"

"I think so. Let's see what Scott and Trent have to tell us at luncheon. Then we can plan our next approach to this investigation."

"I hope it's the graveyard," Emily said. "I do love reading old headstones."

He didn't point out that it might be more difficult when the headstones were covered in snow. Picturesque though it might be.

"Have you enough film left?" he asked her. "Even if we don't find Robertson, you might get some interesting pictures."

CHAPTER 30

hungry by the time they arrived back at their hotel. It felt good to
be inside by the fire, surrounded by the smell of good cooking
and the sound of familiar voices.

And it felt good to share what she and Granville had learned
that morning, and to hear Scott and Trent's discoveries.

Trent was full of the tales of the first miners to reach the
Cariboo—whom he insisted on calling Argonauts—and impatient to visit the creeks. "That's where the real stories are," Trent
insisted. "In the mines themselves."

He'd just spent the morning in the saloons. How much beer
had he had, anyway?

He didn't seem drunk, though. Just cheerful.

"It's November," she told him. "There won't be anyone there.
Where are you going to find those stories?"

"The land itself has a story to tell," he said ponderously.
Sounding faintly absurd to her ears.

Emily caught Scott winking at Granville, and wondered what
thought they were sharing. They'd actually lived on the creeks of

the Klondike in winter. Trent had only second-hand stories. Maybe that was his problem.

That was all she had, too.

"Is he right?" she asked Granville. "Does the land have stories?"

"It does indeed," Granville said. "As do the people who first lived here, long before the miners came. We learned that in the Klondike. Though most likely not the stories Trent is thinking of."

"What? Why not?" Trent demanded.

Granville just shook his head. "You'll see," he said.

And wouldn't say anything more, despite Trent's persistence.

Trent could be rather like a gnat, annoying and persistent, Emily decided, feeling uncharitable even as she did so. Maybe it was just the beer he'd drunk talking. But he didn't seem to know when to give up.

"So we'll visit the creeks on Monday?" she asked.

Again Granville and Scott exchanged glances. This time, it was Scott who spoke.

"The local ones, anyway. Seems we're not getting anywhere in Barkerville itself. Might as well have another look at those drawings our missing man left in his letters. See if we can figure them out, now that we're here"

"Or at least find a starting point," Granville added. "Since no-one here seems to remember him, those letters may be the only help we get."

Trent frowned. "But why are we waiting for Monday? Why not tomorrow?"

"I'm going to church tomorrow," Emily said.

Before he could argue—which it was clear he was about to— Granville shut him down.

"As are we all," he said firmly. "We are visitors to this community. It would be disrespectful to avoid church. Besides which, it's the best way to meet everyone in town. You may be sure they all know who we are by now. And that we're asking about Robertson."

"Then why don't we head for the creeks after church?" Trent said. "That way we don't waste time."

"The days are too short to set out in the afternoon. And we have time," Granville said.

Scott drained his coffee, signaled for more. "We can use the afternoon to go through Robertson's letters home again. See if anything stands out now we have a bit more information about these parts," he said.

"We already did that. Why go over it again?" Trent asked.

Emily wondered why Trent was pushing quite this hard. He was usually more reasonable, especially after Granville had explained his plans.

"Why the rush?" she asked him.

"We've been on this case for more than two weeks, now. And we're getting nowhere," Trent said.

"We have been in Barkerville exactly one day," Granville told him with a grin. "It's a small place, granted, but we've hardly talked to everyone yet. Much less thought through what that new information might tell us. Have a little patience."

"But the weather's just going to get worse. You know it will. By the time we figure out where he did go, if we ever do, we won't even be able to get there."

"The distances out here are too great to just check out every creek," Scott said. We've got to pick up Robertson's trail first. Or we'll end up goin' nowhere. Except maybe back home."

Trent then wanted to argue that they had made enough progress to start with already, but Granville shut him down with a look.

"Progress is learning more about our missing man. Not just his times," he said.

Glancing around at the rapidly emptying dining room, Granville pushed back his chair. "We should be on our way," he said. "While it's still light out."

"Yeah, you two need sunlight to read the headstones," Scott said. "Luckily for Trent and me, that doesn't matter in the saloons. We have hours yet. Have some more coffee," he told his sulking assistant with a quick grin.

"I REALLY DO LOVE READING old headstones," Emily said, looking around her. The Barkerville Cemetery was a smaller site than she'd expected, though she hadn't realized she'd been holding expectations. It lay to the north of the town, on a small, cleared hillside, and most of the markers were of wood.

Quite a few of the grave markers were heavily carved. One of the tidbits of information they'd picked up was that Barkerville had been home to a master carver, who carved elaborate grave markers for those who could afford them. She bent over, brushing off the snow as she tried to decipher one weathered marker.

"I can't quite make this out. Is this 'Roddell' or 'Ruddell'?" she asked Granville, who was examining the marker beside her.

He looked over and squinted a little, which made her laugh. It seemed everything made her laugh these days. Marriage seemed to agree with her. Or at least honeymoons did.

Though the thought of a months-long honeymoon to England to meet Granville's family she found equally exciting and terrifying. It was a generous offer he'd made, and she hadn't even been able to respond. She still couldn't find the words for the confused emotions she felt.

Luckily he'd accepted her change of subject then. And he hadn't brought it up since. That meant he understood. Didn't it?

"I think it's Ruddell," he said after considering the headstone. "Is it important? Either way, there are too few letters to be Robertson."

"And this man was born in Ontario, not Washington," she agreed. "But he was thirty-six in 1868. Which is the same age our client's missing father would have been."

"It is," he agreed. "Why are you checking their ages?"

"To start with, I was checking how many men of Mr. Robertson's approximate age died, and of what causes," she said.

"You're wondering what the chances of dying here were for a man like Robertson?" he said.

Emily nodded, not surprised he'd figured it out so quickly. "But what if he changed his name, the way Trent and Scott suggested? We still haven't found anyone who has ever heard of Thomas Robertson, and neither have they. Either Robertson was entirely unmemorable…"

"Or very secretive," Granville put in.

"Well, yes, that would fit with the letters his son gave us," she agreed. "Or he could have changed his name. And probably he'd have changed where he was from, too."

"Since we don't know what name he changed it to, or even if he actually did so, how are these grave markers going to help?" Granville asked.

Emily didn't answer for a moment as she jotted another name in her notebook, trying not to get the pages wet with snow melt. Which wasn't working terribly well.

It was snowing more heavily now, which didn't help. At least pencil lead didn't run, no matter how damp it got. It did tear the damp paper, though, if she wasn't careful.

"However do you keep your notebook pages from getting wet in these conditions?" she asked.

He grinned. "It's impossible. I usually jot things on the back of an envelope or a separate sheet of paper, then transcribe it into the notebook when I'm somewhere dry and warm," he said.

"Oh. I'll remember that. And to answer your question, I'm noting the names anyone of approximately the right age who died after 1863," Emily said.

She gave him a wry look. "Which is not likely to get us far. And which would be much easier without the snow."

"You're sure you aren't just using that as an excuse to read all of the epitaphs?"

She gave him a laughing look. "They are fascinating, aren't they? Here's one that says 'In Loving Memory of Dr. Thomas Bell. Doctor in charge of Royal Cariboo Hospital. Born York, England on June 8, 1822. Died Barkerville, B.C. On August 12,

1875.' Only 53. Doesn't that make you wonder how he ended up here? And running the hospital."

"Which was probably pretty small at the time. He may well have been the only doctor in town."

It was a good point. Emily wondered how she could find out as she walked on a little further. Then bent over to brush the snow from a grave marker. "Oh, here's one of the miners that Mr. Powers told me about on that first part of our stagecoach journey," she called out. "Mr. Bovyer was only 32 when he died in 1870."

Her eye caught another familiar name a few markers over, the lettering deeply carved into the weathered wood. "And here's Mr. Daniels. Listen to this one: 'Sacred to the memory of Samuel Daniels, Native of Milton Abbott, Devonshire, England. Aged 32 years, met with his death by accident on the 15 of June, 1864 while working in the Prairie Flower ore claim.'

I wonder what kind of accident it was."

A while later she commented "You know, I'm seeing people from everywhere. Canada, the United States, England, Wales, Scotland, Ireland, Germany, Italy, France, even a man from Russia."

He smiled across a row of grave markers at her. "And they all ended up here. The Klondike rush was like that, too. Miners and adventurers poured in from all over. And everyone had a story."

Emily nodded. "I find it fascinating. I'd like to know the story of each name here. Why they left home. How they got here. And what their life was like in Barkerville."

"Old graveyards can be fascinating," he agreed. "And very good sources of information. But unless you want to be caught out by nightfall, I'm afraid you'll have to content yourself with finding Thomas Robertson's story."

She frowned. "We're having enough trouble with just that one. But I'm pretty sure now that he's not buried here. Not under Robertson. And I haven't found any-one that came from Seattle, either.

He didn't respond.

"Are you concerned about what Trent said at lunch?" she asked, suddenly worried about him. "That we've had this case for over two weeks, and so far have made no real progress, I mean? Usually we'd have at least some clues by now."

"Usually we're not working on a thirty-two year-old case," he said. "But yes, I'm concerned that there might be nothing to find."

"Then how could you tell Trent to be patient?"

"Because it's what I tell myself every time I doubt we'll find anything," Granville said. "And because the only way we can guarantee failure is to quit trying. Or to get in a rush and overlook…"

"That telling detail," she said, laughing. "I'm sorry. I wasn't doubting you, you know. It's just—everything about this case feels a little off."

"It has since I accepted it," Granville said. "I believe it feels that way because the case is so old. But we won't know that for sure until we either find the fellow. Or fail to do so."

Emily nodded slowly. "My instincts don't seem to be working very well on this one. I hoped that was my inexperience. But if you're having the same problem…?"

He nodded. "I am. Which is either because such a cold case requires methods none of us are used to, or because I should never have accepted the case in the first place."

"I'm glad you did," Emily told him, looking around the small graveyard, picturesque in the snow. "I'm thrilled to be here, and to have traveled all this way. But… why did you accept it, if you had such doubts?"

He stared off down the hill in silence for a moment, and Emily suddenly wondered if she'd been too bold. Was she asking him to admit to a mistake that had brought them all this way for nothing?

Before she could try to fix it, he turned back to her.

"I'm not sure," he said quietly. "As I say, I had my doubts that we'd succeed. But I couldn't turn our client down. Perhaps it was the challenge I couldn't refuse."

"Pitting your investigation skills against thirty-two years of decaying clues?" she said. "I can understand that. Or maybe it's your instinct to take on this case that's the right one. And the doubts we're all having are just because none of us has a clue about dealing with a case this old."

He laughed. "Trust you to think of the second option. And I love you for it. But are you really intending to spend the rest of the afternoon here?"

"Well, Scott and Trent are visiting the rest of the saloons and bars this afternoon, and we've run out of coffeehouses," Emily said. "Tomorrow we have a congregation to talk to and some letters to reread. Then on Monday we head for the creeks. Unless one of us makes some progress finding Mr. Robertson today. Other than the graveyard, it isn't as if we have any other leads."

"Except for the possibility of dead letters at the Post Office," he reminded her.

Emily made a face. "Why don't you go on and talk to Mrs. Darrow now. I'll wait for you here."

Granville looked around the snowy, deserted cemetery. Glanced at the dark clouds massing on the horizon. "Alone? We're out of sight of the town, and probably out of earshot too. Do you think that wise?"

It was clear he didn't think it was. And he was probably right, Emily admitted to herself. It would be beyond foolish to actually put herself in a dangerous situation, just to prove—to herself? to him?—that marriage hadn't lessened her independence.

"Fine. When we're done here, I'll accompany you to the Post Office."

He was too wise to comment. Emily couldn't decide if she loved that about him, or hated that it left her feeling just a little foolish for fighting a battle that wasn't even there. At least, not with him.

CHAPTER 31

"Well, we can cross off the graveyard," Emily said with a decided air of checking an item off her mental list as they made their way through what was fast becoming a snow storm and turned back towards town.

"Careful where you walk," Granville said, making sure he kept his grip firm on her elbow. Those elegant boots of hers were adequate for travel, but not for Barkerville in the snow. "It's getting slippery."

"It is, isn't it?" she said. "With all this snow, it's a good thing I was ready to leave the cemetery. It was getting hard to read the epitaphs. And it didn't exactly help us find Mr. Robertson."

"You found some possibilities, though? If he'd changed his name, that is."

"I have several names of men that were the right age when they died," she said. "So we can call them possibilities. Would he have been likely to change his name, though?"

"A number of miners in the Klondike did, for one reason or another. Something to keep in mind."

She paused for a moment, and he glanced at her face. She looked unexpectedly serious.

"You know, walking through the cemetery really makes me think differently about the gold rush," she said. "All those names and dates on the grave markers."

"Oh? How so?"

"I have several names of men that were the right age when they died. But most of the men who died in those years were a decade or more younger than Mr. Robertson. Not much older than Trent, some of them. Which just seems wrong."

And not a great many years older than Emily herself. Granville wondered if that had occurred to her. But she was right —it was far too young to die.

"That's the lure of a gold rush," he said. Thinking of the day he'd made his own decision to head north to the Klondike and that rush of energy he'd felt. "Great quests—whether they are called gold rushes or something else—often call the loudest to young men. And while youth and strength helps them survive, their daring and inexperience has the opposite effect."

She nodded. "I suppose. It still seems sad."

"It is sad. I lost comrades on the gold fields, mostly to disaster or disease, and it never got easier."

"I'm sorry. That must have been hard," she said, and they walked in silence for a bit.

"Do you really think that the Dead Letter files Mr. Dunham mentioned will have something helpful?" Emily suddenly asked with a sideways look.

Clearly she'd felt it time for a change of subject. She must have noticed that he didn't like to talk about those losses, even now.

"I think it's a possibility we might find something in those files," Granville said. "Even if a remote one. According to our client, the Post Office here was the only address they had for his father."

"If they really kept old letters this long. And even if they did have a letter for him, what does that tell us?"

"It's hard to say. And we have a little time. Why don't we go and find out?"

"As long as you ask the questions this time; I'm going to pretend to be invisible."

He grinned, but didn't point out that she couldn't be invisible if she tried. She was too vibrant for that.

Though Mrs. Darrow would likely be happy to ignore her, if what they'd seen of that lady so far was anything to go on.

As EMILY STOPPED to look at a metal rack of postcards by the door, Granville strode to the counter and smiled at Mrs. Darrow. Who seemed surprised to see him.

"Your suggestions about who to talk to were very helpful," he told her. "In fact, one of the men we talked to mentioned the Dead Letter files, and said we needed to talk to you about it. So I came back to do so."

She beamed up at him. "Of course. The Dead Letters. I should have thought of those. There are rather a lot of them, I'm afraid. It might take some time."

"I have time," he told her. "If the files are heavy, I could assist you."

Mrs. Darrow's automatic flirtatious look dissolved into a genuine smile. "Thank you, I'd appreciate it. There are several boxes, all heavy. Come this way."

And she lifted the hinged passthrough cut into the counter and gestured him through. Then led him through a doorway in the back wall and into a combination workroom and storeroom.

The far wall was lined with cardboard boxes, all labelled, the handwriting on them ranging from uneven scrawls to neat lettering. The postmistress gestured towards a shadowy corner on the far left. "That's it," she said. "Bottom two rows. What years are you looking for?"

"He was last heard from in the late spring of 1868, I believe."

"Not that long before the fire, then. That helps."

"The Post Office burnt then? "

"No. The Post Office for the region was housed in Richfield

until three years ago, so they were safe. In fact, if we can't find the letters you're looking for, some of the very old ones might still be held in the basement of the government building in Richfield."

So a letter lost to fire had not been a factor in Robertson's disappearance. "That's helpful," he said. "Tell me, how are the letters filed here? By the postmark? Or by the date they arrived?"

She looked surprised, then thoughtful. "I'm afraid I don't know. There isn't really a system, so I suspect it will be a mix of the two."

Which was going to take forever. Granville stifled a groan. "So perhaps we need to look at what you have from 1868 and the following three years?"

He'd deliberately included her in the search, and she looked pleased as she pointed down to the far corner of the bottom shelf.

He crouched down, peering into the dimness as he tried to decipher some of the dates.

"Here," she said. "This might help."

There was a scratch, a flaring sound and the smell of sulphur. Then her hand appeared in his line of sight, holding a lit kerosene lantern.

"Thank you," he said, meaning it. Now he had at least some hope of finding the right boxes.

"Try the middle one," she suggested, looking over his shoulder. "And the others you need should be written in the same hand."

That was helpful. He looked closer, chose a box and pulled it out. Standing easily, he carried it to the worktable, where the light was a little better. Which wasn't saying much.

He placed the lantern on the table, also. That helped. And considered the label. 1868. Or perhaps 1869. It was impossible to be sure.

He glanced at Mrs. Darrow for permission, then opened the box. It was entirely filled with yellowing envelopes, some very weather-stained. He glanced through the first few, and grimaced.

"I"m afraid you are right about the lack of system," he said.

"This could take days, just to find out that there is nothing for Robertson."

"Why are you looking for him, anyway?"

"He spent four or five years here in the 1860's, and his letters were postmarked Barkerville. Are you sure you have never heard the name?"

"I'm sure," she said.

Something about her voice, and the way her eyes shifted away from him told Granville she was lying. Or at least hiding something. Which was interesting.

He brought out his notebook and extracted the sketch Miss Kent had made. "This man?"

Mrs. Darrow held the sketch closer to the lantern, and drew in a sharp breath. It sounded painful. She took her time, though, examining it carefully. Even in the flickering light, he could see her face change, though the light wasn't good enough to read her expression.

She knew him, all right.

"This is Thomas Robertson?" she asked.

Maybe she hadn't known him by that name. "Yes. You knew him?"

"Not well," was the quick response. "I'd forgotten the name. I suppose I was too young. But I knew of him."

"You're sure?"

"I think so," she said, though the pain on her face told a different story. As if wary of showing too much, she changed the subject.

"This is a very good sketch," she said, her tone flat. As if it didn't matter. Her eyes said otherwise. "When was it made? He looked very like this when I first knew him. Knew of him, I mean."

"The sketch is recent, but it was based on a group photograph that was taken not long before he left to come north to Barkerville."

She nodded, still examining the sketch closely. "It is very like him when he first arrived. So the photo must have been taken that same year."

1863 then. "So you knew him—of him, I mean—in 1863?"

"I did," she said absently.

"When did you last see him? Or hear of him?"

"In 1868," she said.

The same year his family had last heard. It struck Granville as odd that no-one else had recognized the name or the sketch, if Robertson had returned to Barkerville often over so many years.

"What was he doing during those years, do you know?"

With a soft sigh, Mrs. Darrow handed back the sketch.

"Mining, mostly," she said. "I know he teamed up with Joe Gordon and another miner for a time, though the little gold they found petered out pretty quick."

"Are either of those men still around?"

"No. Joe was killed in a cave-in a year or so later. And the third man left just after."

"And Robertson?"

"He was out prospecting most of the time. He'd come back to town for a few months, then head out again. It was his pattern, you see?"

"Was there also a pattern to the time of year he headed out?"

She shrugged, and for a moment he thought that was the only answer he'd get. Then she relented.

"He'd come and go at odd times during the year. Or so I'd heard," she was quick to add. "Then he'd stay away for months at a time."

"So no pattern there?"

"None." She bit the word off, as if it offended her.

"And did he team up with others?"

"Not that he ever spoke of. But these creeks mostly can't be worked by one man working alone, so maybe."

"Is there anyone who would have known?"

"There were a few names he'd mention now and again. Maybe he'd worked with them. But they're long gone, now, all of those men who worked the creeks."

"Long gone?"

She shrugged again. "Some moved on. We never saw or heard from them again. Others stayed, or we heard a bit, now and again. Most are dead now, from accident, or exposure, or hard living. Even old age, this many years on."

"Can you think of anyone still alive who worked with Robertson, or knew him well?"

"Not really," she said. "Robby—that's what I... what they called him—he was a bit of a loner. He was pretty good at finding small claims he'd work on his own for awhile, but nothing that earned him more than a month or two in town before he'd head out again. His dreams never shrunk any, though."

That might explain why no-one remembered Robertson. Though it didn't explain why she hadn't recognized the name. Perhaps the fellow had changed it after all. "Robby what?" he asked.

"Just Seattle Robby," she said, quickly enough that he wondered if she'd made it up on the spot.

Well, at least the location fit their missing miner.

"And what were his dreams?"

She sighed. "A fortune in gold. Like all the Argonauts."

"Did he ever talk about striking it rich?"

"He did. But he was always pretty cagey about saying much. What little he did say, he talked in a kinda code that no-one 'cept him knew."

"And he never found that kind of gold?"

"Not that I ever heard," she said. Another lucifer rasped as she lit a cigarette.

"Did he ever register a claim, do you know?"

"Sure," she said, and drew deeply on her cigarette. "Him and Joe Gordon registered one for sure."

That was a lead worth following up. "Where was this claim, do you know?"

"On William's Creek, out Richfield way."

Finally, something concrete, Granville thought. Only to have his hopes dashed a moment later.

"But that won't help you," Mrs. Darrow added. "He sold that claim after Joe died, and he and the third partner moved on."

"Where to, do you know?"

"No. And I never heard of Robby registering another claim."

Not much help after all. "And the last time you saw him—do you know where he was headed?" Granville asked

"Just that he was going back to the creeks. He was pretty secretive about where, though. Always was one to play his cards close," she said with a small, private smile.

"Not that he was a gambler, not like some of them," she said quickly. "But he said he was going to be rich, and promised me… Well, no matter. Not long after that, he packed up his things, like usual, and he left. I never saw him again. Never heard what happened, neither."

"I'm sorry," Granville said, seeing the sadness etched into her face. Tightening her eyes.

As he watched, she tucked it away, and turned to him with a too bright smile. Still maintaining the pretense, even now. He wondered why.

"Those were hard times," she said. "I'm lucky. Times are easier now."

He doubted that, but if the pretense gave her comfort, he wasn't about to challenge it.

"What of these dead letters?" he asked instead. "Might there be a letter for Thomas Robertson amongst them?"

She shook her head. "No. Nothing."

"You'd have known if a letter came in for him? Even one that had been lost in the mail for several years?" He hated to quiz her on what was obviously an open wound, even after so many years. But he had to be sure.

"Yes, I'd have heard," she said, looking down. "In those days, the arrival of the mail was big. Everyone gathered to hear the names called out. And Mr. Cranston—he was postmaster then— he knew to tell me if I wasn't there."

She'd finally given up the pretense that there had been

nothing between her and the missing man. But she was still wary of letting out any details of what exactly had been between them.

How had she known Robertson, and what was her story? Had their relationship become a tie that kept Robertson in Barkerville, and away from his family? Or had she become another unwanted tie for the fellow to flee from?

Who had Thomas Robertson been, really? And what was he really looking for here, so far away from the life he'd built back home?

From the son's story, it would seem that the quest for gold, or wealth in any form, was needed to save their family farm. But he knew from his own experiences that sometimes distance changed a man's perspective.

He'd intended to return to England, after all, rich with the proceeds of all that gold he'd never found. Instead he'd found a rich life here, with Emily.

He knew what Robertson's family thought he was searching for. But what had Thomas Robertson himself thought he was searching for? And what had he found?

It seemed it wasn't a life with the sorrowing woman in front of him. Unless Robertson had been killed after she last saw him, and before he could return to her?

"Let me put this box back," Granville said. "I truly appreciate your help."

The only thing he was sure of at the moment was that the answers didn't lie in the Dead Letter files. Mrs. Darrow would never have left them there if they had.

CHAPTER 32

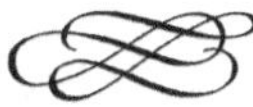

"So what happened? Emily asked, tucking her hand into the crook of his arm as they exited the Post Office. She was clutching a half-dozen postcards she'd purchased from a stone faced Mrs. Darrow. "Was there nothing in the Dead Letter files? And how could you go through them so fast?"

Granville told her what he'd learned.

"Joe Gordon was Mr. Robertson's partner? His was one of the names I wrote down, from the headstones," she said. "That's sad."

"Yes. It is."

"Can that help us find him, though? Their claim?"

"Possibly. The claim would have been registered, at least."

"Then we're on our way back to the Gold Commissioner's office?"

"We are."

"Oh, good," Emily said with a smile, which quickly faded. "But she—Mrs. Darrow, I mean—she thought Mr. Robertson had promised her a future?"

"It seems so."

Emily walked beside him in silence for a moment. "That poor woman," she said softly. And her hand tightened on his arm.

~

Constable McCall looked surprised to see them. "Back again?" he quipped as they shook hands. "How can I help you?"

"We're looking for a claim that would have been filed on William's Creek near Richfield sometime in the 1860's," Granville said.

McCall didn't flinch, just picked up a pencil. "Names?"

"Joe Gordon and Thomas Robertson. And a third man, though I don't have a name for him."

"Can you narrow that date down a little?"

"I think I can," Emily said, reaching into her handbag and pulling out her notebook. "According to his grave marker, Mr. Gordon died in June of 1865. And we were told he was killed in a cave in. So they would have registered the mine before that date."

"And Robertson didn't arrive here until '63," Granville added.

"We might want to start with Gordon's death and work backward, then," McCall said.

As the constable turned towards the bank of heavy metal filing cabinets that took up part of the rear wall of the room, Emily gave him a frustrated look that had Granville hiding a smile.

Then McCall returned with five thick ledgers and thumped them down on his desk. "Here we go. These are the claims filed along William's Creek during that period."

Emily stared from the files to the fellow's calm face. "That's a lot of claims."

He nodded. "Busy time. It calmed down a bit by '65. You'll see that there is only one ledger for that year."

Which explained why he wanted to work backwards.

"Can we help you look through them?" Emily asked.

"I'm afraid not. As the registrar, I need to personally handle any requests. This is going to take me at least an hour. Why don't you come back in ninety minutes or so, and I should have an answer for you then."

"Thank you, we will," Granville said, reaching out to shake the fellow's hand.

When they returned an hour and a half later, Constable McCall rose to greet them with a smile. There was no sign of the ledgers.

"How did it go?" Granville asked.

"I'm afraid I have bad news for you."

"You found nothing?"

"I'm afraid not. Not under those names. And you're sure of the names?"

He thought of Mrs. Darrow's lack of recognition of Robertson's name. "I'm sure of Joe Gordon's."

At that, Emily and McCall both gave him assessing looks.

"Is there any chance a claim could have been registered elsewhere?" Granville added.

"No, I'm afraid not. Everything goes through this office, and is recorded in our ledgers, with copies sent to Victoria."

"Have you any suggestions for a next step?"

"Again, Cranston is your best bet. He'll likely remember Joe Gordon's death, and the circumstances around it."

"Thank you, we'll do that," Granville said. "When is he expected back?"

"It's looking like Thursday at the earliest, I'm afraid. And possibly longer, if the weather turns worse. How long are you planning to be in the area?"

"Until we find our missing man. Or proof of what happened to him."

"Well, I wish you luck with your search. I'll be here if you have further questions."

Granville thanked him, and they left.

On the sidewalk outside, Emily turned to him. "Was Mrs. Darrow lying, then? Or did he lie to her?"

As usual, she'd cut straight to the heart of it. It amused him that he understood exactly what she meant, too. "Our post-mistress didn't seem to recognize Robertson's name, until I showed her the sketch of him. Then she acted as if she'd known it all along."

"So now we may have a nameless missing man," Emily said with disgust. "Who was lying to the woman in love with him. Lying to everyone in Barkerville, come to that. Ugh."

"Unless Mrs. Darrow was lying," he said.

"Well, she wasn't exactly lying about his name," Emily said. "Just not telling you if he was using a different one. Although that's lying too, isn't it? But what about Joe Gordon? He was here. He died here. There's a grave marker to prove it."

"They may not have been partners. Or they might have worked a claim together, but that claim belonged to someone else."

"But if they weren't partners… did she lie to you? Or did he —Mr. Robertson, or whatever name he was using—lie to her?"

"Exactly. We have no way of knowing. And it's the same problem if the claim was registered to someone else. Possibly the nameless third man. We don't know where the truth lies."

"Or why they lied. Whether it was Mr. Robertson or Mrs. Darrow—one of them has to be lying."

"Unless one of Robertson's partners registered the claim solely in his own name and lied to Robertson and Gordon about it."

"Then both Mrs. Darrow and Mr. Robertson would have been telling what they believed to be the truth," she said triumphantly. "Except how likely is that? And it's all very convo-luted and we're no further ahead."

"And our only source so far—the only one who admits to having known Robertson, whatever he might be calling himself here—is either lying about him, or he told her mostly lies about himself and his life," he said.

They looked at each other and began to laugh.

CHAPTER 33

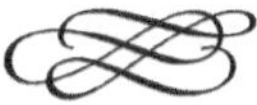

Monday morning dawned cold and crisp and clear. The frost was so thick on the outside of their hotel room window that Emily could see nothing but frost patterns against the thin light.

She snuggled deeper under the covers, and half slid into Granville. Who laughed.

"Time to be up, sleepyhead," he said, dropping a kiss on her nose.

"That's not very romantic," she complained.

"We're married now, remember?"

"You mean now I'm your wife, all I get in the morning is half a kiss?"

His eyes gleamed. "Complaining already?" he said, and set about proving her mistaken. Very thoroughly.

"That's better," she said, emerging from his embrace feeling decidedly mussed. "But I thought you wanted to get an early start for the creeks?"

"Minx," he said, rolling out of bed and reaching for his clothes.

She lay enjoying the show for a moment, then quickly

dragged the blanket around herself against the cold air in the room and hurried into the other room in search of her own clothing.

As EMILY STEPPED out of the hotel several hours later, she drew in a breath and smiled, watching it plume as she breathed out. The air was still, crisp and cold, and every breath felt invigorating.

But they weren't underway yet.

And it felt like half the morning was gone by the time the four of them had all eaten and gathered the horses, tack and supplies they would need for the day. Emily was glad their initial destination was only a mile away. At least they'd easily make it that far before they stopped for lunch.

Unless the snow got worse. Flakes were still drifting lazily down, but it must have snowed heavily for most of the night, judging by the heavy drifts of snow that lay everywhere.

If the weather changed, they'd likely have to turn back before they got anywhere. She hoped it didn't come to that—the Cariboo was so big, and they had so much ground to cover.

But they didn't know the territory, and without a guide, they couldn't risk getting lost in a heavy snowfall. Or caught out in a flood if the weather suddenly warmed. Though they'd been assured there was no danger of that today. Or even this week.

They rode much too slowly for her liking along Main Street, following the wagon road in the opposite direction from when they had arrived. Allowing the horses to find their own footing in the thick snow covering the packed dirt of the street. She had plenty of time to look up at the busy sidewalks several feet above her head. It was such an odd perspective, she felt disoriented, as if the world had shifted while she slept.

Emily quickly shook off the feeling. This was no way to think. Not now they were actually leaving Barkerville to search for the trail of Thomas Robertson.

They reached the narrow, wooden bridge, and the four of

them rode across, turning south along Williams Creek. Their destination was the town of Richfield—or what was left of it. Near where Mr. Robertson had apparently staked his first claim. Or maybe his only claim. If he'd staked it at all, that is.

They still knew next to nothing about the man. Not even what name he'd been known by here.

But it was a place to start.

Richfield had grown around the first mining discoveries on the creek, months before Billy Barker's huge discovery further down the same creek had resulted in the growth of the new town of Barkerville. Oddly—or at least it seemed odd to her when one of the old-timers had explained it—while Barkerville had become the commercial center of the Cariboo during the height of the gold rush, Richfield had been where most of the miners actually lived when they weren't out on their claims. It had also been the home of local government, including the courthouse for the district.

Now only the courthouse was in use, and little was left of the town. A few miners still lived there, especially if they were still working a claim on one of the nearby streams. Not much gold was coming out of those streams though, compared to the yields of the past.

Her roan horse's bridle jingled as they reached the old Cariboo Road, still level and clear of brush, though there had to be a foot of untouched snow covering the road. There were no footprints, human or otherwise, marring that pristine whiteness.

"We'll need to take it slower than I'd like," Granville said, pulling back to ride beside her, leaving Scott and Trent to ride on ahead. "We can't risk losing one of the horses to a pothole we can't see."

Emily reached down to pat her mare's neck. "I'd hate to see that happen," she said. "But it slows us more than I'd expected. Do you think we'll actually be able to get past Richfield today?"

He laughed. "I certainly hope so. But that's one of the benefits of planning only a day trip today. We'll follow the lead Mrs.

Darrow gave us. But we'll also get a feel for the area at this time of year.

And for what we might be up against."

"Yet after a day on horseback in the cold and the snow, we still get to sleep in a warm bed tonight," she said.

"There is that," he agreed with a grin.

"Do you actually expect to learn anything today?"

He shrugged. "I think we've all spent too much time poring over Robertson's letters and those small sketches of his, without actually seeing what he saw when he wrote them."

"You think we might be misinterpreting the letters, because our experience is different from his?"

"I think Randall would call it witness bias."

"He's a lawyer. He thinks everything is witness bias," Emily said. "Or so I've heard."

He just grinned. So she pushed a bit harder.

"But you might have a point," she added. "If witness bias means that people tend to interpret things they see based on their own experience." And she cast her eyes down with fake modesty.

He laughed again. "Marriage seems to suit you," he said.

"You thought it might not?"

"Never. But I suspect you had a doubt or two."

She could feel her face heating, despite the cold, and tried to stop blushing. How had he known?

"Of course I did. I've never been married before, you know," she retorted.

"I'm glad to hear it," he said.

The look in his eyes made her blush again, despite the teasing tone. It wasn't fair he still had that effect on her.

Just wait. One of these days she was going to make him blush.

"So what are we looking for here?" she asked quickly. "We're riding slowly enough, we shouldn't miss a single clue."

"According to Mrs. Darrow, Robertson seems to have gone on his journeys at different times of the year. And it was probably gold he was looking for. At least at first. "

"We'll never see any of the signs he might have looked for that suggest gold deposits," Emily told him. "Not under all this snow."

They'd talked over dinner last night, the four of them, about the kind of mining that had been done in the area in the 1860's, and how and where a miner or a company of miners might look for gold. Several of the other guests, hearing the spirited discussion between Trent and Scott, had joined in.

The fact that gold was most often found here by digging down beneath a layer of blue clay had fascinated Emily. Especially when she realized that 'layer' could be five or six feet deep. And was often found below bedrock, which itself could be ten to thirty feet down.

"That's a lot of digging," she'd said softly, knowing the discussion was too heated for anyone to hear her. No wonder the miners had usually banded together in impromptu "companies" with their fellow miners, in order to stake and work their claims.

And yet, from his letters, Mr. Robertson had sounded as if he'd preferred to work alone. Even Mrs. Darrow was only sure of one time he'd partnered with others to work a claim. And they hadn't been able to find any proof of what she'd said. Not even that the claim had killed one of the partners, and hadn't even paid out.

Yet still their missing miner had stayed. And kept looking for gold. Or so Mrs. Darrow had told them.

If it were her, Emily decided, she wouldn't have kept looking. But what else could Mr. Robertson have been doing, away from Barkerville all that time?

If it wasn't gold he was looking for, what were the "riches" he'd told Mrs. Darrow about? And wrote about in his letters home?

CHAPTER 34

As he and Emily cantered side by side along the wide path beyond Richfield, Granville was surprised that the goldfields of the Cariboo didn't feel more familiar to him. He'd seen more than his share of bare hillsides, shorn of their blanket of evergreens. Diggings half-buried in snow along the banks of frozen creeks. Tiny, thrown together cabins belonging to those hardy souls who were still working their claims year round.

All those were the same.

As were the deep holes in the ground. The smell of fires that had burned all night, softening frozen ground enough to dig. The piles of tailings—taller than a man and frozen solid—that might hold hoped for riches. And might not.

These too seemed as familiar here as they'd been on the goldfields of the Klondike.

Even the wind felt the same, and the bite of snow in it. Smelled different, though. He couldn't put words to it, but up north, the cold had a scent to it that was like you were tasting the frozen ice of the glaciers. Here, the cold had a hint of green to it, somehow. As if it held a trace of the grass frozen beneath the snow.

The feel of the cold was different, too. And the color of the light. Painters knew that about light, but he'd never appreciated the difference in such a visceral way before.

If he fell asleep here, and woke in the Klondike, he'd know immediately where he was. And was not.

Not something he'd ever try to explain to anyone.

Except maybe Emily. She'd probably find the perfect words for it, too. He grinned at the thought.

In a way it was a relief that this area felt so different to him. If they were going to find out what had happened to Thomas Robertson, he needed to see this world through Robertson's eyes. Without any of his own assumptions getting in the way.

He was going to find that easier than he'd expected. Simply because while mining here was similar enough to the work he'd done up North that he could ask decent questions, he found the differences jarring enough that he felt like an outsider.

And he'd been learning that a good detective always looked at the world like an outsider. Questioned everything.

Today's expedition was about all of them getting a feel for the area, and trying to see it as it had been when Robertson was known to be here.

It was also about evaluating the capabilities of the four of them in this setting, before they undertook the longer trip they were planning for the following day.

He especially wanted to be sure it wasn't asking too much of city-born and raised Emily.

He'd been a bit surprised and very impressed by how she'd handled the hardships of the trip from Vancouver. Spending hours on end in a swaying coach wasn't easy at the best of times. Even in England, where good coaching roads criss-crossed the country.

Out here, the main road north from Ashcroft was an amazing feat of engineering, but it was neither entirely safe nor easy to travel. Add in the time of year, and the trip would tax anyone.

Yet Emily had thrived on the adventure of it all.

He expected no less of her today.

But she'd never ridden a horse for hours on end before. Nor spent long hours outside in this kind of cold. Both took their toll on anyone not used to it.

And eventually, even on those who were.

Today, it wasn't his protective instincts that were the problem. Or at least not only them—he'd felt both intrigued by and protective of Emily since the day he'd met her, and now she was his wife, both feelings were even stronger.

But smothering her with his 'care' would kill something in her. Something that made her unique. He could never do that.

No, this was about her survival.

Emily needed to find out how she'd cope with such conditions every bit as much as he needed to know it. Because his new bride —words that still brought an immediate smile to his face—could do pretty much anything she set her mind to. And she would, too. But at a price.

She needed to understand that price on a visceral level. To feel the first aches of sore muscles and skin so dry it cracked. To recognize those first tingles that warned of frostbite. To face the unrelenting cold of a wind capable of freezing you to the bone, and draining the energy you needed to even attempt to find shelter.

Emily needed that knowledge now, before they set off into the wilderness for longer periods of time. It wasn't the things you knew that would kill you in these conditions. It was the things you didn't know, the ones you took for granted. Until the harsh elements taught your error.

Or killed you in the process.

He shuddered at the thought, and set his shoulders firmly.

Not on his watch.

Then Emily sent him an enquiring look that had him easing back in the saddle and smiling at her.

He was pleased that the four of them were making good time along the oldest parts of the wagon trail as it turned away from William's Creek to link up with Lightning Creek. Despite the snow that had drifted deeply here and there. All of their mounts handled the conditions well and seemed to have good stamina, even Emily's smaller mare. Granville would swear his own big gelding was enjoying himself.

The horses were well used to these conditions. Even if their riders were not. With Emily riding easily beside him, he noted that the snow was falling thicker now, and faster. But visibility was still good.

If this continued, they'd need to turn back sooner than they planned, though. He'd keep an eye on it, as would Scott. And Trent.

All three of them had experience in far worse conditions. He rode easier, knowing that it didn't rest solely on him to judge the conditions. Traveling with the three of them, Emily was safe enough.

Barring accidents. Or if she somehow got cut off from them. Or any one of a hundred things that nature could throw at them.

He was beginning to reconsider hiring a local guide for their longer journeys. And if conditions grew worse, would likely do so.

For today, Emily was safe enough.

"Hey, Granville. Does this stuff look normal to you?" Scott asked, reining in his horse and dropping back so he rode alongside him.

They were following the original route of the Cariboo Wagon Road, so the path was wide enough here to ride three abreast. And the quiet hush of a snowfall, punctuated by the soft burble of water running under ice made talking easy. Even Trent, who was still riding ahead of them, could join in.

"Which stuff would that be?" Granville asked lightly, glancing at the remains of what looked to be a fairly normal, if inactive, mining camp. That waterwheel hadn't turned in a while, and one section of the wooden flume had cracked through, but nothing else caught his eye.

Scott just shook his head. Which made Emily laugh.

"It looks like most of the other camps we've passed," she said. "The abandoned ones, at least."

"I think so too," Trent said from behind them. "Not much seems to be happening. Is this really short trip of ours supposed to be helpful?"

Granville and Scott exchanged looks.

"When Thomas Robertson was here in the early-sixties, what do you think it looked like?" Granville asked the lad.

"Busy," Trent said. "I'd guess that someone had staked every possible claim. And worked them hard, judging by how deep some of those holes we've passed still are. That can't be safe, can it?"

"Probably not," Granville said. "Especially if the snow is deep enough to hide it. It's something we'll need to consider when we explore further."

"They had to dig deep, though, didn't they?" Emily said. "Wasn't most of the gold found below bedrock?"

"It was. And then they hit that layer of blue clay, and the real digging started," Granville said.

She grimaced at him, and he laughed.

"Is that what didn't look normal to you?" he asked Scott.

"Nope. I've been trying to figure out the difference between the claims still bein' worked, and the ones that aren't," his partner said. "You got any idea?"

It was a good question. "I think I'd have to know more than I do about local conditions to even begin to answer that one. But it may be key to figuring out where Robertson might have gone. And why."

Scott nodded. "Soon's we find someone crazy enough to be working his claim this time of year, we can ask 'em."

Now it was Trent who was laughing, so hard he nearly fell off his horse. "Says the guy who searched for gold in the Klondike. In winter," he said when he got his breath back.

Scott growled something. Which made Emily laugh. Trent ignored them both.

It was good to hear the laughter, Granville thought. Everyone seemed in good spirits, glad to finally be following Robertson's trail. One of them, anyway.

It wasn't until they could catch glimpses of Bald Mountain that they found several miners hard at work on their claim. Only one of the fellows recognized the sketch of Robertson as familiar, though he couldn't recall a name. Or when he'd last seen him. Or even where.

No matter. The four miners were happy to show them the workings of their mine, and talk about what it had been like here "back then".

"Were there still rumors of gold strikes hereabouts in early 1868?" Granville asked them, mindful of the last time Mrs. Darrow told him she'd seen Thomas Robertson.

"Most of the creeks roundabouts had been staked a few times over, by then," the fellow from Wales told them in a voice that still carried the rhythms of his homeland, though he'd been here long enough that Granville could hear the local accent too.

"Hell, even the trickles were staked," another said.

"Yeah, on William. This part of Lightning, too," said the third. "But it's big country. And there's a lot of streams flowing out of these mountains. Most of them have at least a little gold."

"But not enough to be worth digging for?" Scott asked.

The third miner gave him the nod of one old-timer recognizing another. "You got it. Especially when pay dirt in these regions likes to hide so far below the surface."

"Except for the Chinese miners," the second man said. "A few of them would come in after we'd moved on, take over a played-out mine, and pan out enough surface gold dust for them to live on. Sometimes more than enough."

"Still, we kept trying for that pay dirt," the first miner said. "All of us."

"Hell, we're still trying," the second agreed.

The fourth miner, a short, stocky man with an accent from some part of Eastern Europe Granville couldn't quite place, nodded. "And still, no riches," he said with a quick grin. "Just enough for today. And maybe tomorrow."

And didn't that tell the tale, Granville thought. He thanked the miners for their help, and they rode on. Once they were out of earshot, he turned to Scott. "What are the odds that Robertson sought gold further afield?"

"I'd take that bet," his friend and partner replied. "Given what his lady friend told you."

"And the letters he sent home," Emily said. "The ones where he talked about the riches he'd bring home. It clearly couldn't have been in this area."

"And yet it was close enough that he came back to town on a regular basis," Granville said.

"If it was one place he'd found. And not several, that paid out for a bit, then quit," Scott said. "He'd need to come back to town for supplies, anyway. Plus there's that lady friend."

"That's a pretty good reason, right there," Trent put in.

"Perhaps," Granville said. "Though he either died in 1868, and couldn't come back. Or he moved on, and didn't bother to let her know. In which case, his reason for returning here so often could be that it was a convenient place to get supplies.

"I can't quite work out the timeline, though," Emily said. "What Mrs. Darrow told you is vague enough that it doesn't really help at all. Which makes me wonder if she's hiding something. If Mr. Robertson was as important to her as it sounded, surely she would have a clearer memory of how often she saw him?"

"After thirty years?" Trent said. "Not likely."

"You're not a woman," Emily told him.

Which set him off in another fit of laughter.

Trent certainly seemed to be enjoying himself today, Granville thought. Being cooped up in a coach for several days had been hard on all of them.

Though the lad had clearly been raised without the benefit of sisters. Remembering some of his own sister's courting days, he thought Emily made a good point.

"I think I need to have another chat with our postmistress when we get back to town," he said with a grin.

CHAPTER 35

Tuesday morning saw all four of them all on horseback again. Emily felt another rush of excitement that arced down to her toes. They were headed back past Richfield to Lightning Creek. Then they'd follow the entire length of Lightning Creek to Cottonwood. However long that took.

And they planned to be away for at least four or five days.

Emily couldn't decide if that made her more excited, or more nervous. In some ways this felt like the real start to their case. Here, in the cold and the snow, on the trail that Mr. Robertson himself would have followed all those years ago. She drew in a deep breath of cold air, let it out in a happy sigh.

If those doodles Mr. Robertson had drawn on his letters really did represent lightning bolts, then Lightning Creek seemed the only possible place to start their search. Not only was it one of the earliest places gold had been discovered, but it was the source of any number of smaller streams that might not have been staked back in 1867. There were a lot of reasons for their missing miner to have gone this way.

Even if Trent was still arguing that they were wasting their time. In fact, the four of them had spent several hours yesterday evening, poring over the map and arguing over which direction they would take. As well as discussing whether they needed to hire a guide for this part of their journey. None of them knew the area, and it wasn't easy country. Especially given the weather conditions.

It wasn't snowing now, but there was already a good six inches on the ground, and the skies were overcast. The old timers were predicting even colder weather, and possibly more snow.

Emily had wished she could contribute more to the discussion, but she had so little real experience to draw on. One thing that was clear to all of them right from the start—they were far enough north that they had to be prepared for almost anything, from snow to high winds to freezing rain. Any of which could make it all too easy to lose their way.

And that could prove deadly.

After some discussion, Granville and Scott had decided that since they would be essentially following the old wagon road— which was wide enough to be clearly recognizable as it wound through the forest, even in heavy snow—they could manage without a guide. But to err on the side of caution, they would spend no more than three days searching before turning back. And they'd hire a packhorse, which would allow them to carry enough provisions for a week.

Which meant they had a lot of ground to cover today. So they'd been up and away before dawn.

After so many early mornings on the stage, Emily had been enjoying those lazy mornings in Barkerville with Granville. Even the excitement of a longer trip today wasn't quite enough to make up for that loss.

Still, it was exciting—if a little scary—to know she'd be traveling on horseback and sleeping in tents as she followed in the footsteps of all those who had once called these creeks home. When she was small, she had dreamed of a journey like this. But she'd never truly believed she'd get the opportunity. Now here she was.

Despite her nerves, it felt like an enormous gift.

Several hours later, Emily was less enthused. The bridle jangled loudly as she looked down, past her horse's head. The source of Lightning Creek was in the foothills of Mount Agnes, and there was a trail that Scott and Trent had decided was clear enough for them to follow.

They had been climbing steadily for the last hour. It was a long way down, and Emily shivered inside the thick wool coat she was wearing, partly from cold but partly from fear.

She'd felt confident about her own abilities after their trip to Richfield yesterday. But compared to this, that trip was about as dangerous as an outing in Stanley Park.

Should she have insisted on being part of this first real attempt to follow in Mr. Robertson's path? It had seemed unbearably exciting when they'd talked about it on the train, and at the hotel in Barkerville. But how much of a burden had she put on Granville by doing so?

Now he not only had to deal with finding their client's father, he had to adjust everything to her abilities. Or lack of them.

She'd never told him quite how limited her experience on horseback actually was. Even though she'd suspected that most of their travel once they left Barkerville would be over rough ground. Which meant on horseback.

Or camels, she thought with a fleeting grin, trying to distract herself from the drop below. Apparently there were still a number of two-humped camels roaming free in the area, survivors of a dozen or so of the beasts imported as pack animals at the beginning of the Cariboo rush. She'd actually spotted one of the odd animals on the dry plains just past Hat Creek. Mr. Powers had pointed them out to her from the stage, and explained their story.

Apparently the camels had actually proven decent pack animals in this dry, rocky territory. But their strange appearance, and probably the unfamiliar odor, had panicked every mule train they met. On the steep narrow pathways hanging off the sides of mountains that passed for pack routes at the time, that panic was dangerous. With often fatal consequences for the mules.

Camels didn't make easy mounts for riders, either.

Emily was certainly not about to mount one, even if it had been possible. She was a decent rider, with a good sense of balance both on horseback and on a bicycle, but camels? Not even for the adventure.

Not when she suspected neither her previous experience with horses or with bikes equated to spending days trekking deep into the Cariboo. In November. Much as she loved snow and cold, and had even done a little sledding, she was used to hot chocolate at the end of it, not thick coffee brewed over a campfire.

An icy gust of wind found its way under her long skirts, despite how tightly she'd wrapped them around her. She shivered. The trees overhead swayed and moaned and a clump of snow fell from the branch she was riding under and straight down the back of her neck. She could feel it, so cold it was almost hot, then melting in an icy trickle down her back. And the snow had damped the hems of her skirts, and then frozen. Now they were melting against her legs.

Angrily brushing away what snow she could reach, she immediately had to soothe her horse, made jumpy by her sudden movement.

"What do you think so far?" Granville asked, riding up from behind her.

"It's beautiful," she said. And it was—a cold, white world, so silent. The sun caught the ice crystals that had formed on the branches of the pines above their heads, breaking through in sparkles and rainbows. Which hardly matched her recognition of exactly how dangerous this beauty could be.

And how cold.

But she couldn't tell him that. Not when it was too late in the day to turn around and go back.

It was, wasn't it?

"Have you seen anything that matches what Mr. Robertson mentioned in his letters?" she asked quickly.

He glanced at her, as if surprised—had something come through in her voice? But he answered anyway.

"No, but I really didn't expect to. Not this close to where so many other mines were staked. He'd most likely have looked for a subsidiary creek, one well off the main route."

She looked at him curiously. "You really believe we'll find him? Or at least some word of him? After all these years?"

"I hope to," he said easily. "We knew from the start that this search for a man missing for thirty-two years was a long shot. We're not just going to trip over a clue out here."

Emily laughed. Something in that image struck her imagination. "Though I doubt he was intending to leave anyone clues," she said. Then frowned, as she thought about what she'd said.

"So why did he do it?" she said slowly, as if to herself.

"Do what?" Granville asked, watching her face change with great interest.

"Put those details in his letters," she said, still not looking at him. Her eyes fixed on a bend in the creek below them.

He waited.

"I mean, it's not as if the mail was particularly secure," she said. "There were several instances that I read about where even the express mail was stolen. Which meant it had to happen more often than that."

He nodded. Waited.

"From everything Mrs. Darrow told us, he was so secretive," she said. Then looked up from her examination of the snow covered land. Her green eyes searched his expression. And she grinned.

He grinned back, tempted to kiss her. But at this moment, he wanted to hear her explanation even more.

"You don't know what I'm talking about, do you?" she asked.

"You could be a little clearer," he said. "Though I imagine it has to do with him sharing details in his letters that might lead a thief to his riches, when he wouldn't tell his lady friend anything."

Emily laughed. "I do like being married to you," she told him. "It makes life so much more interesting. And yes, that's it exactly.

But what if it was deliberate?" she went on. "I mean, what if he had reason to worry that he was being watched? And his letters might be stolen. That could be why his family received so few of them."

"So anything that seemed like a clue could be false information, deliberately planted," he finished for her.

"Exactly. Which would mean we are going in entirely the wrong direction, by looking for something along Lightning Creek."

"Unless Trent is right, and that sketch is meant to symbolize Quesnel Forks, which is in the opposite direction from Lightning Creek," Granville said.

"Or both. In which case, those small sketches are useless to us."

"Also possible," he agreed. "Meaning we might as well return home."

She looked horrified. "Surely..." Emily began, then took a closer look at his face. And made a face at him. "Oh, you. That is not funny."

"I found it so," he said, with the grin she loved.

Emily only shook her head at him.

"We have to start somewhere," he said, deadpan.

And then she couldn't keep a straight face and grinned back.

THE FOUR OF them spent the rest of the day just making their way along the beginnings of Lightning Creek. Along the way, they checked out small streams and potentially interesting rock formations that might signal the presence of gold below the surface. With the heavy snow that lay everywhere, it was slow going.

Emily's mare seemed to struggle at times to find her footing on the uneven ground, and Emily often found herself holding her breath, her heart hammering in her chest. As if that would help.

A soft whoosh overhead distracted her and she looked up, startled. A small gray and white bird with a black head was perched on a branch just ahead of her, head tilted so it could observe her. A whiskey jack. It still surprised her to see them away from the coast. And this far north.

Emily smiled as this one cocked its head to the other side, as if to get a better look at her. She looked around for the rest of the flock. Several of the birds had been following them all day. She found them amusing, partly because they seemed so friendly. When they all stopped for a break, the whiskey jacks swooped in, hopping about on their small black feet, looking for morsels of biscuits. As though they'd been invited to a tea party.

Which made her think of Clara, who would definitely not have enjoyed this experience. Emily grinned at the thought of her friend in such a situation. Clara would be miserable. Her friend didn't like being cold, or even damp, and the lack of any shopping would have been worse.

She wondered if Clara was still refusing to see Tim O'Hearn, and what means the resourceful young reporter might be using to get around them.

That thought occupied her for awhile, and took her own mind off the increasingly damp hem of her skirts, which was gradually spreading upwards. She didn't much care for being damp, either, and she hated that creeping chill.

It was late afternoon and the shadows were lengthening when Trent, consulting the map, told them that Van Winkle Creek was just ahead.

Which meant that the town itself—which they had passed through on Monday—would be a little further on, Emily thought. She was surprised to realize how much longer it had taken them this time, compared to that journey by sleigh.

Although, today they had taken the longer route. And gone at least a little way up each of the creeks that they came across, "getting a feel for things", as Scott put it. All of which had slowed them down.

She was beginning to wonder where they would camp for the night. Granville and Scott had discussed it when they all stopped for a lunch of sandwiches the hotel had packed for them, but no decision had been made. Logically, it depended on how far they got before the light began to fail.

And on the conditions, too. Undoubtedly they would have preferences for where to set up camp. Flat ground would be helpful, for instance. And near a creek for water.

But surely it was getting too dark to go much further. And from what she'd seen of the town of Van Winkle, it had shrunk since the gold rush until it was nearly overgrown, with only a few buildings left. They might be able to get some sort of dinner there, but there was nowhere to stay. And she hadn't noticed anything that looked like a camping spot, either.

"From what me and Scott heard in Barkerville, Van Winkle wasn't known as a gold creek," Trent added. "But we might as well take a closer look at it anyway. Just in case Robertson found something there."

"If we start exploring another creek now, we'll never find a place to camp before dark," Emily told him. And if she didn't find a way to warm up soon, she wasn't sure she could go on.

The cold didn't seem to bother Trent. "That won't be hard," he said cheerfully. "And we're here—we wouldn't want to miss something."

He might not want to, Emily thought darkly. But then, he didn't have wet skirts clinging to his legs, did he?

Though wet trousers couldn't be very comfortable, either.

"The shadows are already deeper under the trees," she said, trying to sound reasonable rather than miserable. "By the time we get to the creek, it'll be very easy to miss something."

"I see pretty good in the dark. I won't miss a thing."

"In these conditions? You'll end up in the creek."

"I won't."

Emily's back was really up now. She was about to counter Trent's stupid argument when she caught sight of Scott's broad grin. That would never do.

She looked around for Granville. Who was also grinning.

She frowned at him. How dare he find her amusing.

"Just tell us all where we're to sleep tonight," she told him. "Before I have to push someone in the creek myself."

His grin grew wider. "You'll see," he said. "But we'll hold off on exploring any further until the morning.

She gave him a half-serious glare, then turned to Trent. "You see? It's getting too dark already."

Trent sputtered and started to argue when Granville held up a hand. "I thought we'd all enjoy a steak dinner tonight."

"Steak?"

That shut him up, Emily thought with glee. Then she wondered how you cooked steak over a campfire. And whether the fire would be enough to dry out her skirts.

For steaks, surely you'd need a large fire. And a grill of some kind. She glanced at their saddlebags. Even with the packhorse, there wasn't room enough. Was there?

"And perhaps a hot bath," Granville said, winking at her.

It sounded like heaven. But how was he planning to arrange that? What was he up to now?

CHAPTER 36

Emily woke the following morning in the cozy comfort of a feather bed, the almost-familiar warmth of Granville beside her. She blinked a few times, staring at an unfamiliar ceiling, and the dim light filtering in through unfamiliar lace curtains. This was no tent.

Then it came back. They hadn't even made it to Van Winkle Creek last night, never mind to Van Winkle itself. Instead, they'd had dinner and spent the night in the thriving town of Stanley.

Which she'd never heard of, but there it was, located on the old wagon road, just before Van Winkle Creek flowed into Lightning Creek. From the glimpse she'd had as dusk fell, the town of Stanley was much bigger, and likely more profitable, than the fading township of Van Winkle.

They had eaten a veritable feast at the local steakhouse, and spent the night in the solid, well-appointed Lightning Inn, both conveniently located in the center of town. Somehow Granville had arranged it all before they'd even left Barkerville, but he just smiled when she asked how he'd managed it.

"With so much time spent sitting in a coach over rough roads the last few days, followed by a day spent on horseback in this weather, I thought we all deserved a little comfort," was all he'd say.

He hadn't even asked. Maybe she'd have liked to spend a night in a tent.

Emily glanced across at him, to see him watching her with that smile in his eyes. And remembered her very uncomfortable, very wet skirts.

Infuriating, but thoughtful all the same, she decided. And wound her arms around him.

THE SNOW HAD HELD off overnight, and the day was sunny and cold, with puffs of their breath hanging in clouds in the air. After a hearty breakfast, the four of them spent half the morning exploring up Van Winkle Creek and along some of the larger streams running off of it.

Emily had never spent such a morning. Checking the ice at the edges of the creek as the horses tramped through the deep snow. Watching the swift current where it ran unfrozen in the middle of the creek. It was beautiful, and the snow against the trees, lit from behind by the sun, formed a picture she'd never forget.

But it was hard going, especially in a few areas where there was no trail to follow, and they had to dismount and lead the horses. And she couldn't help but wonder how this was getting them closer to finding their missing miner. Or whatever he'd been.

She still wasn't entirely convinced it was gold Mr. Robertson had been looking for. Or at least not all the time.

Yes, he'd done some mining, alone and with various partners. That much was clear. At least, it was clear if Mrs. Darrow was to be believed. So far, the postmistress was the only person they'd found who remembered Mr. Robertson. So they had no way to check anything she'd told them.

Still, if Mr. Robertson hadn't been looking for gold, what had he been doing? How else to interpret all those half-hints in his letters?

As her mare picked her way through along a tiny trail between the trees, Emily shook her head. As if that would shake something loose, she thought with a quick grin as she caught herself. But she just didn't have a better explanation for what Mr. Robertson might have been up to. Not yet.

And she couldn't stop thinking about it.

She hadn't said anything to the others about her doubts, though. Except for the questions she'd asked Granville yesterday, which hadn't really gone anywhere. It seemed too soon to raise it with him again, when she hadn't worked it out herself. Or even sorted out quite what was bothering her so much.

It was definitely too soon to raise it with the other two. Scott wouldn't say much, even if he thought she was wrong. But Trent would say she just didn't like the wilderness, and wasn't that a convenient way to get out of it.

And he'd be wrong. At least partly. This was a journey she'd dreamed of all her life.

But until the last few days, she'd not really understood how immense this area was. And what a wilderness really looked like.

Though they had spent the night in a decent inn, which probably meant this didn't even qualify as a wilderness. But it felt like one.

The minute they'd left the wagon road behind, everything changed. It felt as if they'd lost any connection to the world she knew.

Not that they'd get lost. Not as long as they followed the creek. In the hush of the forest, with the snow muffling sound so it felt even more as if they were cut off from the world, she could still hear the cheerful burbling beneath the ice. Even when she couldn't see the creek.

All they had to do was turn around and follow the creek back. And yet. It all felt overwhelming.

Nothing she could see as they rode bore any signs of human presence. And it took forever to get anywhere.

She looked at the snow-covered trees rising high above her, the thick underbrush they had to fight their way through. Everything was so big. And so quiet. Even the wind hushed through the trees, almost too soft to hear.

She couldn't imagine anything more different than the bustling streets of Vancouver, the cheerful ringing of the trolley bell, ready to take her quickly to her destination.

How would they ever find any trace of a man missing for thirty-two years in an area this big? And this empty.

By noon they had followed the creek back to Lightning Creek. They'd found nothing that moved the case forward, as far as Emily could see. Tired and hungry, she heartily agreed with Granville's suggestion to detour back into Stanley for lunch before resuming their exploration of Lightning Creek.

"As long as there's hot coffee," Scott had added with a sly look at Granville. Who laughed.

In the sudden warmth of the Stanley Cafe, Emily suddenly became aware of how cold she was. And how tired. Her leg muscles ached, and her back was sore.

She sank into a high backed wooden chair with relief. It felt so good to sit down. And the mingled scents of baking bread, of fresh coffee and roasting meats—everything smelled wonderful.

They ate thick sandwiches of sliced roast beef, served hot with fried potatoes, and ended the meal—again—with apple pie. And coffee. Lashings of coffee.

Emily thought she'd never tasted anything quite so good. Or maybe she had never been quite this hungry.

Barely an hour later, they were back on the road—quite literally—as they followed the old wagon road towards the junction of Lightning Creek and the Swift River. There would be the remains of old mines scattered throughout the area, though it didn't sound like there were still any active mines, as there were around Barkerville.

Granville, Scott and Trent were riding ahead, discussing the possibilities ahead of them, and Emily was happily bringing up the rear. Lunch hadn't been a long meal, but sitting still in the warmth for even an hour had felt so good, she thought with a contented sigh. Despite the crisp air, she felt relaxed and a little sleepy. And judging by the map they'd discussed over lunch, they had quite a distance to go before the next creek they wanted to explore.

Was it possible to doze on a horse? Or would she fall off, and outrageously embarrass herself? It might be worth it, she decided as her eyes began to drift shut.

Only to startle awake as Granville rode back to join her.

"This area has an interesting history," he said. "Since it is where the old and new wagon roads merged. If Robertson did spend time here, it's worth exploring some of the smaller creeks in more detail. We'll definitely be camping tonight."

Emily blinked at him, then decided she was glad about that. She was here for the adventure, she reminded herself. "What are we looking for this afternoon? Exactly, I mean."

He laughed. "Yes, I understood. And this is the part where I say something annoying, like 'we'll know it when we see it'. Only the reality is, we may not recognize it."

"You mean because we're looking for something left more than thirty years ago?"

"That is one reason. And a good one. But the thing I find the most challenging about investigations is that we don't always recognize the bit of information that leads to breaking a case."

She nodded. "You mean like the puppet master case. He hid in plain sight."

"Exactly. And we put together piece after tiny piece of information, until he had nowhere left to hide."

"Plus he shot you," she said with a sideways glance.

"Plus that. Though I needed him to shoot at me, at that point. We needed a reason to have him arrested, if you recall."

"I don't recall you needed him to hit you," she said, keeping a straight face with difficulty.

"Ricochet. You can't predict 'em."

"Now you're quoting Scott?"

"There's a reason we're partners."

"I see," Emily said primly. Then spoiled the effect by bursting out laughing. The sound rang in the clear air and had Scott and Trent turning from where they rode ahead to look back at the two of them.

"Newlyweds," Scott said to Trent. Who rolled his eyes and grinned. Then the two faced forward again.

"Now see what you've made me do," Emily complained to Granville. "Trent's annoying enough without giving him ammunition."

"I thought you'd given over being annoyed by the lad," Granville said.

"That was back in town. He's too much of a know-it-all out here." Hearing herself, Emily laughed quietly. "Or maybe I wish I knew as much about this kind of investigation as he does."

"He knows about living rough," Granville said. "He had no choice. But you have a much better feel for investigations than he will ever have."

She flushed a little. "That's good to hear. I've been feeling less than useful ever since we left Vancouver. I don't like the feeling."

"Who does?" he said gently. "And it is in no way true. In this particular investigation, we have none of us been very useful so far."

"That's not true, either. You got a lot of information from Mrs. Darrow on our missing miner. Or whatever he is."

"I did. And as you pointed out earlier, she is our only source to date. And she has a lot to hide. It may not be in her best interests for us to learn any more about him."

Emily reined in her mare and turned to stare at Granville, who had halted as well. "You don't mean you think she has something to do with his disappearance?"

"She'd have to be a very good actress," he said. "But it's a possibility I'm not ready to rule out. We know too little."

"True. And if she did…" Emily blinked up at him as her mind raced. "It could work. She is a woman who survived, on her own, in a gold rush town.

And back then? It was a very rough and tumble time, as Papa used to say. Good manners didn't get you very far. She could have killed him—or had him killed—for something he'd found.

Who would know? Or remember?"

"Just so," he said, watching her with appreciation.

Emily didn't notice. She was still thinking about what that might mean. "But if that's true—or if you're thinking it could be true—what in the world are we doing out here? Chasing ghosts and ghost mines."

"Ghost mines? I like it," he said, still watching her expressive face.

"Well, what else are they? But never mind. We haven't found a single other person with a motive, or with the means to make him vanish. She has both."

"However, she's also the only person we've found who claims to have known him. That doesn't mean there aren't others with both motive and means."

"Then why haven't we found them?" Emily asked. Then held up a hand. "I know. Because we don't know who to ask. Or even where to find that who. Because we don't know where Mr. Robertson went. Which is what we're doing out here, on this abandoned road."

She looked around her, then back at him. "As if we expected to see history, if only we looked hard enough."

"And isn't that what both of us do, on every case we work?" he asked her.

Emily blinked at him. Then smiled. "I suppose it is. In a way. But I don't know how to make this particular history speak to us. It's not like we can interview a creek."

"This is harder for both of us, because the case is so cold. He's been missing for more than thirty years, after all. People have moved on. It's much harder to find the people we need to interview. If they're even still alive. And it's harder still for you, because the whole environment is new to you."

She nodded slowly, thinking about it. "I understand cities, and how to talk to people who knew a victim. I know nothing of mining, or this kind of wilderness, or even frontier towns. I'm beginning to understand why you didn't want to bring me on this case."

"And I was wrong," he said. "I was worried it would be too much for you. And you've proven me wrong by thriving at every turn. Don't underestimate yourself now.

People talk to you. The stagecoach drivers, the other passengers, people at every place we've stopped. If there was information to be learned, you dug it out."

"Not Mrs. Darrow," she said. "And she's the one who counts."

"You're a woman," he said. "And she was never going to open up to another woman."

"No, I suppose not," Emily said, thinking about that day.

"Though your presence helped spur her to talk to me," he said with a sideways glance.

Which she ignored. "Maybe, but we still haven't got very far in finding our missing miner."

"And we haven't been here that long."

"It feels longer."

"That it does. But we aren't just looking at mining sites. We're talking to people along the way. Mrs. Darrow won't continue to be the only one who remembers our missing miner." He smiled at her. "Besides, I don't mind if our honeymoon stretches out a bit."

And Emily suddenly realized she didn't either. There was no real rush to solve this very old case, after all.

And she would never have this particular adventure with her new husband again. "As long as we're back home by Christmas," she said in deliberately faked lecturing tone.

He grinned, hearing what wasn't said. "Six weeks from now? I'll take it."

THE FOUR OF them spent the rest of the day following Lightning Creek and exploring its various tributaries until the light began to fail. They based their explorations on whatever sketchy information they had on which creeks had yielded the most gold, combined with their best guess about Mr. Robertson's journeys, based on his letters.

The approach didn't feel quite right to any of them, but it was the best they had for now. Granville tended to smile and tell them that detection was an inexact science whenever Trent got annoyed over a wrong guess.

Emily was surprised how much she enjoyed all of it, now that she'd stopped worrying that she didn't belong here. Even her damp hems didn't irritate her. Nor did Trent at his most irritating.

That evening, she had her first experience of eating food cooked over a smoky campfire on a clear cold night. And sitting around the campfire afterwards, sipping the hot chocolate Granville had brought just for her, and watching the stars far above them.

She finally got to spend her night in a small tent, wrapped around Granville for warmth. Yet another memory to cherish. She added it to the ones she'd begun compiling.

Though trying to find a way to hang her damp skirts inside the small canvas tent so they'd dry had proven frustrating as well as fairly useless. And sleeping on the ground was over-rated, no matter how well-folded the blanket they lay on was.

Despite that, she wouldn't trade this experience for anything. But the next time Granville booked a hotel for them without telling her? She was not going to argue about it.

CHAPTER 37

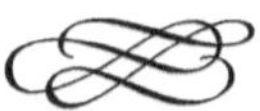

Thursday, November 15, 1900

On Thursday morning, Granville pushed back the tent flap to find it had snowed overnight. They had camped on a wide flat near the creek, and there was at least two inches of fresh snow now covering everything. No wind though, which was helpful. That two inches could have drifted up against the tent flap and made getting out this morning a little tricky.

Especially for Emily. Turning his head to watch her sleeping face, he marveled at his wife—and he did love thinking of her that way. It seemed he'd been waiting forever to marry her—and how well she'd taken to this journey of theirs. Nothing seemed to faze her.

His glance went to the improvised hook at the far corner of the tent that he'd rigged up to help dry Emily's long skirts. Stretching out one hand, he tested the fabric. Between last nights fire and their body heat within the tent, it had largely dried. But the hem must have still been damp, because it was covered in frost and had half-frozen into folds.

That would be a very uncomfortable garment for her to put on. And a difficult one to pack. It was a problem he'd never encountered before. In fact, he hadn't even considered it, since he'd never traveled under these circumstances with a woman.

Now he had Emily. Who would probably insist on joining him wherever she could. And to his surprise, he wouldn't have it any other way.

Which meant they needed a solution for the problem of wet skirts. And fast.

He knew there must be one. There were whole families that took the gold rush trail to the Klondike in '98 in cold much worse than this. He'd seen women in skirts making their way up the impossible grade that was the Chilkoot Pass.

He'd seen a few women wearing trousers up north, too, though he wasn't sure how he felt about Emily traveling wearing men's clothing. Or how she would feel about it.

He stared at a tiny icicle hanging from the edge of her serviceable navy skirt nearest the tent wall. Under his gaze, a little drop of water formed on the end of the icicle, hovered. And dropped.

Perhaps trousers weren't such a bad idea, after all. She couldn't travel too far wearing that skirt. Though he knew she had another in her bag. And he had planned that by tonight they'd be in Cottonwood, and staying at the Cottonwood House. She could dry out anything that needed drying overnight there.

But that wasn't a solution that would work very often. Depending where this case took them, they might be camping in tents for days on end. He gave the makeshift hook he'd come up with last night a considering look.

If there had been a way to hang the skirt closer to the campfire last night… And a second hook in the tent, higher up, so that the folds of cloth could be spread wider when they brought it inside? Then perhaps the skirt could have dried overnight.

And on future journeys—which after less than a week married to Emily, he was sure would occur—perhaps there was a better fabric for her traveling skirts? He'd have to discuss it with her.

He'd worn trousers made of hardwearing corduroy or duck

cotton in the Klondike, with thick woolens underneath, after all. And the Tagish women who lived in the region often wore deer-skin skirts, which would be more impervious to the weather. And might help keep Emily warm.

Anything was better than what she had, he decided, glaring at another drip forming on the edge of her skirt.

HALF AN HOUR LATER, the four of them were gathered around the campfire enjoying a hearty breakfast of baking powder biscuits, bacon and coffee. Trent had built the fire while Granville and Scott had prepared the breakfast with the practiced moves and coordination they'd developed in a year and a half living on the goldfields of the Yukon.

It amused Granville to see Emily watching them with wide eyes, as if amazed that he could cook. He wondered if she had ever learned how, or if her training had been limited to how to hire and manage a cook. Not that it mattered. The investigative business was doing better than he'd expected. They could afford a housekeeper.

He nearly laughed at the blissful expression on her face as the aroma of grilling bacon and fresh coffee joined the smell of fresh air and woodsmoke.

This was one of his favorite parts of camping out. Cooking over a campfire, then sitting eating, talking and watching the flames dance. Weather permitting, of course.

It wasn't nearly so appealing when the weather turned against you. And he'd been in too many storms where they could barely manage to light a fire, and anything they managed to cook was eaten quickly in whatever shelter they could find.

He wouldn't want to put Emily into some of the situations he and Scott had survived.

Though he was beginning to suspect that she would thrive in that kind of crisis, just as she had with anything she'd been faced with so far.

As they finished their meal, Granville brought up the idea of staying at Cottonwood House that evening.

Why there?" Trent asked. "We don't even know how far we'll get today."

"To begin with, Cottonwood is about the same distance from here as what we traveled from Stanley yesterday," Granville said. "Which should give us time to see everything we're interested in today. And save us the time it would take to set up camp this evening."

"Food's good, too," Scott said with a broad grin. "Plus it's where the Swift River meets the Cariboo Wagon Road. And not far from where the Swift joins Lightning Creek. They took a lot of gold out of that area."

Trent was nodding. "We heard some good stories about that gold," he said. "Robertson might well have tried his hand there."

"Might have," Scott said.

"Cottonwood House may be a good place to mingle, as well," Granville said. "The more people we talk to, the likelier we are to meet someone who knew our missing miner, as Emily calls him."

It worried him that they still hadn't found anyone other than the Barkerville postmistress that recognized either Robertson's name or the sketch of him. It was too early in their investigation to make too much of it, though.

"Think they'll serve steak, like last time? It was really good," Trent said.

"I think you can count on it," Granville said. "And if we need more time exploring the region, we might need to spend a second night there."

He drained his coffee, scrubbed the empty cup out with snow, and stood up. "Or just enjoy one of their luncheons, if we're headed back this way sooner."

Which would give him more time to work out a solution for drying Emily's skirts.

Trent smacked his lips and Scott's grin broadened as they both stood and began to pack up camp.

Granville glanced at Emily, who hadn't said a word. She was

finishing off the last of her bacon, but she didn't seem upset or concerned by their current plans.

Not like she had been when he'd surprised her with a room booked at Lightning House. He'd wondered then if she was hoping they would spend most of their journey camping out.

Apparently not.

Which was good to know. Though those frozen skirts this morning might have changed her mind.

CHAPTER 38

Once they broke camp, the day's journey unfolded much like the previous one had as they explored Lightning Creek, following several tributaries upstream for a bit. Which made for a long day, because the fresh snow made the going harder. And the creeks that flowed into Lightning Creek were overall more challenging to follow than the ones the previous day, being steeper and more overgrown.

They met no-one during their explorations, and saw nothing that reminded any of them of Robertson's letters. Or suggested a different interpretation of any of his squiggles. It still felt good to be outside and doing, but Granville could tell that initial enthusiasm was waning in all of them as they kept running into investigative dead ends.

He'd clearly underestimated the problems of attempting a thirty-two year old case in what was still largely wilderness. Only Emily's interest in everything around her kept him from regretting that he'd ever taken this one on.

They stopped at noon for leftover bacon and biscuit sandwiches, and since they wouldn't have to spend time searching for a campsite later, took time to build a fire and make coffee. He'd saved some tea leaves he'd begged from the Lightning Hotel for Emily, but she'd thanked him and informed him she preferred coffee when they were camping. Which made him smile, though he couldn't quite say why.

The rest of the afternoon passed much as the morning had with nothing much learned, though everyone's spirits picked up as they grew closer to Cottonwood. Granville couldn't decide if it was the siren call of a hot dinner that made the difference. Or the possibility that conversation with their fellow guests could end in a lead, no matter how unlikely that might be. Though he rather suspected it was the latter.

They needed something more to go on than what they'd come up with to date.

As the light faded in the late afternoon, all of them began spotting landmarks they recognized from the earlier journey by stagecoach.

"That's the big cottonwood tree," Emily said. "I can just see the top of it. Before long, we should see the river."

As they got closer they saw several discreet signs for the road-house. It was a popular place. And a busy one, as it turned out.

In addition to the four of them, there was a party of miners, and a family returning home to Stanley. Before a generous dinner served at the long pine table in the dining room, drinks were served for all the guests in the spacious parlor. Emily was quick to make friends with the mother and daughter, while Granville and Scott joined the miners. The father and his almost grown son joined them, and the talk turned to mining for gold. As it was now, and as it had been "back in the day."

No-one there was old enough to have been alive in the 1860's, so Granville didn't hold out much hope for any information on Robertson.

But he was wrong. It turned out that the tales of "back in the day"—and the men and women who had pushed into this land, hoping to win fortunes or a new life for themselves—were still very much alive.

And before long, their fellow guests were telling their favorite stories of those days, those people. And not just telling them. Competing to top each other's stories.

It didn't take long for the women to join the men, and it was the daughter who told the story that had his eyes meeting Emily's in sudden interest.

She told a tale about a young woman who danced at a saloon in Barkerville, and how she had found, and lost, her one true love.

"It was in the early years, when the town was growing out of nothing," said the girl, whose name, improbably to his ear, was Candace. "And a young dancer took a job at one of the saloons. Most of the dancers back then were hurdy gurdy girls, brought in from Germany for their stamina as much as their looks, since the popular dances of the day called for much flinging a partner about. This one, though? She was a delicate, graceful beauty. She might even have studied ballet, because she danced as though she had wings. And unlike many dancers, she sang like a nightingale.

The miners loved her, and were so careful of her. Who she really was, and where she came from no-one knew for certain. But she took the stage name of Belle, and she was.

They called her the Belle of Barkerville, and she danced every night except Sunday. She made good money for those days, and better tips, as the tips were in nuggets and gold dust.

Until a man with dark hair and hazel eyes came back from the creeks, and walked into the saloon where she danced. He greeted his friends, and called for a whiskey, and then he saw Belle. He watched for a time, his eyes fixed on her, then he asked her to dance."

Candace paused to take a breath, then clasped her hands together. "They say that when their eyes met, they fell in love in an instant, and their first dance sealed it. There was no one else for either of them after that moment. They say that watching the hazel-eyed miner dance with Belle was like seeing the most beautiful song.

After that, Belle never danced with another man."

"How did she make her living, then?" asked one of the miners with a grin. Which faded when the girl's mother glared at him.

Caught up in her tale, Candace didn't notice. "He found gold, at least some, and gave it to her," she said. "Only it wasn't enough gold. So he left town to find more. Then he'd return, and they were blissful again for a time.

But always the gold ran out, and he had to leave again. Until the last time. When he never returned. And no one heard from him again." She sighed. "It's such a sad, romantic story."

"What was the hazel eyed miner's name?" Emily asked carefully into the silence that followed Candace's heartfelt sigh.

"Belle called him Robby," the girl said, too caught up in her tale to notice Emily's startled look. "But everyone else called him Beau. Or Brody, since his real name was Robert Brody."

And there it was. If this was Mrs. Darrow's Robby—and she'd lied about his nickname? Then no wonder they hadn't found any trace of Thomas Robertson. He'd taken, not just a nickname, but a completely different name.

"So what happened to this Brody?" Trent asked.

"No one ever saw or heard from him again," Candace said.

Someone had, Granville thought. Likely his killer. Or perhaps the fellow had simply moved on, and changed his name again.

He exchanged glances with Emily over Candace's oblivious head, while Trent rolled his eyes at Scott.

What if the hazel-eyed Robby (Beau) Brody was indeed their hazel-eyed missing miner, Thomas Robertson? Did that make Mrs. Darrow the Belle of Barkerville? Or had she just heard the story, and had some motive of her own to call Thomas Robertson by that same name.

Or perhaps she just thought it romantic.

Either way, it was too many coincidences to actually be one. At least it was a potential lead. And it gave them another name to fit into the puzzle of their missing miner.

Perhaps they might actually solve this case, after all.

CHAPTER 39

FRIDAY, NOVEMBER 16, 1900

On Friday morning Emily woke early in the comfort of soft cotton sheets and a featherbed. She stretched gently, just to see. The stiffness from sleeping in a tent and a day out in the cold had completely vanished. It felt so good.

She definitely preferred traveling in comfort to camping out. Or at least, to the sleeping in a tent part.

She still wanted to try spending a week in the wilderness, though. And camping out every night. Somewhere that didn't have a hotel or a roadhouse conveniently at hand. Just to see if she could.

When she'd read the articles about women climbers and women explorers, it had sounded so brave. To dare the elements, to go places no-one had been before. And yes, so romantic.

She'd never appreciated the difference between romance and reality quite as clearly as she did at this moment, lying here in her warm little nest.

One night in the wilderness and you're suddenly a realist? she scoffed to herself. Or just not quite the explorer you thought you might be.

Which was an unsettling thought.

"I refuse to be an armchair explorer," Emily muttered to herself. "It's far too limiting."

"What's that?" Granville asked, opening the hall door and coming into their room with a tray smelling invitingly of coffee and breakfast pastries. "What is too limiting?"

"Oh, nothing," Emily said, trying not to blush. "I was just thinking out loud."

"Not about being married, I hope?"

Surely he wasn't serious? "Of course not. I was just thinking about the case."

It wasn't exactly a lie. It made her squirm, though, because it wasn't quite the truth either. But she couldn't bring herself to tell him exactly what she'd been thinking.

Because she didn't believe that about herself? Or because telling him might make it real?

That was no way to start a marriage. Hiding from herself? And from him? When she'd just been thinking about those women who dared to go places women just didn't go? Where was her own courage?

"Actually, I was appreciating the comfort of this hotel compared to sleeping in a tent," she confessed, hoping she didn't look as uneasy as she felt. "And wondering if it meant I lack the courage to be a detective. One who joins you on all of your investigations, not just the ones where I can stay safely in a town."

"You? Lacking courage? Hardly," he said with a grin. "You are braver than any woman I've ever met. And most of the men."

Now she did blush. "But the camping..." And cringed when she heard her voice trail off weakly.

"I prefer sleeping in a comfortable bed, too," Granville said, walking across the room to put the tray on the bedside table. Taking her hand, he squeezed it gently. "That just means you're no fool."

"But..."

"If I told you we were going to need to camp out for the next few days, would you argue with me?"

"Of course not," she said immediately.

"Or refuse to join us?"

"Never. We follow the case."

"Exactly. Just listen to yourself," he said. "You might prefer not to sleep on the ground. Or wake in the morning to find icicles dripping from your skirts. But you won't let it stop you."

That was true. Maybe she was braver than she'd thought. "I guess not. I did enjoy the campfire cooking, and sitting around the fire. Though the ground was rather firm. And I didn't appreciate the icicles on my skirt."

"There isn't much I can do about the hard ground. But I might have a solution for those icicles, at least," he said. And bent down to kiss her.

THE SUN WAS JUST RISING when Emily and Granville met Scott and Trent in the dining room, and ordered a hearty breakfast. Then Granville placed the now familiar map on the table and they all bent over it. They had some planning to do. And a long, cold ride ahead of them, Emily thought, unless she missed her guess.

The early hour meant they were the only guests in the dining room, giving them an opportunity to talk freely about the case, and about the implications of last night's discussion. If any.

Trent, however had other ideas.

"Y'know, we haven't found anything that helps us find our missing miner since we left Barkerville," he said eagerly. "What if we were wrong about Lightning Creek being the symbol he drew in that letter?"

"You got a better idea?" Scott growled into his coffee. He didn't look like he'd slept much.

"We talked once about Quesnel Forks, but that didn't fit. It's too far, and it isn't easy to get to from Barkerville. But what about Antler Creek?"

"We have nothing telling us he went that way," Granville said.

"And nothing saying he didn't, either." Trent tapped the map. "Look how close it is to Barkerville."

Granville ran a careful finger from Barkerville to the closest access to Antler creek. "It may not be far on the map. But those are mountains he'd have to cross."

"Doesn't mean he didn't go there."

"True enough. And well worth looking into," Granville said. "But I gather none of the sources you talked to about Antler Creek recognized Robertson's name or photo?"

And he glanced over at Scott, who shook his head.

"Then it may benefit us to have another chat with Mrs. Darrow before we head that way," Granville said.

"You mean because of the stories from last night? Those old stories that grow in the telling aren't worth much," Trent said dismissively.

"There's often a kernel of truth in even the wildest of tales," Granville said.

"Maybe, but which kernel?" Trent asked. "We'll end up chasing tall tales."

"Especially if it's the romantic story the young daughter told," Scott said. "Most stories like that one are exaggerated, thirty plus years later. Not sure we can trust any of the details."

"I agree. Especially from a story that's been romanticized as much as the one Candace told," Emily said. "I sincerely doubt Mrs. Darrow goes by Belle."

"She might have. Once," Trent said, surprising her. "The names don't matter, anyway. Thirty years from now, who's going to remember any of us? At least she's part of a story that still gets told. Even if it won't help us find Robertson."

Emily had to smile. Trent was a romantic at heart. Who'd have thought it?

Catching her expression, Trent made a face at her, then broke off as the cook and her helper brought in a huge platter laden with heaping plates of bacon, sausage, eggs and fried potatoes. Baskets of biscuits and toast were passed around, and coffee was poured.

CHAPTER 40

WHEN THE COOK AND HER HELPER HAD LEFT AND THEY HAD THE room to themselves again, Granville watched in amusement as Emily turned back to Trent. He could see her enjoyment of the debate. And perhaps a little relief? They'd been chasing their missing miner with no result for too long now.

"In this case, the names in that romantic tale might just give us the best clue we've found yet," she told him. "You're the one who raised the possibility that Mr. Robertson might have taken another name. If that name was Brody, we finally have a starting place."

"And if it wasn't?" Trent retorted. "You've got nothing to connect our missing miner to the story that girl told us."

"We have the postmistress telling us she called her fellow Robby. And she identified the sketch of Robertson as being her Robby."

"Doesn't mean it's the same Robby. And anyway, maybe she's remembering it wrong. It's been decades."

"The descriptions match."

Trent snorted. "Hair and eye color is barely a description."

"Emily is right," Granville said. "If even some of the

elements of Candace's tale are accurate, it matters. And if Mrs. Darrow was once Belle…"

"Then the hazel-eyed Brody could well be our missing miner," Emily said. "And the postmistress may be the only one who knew her Robby's real name."

"Or perhaps not," Granville said thoughtfully. "Mrs. Darrow hesitated, just a little, when I named the sketch as being of Thomas Robertson. It didn't strike me as important at the time, but if she hadn't known his real name, she covered it well by quickly agreeing that the image was her Robby."

"You mean that might have been the first time she'd heard the name Thomas Robertson?" Emily asked.

"We can't discount that possibility. She never mentioned the name Brody, but she never called "her Robby" Robertson, either. However, if she hadn't known his real name before I showed her the sketch, she's a much better actress than I'd realized. Which we would need to factor in."

Emily nodded, her brows drawing together a bit. Which he'd come to know meant she was thinking hard, most likely about her impressions of the woman.

"But Robertson's letters from home," Trent said. "They would have been sent under his own name."

"Or so our client told us," Granville said. "But we have no evidence of that, either. And our client probably wasn't the one that wrote out the envelopes for the letters they sent to his father."

"That would have been his mother, most likely," Emily said. "You think our missing miner might have asked his wife to send his letters to this Brody name? If it proves to be him, I mean. And without telling their son?"

"It's a possibility," Granville said. "One we can't ignore, since we've had no luck at all finding anything on him as Thomas Robertson."

And that possibility was enough to make him question whether Thomas Robertson's disappearance might be rooted in their quarry's former life. Their client believed it was the looming bankruptcy of their ranch that had driven his father north to

Barkerville and gold. But was the reality different than his son, only ten at the time, had understood?

That answer could cast an entirely new light on the father's disappearance.

Which meant he needed call Foster at Pinkertons in Seattle and ask a few pointed questions. Just as soon as they got back to Barkerville, where the hotel phone wasn't on a party line.

"Well, we had some luck with Mrs. Darrow," Emily said. "She at least says she knew him. Though she never mentioned the Brody name. And it never made sense to me that she was the only one who remembered him, out of all the people we've talked to."

"That's for sure," Trent said. "It's why I've said all along that she's lying."

Granville bit back a grin at the lad's vehemence, when he hadn't even met the lady in question.

Emily simply ignored Trent's comment, turning back to Granville. "But why would Mrs. Robertson agree to write letters to her husband under a fake name? If she did so?"

"It's possible we haven't heard the real story about why Thomas Robertson headed north to chase gold," Granville said. "Or at least not the full story."

"You think he might have been involved in something criminal?" Scott asked, looking more alert now. "So he had to travel under a fake name?"

"We've seen it before," he said.

Scott nodded. "You think he might have been running from something in Barkerville?"

"Other than Mrs. Darrow and her expectations?" Granville asked, only half joking. "Perhaps. If Thompson really is Brody, it might be more likely that something caught up with him there. If he's run once, he could do so again."

"Something? Like what?" Trent asked.

"That's up to us to figure out," he said. "To start with, I think we need to find out if anyone remembers one Beau, or Robby

Brody. Or better yet, recognizes the sketch of Robertson as being Brody."

Trent nearly choked on a slice of bacon, dropping his fork with a clatter. "You mean now we not only have to go back to Barkerville, we have to talk to everyone again? Just to see if they've heard of this Brody?"

"That's it," Scott said, whacking him on the back. "You got a better idea?"

"Sure do."

"Go on," Granville said dryly.

Might as well get this out of the way so they could get on with finding Robertson.

CHAPTER 41

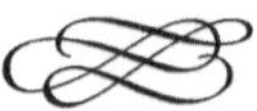

Emily looked from Granville's amused expression to Trent's stubborn one. Of course Trent had a better idea, she thought, hiding her grin behind her napkin. Or was convinced he did. Why had Scott even asked?

At this rate, they'd be here all morning.

"What about what the guy last night was saying?" Trent said. "About all the claims along the Swift River, and how much money some of them made?"

He obviously hadn't given up his desire to explore further. Emily wanted to argue with him, just because he was so sure of himself.

But she didn't truly understand what they were up against in this wild land. Not the way the other three did. So she sat back and waited to see what came next.

"Since we're already here, we could check those out, follow the Swift all the way down to Quesnel," Trent was explaining. "And then from there we could go back to Barkerville. Or we could head for Antler Creek. A lot of people mined on Antler. It was nearly as productive as Williams, but for more years. It would make sense that Robertson would have been searching there. No matter what he was called."

"The lad's right about that," Scott said. "We heard a lot about Antler Creek in the pubs. And it would fit that forked scribble on our missing miner's fourth letter."

"It's a good thought," Granville said, and Trent grinned. "Except that from what I understand, following the Swift at this time of year is much more difficult than the route we took here. The path is a great deal steeper and already deep in snow. We'd be climbing up and down the sides of mountains much of the way."

"But we could do it," Trent said.

"Yes, we could," Granville agreed. "If we had at least a week to plan it. Since there's no path, we'd need to hire an experienced guide."

"So? There have to be guides around," Trent said.

He wasn't about to give up, Emily recognized. And especially not when Scott seemed to be agreeing with him.

Her money was on Granville, though.

"Undoubtedly," Granville said. "Though it could take some time to find the right guide. Given the time of year and the fact that we'd be putting our lives in this fellow's hands. And even then. We'd also need to plan to be traveling for at least a week, more likely two. Probably in steadily worsening cold, and nasty weather."

"So you're saying we shouldn't go?" Trent asked. "Just give up on the whole area?"

"I'm saying we'd need to ask a few more questions of folks who know the area before we attempted it," he said. "For now, we might be best to break our travel into two journeys. One back to Barkerville. And then another from there to Antler Creek and onwards."

"I think that might be harder," Emily said, still feeling out of her depth. Of them all, she had the least wilderness experience. But she couldn't say nothing.

"When Candace's mother and I were talking last night, she was telling me about some of the areas, and how even now Antler Creek and the Keithly River area are barely accessible even in summer. And this time of year it's much easier to get to Antler by following the creeks inland from Swift River than it is from Barkerville."

"If the case is taking us there, then we'd need to look hard at that route," Granville said. "But Antler Creek may no longer be relevant. If Robby Brody turns out to be our missing miner, then the trail leads back to Barkerville. Not down the Swift to Antler Creek.

"Granville's right," Scott said. "Exploring further here before we check that out is wasting our time."

Trent looked like he was gong to explode. "So we come all this way, then head back to ask more questions in Barkerville? Before we even explore Swift River?" he demanded

"Yes," Granville said.

Trent muttered something about the trail already being cold, then subsided when Scott raised an eyebrow.

Emily couldn't hide her grin at the byplay. Because that excitement was bubbling inside her. The kind that said that they might be close to a breakthrough on this baffling case.

She turned to Granville. "Are we packing up and leaving for Barkerville this morning, then?"

"We are," Granville said.

"We'll take the same route back?" she asked carefully. It seemed a bit of a waste, since they'd just explored that way, but after Trent's outburst she didn't want to stir up anything.

"We'll stick with the wagon road, but on this trip, I'd suggest we take the newer road, as it's better maintained. The weather is too unpredictable now to do otherwise," Granville said.

He glanced across at Scott, who nodded.

"Shorter and faster," Scott said. "Good idea. We can be packed up in an hour?"

Trent just shrugged, and Emily nodded.

"Done," Granville said.

By NINE THEY had packed up, left the hotel, and headed east. Granville and Scott had overseen the packing and the provisioning. Emily had made short work of her own packing, and watched their efforts with fascination.

They worked together as if they'd done so many times before, with very little conversation about what supplies were needed, and who would pack what. She supposed there had been times when their survival had depended on that coordination. In a blizzard, there would be no time to decide on the details.

She shivered at the very idea of being caught out in a blizzard, her imagination supplying a vivid picture of the freezing cold and the blinding snow. Until she'd camped out with them the other day, she'd been cold before, but she'd never truly understood how very cold it could be, when there was nowhere warm to go to get away from a storm.

As she thought this, she watched their competent hands packing flour, along with sugar, coffee, baking soda and salt. Adding a container of lard, a rasher of bacon and filling their water flasks. They added in a stack of sandwiches the cook had made for them, using most of a loaf of bread and a good portion of last night's roast, sliced thick, as well as half an apple pie.

The amount of supplies they packed, and the fact they'd managed to fit everything into the various saddlebags, astounded Emily. It was a very good thing they had a packhorse with them.

Weather permitting, they should be back in Barkerville by mid-afternoon, surely? As she continued to watch, she realized they were packing for an emergency. If the weather trapped them on the trail. If someone was injured and slowed them down. If they were lost.

Things she would have never considered before. Things that might save all their lives in a bad situation.

And she was relieved she hadn't spoken up earlier to argue for spending more time exploring along the Swift River.

Trent hadn't given up on his argument, though.

"We could have taken a day to explore," he said again as they mounted up and set out. "What difference would that have made?"

Obviously he hadn't had the same revelation she had, Emily thought. Probably he was more used to the preparations that were needed for travel in the wilderness.

Or maybe he just thought he was right.

Whatever his reason, Trent's question went unanswered as Granville, in the lead with Emily beside him, swung his horse's head towards the wagon road and away from the much less traveled path that ran along the river.

But Trent wasn't done yet. "The way is clear in every direction," he insisted. "And we're hardly going to find anything new about Robertson on a road that's this well traveled."

The other two ignored him, though Emily had to bite back a few choice words. She wasn't quite sure why he was being so annoyingly persistent.

Except to be fair, she too had been feeling a little like they were wasting time. It was hard to backtrack like this when the air was fresh and clear, the day just beginning. And they had found a new lead at Cottonwood, and had a new area to explore right there.

Until she'd watched Granville and Scott packing she'd still half-agreed with Trent. But at least she'd recognized that she knew nothing of winter conditions in this kind of landscape, and even less about investigating very old cases. So anything she could have said would probably be wrong. And maybe even petty.

Like Trent sounded right now.

They'd hardly ridden for half an hour when the road began to rise ahead of them. "A lot of climbing going this direction," Scott noted.

"No joshing," Trent said as the path turned a bit east. And they hit snow.

It wasn't falling heavily now, but it must have been earlier, because the horses were stepping their way through a good three or four inches of fresh powder. And to Emily's admittedly non-expert eye, there were dark clouds in the distance that looked like they held more snow.

"It's a good thing we're on a well-marked route, then," Scott commented as the wind rose, driving little white flurries hither and yon.

Trent scowled at the reminder but said nothing.

Emily hid a smile. He didn't have much of an argument for taking the other path now. The snow was silent proof of Granville's concern that higher elevations and the season hastening towards deep winter was a challenging combination for travelers.

She felt relieved all over again that she'd managed not to say anything more about her own concerns. Since they had been even less well-founded than Trent's.

As they climbed, the snow began to fall in earnest, muffling sound, building up in soft mounds on the green sweeps of evergreens and along the sides of the road. Even on the road itself, the big white flakes clung stubbornly, hardening under their mount's hooves.

Emily was glad of the hood on her thick coat, which kept her hair mostly dry. It made it harder to hear the others, though. But the aching quiet of the falling snow helped with that.

"There's one thing I don't get," Emily said, turning to Granville after they'd ridden for several hours. It had finally stopped snowing, and the sun was glinting off the ice crystals that had formed in the snowbanks.

"Only one?" he asked with a sideways glance.

She wasn't quite sure if he was teasing so she just asked her question. "This, everything we're investigating, it all happened years ago. Our missing miner hasn't been seen in decades. If Mrs. Darrow did know that Thomas Robertson and Robby Brody were the same man, why wouldn't she just tell us? Unless she has something to hide."

"Or protect," he said.

Emily tilted her head to one side as she thought about it, then realized he was watching her with that little smile that made her insides melt.

Hurriedly straightening, because, well, she wasn't quite sure why, she blurted out her thoughts. "You don't think she murdered him, do you? She didn't say anything because she'd hang for it?"

"It's possible, but I doubt it."

"Then you think she could have been protecting him? After all these years? What could he have done?"

"That's an excellent question."

She made a face at him. "Yes, that's why I asked it. Stop being so inscrutable."

He grinned at her. "You seem to think I have all the answers."

"Well, sometimes you do," she said, as if thinking it through. Then grinned back. "But mostly that's what you get when you drop hints like that one, and then don't tell me anything. It's annoying."

He put his hand against his heart, as if wounded. "One week married and already I'm annoying."

"Yes," she said decidedly. "I don't think I could live without you. But definitely annoying. Now, let's solve this case."

He slanted her a look that melted her knees. Then winked at her. "That's why we're here."

Widening her eyes in mock wonder and looking around her, Emily said, "We're stuck in the snow in the middle of a near wilderness with no-one anywhere near us to question? And that's going to help us solve this case?"

"It's hardly a wilderness when there's decent food and lodging within a day's ride in any direction," Granville pointed out. "Unless we get caught out in a blizzard, of course. But yes. This is how our missing miner would have traveled. And this is how we will solve this case," he said.

And threw a snowball at her.

∼

EMILY HELD that light-hearted moment in her heart as a talisman as the cold hours passed. The road back to Barkerville was mostly uphill, and the weather worsened as the day wore on.

As the conditions worsened on their chosen route, with high winds driving an icy snow straight into their faces, Emily's enjoyment faded even further. She was suddenly very glad of the provisions she'd seen packed that morning. But she hoped with everything in her that they wouldn't actually need them today.

They stopped at noon just long enough to eat half of their sandwiches, leaving the rest for later. They did eat all the pie, though. All of them were too hungry to even think of leaving any for later. Especially since, as Trent was quick to point out, it might well have frozen solid by then.

As they set off again, visibility shrunk to a few feet, and drifts had begun to obscure the route they followed. After a quick conference Granville and Scott made the decision to push through to Barkerville, and make the best time they could.

Rest stops were cut to a minimum, and they rode bent forward into the wind, with Scott and Granville switching off the lead position, eyes focused on the path in front of them.

It took them more than eight hours to make the journey back to Barkerville, and Emily had never been so glad to see anything in her life as she was to see the lights of their hotel glimmering through the driving snow.

CHAPTER 42

Saturday, November 17, 1900

Saturday morning, Granville was relieved to wake in their now familiar room in Barkerville, with Emily sleeping quietly beside him. Yesterday's storm hadn't been the worst he'd ever encountered—an ice storm on the creeks of the Klondike that had nearly killed him had earned that title. But it was worse than he'd expected this early in the year. And far worse than he'd hoped to face while Emily was traveling with him.

Though she'd more than held her own. As she had with every hardship he'd seen her face. He supposed one day he might even get used to it.

She'd probably make sure of it, he thought with an inward grin.

When they'd arrived last night, shaking from cold, hungry and exhausted, dry clothes and a hot meal had been everyone's priority. They'd eaten in the private parlor, too tired to face the interest and questions of their fellow guests. After dinner, he'd expected Emily to be the first one to head upstairs for the night. Instead, with her eyelids drooping and a small frown of concentration between her brows, she'd insisted on checking her list of those buried in the graveyard here.

"It's as I remembered," she said at last, looking up with a beaming smile. "There is no-one named Brody buried here."

"Well, there wouldn't be, would there?" Trent said matter-of-factly. "Candace told us that Brody never returned. And Belle never knew what became of him."

"I thought you didn't believe in tall tales?" Emily had said.

To Granville's amusement, Trent had flushed a little and muttered something about still needing to check facts. Emily shared a laughing glance with Granville, but refrained from embarrassing the lad further by pointing out that checking the facts was exactly what she'd been doing.

Instead she'd excused herself, and gone upstairs. He'd been not long behind her.

This morning, the sun was rising clear and bright, the storm having blown furiously half the night but quietened by morning. Perhaps they should have overnighted in Stanley last night, after all. He and Scott had debated it, but neither was willing to risk finding themselves stranded there, with the storm increasing in fury around them. Even in retrospect, it was still a hard call.

But they were all here now, all safe. And ready to resume their hunt for Thomas Robertson. Or, perhaps, for one Robby Brody.

AFTER A GOOD BREAKFAST in the dining room of the hotel, the four of them split up to begin their search for anyone who remembered Brody. Granville and Emily were headed for the Post Office and Mrs. Darrow, of course.

They were in luck. She was working behind the post office counter, just where they'd expected her to be.

"Does this mean this case is finally going to go our way?" Emily asked him under her breath, just before they opened the door to go inside.

"Hush. Don't jinx it," he said with a wink. He didn't believe in jinxes or fate. And he wasn't a fan of coincidences, either. Though sometimes, he had to wonder.

"Good morning," Emily said as the bell over the door jangled cheerily.

Mrs. Darrow looked up from the stack of mail she'd been sorting. Dressed today in a gray gown that looked dreary even in the bright sunlight streaming through the windows, she looked more severe than she had. And she smiled broadly to see them, Emily in particular.

He was surprised to see Emily turn a shade paler under that smile. Did she really dislike the postmistress that much? Or was this something else?

"I have a letter for you," Mrs. Darrow was saying gaily.

Ah, that explained it, Granville realized as he watched Emily's lips tighten and her face pale even more. She looked as if she was bracing herself for an attack.

He'd forgotten that she'd been expecting a letter from her mother. A response to their elopement.

His gaze went back to Mrs. Darrow's cat with the canary look.

So that unfortunate post office practice of steaming open letters to tease out gossip had migrated from Britain to the colonies. And Emily's letter had to contain a bombshell.

Which was about to explode.

If he didn't miss his guess, the postmistress knew exactly what Emily's letter said. And was about to hand Emily's pride to her on a platter.

He needed to get Emily out of here. Now. Before the woman could utter whatever meanness she'd been saving up to say to his new bride.

But he'd underestimated Emily. Again.

Before he could act, Emily stepped forward. All signs of strain gone from her face, she smiled, and plucked the letter from Mrs. Darrow's hand.

"Thank you for telling me," she said, glancing at the return address. "I'd been hoping this would arrive today."

"Actually it arrived last Thursday," Mrs. Darrow began.

"Then thank you for holding it for me," Emily said with another, seemingly genuine, smile. "I can't wait to read it." And she turned and swept out the door, which he'd held open for her.

"Do you need to read that in private?" he asked when he caught up with her on the walkway. A little worried she'd be in tears.

And she was. But they were tears of laughter.

"I could use a cup of tea," she said. "Did you see Mrs. Darrow's face? Whatever can Clara have said to give her such satisfaction?"

"Clara? I thought perhaps your mother?" he said, tucking her hand into the crook of his arm as they strolled in the direction of the coffeehouse.

"Mama? Oh, whatever Mama may think about our elopement—and trust me, we will hear about it—will be couched in such a way that no-one else will take her words for anything but pleasantries. She's an expert at dealing with the Mrs. Darrows of the world."

He thought about that for a moment, then grinned back at her. "You have no small expertise yourself. I wondered where you'd learned it."

She laughed aloud. "Thank you. I think."

"It was a compliment. I trust you'll translate your mother's words for me when her letter does arrive?"

"Of course. They will be aimed at both of us, you may be sure of that."

Somehow that didn't surprise him in the least. He'd begun to take his new mother-in-law's measure quite early on. "I suspect she won't appreciate our solution to the wedding problem. But she'll have a plan already in place to deal with whatever damage we may have caused."

Emily nodded, but her gaze was distant.

"What is it?" he asked after a moment.

She shook her head as if clearing it. "It just struck me—we may have been following her plan all along."

"What? By eloping?"

"Exactly," she said. Then laughed. "Granville, the look on your face…"

"You'll need to explain, I'm afraid. How could she have planned our elopement?"

"Not planned, exactly. More like made it inevitable." She glanced at him, and explained. "It never made sense, the way she kept putting off our marriage. Even it if was what society expected—Mama has always been good at twisting society's expectations to fit her own plans. No, she didn't handle any of it with her usual panache. Not if she really wanted us to wait *four years* for our marriage."

"So it had to be deliberate?" Knowing the lady, he could almost believe it.

"You know, talking about it? I think it did," she said. "In fact, I can't believe I didn't see it sooner."

"You were a little busy at the time," he pointed out. "And most women would never have figured it out."

"Most women weren't raised by my mother," she said. "And just thinking about it all now? I really need that cup of tea."

"Then it's lucky we're here," he said, opening the coffeehouse door for her. And wondering, as he followed her into a room smelling richly of pastries and buzzing with gossip, exactly what impact being raised by Mrs. Turner had made on his new wife.

He'd known his life with her would be interesting. He was beginning to suspect he'd badly underestimated that, as well.

He smiled at the thought.

Anyone who accused him of "settling down" didn't know Emily.

Once they were served and Emily had poured tea for both of them, she pulled her letter from her purse and raised an enquiring eyebrow.

"By all means," he said. "I'm impressed you held off this long."

"So am I. When I think of Mrs. Darrow's face, I'm dying to know what Clara said to put that look there."

"But Clara was nothing but supportive of our elopement."

Emily gave a little snort. "Clara? She suggested it."

"The elopement?"

"The idea of it, yes."

"I see. Then what could she have written?"

Emily looked up from her letter. "Clara has a flair for the dramatic. Especially when she takes pen in hand."

"She doesn't realize that when it comes to letters, the walls really do have eyes?"

"I think it inspires her."

He closed his eyes for a moment. "I see."

She reached out across the table, put her hand on his for a moment. "I don't think you do," she said quietly, and went back to reading her letter.

He watched her, intrigued by this side of her.

Then she started to laugh. "Oh, you have to hear this."

Clearly he did. "Read it to me, then."

She leaned closer, and lowered her voice a little. "This is dated the day she got back to town, and it begins:

I had Bertie leave your letter in your mother's parlor, tucked into her embroidery hoop. No-one else would look there, and she'll find it this after-noon. She's going to burst, she'll be so mad.

Emily, what will you do?

I can't ever face your mother again. Not when I knew. And she goes everywhere.

I'll have to become a hermit, a social outcast. And all because of you.

Emily put the letter down and met Granville's eyes. Hers were dancing. "See what I mean? She's discreet, in her way, because she never says exactly what happened. But everything is a drama, and every problem is a crisis. And the unwary reader will assume the worst."

"And look like a fool if they talk about it," he finished. "You have interesting friends."

"Yes, I'm very lucky," she said. "But Clara is unique."

"She is indeed," he agreed, certain that wasn't how he'd describe her. "No wonder Mrs. Darrow looked so smug."

Which made Emily smile.

"Perfect," she said. "I'll have trouble keeping a straight face next time I see her. Which brings up the next problem. Granville, how are we ever going to confront Mrs. Darrow about Robby Brody after this?"

"And which of us has to face her?" he added.

CHAPTER 43

It turned out to be easier than Emily had feared. Once she and Granville put their heads together and began playing with possible scenarios, it became clear to her that she, and not Granville, had to be the one to go back and confront Mrs. Darrow.

Her plan was to go with sympathy. She was never afterwards sure if she'd thought of it first, or Granville had. But either way, they both agreed this was the best approach to find out if Mrs. Darrow really had known Brody. Or if they were just reading too much into a tall tale.

At least it felt like the best approach. Right up until the moment Emily stood outside the post office, reaching for the door knob. Then she was hit with a wave of doubts, suddenly certain she'd be laughed out of the post office. For a long moment she froze, her hand outstretched and her knees threatening to betray her.

Then she took in a deep breath, admonished herself to be brave, and walked in.

Mrs. Darrow looked up when the door bells jangled, and couldn't quite hide the look of surprise at seeing Emily, alone.

She did better with the gleeful look that followed it, stuffing it down so fast Emily wouldn't have caught it if she hadn't been watching for it.

"Can I help you?" The words were formal, the tone indecipherable.

No matter. Emily had a role to play. "I hope so. I got some… difficult news."

"The letter? I'm sorry to hear that."

Not much sincerity behind that one, Emily judged. Which was helpful, given what she had in mind.

"Thank you," she said, as if she'd believed every word. Or was too steeped in grief to notice the nuances. "It's just—I don't know what to do. Or who to talk to. And you… you've obviously been around long enough to have seen pretty much everything."

She kept her tone young, naive. The words still had Mrs. Darrow giving her a hard second look.

"I really don't know what to do." Emily was proud of the near wail that came out in.

"There, there. Perhaps I can help." The words were right, at least. And perhaps even said with a hint of sympathy. This just might work.

Emily pushed back a grin. Gloating was not what she was aiming for here. She needed a connection with this woman, not payback.

"My friend—she took a letter to my mother, and it was bad. Now I'm afraid my family will disown me. And then what will I do?"

"What about your fella?" Mrs. Darrow was leaning forward a little now, and something in her expression was different. She didn't look quite so disdainful now. Or so tightly buttoned.

Emily thought hard about how she'd feel if Granville ever left her. And let those thoughts show on her face.

"Oh, you poor thing." There was no pretense now. "You'll make it, I promise," Mrs. Darrow said. "I did."

"How?" Emily didn't have to try for a wail now. It was there in her voice, put there by the thought of losing Granville. "How could you?"

"I had my memories," she said, proud for a moment. "And no other choice."

There was a raw honesty in the words that Emily hadn't expected.

"This was your Robby you lost?" she asked. Then at the look the other woman gave her, was quick to say, "My Granville told me."

And if Emily's voice quavered on the words, it wasn't on purpose.

The other woman's face softened. "You're younger than I thought you."

"I hide it," Emily said. "He's… older."

"He is. Only a few years, though. And worth hiding things for, I suspect."

"Yes," was all she said.

It was enough.

"Yes, it was my Robby," Mrs. Darrow said. "He left one day, like usual. And he never came back."

An flash of old pain in the woman's lined face told Emily that this was the moment. "Were you a singer, like in that love story I was told?" Emily asked as naively as she could.

It earned her another hard look, anyway. But it also earned an answer. "I was, though I started as just a dancer. They called me Belle. Before. I wasn't Belle any more, not after. When he didn't come back."

"But you stayed. And you survived."

"I did. Nowhere else to go," was the blunt answer. "But I wasn't giving in. And I wasn't leaving. Just in case…"

Emily gave a short nod. "In case someday he came back." It surprised her to realize that she'd do the same. If ever….

Though she'd probably go searching for Granville first, Emily decided. Not sit and wait forever, as Mrs. Darrow seemed to have done. It would be too hard, just waiting like that. For decades.

Nearly choking on the sudden empathy she felt for the other woman, Emily hastily turned her thoughts back to the case.

"You knew him just as Robby?"

"Robert Brody."

"We're… Granville is… looking for a Thomas Robertson. Not Brody."

"I didn't know him by that name," Mrs. Darrow said. "Though the sketch he showed me is right. He was Brody to me. My Robby. Always will be."

Emily nodded, finding herself with nothing to add. No questions it felt right to ask.

Seeing it, the other woman offered comfort. "You can do it too. There's always memories. And you never know. Sometimes they come back. Even years later."

"You still believe that?"

"I have to."

"Oh." It was so sad. "I have to go now. Thank you. And I hope… your Robby does, one day. Come back."

The older woman smiled faintly. "I'll hold your letter for you, when it comes. Who knows, it may not be as bad as all that."

Her eyes tearing a little, despite her best efforts, Emily just thanked her and turned to go.

EMILY WAS SHIVERING a bit as she rejoined Granville in the cozy warmth of the coffeehouse where she'd left him, even though she'd only walked a block or so. He looked up as she approached the table.

"You look half-frozen."

"The wind's come up."

"Ah. Let me get you a fresh cup," and he signaled the waitress, who hurried over with a steaming teapot and a plate of hot scones.

"How did it go?" he asked as she added milk to her tea.

"Quite well," she said, taking a grateful sip of the hot drink. "All things considered."

He gave her a quizzical look, but all he said was, "Did she admit to any of it?"

"I asked if she was the singer from the story, and she told me that she was once Belle. And that her lost love was one Robert Brody. Thank you for the scones, by the way."

"It was my privilege," he said, leaving her feeling flustered. He was taking care of her again.

"Mrs. Darrow did recognize Brody in the sketch you showed her, but not by that name," she added quickly.

"She told you?"

"Yes. And I believed her. There was something in her eyes. She looked so very sad."

"She's lied to us before. You believe she was telling you the truth this time?

"Yes, I do. I truly felt I was seeing the real woman, finally. What she told us before was a hard mask she'd built to hide her loss and sorrow behind."

"So she didn't kill him? It's what we were both wondering."

"I know. The woman she pretends to be might have done so. The grieving woman I saw today?" Emily paused and sat back for a moment, sipping her coffee, then shook her head. "No. She just couldn't have."

Granville nodded, and offered her the plate of fragrant scones. She took one, buttered it, and popped a piece in her mouth. Delicious.

"Since Mrs. Darrow confirmed that Robert Brody really was —or is?—Thomas Robertson," she said when she'd eaten half the scone. "What does that do for our case?"

"It opens it up again. For starters, we need to revisit everyone in town we asked about Robertson, see if we get a different answer with his Brody name."

He drew out his pocket watch, glanced at it. "Scott and Trent will already have started in one of the bars by now."

"Well, we'll need to revisit everywhere except the graveyard,"

Emily said with a little quirk of pride that she'd been thorough enough before to save them time now. "Do you want to talk to Mrs. Darrow again?"

He shook his head. "I think you got more from her this morning than I would have. More questions will likely only irritate or upset her."

"And I'll have to go back to collect Mama's letter in any case," Emily said. "I can talk to her then. Who knows, we might even have learned something new by then. Meanwhile, we should probably talk to the stage drivers, too. When is the next one due in town, do you know?"

"Probably next Tuesday, if the storm hasn't stopped them. Our host will know."

"We need to go back to the other coffeehouses we visited last week. Especially the one where the old-timers were. Then maybe we should track down Scott and Trent. We could split their remaining bars and coffeehouses with them."

"It might be more useful if we each re-interview the same people," he said. "Especially the ones who almost recognized an out-of-date sketch the first time. With the right name, they might actually know him."

Emily nodded. "That makes sense. And then?"

He made a face. "The stores."

She laughed at his play. "Well, I don't love shopping the way Clara does, but I can think of worse ways to spend the rest of the day."

"I can't."

She gave him a thoughtful look. He wasn't entirely serious, but he'd probably rather be visiting pubs with Scott than stores with her. And he had done so much to make this trip easier for her.

"What about the Masonic Lodge?" she asked. "If Mr. Robertson was a mason, they might know what became of him. You could start there, and I could begin with the general stores. I'm told they carry a fascinating variety of merchandise."

"That's a generous thought. I have no idea if Robertson was

a Mason, but the lodge here wasn't established until the year after he left town for good, so I'm afraid they wouldn't be much help.

"No, I'll have to join you in talking to shopkeepers, I'm afraid. But why don't we begin with the old timers we've talked to before."

He still didn't look very happy about it.

"You know, fascinating though the general stores might be," Emily said. "Most of them are unlikely to be run by anyone old enough to remember Mr. Brody. But Mr. Powers, the stage driver? He told me that after the big gold finds of the Cariboo had been made, a lot of the miners would leave a claim they had staked that wasn't paying out, or was yielding just a little gold, and move on in hopes of staking a richer claim."

He nodded. "The same thing happened in the Klondike. Part of the issue there was the isolation. That and the climate drove the cost of basic goods like beans, flour, lard and salt so high, very few claims paid out enough to cover the costs of working them. Miners eat a lot, especially in winter," he added with a grin. "It seems the Cariboo mines were similar."

"Exactly," Emily said. "Except that here, the Chinese miners —those who had been working building the railroads—took over claims that had been abandoned, and worked together to bring out enough gold to survive on. In some cases, they would hit another seam of gold—do I have that right?"

"You do. Though depending on the claim, it could be a deposit of loose gold, like from a stream or a glacier, rather than a seam running through rock."

She smiled and continued. "So sometimes the formerly abandoned claim paid off very well. In any case, it seems that after the peak of the gold rush more than half of the miners still working in the region were Chinese. And still are."

He narrowed his eyes a little. "So you're thinking that by 1868 a lot of miners might have moved on in search of other gold rushes with richer payouts."

"That's it exactly," she said, not in the least surprised at how quickly he'd put it together. "Apparently the Chinese-owned stores in town then became the social hub for most of the active miners. Some of those stores, or their successors, still exist."

"So those stores might be the place to find information on where Brody went each time he left Barkerville," he said, finishing the thought. "Or we could talk to the local tribes."

"Those might be interesting places to start, at least," she said.

"Then we can add both to our list," he said, draining his teacup and signalling for the bill.

CHAPTER 44

GRANVILLE AND EMILY FOUND SILAS DUNHAM, ALONG WITH HIS three cronies, at the same coffeehouse where they'd met him a week ago. But it was Dunham they were most interested in. He was the one who'd lingered longest over the sketch of Thomas Robertson, finding it almost familiar.

Dunham recognized the two of them immediately. Nothing wrong with his memory, anyway. With a fresh cup of coffee in front of him, he was happy to chat, especially with Emily, Granville noted with a grin. And clearly curious about why they were back.

Emily didn't miss any of it. She produced the sketch and placed it in front of the old miner. "You almost recognized this the last time we chatted," she said.

It wasn't quite a question, but Granville noted it sparked the fellow's interest and drew him in immediately. She was good at this.

"I did," Dunham said, leaning forward and tapping the sketch with a gnarled finger. "Doesn't bring anything new to mind now, though."

"What about in connection with the name Robby Brody?" she asked.

"Brody?" the old miner asked, peering at the sketch. Glancing at her for permission, he picked up the sketch and held it towards the light from the window. "I remember Brody well. Or at least as well as I remember anyone from back then. This isn't him."

Deliberately sitting back to let the conversation play out, Granville looked from the deep frown on the fellow's face to the flash of disappointment on Emily's. Seconds later she'd hidden the emotion and showed only interest. "Go on," she said.

It was impressive. She'd already learned not to be discouraged when a lead didn't pan out, Granville realized. Some investigators never learned that. No matter how seasoned they were.

"But then again, it isn't *not* him, either," Dunham said as he angled the sketch this way and that. "The features are close, but the expression, the way he stands? No. This," and he put the sketch down, tapped it again, "is an older man."

Emily wisely said nothing as Dunham reached for his coffee cup, still frowning slightly. The fellow took a sip, put the cup down with a clatter and reached for the sketch again. This time he tilted it back and forth, seemingly watching the play of light across the image.

"When the light moves and changes, I do see Brody in this," he said after a few silent moments. "He had an expressive face, with quicksilver changes of expression. He moved the same way. Quick. And his enthusiasms—they lit up the room, drew people to him. He could draw anyone into one of his schemes, that boy, and no-one ever blamed him, even when something went wrong.

This man?" and he turned the sketch towards them. "He's Brody's opposite. You can see the responsibility heavy in this man's face, in how he stands. Weighing on his shoulders. And yet the likeness is there. An older brother, perhaps?"

"This sketch is of a man named Thomas Robertson," Granville said, joining the conversation.

"A cousin, then?"

"It's a possibility," Granville said. If Mrs. Darrow was wrong about this being her Robby. Or if her memory of her long lost love had been clouded by too many years and too much disappointment. "We know very little about his family, unfortunately."

And that wouldn't be easy to change from here. He exchanged a glance with Emily.

Who smiled at Dunham and leaned forward a little. "Which makes anything you can tell us about Robby Brody of great interest to us," she said. "Whatever became of him? I noticed you spoke of him in the past tense?"

The old miner nodded. "I did. Though I don't know for sure that he died. Went off on one of his trips one spring—must have been in '68, because it was the year of the big fire. And he never came back."

He paused, sipped his coffee. "No-one ever heard from him or of him after that, either. We kinda figured he'd been killed off mining somewhere."

"Not moved on?" Granville asked.

The fellow shrugged. "Even the ones that left, someone generally heard where they'd gone. Or someone knew someone who'd seen them or heard something about them."

Granville nodded. "The goldfield telegraph."

Dunham laughed. "We just called it news from outside."

Then he sobered. "With Brody, there was none of that. And Brody was someone people remembered, talked about. If he were alive, we should have heard something, eventually. And we didn't."

"You never heard that he died? Or been injured?" Emily asked.

"Nothing. But that isn't unusual in these parts. Especially for miners. No, he's dead."

"Or living under another name," Emily said. Her attention was fixed on Dunham.

Who stared at her in silence for a moment. But his expression never changed.

"You think Brody is this Robertson," Dunham said slowly, tapping the sketch as he spoke. "And that he's what? Some kind of chameleon? One who changes his mannerisms along with his name?"

The thought didn't seem to bother him much.

Granville sat forward a little. Now this was interesting. It wasn't a direction they'd considered before—but when Emily raised the question that way, it was plausible. Especially given Dunham's earlier reaction to the sketch.

Though the fellow's lack of reaction to the idea was decidedly odd. As if it wasn't the first time he'd considered the possibility.

Had he guessed that Robby Brody wasn't really Brody? And not cared? Or had he cared too much, for some reason of his own?

Either way, Silas Dunham could be a possible suspect in Brody's disappearance. And finding those answers was not going to be easy.

They really knew too little of Thomas Robinson, and that little was colored by time and the views of his then ten-year-old son. And the fellow's letters home, of course.

Letters which could give exactly the impression a chameleon wanted them to.

To start with, they needed to run with the Brody name as far as it would take them. And see if that gave them any new leads.

Granville had seen such things on the goldfields of the Klondike, and wondered idly what would happen when those miners returned home. Though some of them never did.

Just like Robertson hadn't.

Were they going to find the fellow, as Robby Brody, alive and well somewhere?

Though if their missing miner was alive, he'd already left Barkerville behind. And his supposed sweetheart along with it. What was to stop him taking on yet another new name, and going in search of a new life?

Or had something found him first?

CHAPTER 45

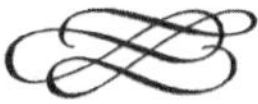

JUST AFTER ONE O'CLOCK GRANVILLE AND EMILY MET UP WITH Scott and Trent in the small private dining room in their hotel. Granville was looking forward to a hearty lunch. Scones weren't his favorites, though Emily loved them. Even more, though, this gave him—gave all of them—the privacy to compare notes on what they'd learned that morning. And to discuss exactly where they were at with the case.

"You'll never guess what we found," Trent said as soon as the door closed behind their hostess and her helper. Grabbing a quarter of an egg sandwich in one hand and his cup of coffee in the other, he grinned widely.

"What did you find?" Emily said, playing along. And hiding her smile as Granville rolled his eyes at the two of them.

"Everyone we talked to had heard of Brody," the lad said gleefully. "I didn't find anyone who'd actually met him, but they all knew about him."

"What did they know?" Granville asked. "More tall tales about fated romances? Or had some of them heard something about who he really was?"

"Well, that's the thing, see," Trent said. He paused to inhale his slice of bacon and gulp down some coffee. "It depended."

"On?" Granville asked, ignoring the smirk Scott was sending his way. Usually their assistant more than pulled his weight, but sometimes his enthusiasm—not to mention his love of puzzles and games—could be trying.

"On whether they'd actually met him," Trent said, producing one of the copies of the Robertson sketch, as if expecting applause. "The ones who recognized this? They'd met him. Back then, I mean."

"I thought you said you didn't find anyone who'd actually met him," Emily protested.

"Well, I didn't. Not today, anyway," Trent said.

"So how do you know that the men who recognized our missing miner really knew him?" she asked.

"Well, it stands to reason, yeah? How else would they know? And they all—to a man—were old geezers—plenty old enough to have known Brody himself."

Emily looked at Granville with dancing eyes, and sat back in her chair. Over to him, was it? He hid a smile, and met the barely suppressed mirth in Scott's eyes.

"Care to fill us in on how your morning's work actually went?" Granville asked his partner.

Trent put down his coffee cup. "But I just told you…" he began.

Granville simply looked at him.

At which the lad shrugged, grinned and sat back in his chair.

"It was worth a try."

Not that Trent said the words. But Granville knew exactly what the boy was thinking, could practically hear him saying it. And he couldn't have kept a straight face if he had.

"We split up," Scott said. "Thought we could cover most of the bars before lunch. While people were still sober."

"You're the one who talked to the men who'd half-recognized the photo earlier, then," Granville said to him.

"That's me."

Emily put down her coffee cup and leaned forward again. "What did they say? And how did they react when they heard Brody's name?"

"There was a blank look, then as soon as they heard the name Brody? That moment of recognition, almost a double take. And then each of them reached for the sketch, examining it as carefully as if it could tell them something."

"Like what?" she asked.

He shrugged. "What had happened to him, maybe. Who knows?"

"They didn't know? What happened to him, I mean."

"Didn't seem to."

What Scott was saying matched what they'd heard from Dunham. Part of it, anyway. Emily glanced over at him, her eyes sparkling.

He wondered what conclusions she was drawing. She didn't say anything yet, though. Just nodded, and poured them all a little more coffee.

"If they didn't know what happened to Brody, what did they tell you?" he asked Scott. Clearly there had been something.

"All of 'em agreed it was Brody. No question. In fact, as soon as they heard the name, there was that "of course" look on most of their faces. And you have to understand, this wasn't a case of one guy in a group recognizing him and the others agreeing. I was only talking to one or two of these guys at any of the bars. "

"Not many of 'em left," Trent put in, then focused on his plate at another look from Granville.

"And every one I talked to had the same reaction," Scott finished, ignoring the interruption.

"What else did they have to say about Brody?" he asked Scott.

"He was a hard worker, but he either wasn't much of a miner, or he was the unluckiest one they'd ever met. Stories differed on that one," Scott said. "But they all agreed that Brody was a good guy, easy to get on with, the kind that made any party better. Everyone liked him, and he seemed to like everyone."

"He was memorable," Emily noted. "Brody, I mean." She sipped coffee, then speculated out loud, "I wonder if Thomas Robertson was equally memorable? Or if leaving his old life behind and heading for the frontier allowed him to become a different person?"

Then she waited, watching Scott and Trent closely.

"Could be," Scott said. "We don't know enough about about Robertson to even guess. But I met a couple of very buttoned-down men on the boat to the Klondike. Both of 'em seemed to lighten up with every mile we covered. The closer we got to the goldfield, the more outgoing they got. It takes some that way."

Emily nodded, seemingly not feeling the need to add anything further.

So Granville took the lead. "And no-one seems to know where Brody went after he left here?"

"If they do, they aren't saying."

"What about when he was last seen?"

"Not much agreement there, either."

"Could they tell you where they last encountered Brody?"

"Or what little they remember, anyway," Trent muttered.

This time both Scott and Granville turned and glared at him.

Granville wondered what was up with Trent. He wasn't usually disruptive like this. Not on purpose, anyway. Was he still sore about their return to Barkerville?

"I've got notes of every place that got a mention," Scott said.

"Good. We'll add those to our map, and see if it gives us any insight into our missing Romeo of a miner," Granville said.

"Or at least which direction to head next," Scott said. "But what did you two find out?"

"Mrs. Darrow confirmed that her Robby was indeed Robert "Beau" Brody," Emily said. "She hadn't known his real name, either. Not before Granville told her last week."

"And we visited Chinatown, since one or two of the general stores have been in operation for thirty years. Several of them had satellite stores in other areas, but no record of him as a customer. And no rumors about him, either."

"We should check those locations against the places Trent and I heard about today," Scott said. "Tomorrow is Sunday, which gives us plenty of time to work on it."

"Good idea," Granville said, clapping his partner on the shoulder. "Meanwhile, we need to visit anyone else in town who might have known Brody."

It was, finally, a start.

CHAPTER 46

On Monday morning, Emily braved the heavy snow that had fallen overnight, and made her way back to the Post Office to see if there was a letter from Mama. Mrs. Darrow looked pleased to see her, and nodded as if Emily had asked a question.

"It's here," she said. And turned to retrieve the stiff white envelope with the familiar writing on it. As she passed it to Emily, the postmistress said softly, "I didn't look."

"Thank you," Emily said, meaning it. "If I may?"

And she waved toward a quiet spot by the windows, where the bright sunlight would make reading Mama's cramped handwriting easier.

"Of course."

With a nod of thanks and a smile, Emily slid into a sunlit chair. Tearing open the envelope, she unfolded her letter and skimmed the closely written words. Yes, Mama had been careful, just as she'd expected.

If Mrs. Darrow *had* steamed it open, there was nothing to tell her that Emily's mother had been upset about her elopement. Or indeed, that there had been an elopement at all.

Knowing her mother well, Emily could see the emotions behind the carefully chosen words. And as she'd expected, Mama had a solution to the inevitable social problems caused by the elopement of her youngest daughter. It seemed that the celebration of their marriage that she and Granville had intended to host on their return was going to be much bigger and more elaborate than either of them had planned.

In fact, as Mama waxed lyrical about the party, it sounded more and more like the kind of event Mama had intended to turn their wedding into, once her older two sisters were safely married. Only, her sisters were both unmarried still.

So instead of her parents hosting an elaborate wedding party for them, she and Granville would end up hosting a nearly identical grand event as a married couple. Ensuring society's rules and expectations would be met.

She'd been right about Mama's schemes. Though this was even more devious than she'd expected, she realized as she reread a paragraph. Mama's current plans meant Emily and Granville would be paying for the event. And doing all the work, she thought with a wry grin.

While Mama basked in the social glory. And invented stories to smooth out the prickliest sticklers. Wait 'til she told Granville.

It was a good thing this case paid well, whether they found their missing miner or not. Given how much this party was likely to cost.

Unless… Could Mama be outmaneuvered?

Emily would have her own household now. She would be the one responsible for any entertaining she did, not her mother. Mama would still attempt to manipulate everything from behind the scenes, of course. But Emily had watched her do so for years. And she'd learned.

The possibilities were intriguing.

"You don't look too upset," Mrs. Darrow said with a trace of her former sharpness. She was standing at the far end of her counter, angled so she could sort the mail and still see Emily's expression where she stood over by the window. "Your news was good, then?"

So the postmistress really hadn't read the letter. That made it easier still. Tucking it into her handbag—and her unruly emotions along with it—Emily walked quickly back to the counter.

"I won't be banished, in any case," she said.

Thinking what a good thing it was that the post office was empty except for the two of them. The last thing she needed was to trigger gossip here about her recent marriage. "Though I may have to pay for my misdeeds. And for quite some time, I suspect."

Mrs. Darrow gave her a thoughtful look. "Was it worth it?" was the only question she asked.

Emily nodded. "Oh, yes. Isn't it always?"

Another thoughtful look. Mrs. Darrow seemed about to say something, then paused, and frowned a little, glancing over towards a small pile of letters tied with faded postal twine. "You're not as young as I thought you, after all," she said slowly. "And yes, it is."

"We're still looking for your Robby," Emily said after the moment of silent recognition between them. "Do you want to us to tell you if we find out anything?"

She'd expected a pause before the other woman answered, but there was no hesitation in Mrs. Darrow's voice. "Yes, of course. As soon as you can."

Emily hadn't been sure if, for Mrs. Darrow, not knowing was better than hearing the worst. But this was the choice she herself would have made.

And it was the other woman's choice that let Emily ask the next question.

"We're trying to put together a map of all the locations Mr. Brody went," she began. "And who might have seen him there. And when."

"How can I help?"

The question threw Emily off a little. She'd been working up to it, but hadn't expected the offer. Especially when the postmistress had avoided Granville's similar questions only a week ago.

"I know he used Barkerville as his base," she said. "Anything you know about where he was going each time he left here—even just the direction—would be very useful in trying to narrow down where he might have gone that last time."

Mrs. Darrow looked at the snow that had begun to fall again outside the window, glanced around at the empty post office. And smiled.

"I have the time," she said. "If you'll write my words down, I'll make us some tea."

"Done," Emily said, and drew her pencil and notebook from her purse.

LESS THAN AN HOUR LATER, Emily hurried towards the private dining room at their hotel, where she found Granville, Scott and Trent working on uncovering exactly what their missing miner had been up to from the time he arrived in 1863.

Somewhere they'd found great sheets of butcher paper, and spread them from one end of the long dining table to the other. All three of them were using grease pencils to make lists and interconnected events on various large sheets of the stuff.

She paused at the doorway, her lips quirking up at the unexpected sight. She'd never seen anyone work a case like this before. But the big diagram they were currently working on, all notes in boxes with circles and arrows, would certainly make it easier to see how the missing miner's search for gold—if gold was indeed his goal—had unfolded. And spot the gaps that might tell them what they were missing.

"You might want to stop for a moment," she said as she swept into the room. "I have information that may change everything."

It was a lovely, dramatic thing to say, and she savored every moment, even as she was amused by the high drama of it all.

She'd always longed to sweep into a room and make a proclamation like that.

And here she was.

She almost laughed at the expressions the three men turned on her. Granville had laughter dancing in his eyes. Scott looked worried. And Trent just looked annoyed.

It was a good thing she'd married Granville, and not someone else. Not that there had ever been any one else. But the more difficult this case became, and the longer it dragged on with no good answers, the more she learned of the man she'd married.

And the happier she was with her choice.

"Your mother's letter came?" her new husband said. "What did she have to say?"

"Yes, it did. And nothing that can't wait," Emily said, waving off the question. She preferred to tell him in private exactly what schemes Mama had in store for them.

"But I also spoke with Mrs. Darrow at some length. And she's given me a list of where he planned to go every time he left Barkerville. And when each trip occurred."

"Who is he?" Trent asked sarcastically.

"Our missing miner, of course," she said, pulling the list out of her bag and extending it to Granville. "I'm hoping this will give us context for all of the other information people have been giving us about when and where they saw Mr. Brody."

SEVERAL HOURS LATER, Emily stepped back and stared at the information she'd just put up in one of the Barkerville sections of their timeline. Then she took another step back and looked from one end of the wall they were using as a type of blackboard to the other. She even squinted a little, to see if that helped. Then she nodded to herself.

"Whatever it was that happened to Mr. Robertson, it must have started long before he disappeared," Emily said. Half thinking out loud, half because she could use another perspective. Three pairs of eyes focused on her.

"Don't you mean before he left?" Trent said, frowning at her careful notes, then at her. "You don't think he's still alive, do you?"

Emily shrugged one shoulder and shot him a smile, then turned her attention back to the timeline. There was something…

Behind her, she could hear Granville say to Trent, "I don't think she does."

In her head, Emily could almost hear Papa's voice, telling her child self how the Fraser River Gold rush had moved upstream until the new strikes diminished, then become the Cariboo Gold Rush as the miners explored the rivers and streams north and east along the Fraser. Then came the Omenica Gold Rush, a few years later and still further north. And with each new discovery the miners followed.

For some, it had been the discovery of rich goldfields in Australia that called them even further. And finally, the nugget-rich creeks of the Klondike, which had drawn Granville from England to Canada. And Scott from the United States.

She glanced at the two of them, and thought about the detective agency they'd formed together, and the difference it had made in her life. She felt a sudden rush of gratitude for the chain of coincidences sparked by the siren call of a gold rush, which had made her new life possible.

"If there's so much gold, why do they leave?" she'd asked her father every time he told the tale of the gold rush days.

He'd laughed, a little bitterly she'd realized years later. "No man can ever have enough money. Or enough gold," he'd told her. "The lure of the big strike, of hitting that jackpot, was too strong to resist. Even the journalists fell for it. You can see it in the reports covering the story."

He'd been right, too, at least about the journalists. There was a kind of breath-holding excitement that filled the headlines and hid behind even the most prosaic of stories. Even the ones written long after the gold rush itself.

And always the focus was on the first big strike, and the bigger ones that followed it.

Granville and Scott had said much the same about the lure of that one big strike. Though unlike some, they left the goldfields of the Klondike to pursue other dreams.

She stared at their attempt to record the journeys their missing miner had taken, the way he'd spent nearly a decade covering trails that spiked out from the area around Barkerville like the spokes of a wagon wheel. Instead of chasing the next big strike, he'd followed what looked like a consistent, determined pattern.

All while writing cheerful letters home, and promising them riches.

"Have a look," she said, gesturing towards the work they'd done. "Our missing miner kept returning to Barkerville? Why?"

"Love?" Trent said.

"That doesn't explain his letters home," Emily said. "It's as if he was looking for something he was convinced was there."

"Sounds like gold to me," Scott said. "Lot of miners I've known thought that way. Probably searched like this too, if we'd ever had this much information on them."

It made sense, Emily admitted. Wasn't that what he and Granville had been saying all along? But she couldn't help feeling they were missing something.

"By 1867, most of the other miners had long moved on to new finds. But not Robby Brody. What did our missing miner know, or think he knew, that kept him tethered to this area? It doesn't make sense. And yet it must have made sense to him."

"There's no way to be sure," Granville said. "Not with the information we've managed to gather so far."

"But surely there has to be a way to find out more about where he'd been, before he vanished?" she said. "Looking at what we do know, is there a next logical step? Or maybe he'd said something more to Mrs. Darrow, something she hasn't told us. Or something she never realized was important?"

Emily looked from Granville to Scott to Trent, hoping to see a spark of what she was feeling. They were all missing something, she just knew it.

"Maybe it was something Mrs. Darrow hasn't even considered over all these years since, no matter how often she thought about him," she added, half to herself.

"But what?" Trent asked.

He didn't see it. None of them did.

And she didn't have an answer, just this uneasy feeling. There had to be something more for them to detect. Otherwise, they might have to admit defeat and return to Vancouver with no answers.

And that would be a shame, after they'd come all this way. It had been such an amazing trip—too marvelous to end like this, with nothing to tell their client.

Granville seemed much more resigned to not solving this case than she felt. Maybe a good detective got that way by learning from every case, even the ones that couldn't be solved?

And not wasting too much time on them.

Or was he simply putting on a better front than she was, to keep up morale? Probably her morale, especially.

The thought touched her and irritated her at the same time. This marriage thing was more complicated than she'd imagined.

"We could talk to Mrs. Darrow again," Granville said. "See if the right question can jar something loose in her memory. Or we can finish putting the information we do have on the timeline, see if there's some detail that gives us some better questions to ask her. What do you think?"

He was making it easy again. And undermining her irritation in the process. She wanted to be annoyed with him for it, but couldn't quite manage it. Especially when he made sense.

"Yes, let's finish this timeline with the information we do have, and then see," she said.

CHAPTER 47

After the four of them had been working with intense focus for most of the morning, Granville stepped back to consider what they had accomplished. It had taken six big sheets of butcher paper to capture all of the journeys Robertson had made as Brody. And that was before they even began to include all the recent bits of information.

It was a lot of work, but it was looking good. While the others finished off their respective charts, Trent had gone to beg some more pins to hang the charts.

Once the various charts were done, Trent and Scott pinned the sheets to the decorative rail that ran at head height around the walls. Granville tacked up the larger map of the area they had been using beside the last page.

They all stood back and looked in silence at the timeline they'd created.

Finally Trent spoke. "See, I told you we needed to go look at the Antler Creek area.

"Not so fast," Granville said.

All three turned to look at him. Emily was the first to speak.

"What am I missing?" she asked. "Brody does seems to have

spent a lot of time at and around Antler Creek. Yet you see something different?"

He smiled warmly at her, oddly pleased to see her fight back a blush. Then he explained, keeping his tone professional, and including all of them.

"Look at the timing. When Brody left town for the last time, everyone here, including his Belle, expected him to be coming back."

"So? Maybe he was tired of her," Trent said impatiently. "Or he was killed in a mudslide or something. Near Antler Creek."

"Have another look at the letter he sent home two days before he left here for the last time," Granville said.

Impatient, Emily reached for it before the others could. And began to read it aloud. Only to stop on the words in the second paragraph. "He's talking about riches again. And about being home soon."

"Meaningless," Trent said, and Scott nodded his agreement.

"Are you sure?" Granville asked.

"Why aren't you sure?" Trent asked.

"I'd have thought it was obvious," he said with a straight face.

"Obviously not," Emily said, unable to hide her grin. "Have a heart. Clearly we can't see whatever you've just put together. Give."

He winked at her. "Take a look how much information we have from around that time. He seems to have talked to everyone he knew before he left."

"Yet they all said he was acting normally," Scott said. "Buying the usual supplies for at least a month. Getting his gear clean and ready. Hiring a pack horse. Updating his maps."

"Everything was the same. So what?" Trent said, in a tone as heated as his face.

It looked to Emily as if he hadn't been able to hold the words back another moment. He should have known Granville better by now, she thought.

Just like she should be able to see whatever it was her husband was seeing.

Refusing to be distracted by the reminder they were really married, Emily stared at the timeline. Running everything she knew about that time through her head. "What am I missing?" she muttered, and Granville grinned.

"Need a clue?" he asked.

"No, I do not. I need an answer, not more clues."

He laughed, a full-out sound that raised her spirits at the same time it irritated her all over again.

"You're not helping," she muttered.

Meanwhile Trent was still sitting back with his arms crossed and a mutinous look on his face. Scott was staring at Granville intently, then switching his gaze to the timeline they'd been creating. Again. And again. And…

"I get it," Scott said at last, a huge smile cratering his thick dark beard. "Brody was going backwards. Revisiting his assumptions in reverse order. Look, he'd started around Lightning Creek way back in '63. Worked his way down to Antler Creek over the next few years. Spent a few years in the Antler Creek area, seemingly exploring all of the creeks in the area."

"We know his stated goal was the Antler Creek area then," Granville said. "We don't have enough to tell us where he actually spent his time over the course of those several summers."

"So? How is any of that helpful?" Trent asked.

"What if he was eliminating things?" Emily said slowly. "It looks to me as if he had some kind of theory about where he'd find gold. He seems to be testing that theory. And it looks like he worked backwards. Or maybe he eliminated the most likely areas first. However it was, he was done with Antler Creek."

"That would fit," Granville said. "Then he ends up revisiting the area between Barkerville and Lightning Creek, as far as we can tell. Not far from the only claim we've been told he staked, even if it was with a partner."

"But that suggests he'd finally found his treasure," Emily said.

"What makes you say that?" Trent demanded. "How could you know?"

"Just look at how he ends the last letter they ever got from him," she said, reaching across to pick it up, and reading out the last line. The date is too blurred to read, but he wrote, "*I miss you, my dear ones, and look forward to seeing you before the next harvest moon.*"

Emily passed the letter to Trent. "I think that's the first time he's written anything stronger than hoping he'd soon be with them once again."

"It's sappier too," Trent said in disgust. "I thought he and Belle were the love story of the Cariboo."

"Belle thought so too," Emily said sadly, glancing at Granville. "But love story or not, it seems her Robby never stopped hunting for gold. So perhaps he never stopped planning to go home and rescue his family."

"Certainly his wife thought so, from what our client told me," Granville said.

"Then why the big romance?" Trent said.

"Those were hard times," Granville said. "The land was unforgiving, and people died easily."

"So people enjoyed life any way they could?" Emily asked.

"Good way of putting it," Scott said. "A lot of tall tales grew out of that time. You can't believe half of it. And people invented new names and new lives for themselves. Made life more interestin'."

"But… You mean he lied to her? Maybe he deserved to die and never make it back to Belle. Or his wife," Trent muttered.

"Maybe," Emily said. "Or maybe he didn't really take their 'romance' seriously, and didn't think Belle would either."

"And found himself trapped in a romance story he didn't believe in?" Trent stopped looking belligerent and traced a finger over the lines of the letter he held. "In a town this small, where people depended on each other to survive, that must have been awful."

"If that is what happened, it probably was," Granville said.

"Then why didn't he just leave?" Trent burst out.

"And the answer to that question is what will help us find our missing miner," Granville said.

"You think he really found gold?" Scott asked.

"Or thought he had a good chance to find it. I can't think of any other reason he'd stay in this area so long, can you?" Granville said, meeting his fellow Klondiker's eyes.

"Most of the other miners had already moved on," Emily pointed out.

"Then no," Scott said with a grin. "If it had been us," and he pointed from himself to Granville. "We'd have been long gone. Rumors of nearby gold strikes are pretty much impossible to ignore."

"Exactly," Granville said. "So why was our missing miner so determined to stay in Barkerville? What did he expect to find? And how is that related to his sudden disappearance?"

"Wait," Scott said, moving to stand in front of the map. "If he did find gold somewhere along here, and planned to mine enough to count as "riches", that would have taken months, if not years. Someone should have seen him."

"Maybe they did," Emily said.

"And said nothing?" Scott said.

"If they were leaving the Cariboo, that's possible," she said. "Especially if Mr. Brody gave whoever it was a little gold to hasten their journey."

"Or they killed him for it," Trent said. "That would explain his disappearance, too."

"There's no record of a rich strike being made there in '68," Granville said. "And no rumors, either. Miners talk. If there was a strike rich enough to be worth killing for, the gossip would spread like wildfire. And no-one would walk away from it."

"Unless Brady had worked the mine secretly, and dug out enough to buy a stake somewhere else?" Trent said.

"There would have been signs," Scott said. "And taken years. Gold is found deep here, and the tailings would be too high to hide."

"What if he'd found someone's stash?" Emily said. "Gold that had already been mined, and then hidden in another location."

"It could be a stash from a robbery, too. There were a few ambushes in the area back then," Trent said, his eyes bright. "I heard the stagecoach taking gold out was even hit a couple of times in the early days."

Emily nodded. "Miners traveling alone with their gold would be easy targets. If they went missing, no-one would even know to look for them."

It was an interesting angle. One he'd not considered. Had their missing miner actually found gold rather than a mine? But he'd never made it home, either.

Trent's scenario that Robertson, aka Brody, had been ambushed and killed for his newly acquired gold was definitely possible. But there was another possibility, one that Robertson's name change to Brody had started him thinking about. In his experience, would-be gold miners tended to change their names when they had something in their past they wanted to keep secret.

So what secrets was Robertson hiding while pretending to be Brody? Could something from Robertson's past have finally caught up with the fellow?

He'd made a call to Seattle earlier, and he was hoping for an answer that would tell him more about Robertson's background. Until then, Granville knew they might as well be whistling in the dark on this case.

BEFORE THE DISCUSSION could get any more heated, a knock at the door heralded the arrival of the cook and the kitchen maid with the late luncheon he'd ordered earlier. Cook carried a heaping tray of sandwiches, while the kitchen maid carried a heavy tray of plates, coffee cups, utensils, cream and sugar. He and Scott were quick to relieve them of their burdens, and setting the trays on one of the tables they'd pushed to the side of the room.

It was a welcome distraction. They were all hungry, and running out of ideas. But none of them were ready to give up.

The food was good, the coffee strong and hot, but neither was enough to make any of them stop their work. Instead they pulled the table back far enough to contemplate their incomplete charts while they ate. Lunchtime chatter was limited to pointing out gaps in the data, or questions they might want to find answers to.

None of which seemed to help. A gloom began to settle over the table. Granville was about to suggest a brisk walk in the snow to break the mood when there was another knock at the door.

"Come in," he called out.

It was their hostess.

"I'm sorry to interrupt, but there's a call for you, Mr. Granville," she said. "He says it's urgent."

There was only one person that could be. With a nod of thanks, he folded his napkin, stood up and excused himself. He could feel the team's curious eyes following him, but at this point in the case, he didn't want to dash any more hopes. He hadn't even told Emily about calling the Pinkerton's.

He followed their hostess as she made her deliberate way back down the hall. He crushed back his impatience, thanking her politely as she showed him to the small, cramped office where the telephone lived. Then grabbed the receiver.

"Granville here."

"Granville? It's Bill Foster from the Seattle office. I got your message, and have at least some of the answers you were looking for. And I may need to apologize for referring Stephen Robertson to you."

CHAPTER 48

WHEN GRANVILLE RETURNED TO THE PRIVATE DINING ROOM THAT had become their chart room, his expression was hard to read, but Emily thought he was pleased about something. But he looked fierce, too.

"What happened? Who called?" she asked before the other two could do so.

He smiled at her, but took the time to look at their wall of charts before answering. "That was Foster, who heads up the Pinkerton's office in Seattle. I left a message for him earlier and asked him to look into Thomas Robertson's past. Especially what the fellow was up to before he came to the goldfields."

"And conveniently changed his name," Scott said thoughtfully. "Does he have one?"

"He does. A particularly brutal one."

"So his son didn't know?"

"Apparently not. Or if he did know, our client is a very good liar. And I'm not as good at reading motives as I believed myself to be. Unfortunately, on this particular case, both are possible."

"But I thought our missing miner was a struggling rancher," Trent said.

"That's the story we were told," Granville said. "It's a long way from the truth."

Trent stared at him. "You mean he might have brought this on himself?"

"Almost definitely. Unless his disappearance from Barkerville was the next part of a larger plan. Just as his disappearance from Seattle was."

"Wasn't he supposed to be part of a cattle drive north?" Scott said. "Which doesn't sound like a safe place to hide to me. Not if there was any serious heat on his tail. Too slow."

"Indeed," Granville said, his tone deeper and angrier than Emily had ever heard it. "But it might have made an excellent cover to get out of town. I doubt he stayed with the drive long after that."

"But what did he do?" Trent asked, his voice avid.

"Cattle rustling," Granville said. "Made good money at it too, from what Foster said. Cattle was a valuable commodity because of the gold rush, and there were plenty of gangs happy to take advantage of that. Robertson ran one of the most ruthless from his supposedly failing ranch. The local law eventually figured out that he was the one behind it all."

"And then he used a legitimate cattle drive to hide his escape? Man has a sense of humor," Scott drawled. "What do the Pinkertons have on him after he left town?"

"Not a thing," Granville said. "He wasn't one of their cases, and once he left town, the local law had other priorities. It seems his name change was sufficient to confuse his trail for anyone else."

"So he changed his name after he left the cattle drive?" Emily asked.

"Pinkerton's couldn't find any record of the senior Robertson after he left the Seattle area, so that's probable. I've asked Foster whether they have any record of Brody."

"Sounds like a long shot," Scott said.

"Probably," Granville replied. "Foster will get back to me, but he warned it could take some time."

"Time we might not have. Not the way the weather's been closing in," Scott said.

Looking from one to the other, Emily wondered again if they'd ever manage to close this case. It seemed everything was against them. Every time they made a tiny bit of progress, another problem came up.

"Our client must have known about his father's reputation, though," Trent said, clearly following an earlier thought. "He was what? Ten? That's old enough to suspect something is wrong, even if you don't know what."

"And he's had plenty of time to ask those questions in thirty years," Scott put in.

"Unless he was desperate not to know," Emily said. "It can be hard to see those you love clearly."

"Most especially a son for a father," Granville agreed, smiling at her.

"And if his mother had known about his father's lurid past, and not told him, that might have made it even harder for the son to admit anything was wrong," Emily said. "Didn't you say that being able to tell his own son what happened to his grandfather was the major reason our client was searching for the man now?"

"That's what he told me. And I suspect watching his own son grow to the age he himself had been when his father disappeared may have raised questions he'd either forgotten or successfully ignored for years."

"I can see that," Trent said.

"In any case, it isn't up to us to condemn our client, however torn his loyalties might have been," Granville said. "But there seems to be little doubt that Robertson Sr. was a criminal who fled north to escape the law."

"Not unheard of in a gold rush," Scott said, exchanging a grin with Granville.

"More like the norm," the latter said.

Emily narrowed her eyes as she looked at the timeline they'd tacked to the wall. "If our missing miner was a criminal, then why did he stay in the Cariboo?" she asked. "From everything we've heard about his life as Robby Brody, he was broke as often as he was flush. Maybe more often. I assume in his former profession, he'd be accustomed to an easy flow of money. So why stay?"

"From what Foster told me, his gang was raking in the money. So, why indeed?" Granville said, turning to look at the section of the timeline that had caught her eye.

"Emily's right. Makes less sense now than it did before we knew he was crooked," Scott said.

"Was the possibility of gold enough?" Emily said. "He seems to have been pretty determined to find a major strike, judging by his travels."

"Unless he really was in love," Trent put in. "And he'd leave town and pan the gold streams until he found enough for the two of them to live on for a time before he went back to her. Sounds like Belle was a beauty in her day."

Emily had to pretend to cough to hide her smile. Trent really was a romantic, no matter how much he denied it. She probably shouldn't find that as funny as she did.

"If that's true," she said, keeping the laughter out of her voice with an effort. "Then it raises another question. Why did he leave when he did?"

"The law caught up with him," Trent said.

"After five years?" she asked.

"More likely to be other bad guys," Scott said. "You don't run a successful crime ring without making enemies."

"Five years," she reminded him.

"If he was chased off the farm, he probably left with a bunch of money unaccounted for," Scott said. "Maybe he hid it, or they thought he did. They may not have been actively looking for him, but they wouldn't forget about him, either."

"That could apply to the good guys, as well," Granville said. "And if our missing miner had finally found a rich strike somewhere in the Cariboo, after all this searching," and he nodded towards the timeline. "Then that would have made him a target for a whole new set of bad guys."

Emily had to laugh. "We seem to have gone from having no

motives for his disappearance to having too many. What if he isn't dead?"

"Then he found gold and ran off to live as a rich miser some-where," Granville said promptly.

Scott was nodding. "Either that or enough time had passed it was safe to retrieve the loot from his earlier crimes. It's the only thing that fits," he said solemnly before the two of them exchanged glances, and Scott's belly laugh filled the room.

"Except it doesn't explain his last letter home," Emily protested, and shook her head at them. Then she gave in to her own laughter. It felt good.

Even if it didn't help them solve this thrice benighted case.

WHEN EMILY finally looked up from her fit of laughter, Trent was looking back and forth between the three of them, his scowl growing darker with every moment.

"I don't get it," he burst out. "This isn't funny. And even with Pinkerton's help, all this work we're doing," he waved dismissively towards their makeshift blackboard. "Isn't getting us anywhere. So why are we sitting around this stuffy room instead of getting out there and doing something?"

"Like what?" Scott asked him. "You going to conjure the answer out of the snow?"

"There must be someone who'll talk to us. Someone who knows what really happened. Or what this guy was up to."

"Between us all, I'm fairly certain we've talked to everyone," Granville said. "But by all means, go and see what you can find out."

"You don't mean that," Trent accused him, pacing from one end of the small room to the other.

To Emily, it looked as if he had to burn off energy before he exploded. And going by his expression, she worried that pacing wasn't going to be enough. But picking a quarrel with Granville or Scott wasn't going to help.

"No," Granville said. "It doesn't make sense to go flying off. Not on your own, anyway. If there is anyone still in town who knows what really happened to Brody, it's likely that person is his killer."

That stopped Trent in his tracks. "What do you mean?" he demanded, turning to face Granville. "They'd be too old."

"Guns don't care how old you are."

Trent blinked at him. "But…"

"Think about it," Scott said.

Trent stared from Scott to Granville. "It still doesn't make sense," he said. "And we're just sitting around. We're not *doing* anything."

"We've never tried to solve a thirty-two year old case before," Granville said. "Most of the information we're used to looking for is long gone. Along with the people who knew it. But a killer is a killer. Confronting one is never a good idea."

"Yeah, like you keep doing," Scott told Granville.

"I usually at least suspect them before I do so," Granville said. "In this case, you could easily end up confronting a killer. One you think is just a witness."

"A killer who's been hiding what they are for a very long time," Scott added. "Probably not goin' to take kindly to being exposed."

"But…" Trent began, then abruptly turned back to the time-line sheets. "A very long time," he said slowly, looking at one sheet in particular. "A very, very long time."

"Nearly twice as long as you've been alive," Granville said softly, watching him. "What are you thinking?"

"What if it wasn't gold?"

"What?"

"He wasn't a miner," Emily said softly, more to herself than anything.

Trent heard her, and turned towards her eagerly. "He was a cattle rustler. A big bad guy. What did he know about mining?"

Emily caught the quick glance Granville and Scott exchanged. Neither of them had been miners, either, before they headed for the gold creeks of the Klondike. Apparently lack of credentials had nothing to do with the lure of gold.

Of course, neither had come home rich, either, so maybe it did matter.

Either way, she wasn't going to break Trent's train of thought. "Very little, I suspect."

He nodded vehemently, his gaze still fixed on one segment of the timeline.

She tried to follow his line of sight, but whatever had caught his attention, she didn't recognize it as a clue.

"But he knew about ranching. Enough to know he couldn't make money at it. And he knew about rustling, and getting guys to work for him."

"I guess he must have," she said. It was an interesting way to look at the problem.

"He might even have had money with him. If he didn't bury it, or something."

"Didn't I just say that?" Scott asked Granville.

"I believe you did."

Trent ignored both of them. "But he'd need to hide. So what does a guy like that do in the Cariboo when he needs to hide?"

"Pretends to be a miner?" Emily suggested.

Trent nodded. "So how did he end up in Barkerville?"

"What's one more gold miner here?" Granville said. "There might have been a limited number of men driving cattle north. But there was no shortage of would-be gold miners."

"Pretty good place to hide," Scott said.

Emily glanced over, surprised at his approving tone.

Scott caught it, and grinned at her. "Strategy," he said. "Keeps people alive. You have to admire it, even when they're crooked."

"And it might tell us something about the man we're looking for. Something different than what his son's story might have led us to look for."

"What d'you mean?" Trent asked, finally turning away from the timeline to stare at Granville. "Why would that matter?"

"Because a failed rancher who thought he'd turn his hand to gold mining is very different from a ruthless thief who eluded capture and chose to hide in the Cariboo gold fields."

"Oh. Yeah," Trent said, and turned back to stare at that piece of timeline again.

Finally Emily couldn't stand it any more. "What are you looking at?" she asked Trent. "And why does it being thirty-two years matter? Aside from the obvious."

"What obvious?" he demanded.

"Old information. People missing. Or dead. The part Granville said earlier."

"Oh, that part."

"So what are you looking at?"

"The people we talked to. Me and Scott."

"And?"

"Our guy went missing a long time ago."

Emily rolled her eyes and turned to Granville. "Is he making sense to you?" she asked.

"Not yet. Doesn't mean he doesn't have a point, though."

Emily was getting tired of Trent's attitude, though she didn't think Granville was playing games. Maybe Trent wasn't either. So she didn't demand to know what point he meant. Even if she couldn't see it.

She took comfort in the fact that Granville didn't get it yet, either. It was this case, this frustrating case.

So instead of saying the wrong thing, Emily promised herself hot chocolate later, and perhaps one of Clara's favorite pastries. And tried to think about what Clara might have said to all of this. Suddenly she missed her friend, and the chance to talk the case over with her. Fiercely.

No matter how wonderful it was to be married to Granville, and to be in Barkerville and working this case with him, sometimes she felt like she was speaking a different language than the men were. Even Trent, who was still just a boy, no matter what he thought.

On other cases, talking things over with Clara had helped her to clarify her own thoughts. Right now, here? Nothing about this conversation was helping her clarify anything.

She drew in a deep breath, reminded herself to be patient, and settled back to listen. Eventually, some of these pieces would settle into place. They had to.

CHAPTER 49

GRANVILLE SHOT A CONCERNED LOOK AT EMILY. SHE SEEMED
deep in thought, but she had an odd look on her face.

"Go on," he said to Trent. The lad was on the track of something, even if he couldn't put words to it yet.

He glanced back at Emily, who was now sitting back, her lips firmly pressed together. Which was unusual for her. In fact, this was the first time he'd seen her distance herself like that since they left Vancouver. It worried him, partly because he'd expected this reaction earlier. And she'd met every experience with a smile.

No smiles now.

This case was taking its toll on all of them. Perhaps more so now. Every time it seemed like they might be getting somewhere, whatever lead they were following drifted out of reach. He took another look at the timeline as he waited for Trent to collect his thoughts. What were they missing?

"It's old information," Trent said.

"It is," Granville said.

"About men who were here more than thirty years ago."

"Yes," he agreed. Noting Emily's lips tighten a little at the inane exchange. That wasn't good.

"Why do they remember him at all?" Trent said. "Brody, I mean. If he was one of dozens who came and went for five years or so?"

"More like hundreds that came and went," Scott said.

"So why do they remember him at all?"

"Brody and Belle?" Emily asked, sitting forward a little, her eyes suddenly bright.

"The romance of it?" Trent scoffed. "I thought you said it was such a tall tale."

"People like telling tales," Emily said. "Especially tall ones. They may forget the people behind them, but they remember the tales."

"Huh."

Now it was Trent's turn to sit back, as he stared at the time-line again.

Granville was just about to see if he needed help putting words to those thoughts when the lad turned to Scott.

"All those old-timers we talked to. How many talked about Brody as if they remembered him clear as anything, once they'd seen the photo? And didn't mention Belle?"

"One or two," Scott said. "Why?"

"The killer, if he *is* alive and still in town? He wouldn't forget a single detail about Brody. Or how he died," Trent said. "And not because of Belle, either."

"You're right about that," Scott said, and stood up, reaching for his notebook in the stack of information they'd collected. "It may be a small clue, but it's all we've got. We need to talk to at least three of those men again."

"Trent, that's brilliant," Emily said, all frustration evidently forgotten.

The lad made a face at her, and joined Scott in gathering their written notes.

Granville was relieved to see all was well with his team. And particularly with his wife. He suspected finding Robertson's killer, if there was one, wasn't going to be quite so easy. But he was willing to go along, for now.

"Silas Dunham," Emily said suddenly, turning to him. "When the two of us spoke with him, he remembered Brody very well indeed, didn't he? Though he did talk about Belle as well. Maybe we need to talk to him again, though."

"Perhaps we do," Granville said.

THEY DIDN'T FIND Dunham at the coffeehouse, but at a smoky bar down the street, which was apparently his watering hole of choice. At least in the afternoons.

He didn't look surprised to see them, just waved them over and signaled the bartender for a round. Which Granville obligingly paid for.

"What can I do for you two?" Dunham asked.

"We just have a few more questions about Mr. Brody," Emily said. "If you would be so kind?"

"Happy to help, if I can," was the reply. "What did you need to know?"

"We're trying to work out what route Brody might have been following when he left Barkerville for the last time," Granville said.

"You're trying to backtrack him? Smart," Dunham said, then lit a fresh cigarette and sat back. "Except that it's been more than thirty years. What do you expect to find?"

The slight edge to his voice was interesting. Granville didn't pause to consider the reaction—he didn't want to lose momentum. "We don't know, exactly. That's why we're asking. It could be some unimportant detail that you'd never have thought to mention that gives us a lead."

Dunham raised his glass, contemplated the golden contents for a moment. Then winked at them. "Just keep these coming and I'll answer whatever you want to ask. And don't blame me if you're bored cross-eyed."

"When was the last time you saw Mr. Brody?" Emily asked him.

"It was April 20th, the last Saturday of the month. And the year of the big fire, as I told you yesterday."

"Take us through that day," Granville said, ignoring the gibe.

"Everything?"

"Every detail you can remember."

The fellow took a drag from his cigarette, tapped the ash from the end into an empty beer bottle. "Well, you asked for it." He sat back, and started talking.

Granville suspected Dunham was deliberately trying to be as boring as possible, but he got too lost in his own memories to maintain it for long. Details poured out of the old miner, small things and bigger ones. The minutiae of living. Dunham remembered it all.

Probably more clearly than he remembered any day he'd lived recently. And with too many details for a memory he hadn't revisited in thirty-two years. Certainly for a day that was as dull as this one sounded.

Granville listened for anything out of place, a detail, even a tiny one, that could give them something new. A quick glance at Emily told him she was doing the same, her eyes sharp and her expression intent. Did she have the same reaction to what they were hearing as he did?

She looked up and they exchanged glances, the same question in both their eyes. Had they found Brody's killer? Or was there another reason Dunham remembered this day so well?

"I'm amazed you remember it all so clearly," Emily said, leaning forward. "It's so amazing, hearing all these details about a time before I was born. I've always been fascinated by the gold rushes, and newspaper reports of the day only give a hint of what it was like. You actually lived it."

Trust Emily to come right out and ask the question, but do it in such a way as to feed his ego. It was working, too. Dunham was beaming at her, showing no sign of hesitation or nerves, as he might have done had Granville asked something similar.

Of course, the fellow might be innocent of any wrongdoing. But he doubted it.

"It was an extraordinary time," Dunham was saying. "We knew it, too, most of the time. So many fortune seekers, all in one place. They came from everywhere—the United States, Canada, Europe, Britain and the Commonwealth."

"Is that why you remember everything so clearly?"

Dunham laughed. "Hardly. Trying to wrest gold out of the ground in a place like this? In a raw town that grew from nothing overnight? Most of it was backbreaking work and endless struggle, day after day. That was one of the few good days I can remember from that entire decade."

"And what made it a good day?" Emily asked.

"My partners and I had just opened our claim for the year, and taken more nuggets out in a single day than ever before. So we'd quit early, dressed in our finest, and hied ourselves off to the Wake Up Jake for a drink and a bit of dinner."

"Was Brody part of that?"

"Wasn't supposed to be. He was heading for his claim the next morning. Not that he ever admitted there was a claim. It was pretty obvious, though. He wasn't supporting himself and Belle on moonlight, after all," Dunham said with a sly grin.

"How did Mr. Brody and Belle end up at your dinner, then?" Emily promptly asked. "Wasn't the dinner to celebrate his departure?"

"Well, it was and it wasn't," Dunham said. "We were in the mood to celebrate our own improved fortunes, and young Lopes piped up and invited the two of 'em along. Said we were in the money, and why didn't they join us to celebrate Brody's departure for the creeks."

"It doesn't sound very memorable," Emily said, hitting just the right note.

"Well, it does when you know that Brody and Lopes hated each other. Which made it the best entertainment I'd seen all year. And I had a front row seat. Along with enough gold dust to pay for a really first rate meal. Bacon and beans gets beyond tiresome after the first month or so, y'know."

Emily didn't look convinced, but Granville nodded in recognition.

"That's true," he said. And the story was plausible enough. "Tell me more about this Lopes. Where is he these days?"

But it seemed young Lopes had been killed in a cave-in the following year. Yet another dead end.

One that didn't quite explain Dunham's clear memory of that day. Which didn't make him the villain. But it didn't clear him either.

On the other side of town, Scott and Trent would be asking their own questions. Granville spared a moment to wonder what details they were hearing. Perhaps they would be the ones to find a viable lead. He'd know soon enough.

CHAPTER 50

A FEW HOURS LATER, THE FOUR OF THEM GATHERED AGAIN IN THE private dining room at the Barkerville Hotel. Their lists and time-lines were still tacked to the walls, since the proprietress had obligingly locked the room for them, and given Granville the key. Once he'd handed over a substantial deposit, of course.

He considered it well worth the cost. It made their detecting easier when they could leave those charts in place. As long as no-one else saw them.

"They mostly couldn't remember much," Trent burst out as soon as they were all seated. "The old miners, I mean. Not even enough to pin down exactly when they'd last seen Brody, or what they'd talked about then. And we questioned them separately too. So it's not like they were stealing each other's stories, or something."

Scott nodded agreement. "Other than trying a couple of really nice ales, it feels like we wasted the afternoon," he said.

"Unless not being able to remember is the sign of a killer trying to hide his tracks," Trent said.

Emily was watching them carefully. "Which one, though?"

she asked. "If there were three of them who couldn't remember, how does that tell you one of them is a killer?"

Trent looked annoyed, then he lit up. "Maybe they all are?" he said.

Granville fought back a grin. "Working together, then?" he suggested blandly.

"Why not?" said Trent. "A conspiracy, right? It would explain why we can't get any answers."

"It's one possibility," he said diplomatically. "But then, what do we make of an old miner who seems able to remember every single detail of the last day he saw Brody?"

"Every detail?" Scott leaned forward. "This is Dunham you're talking about?"

"It is."

"You're not telling me he remembers what he ate for breakfast, on a particular day thirty years ago."

"Oh, but I'm afraid I am," Granville said with a broad grin.

"And it was *not* in any way an interesting day," Emily added with heavy emphasis.

"Then he must be our killer," Trent said, abandoning his previous theory without a qualm.

"Must he?" Granville said. "Why?"

"Well, because he's doing exactly what we thought the killer might do. He remembers every detail of the day Brody died."

"That won't stand up in court, I'm afraid."

"Well, Mr. Randall is a terrific lawyer. I'm sure he can talk this Dunham into a legal corner." Trent looked pleased with the thought.

Granville shook his head, more amused than before. Josiah Randall was their company lawyer, and the best defense lawyer he'd ever seen. He would definitely make mincemeat of Dunham's story. If he ever got the chance. "We'd need a prosecutor for a murder case. Not Randall."

"Well, the prosecutor can question Dunham until he confesses, then. If he's the killer, he'll crumble under the pressure."

"They won't prosecute without a body. And even if we found Robertson's remains, we don't have any evidence that Dunham is the killer."

"Can't the prosecutor grill him and make him confess?"

"I gather from Randall that it's not a good idea to ask questions you don't know the answer to on the witness stand," Granville said. "If there is another reason Dunham remembers that day so clearly, it could blow a hole in the best prepared case."

"Well, but…"

"Which day does your suspect remember so clearly?" Scott asked, cutting across Trent's argument, whatever it was going to be. He'd obviously had enough of the lad's theories.

He wasn't the only one. Emily was looking irritated, and his own patience was wearing thin.

"April 20th, 1868," Emily answered promptly.

Before Trent could get another question out, Granville noted with some amusement.

"And what else was goin' on that day?" Scott asked.

The question had everyone turning to look at the timeframe. Nothing else was listed for that specific day. And only Brody's departure was listed in the week following.

The room was silent for a moment.

Emily looked up from consulting her notebook. "Granville, Mr. Dunham only told us about seeing Brody once that day, at a dinner with several others. If that was really true, what happened at that dinner to fix the day in his memory? Do you recall him mentioning anything else that might have been important that day?"

"No. In fact, his description of that dinner was the only interesting thing he mentioned, apart from a supposed feud with another miner, Lopes."

"What kind of dinner?" Scott asked.

"A celebration, according to Dunham."

"For Brody?"

"No, for a good day on his new mine. Lopes was the one who invited Brody to join them for dinner."

"I thought he was the one who hated Brody."

"According to Dunham, who found the matter amusing, he was."

"Huh," said Trent. "Who else was there?"

Emily flipped forward a few pages, ran her finger down a few lines. "There were five men and two women. The men were Dunham and his three partners, and Brody. Belle was one of the women, and the other a dancer named Hildy."

As she spoke, Granville added the two names to the appropriate date on their timeline.

"What about the men?" Scott asked, leaning forward. "Do you have those names?"

Emily nodded, and read them off.

"None of those are men we spoke with," Granville said as he added them to the list. "The names aren't familiar to either of us. Scott? Trent? Do you recognize any of them?"

Scott and Trent exchanged glances.

"Two of them were among the men we just talked to," Scott said.

"You mean two of the three who remembered Brody clearly?" Emily asked.

"No," Trent said. "You'd think that, wouldn't you? O'Grady remembered him well. But McKillip? Well, he didn't."

"Or so he said," Scott added. "Which seems odd, given what Dunham told you."

"Did either of your two mention the send-off dinner on the 20th?" Granville asked.

"No. Someone has to be lying."

"They do," Granville underlined the two names, adding a large question mark behind the second name. Then another behind Dunham's name. "The real question is who. And why."

"What's your take on Dunham?" Scott asked.

"It's hard to imagine him being a killer. He seems so old," Emily said.

"He wouldn't be, thirty years past," Scott said. "We'll need to look deeper into Dunham and these two men."

"We should talk to Belle again," Trent said.

"No," Emily said. "You didn't see her face, while she was telling me the story. She was reliving all of it. And she looked so sad."

"Did she mention this dinner Dunham was talking about?"

"No," Emily said thoughtfully. "She never did."

"Then maybe she didn't tell you everything," Trent said.

"Or maybe Mr. Dunham was lying," Emily said fiercely.

Granville couldn't tell if she was angry on Belle's behalf, or if she was annoyed with Trent again.

"You think he was lying about who was at the dinner?" Trent said.

"Or perhaps about the dinner itself," Granville put in. "We don't know yet."

"Well, that's no help," Trent said.

"Maybe not. But that's detective work."

Emily looked from his face to Trent's scowl. "I'll talk to Belle," she said. "Thirty-two years is a long time to remember a dinner. Maybe something in Mr. Dunham's story will spark her memory."

"Maybe it'll help," Trent said. "But I still don't get how this dinner Dunham talked about is related to our missing miner really being a cattle thief. And if that's the newest information we have, why aren't we following up on it?"

"We will follow up," Granville said. "Finding out more about this dinner party that may or may not have happened will give us an excellent opportunity to do so."

"When do we get to say this is a waste of time, the case is too old, and go home?" Trent asked.

Trent's stubborn clinging to his current idea wasn't new. But it was time he learned the merits of flexible thinking.

"Not now," Granville said with a finality that had Trent staring at him with wide eyes.

Scott looked amused and Emily smiled a little.

Arguing in circles was getting them nowhere. But unfortunately the lad was right. If they didn't find a solid lead soon, with winter settling in fast, it would be time to head home. Much as he'd hate to leave with no more answers than they'd arrived with.

But it had been a long day, and they were all tired. Tired of the case, tired of talking about it, tired of not finding answers.

"We have a lot more information than we had yesterday, and we could all use a break. Let's have dinner, and start fresh tomorrow."

CHAPTER 51

By the following morning, Emily had decided it really did make sense to talk to Mrs. Darrow—Belle—again. The snow had let up overnight, and the sun was just rising. The early morning air was crisp and cool, and every breath felt invigorating. On a morning like this, even solving impossible cases felt possible.

The trek through the snow from the inn to the post office was a familiar one now. But all those stairs she had to climb up and down were icy, so she had to watch every step. A fall could mean disaster.

It wasn't until she reached the post office door that Emily wondered how she was going to ask Belle yet more questions. Standing outside the far too familiar door she wished she'd asked Granville to talk to the postmistress. Belle had a soft spot for him. And maybe his way of asking questions would spark a memory for her.

Too late now. He'd already gone to talk to Mr. Dunham again. And Scott and Trent were taking another shot at getting some clarity from O'Grady and McKillip, the other two names on their short list. So it was up to her to tackle this one.

She'd need to find the right balance of asking hard questions without hurting the poor woman further. Or offending her so badly she'd never talk to any of them again.

Was she up for it? She'd have to be. Drawing in a deep breath, Emily pushed the door open before she could change her mind.

The main room was empty except for the postmistress, which was a stroke of luck. Belle looked pleased to see Emily, though her tone was wry. "Didn't you ask enough questions last time?"

She smiled. "I thought so, but apparently not. I hope you don't mind?"

Belle looked world-worn this morning, blinking darkened lashes as if fighting back tears as she shook her head. "You're still trying to find out what happened to my Robby?"

"Yes, ma'am."

"Then ask."

"It's about that send-off dinner for Robby that the two of you attended before he left town."

"What dinner?"

"On the last night he was in town? I was told there was a dinner that night, partly to bid him farewell, with the two of you, and five others attending," Emily said.

"Who have you been talking to?"

"Dunham."

"He's mis-remembering, the old fool. There was no dinner. Brody packed up one morning, and was gone that afternoon. He hated goodbyes. He'd never have agreed to a "send-off" dinner if that's what Dunham is saying."

"You're certain? It was a long time ago. And Mr. Dunham described the event in great detail," Emily said, working hard not to show how important this was.

"More fool him. And of course I'm sure. He was superstitious, was my Robby. Though he'd never have admitted it. He didn't like to announce his plans to all and sundry."

Or maybe he didn't want to be ambushed along the way,

Emily thought. Which would be of particular concern if he really had found gold. His own, or someone else's.

And he really wouldn't want anyone to know his plans if they included leaving the area for good. And taking the gold with him.

She didn't mention that possibility to Mrs. Darrow now. There was no point. The woman had suffered enough, in her grief over her missing lover.

"Do you remember a dinner party with yourself and your Robby, Mr. Dunham and his three partners, and a Miss Hildy?"

"Which three partners?"

"Lopes, O'Grady and McKillip."

Mrs. Darrow frowned a little, then laughed. "Dunham told you those were the attendees? He's having you on, that one. Or he's gone soft in the head. My Robby and Lopes couldn't stand each other. And Hildy and I weren't exactly sociable. My voice was always better than hers, and she resented it, she did. Long time ago, that was."

There was no doubting the certainty in her voice. Emily even felt a little sorry for Miss Hildy, whoever she'd been, having to face Belle's disdain. And she couldn't help but wonder exactly how good Miss Hildy's voice really was.

After a few more equally unproductive questions that served to confirm that in Mrs. Darrow's mind, there had been no dinner remotely resembling the one that Mr. Dunham had so carefully described, Emily was almost ready to take her leave. "One more thing. Do you know what happened to any of them?" she asked.

"Hildy got the chills the following year and died that spring. Dunham, O'Grady and McKillip are still around. And I heard Lopes had some luck at a mine along the Chilcotin, and ended up back in Victoria."

Lopes was still alive? That wasn't the story Mr. Dunham had told. "I'd like to talk to Mr. Lopes," Emily said neutrally. "Do you know where he was working?"

"No idea. Something about running a sawmill, I think. Though I doubt you'd find him, now. It was twenty years ago, at least."

Emily jotted down a quick note, then looked up. "As the postmistress, and a long time resident, you'd know a great deal about the people who live here, wouldn't you?" she asked.

"I would," Belle replied. "Why? What do you want to know?"

"What can you tell me about Mr. Dunham?"

"How do you mean?"

"What kind of man is he? And why did he remain in Barkerville?" Emily said. "Any details or quirks you might remember about him from the time before your Robby vanished might be really helpful."

That earned her a hard look. "You think he had something to do with my Robby's disappearance?"

She should have phrased her question better, Emily realized. Belle was a sharp one, and when it came to her lost beau, she didn't miss much.

"I think Mr. Dunham told us a story that you just proved untrue," she said carefully. "And without knowing more about the man, we can't judge if he's just an old man mis-remembering his past. Or something else."

Belle's eyes narrowed a little and the corners of her mouth hardened as she considered Emily's face. "Is that true?" she demanded.

"Yes," Emily said, glad she could give her an honest answer. "Finding what happened to your Robby is too important to settle for easy answers and assumptions."

The other woman nodded at that, and her expression softened. "I'm glad to hear you feel that way. And I'll tell you what I can."

"I appreciate that."

"Well, let's see. I don't remember what year Dunham arrived in Barkerville. He was just one of the miners, coming and going. But he was a generous tipper, and when he was flush, which wasn't often, he'd stand a round or two for the house. I first remember noticing him sometime after Robby and I got together."

"So several years before Robby vanished?"

"That's right. Like all the miners, he was in town for months, then gone for months more. Dunham blended in, mostly, wasn't a violent man or a mean drunk like some, but he wasn't the fancy dancer or smooth talker others were. He was… one of the miners. Now I think about it, they blurred together over the years. The ones who didn't stand out."

Emily found the description interesting. Especially compared to the thirty-two-years-older man she and Granville had met. Who was a talker, and personable, if not smooth.

Had thirty-two years polished him? Or simply perfected his act?

"Were your Robby and Mr. Dunham friendly?"

"They never seemed unfriendly. But he wasn't one of my Robby's intimates. And when we did socialize, he might be there, but only on the fringes of any group."

"So your Robby wouldn't have confided in him?"

"Never. Robby seldom shared information, even with me."

"Do you remember any interactions between the two men in the months before your Robby left town for the last time?"

"No. I doubt I ever saw them together in that last week, and surely not in any way that was memorable."

"Did you ever get the sense they had known each other before Barkerville?" Emily asked on impulse.

"Before the gold brought everyone here?" Belle's eyes sought the rough board ceiling she looked as if she was revisiting those years for a moment. "No, I never got that sense."

"No tension between them? Or harsh words?"

"Not that I recall. And everyone loved my Robby. I'd have remembered quarrels, or even tension, I think. It was so unlike him, you see."

"Mr. Dunham, you mean?"

"I was thinking of my Robby, but him too. Neither of them showed their feelings much in public."

That struck Emily as an odd trait for Belle's Robby and the man who'd told her about the dinner party in such detail to share. But for Thomas Robertson, the Rustler King, and the

Mr. Dunham of thirty years ago? It could be a very telling trait.

Granville had told them the Pinkerton's records described Mr. Robertson as a ruthless criminal with a brutal past. Until the law got too close and he lost himself in a crowd of fellow miners.

What might be hidden in Mr. Dunham's past?

"How did the two of them interact then, do you remember?" she asked, pushing a little.

Belle frowned. "Well, I don't know that I noticed. Not really. Dunham was just there, like wallpaper. And Robby mostly ignored him."

And that was even more interesting, given what she'd just said about how friendly her beau had been. "Did your Robby ignore many people?"

Belle stared at her. "No, now that you ask. My Robby was easy with people, enjoyed them. Ignoring Mr. Dunham? It wasn't obvious enough even for me to notice at the time. But when I think about it now—it was there. And out of character for him."

"So would that suggest to you that the two men might have known each other before Barkerville?" Emily persisted.

"I could be wrong about what a very old memory means. But yes, I suppose it could."

Belle's face was bland, but there was an edge to her voice that suddenly alerted Emily to a danger she hadn't suspected. And left her wondering if she'd just stepped into a pile of trouble.

Was Belle now suspecting Dunham might be an old enemy, with reason to kill Robby Brody, as Emily was? She needed to distract her.

"Granville will find out for you. If they did know each other, that is. Though it probably isn't relevant," she said quickly, hoping Belle would respect Granville's obvious expertise. "And I'll tell you the minute we learn anything."

Belle nodded, but her lips had tightened in a way that only increased Emily's concern.

"Until we do, please don't let on to Mr. Dunham or anyone else that you've remembered a possible tension between them. It could slow down our search for your Robby," Emily said, trying to sound firm and confident without giving Belle any ideas she hadn't already come up with.

And hoping she hadn't made things worse.

Belle nodded, and gave her a small smile. Which didn't help.

It left Emily with a lot to think about, but no questions that felt safe to ask Belle.

Not yet, anyway. She had a lot of thinking to do first. And she needed to talk to Granville. Maybe even warn him?

CHAPTER 52

As Emily climbed up the last slippery steps and crossed the snow covered sidewalk towards the inn door, she pondered everything she'd just heard. And wondered just how much of a mess she'd made of her conversation with Belle.

The conversation had started out so promisingly, too.

If Belle was telling the truth, and that dinner of Mr. Dunham's had never happened, why would he tell her and Granville about it in such detail? His story was so over-explained, it drew attention to itself.

Was the old man remembering a different occasion? Had Belle simply forgotten the dinner? Or was something more sinister at work, as—thanks to her questions—both she and Belle had begun to suspect.

Had Mr. Dunham's story been a bold-faced lie from beginning to end? But why would he bother? What was he really up to?

After this many years, Dunham's story would be hard to prove or disprove. And his motive for telling it even murkier.

It could be some form of misdirection, enticing them to look in one direction when the reality lay in another direction entirely. Such as in Mr. Dunham's past. The one before Barkerville.

His perhaps questionable past? Tall tales aside, something in Emily was convinced he had one. And a lot to hide. Though she couldn't pinpoint exactly when she'd begun to feel that way.

Given how difficult tracking down Mr. Robertson's history had proven, Mr. Dunham's past was likely to be even trickier. Unless the Pinkertons had a file on him, too?

She stopped walking to consider it. If they had a file on Mr. Dunham, would they be willing to share it with Granville, like they had Mr. Robertson's file? But what if Mr. Dunham had also changed his name before arriving in Barkerville? Then what?

The wind picked up again. Emily shivered as a cold draft sneaked under her scarf and down her neck. She resumed walking towards the inn, her steps brisk and her mind entirely focused on the case.

Whatever Mr. Dunham was hiding, it would have to be some-thing very different from the story of a cosy good-bye dinner with friends, for sure.

And Belle's recollections of those days suggested that the opposite might be true—that Mr. Dunham was an enemy, not a friend. Maybe even the killer, as Belle seemed to have so quickly assumed.

That thought still made sense to Emily, too, though she wasn't basing it on very much proof. And it only worked if Mr. Robertson was indeed dead, of course.

If he was, and Mr. Dunham had killed him, everything fell into place.

Except the motive. Which grew murkier with every detail they learned.

For one thing, which of the two identities sharing one body had Mr. Dunham wanted dead? Robby Brody? Or Thomas Robertson?

From everything they'd learned so far, the two were very different, inspiring very different reactions in the people they'd met.

And inspiring different reasons to kill them, too?

It seemed logical. Which only confused the situation further. And brought her straight back to motive.

How could they prove murder if they couldn't find the killer's motive? And a motive for killing Thomas Robertson seemed much more obvious than a motive for killing his seemingly charming alter ego.

Thomas Robertson was a ruthless criminal. What was Robby Brody? Other than missing.

She turned that thought over in her mind. Again. Maybe Trent had been right. That information changed everything. If not exactly the way that he thought it did.

After all, given Thomas Robertson's past, how likely was it that such a man had "gone clean", as the penny dreadfuls liked to put it? No matter how well the people here thought of Beau Brody.

And if he hadn't changed? If Beau Brody was just a front? Then it put the years their missing miner had spent in the Cariboo in a whole new light.

Even if he'd found a mine, would he have been willing to do the work to make it pay off? Yet how else could a crook, even a successful one, make a fortune out here? All without making any of the locals suspicious. It wasn't possible.

Probably.

Unless it was.

And even more annoyingly, the fellow could still be alive, somewhere. Under yet another alias. Probably building a criminal empire of some kind.

This case had done it again. There were too many possibilities, and an equal number of unknowns. It made her head hurt.

And what if Belle ignored her warning and went to confront Mr. Dunham herself. Then what?

Surely the postmistress wouldn't be that foolish.

Except there had been that look in her eye.

She needed to talk to Granville about Mr. Dunham. And Belle. And especially about Beau Brody.

Before Belle went looking for Mr. Dunham.

Sʜᴇ ɢᴏᴛ that chance a half hour later. Since they arrived in Barkerville, she and Granville had embraced the habit of stopping for a mid-morning break, just the two of them. She'd suggested it, as a chance for a little privacy in the middle of the chaos that was their current case. Granville seemed to value it, too. It was proving to be one of their favorite times of the day.

Today they'd retreated to the quiet of their hotel room and asked that tea and biscuits be brought up for them. It proved the perfect place to tell him about her recent conversation with Belle.

Her new husband was a good listener, and Emily was already feeling somewhat less tense. He didn't miss that, either.

"You're still worrying about it, aren't you?" he asked. "We're investigators. We have to ask leading questions if we're to learn anything."

"Surely there are limits?"

"Of course there are. And I trust your good judgement of people to keep you from pushing past that limit."

"But in this case…"

"Did you learn something from the conversation that will help us move the case forward?"

"Maybe…?" she said, unwilling at this point to rely on any lead actually helping them solve this miserable case."

"Did you ask the question in a way that would make clear your own suspicions?"

"Well, no." Emily thought about it for a moment. "She guessed, though. Just from what I did say."

He gave her a shrewd look. "Because you had to tell her something she didn't know."

"Yes."

"And you needed to find out if that information was accurate."

That was true, too. Emily nodded.

"Was there any way to uncover the information you needed without asking Mrs. Darrow?"

"No. No, I don't think there was."

"You had no choice."

Emily wasn't quite convinced of that. "I couldn't see another one," she said.

He laughed. "Fair enough. Look at it this way. These are both adults. Even if Mrs. Darrow confronted Dunham and outright accused him of murdering Brody—which is unlikely—he isn't going to react. What could he do, after all? Shoot her?"

"I suppose not," Emily replied. "It would hardly help him, would it?

She laughed a little, ate the last bite of her pastry. "Thank you, I do feel better for talking about it. But I'd feel better still if we talked to her together. And soon," she said.

A loud rap on the door of their room had Granville striding to the door and flinging it open.

Trent stood there, breathing hard. "Come quick. There's been a shooting."

CHAPTER 53

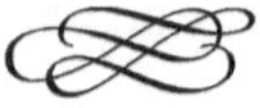

"Where is the shooting?" he asked Trent.

"Down at the Ace of Clubs pub."

"Belle?" Emily said quickly, the frown back on her face.

"The postmistress?" Trent said. "I don't know. She was there. I think. Maybe. Come quick."

"Anyone dead?" Granville asked.

"I don't know that, either. Scott's gone to see."

"Then we'd best join him, and find out," he said. "Go on ahead. I'll be there in five minutes."

As he closed the door, Emily moved to stand beside him, and put her hand on his arm "Is this my fault? I'm the one that talked to her about all of it."

"Were you holding a gun?"

She just looked at him.

"Then it isn't your fault."

"Maybe not in a court of law," she said. "But it doesn't mean my actions had nothing to do with it."

She was right, of course. "That's possible, but we don't even know what happened yet," he said, crossing to the bureau and reaching for his gun and holster.

"Then I'm coming with you. I'm part of this case, too. Especially when something I said might have triggered this."

One look at her face told him he'd have difficulty arguing her out of it. Even if there had been time. And she had a point. She was part of the case, very much so.

"If anyone is still shooting, we'll need to keep well back," was all he said.

She gave him a strained smile and quickly gathered her things.

NOT QUITE TEN MINUTES LATER, he and Emily joined an eerily quiet crowd clustered on the sidewalk outside the Ace of Clubs. There was no blood in the crusted snow, no sign of an injury. Or a body.

"Dunham's favorite watering hole," he murmured to her.

She nodded, her eyes fixed on the door, which was ajar. If there was trouble inside, they couldn't hear it. If there had been shooting, it had stopped. Why?

What was going on in there?

He glanced around for Scott, who was easy to find, being the tallest in the crowd. Feeling Granville's eyes on him, his partner turned his head, then worked his way through the onlookers to join them, Trent at his heels.

"You know anything?" he asked them.

"Not much," Scott said. "Everyone was outside when I got here. An argument and some kind of gunfight is the best I've got."

"The gunman still inside?"

"Gunmen, I think. But you know witnesses. Everyone saw something different."

Granville nodded. It still amazed him just how different those stories could be.

"No police yet?"

"Constable McCall went to Richfield this morning. Some-one's gone to fetch him."

"Good. Anyone dead?"

"Don't know that either."

"It sounds pretty quiet now. Time to go inside," he said. "You with me?"

"Lead on," his partner said.

Granville put a hand on Emily's arm. "Stay here?"

She gave a tiny nod and he squeezed her arm. He looked over at Trent. "You too."

Trent looked at him as if to argue, then glanced at Emily and changed his mind.

A sudden shriek coming from inside the tavern had them all freezing where they stood. It was a woman's voice. Mrs. Darrow?

Emily might have been right to worry about her.

Granville drew his gun. He hadn't heard a shot, but he wasn't taking any chances. With a glance at Scott, who drew his own gun and nodded back, he stepped inside.

AT FIRST GLANCE the bar was empty. Gunsmoke hung thick in the air. Several shots had been fired at some point, but if there was blood, he couldn't pick up that coppery smell over the reek of gunpowder, stale beer and spilled whisky.

His eyes swept the room, taking in the chaotic remains of whatever had happened here, trying to make sense of it. No sign of a gun. Or a body. Overturned chairs and bar stools spoke of a fight.

But where were the combatants?

Where was the woman who'd cried out?

He spotted the bartender, still crouched down behind the bar. Catching his gaze, he asked a silent question. A shake of the head was his answer. The gray-haired bartender didn't move from his defensive position.

At least one other person was still here. The woman who'd shrieked. Probably the shooter—or shooters—was still here, too. But where?

Scott had stopped just inside the door, gun drawn. They exchanged glances. Judging by his partner's intent look, and the steady aim of his revolver, he'd reached the same conclusion.

He caught a slight movement behind Scott from the corner of his eye and swiveled, gun at the ready. Emily!

"You need to wait outside until it's safe," he said quietly. "Now."

To his relief she didn't argue, just melted back through the door.

Granville checked out the room again, his gaze moving slowly over the debris littering the sawdust floor. A flash of movement behind an overturned table against the far wall caught his eye. He focused on that area, a tilt of his head signalling Scott of what he'd seen.

Then, nothing. The two of them watched the room, like two hawks he'd once seen in Alaska, waiting for the slightest twitch to give away a prey's location.

There.

Another tiny motion behind another overturned table, maybe ten feet away from the first. Two opponents, then. Were there more?

He still couldn't smell blood. No way to know if either of the combatants was injured.

He held his gun ready, finger loosely on the trigger. He let his eyes take in the entire scene, his whole body focused on that next hint of motion. But there was nothing more.

Only two then? And if one or both were injured, perhaps dying, they'd need help, and fast.

The reek of gunpowder was fading, dissipating despite the stale air. The last shot had been a while ago. Time to move.

He turned to Scott, gestured his intentions. Scott nodded. "I'll cover you," he agreed softly, his gun continuing to sweep the room.

His own revolver at the ready, Granville circled around, picking his way carefully through the mess towards where he'd seen the first flicker of movement. As he rounded the overturned table nearest the bar, he could see a dark figure huddled motionless behind it, clutching his arm.

It was Dunham. With a small pistol laying beside him, as if he'd suddenly dropped it. There was no blood on the floor, and only a trickle running through his fingers.

He was alive then. But very pale. Being shot was no joke at any age, but for an old-timer like Dunham? Some wouldn't survive it, or the infection that often followed.

Granville quickly checked Dunham's pulse, which was steady, if weaker than he'd like. Shock, most likely. With luck it wouldn't be something worse.

Moving more quickly now, gun still drawn, Granville approached the other hint of movement he'd seen. As he got angled closer, he saw another still figure. Her full skirts told him it was a woman, lying crumpled on her side.

What had happened here?

Closer yet, he could see the dainty pistol still clutched in her hand.

Belle.

Emily would be upset. At least the postmistress seemed to be breathing. He couldn't see blood on her, nor any sign of a wound. Her face was ice pale, and she wasn't moving. Unconscious?

Her pulse was strong but uneven, and there was no obvious sign of an injury. But she hadn't stirred, which meant trouble.

Both of them needed a doctor. Immediately.

But there was one thing he needed to do first.

Knowing Scott had his back, he holstered his own revolver and collected both pistols. Shoving them in the back of his belt, he returned to the bar,

"Call a medic. It's safe now. I've got their guns."

"It's too early in the day for a gunfight," the bartender grumbled, rising slowly and wincing as he did so. "This isn't the old days. What were they thinking?"

From the heavy lines in his face and his gnarled fingers, Granville suspected his joints were paining him. His reflexes in a gunfight would be poor. Probably why he'd drawn the early shift. Drunken fights grew more likely as the night wore on.

"They'll both need a doctor. Can you call one here?"

"Dunham's still alive? He went down like a rock," the fellow sounded stunned. "And the woman?"

"Both of them," he said. "But possibly not for long if that doctor doesn't get here fast."

The bartender nodded and turned to the phone on the wall. "I'll tell him it's urgent."

CHAPTER 54

A COMMOTION FROM BEHIND HIM HAD GRANVILLE SWIVELING around, his gun drawn.

Both of the combatants appeared to have revived, and against all odds they were standing glaring at each other across the ten feet of overturned furniture that separated them. Given their expressions, he was very glad he'd already taken away their weapons. He just hoped the doctor would arrive before one—or both—of them collapsed from overstrain.

Or figured out how to kill the other one.

"You shot me!" Dunham accused her.

Mrs. Darrow snorted inelegantly. "I barely winged you. You're just lucky I'm a good shot. I could've killed you if I'd wanted."

"You! Ha!"

"Better than you," she said, holding up her arm to show him the neat bullet hole through the widest part of her sleeve. "You didn't even get close to my heart."

"You were trying to kill me."

"So you figured you'd kill me in return?"

"What else was I supposed to do? You pulled a gun on me."

"You're still alive, aren't you?"

"Because you can't shoot straight."

"No, because I have some questions about my Robby. If I don't like your answers, *then* I'd kill you."

"Oh, you're going to kill me because your boyfriend left you? *Thirty-two years* ago?"

"Wrong again. Because he didn't leave me. Someone killed him. Was it you?"

"You're just lucky he's dead!"

"I knew it! I knew you were the one as killed him!"

"You don't know anything, you stupid woman."

"I know you killed my Robby!" she shrieked. "We should have had years together."

"He'd have killed you long before now," he said. "You were living in a fairy tale. A deadly one."

"How can you say that? I was his Belle, and he was my Beau."

Dunham snorted. "Your Beau? He's a flat out con artist and a thief. Probably a killer too. I saw it in his eyes. You don't know him at all."

"How can you say that?

"Because it's the truth, whether you like it or not."

"You're just trying to justify your killing him. And for what? He was broke. It's why he left—to dig out more money for us to live on."

"He dug out money, all right. Right out of other people's pockets."

"You're just making up lies to justify killing him. Which you did, as soon's he left town."

Still clutching his bleeding shoulder, Dunham glared at her. "Fine talk from a fool who just tried to kill me."

"I told you, I wasn't trying to kill you."

He ignored that. "And over a man who's not worth spit."

"Not worth spit…?" she shrieked, pulling out a second pistol she'd concealed somewhere in her skirts. "I'll show you not worth it!"

It was time to break this up, before these two really did manage to murder each other. Granville stepped forward from one direction, Scott from the other, each with a gun pointed directly at one of the combatants.

"You'll be dead before you can pull that trigger," he told Belle, his revolver centered on her heart. "And I guarantee I don't miss."

She glared at him, her small pistol holding steady.

"What if your Beau is still alive?" he said. "If you kill Dunham now, you'll never know."

"What? No. That's not possible. You're lying, just trying to save this snake."

Granville watched the pistol waver, just a little, as her finger tightened on the trigger. He didn't want to shoot her. He had to find the words to stop her.

If only for Emily's sake. She seemed to quite like the post-mistress.

"That snake referred to your Beau in the present tense," he said firmly. "Did you notice?"

"But… What? What are you saying?"

He watched her pistol lower a little. And released the breath he'd been holding. She was listening, at least.

He risked a glance at Dunham, who was standing very still, his eyes riveted on Scott's revolver, which was trained on him.

Good.

"I'm saying if Dunham thinks your Beau is alive, then he didn't kill him."

"And you… You've been investigating, looking for him. For my Beau. Is he alive?"

"He could be. We haven't found anything that tells us otherwise."

"But… He didn't come back. Why didn't he come back, if he's alive?"

The pistol hung at her side now. She was focused on him, Dunham forgotten.

"Perhaps he couldn't."

She stared at him. "You mean… he was injured, maybe lost his memory?"

"Or he's in jail for his crimes. Unless he found himself another Belle, a younger one," Dunham spat out, apparently unable to resist now that she wasn't pointing a gun at him.

He'd forgotten about Scott's revolver. Which fired, the bullet lodging itself in the wooden pillar right beside Dunham's ear.

Granville fought back a grin. Apparently his partner found the fellow irritating too.

Both of the would-be combatants jumped, and cringed. Neither were seasoned fighters. Not anymore, if they ever had been. Good.

"Enough of this," Granville said.

Striding up to her, he relieved Belle of her second pistol. His gun held at the ready, as was Scott's, his attention shifted to Dunham.

"What do you know?" he asked. "And let's have the truth, this time."

"I told you the truth."

"Perhaps. But not all of it. Now let's have the rest. How do you know Brody was a criminal?"

An outraged shriek from the postmistress vanished the moment Scott raised his revolver. Granville ignored the byplay, focusing on the emotions shifting across Dunham's face.

"Well?" he said as the silence stretched.

"He was blackmailing me," Dunham burst out. "We finally made a big strike, and he wanted a tenth of it. A tenth! After all our hard work, he does nothing and gains more than any of us?"

A quick motion from Belle, stilled when Scott glared at her.

Granville gave Dunham a hard look. "Tell me about the blackmail."

"I can't."

"You will."

"But… I haven't done anything wrong. She's the one that shot me. I'm the victim here," he said.

"He shot at me, too!" Belle said. "And he missed twice, the idiot." She gestured towards the wall behind her.

Granville turned to look. In addition to the rent in her sleeve he'd seen earlier, there was indeed a bullet hole in a beam just behind her head.

If it was fresh, that hole in the wall corroborated her story. He swung his gaze back to Dunham, who paled, and flinched. Yep, it was fresh.

"About the blackmail. You were saying?" he prompted the fellow.

"So maybe I was known in Seattle. And maybe the sheriff would have been happy to know where I was. Then," Dunham spat out. "This many years later, no-one would care."

Interesting. "But when Brody was blackmailing you, it was five years later. And obviously you thought the sheriff would have cared then. So what did you do?"

A stubborn silence.

Even more interesting. But for the moment, finding what had happened to their missing miner was his priority. "How did Brody know about you?"

"I don't know! And I never found out. But he had details… He knew too much. And he wasn't just trying it on, conning me. He would've turned me in. I had to pay. And keep paying."

Dunham didn't seem to connect Brody with the gang of rustlers the fellow had led as Thompson. "So why should we believe you didn't kill him?"

"Because I couldn't. He was a better shot, and impossible to sneak up on. Then, when we hit our strike—I wasn't lying about that part—I suddenly had money. Enough to get free."

"How?"

Dunham shrugged. "He said if I gave him enough, he'd leave town. And never come back. So I did. And he did."

"Where was he going?"

"No idea. He never gave a thing away, that one."

"He's alive?" Belle said, her voice gone thready. "And he was leaving me?"

A COMMOTION at the door signaled the arrival of Constable McCall, who rushed in along with Emily and what looked like half the gathered crowd right behind him.

Seeing Granville and Scott had the situation well under control, the constable headed straight for them. Emily spotted Mrs. Darrow where she'd landed in a sobbing heap on the floor, and arrowed straight to her.

Deciding she wasn't in danger, he turned to meet the constable's barrage of questions. He barely had time to give him a quick overview of his part in this when the doctor arrived, out of breath.

"Where are the victims?" he demanded.

It was some time before things were straightened out. Once the combatants were carried out on stretchers, heading for the hospital to be treated—one for a gunshot wound, the other for shock—Granville and the constable turned to the bartender.

"You were here when this started?" McCall asked.

The bartender paled and nodded.

"What exactly happened here? And who started the shooting?" the constable asked.

"I didn't see all of it," the bartender said, quickly pouring four whiskeys. He passed one each to Granville, Scott, and McCall, and downed the fourth. Tipping his glass in thanks, Granville followed suit, as did Scott.

McCall waved his away—"On duty, after all," he said.

Granville savored the harsh burn of the whiskey. It felt good in the aftermath of the shooting, even at this early hour. The bar was cold and smelled of gunpowder and cold air from the doors that had been left open. Behind them, the other patrons surged inside, full of questions and chatter, retelling their own experiences.

"So what did you see?" Constable McCall asked the bartender.

"Dunham was over there, at his usual table. Along with his

buddies," and the fellow pointed to the same table where Granville had found Dunham the day before.

"Mrs. Darrow came flying in, and before I had time to do more than look around, she was confronting him. Screeching, she was. Holding a pistol on him and demanding answers."

Shaking his head, the fellow reached for the whiskey and refilled all three glasses without even asking. He threw back his own drink and wiped his mouth with a not too steady hand before continuing. "Her voice was out of control, but her face wasn't. Harsh it was, and focused. I've seen that look before, you can't mistake it. You're sure Dunham's still alive?"

Hadn't the fellow seen that last confrontation? "For now," Granville said. "What was she asking him?"

"Mrs. Darrow? I couldn't make it out. It was busy in here this morning, and most hadn't noticed the confrontation yet."

He nodded. Given the circumstances, that made sense.

It seems it made sense to McCall, too. "What happened then?" he asked.

"She was waving that pistol round, and then he stood up suddenly and drew his own and aimed it at her. For a second I was sure she'd be dead, but somehow she shot him first. His shot went wide."

"He shot her, too?" McCall asked, looking surprised.

"Tried to. Shot went wild, I guess."

So shooting women wasn't acceptable in Barkerville, either. Granville and Scott exchanged glances.

"Any idea why she was unconscious when I got here?" Granville asked. "Did someone hit her?"

"Don't know. People were panicking. Mostly trying to get out of here. Last I saw, the two of 'em were both still standing, facing each other with guns drawn."

"Were there more shots?"

The bartender shrugged. "If there was, I couldn't tell."

The fellow reached for the whiskey bottle and offered it around again, but Granville waved it off. It was far too early for heavy drinking, though he made no comment as the bartender poured himself a third drink.

"Thanks for the info," he said instead.

"I may have more questions for you later," McCall said to the bartender. "But if you think of anything else in the meantime, let me know."

The fellow nodded, and McCall turned to Granville. "I need to take a better look at the scene before it gets any more trampled. I'd appreciate hearing what you saw unfolding here."

The three of them turned to look at the area McCall had cordoned off once the two shooters had been taken to the small local hospital. The bar patrons who'd waited outside had since hurried to seat themselves at tables as close as possible to the site of the attack, and the buzz of conversation had been rising steadily higher.

Granville couldn't see Emily, though. He scanned the room twice before he spotted her. She and Trent had seated themselves at a crowded table, and both appeared deep in conversation. Granville recognized a couple of the old miners as part of the group.

No guessing required as to the topic of that conversation. Not something he wanted to bring McCall in on just yet, though.

"I wouldn't mind having a closer look at the scene myself," Granville told McCall. "There are a couple of things that have been bothering me."

CHAPTER 55

IT WAS MID-AFTERNOON BEFORE EMILY FINALLY GOT A CHANCE TO talk to Granville. By which time she was dying to find out what he'd learned. And to tell him what she'd uncovered.

To her surprise, it wasn't the conversations she'd had with Belle that had been the most enlightening—not the one in the bar, or the one in the hospital. No, it was the chat she'd had with Mr. Dunham's buddies in the bar. After she'd talked to Belle the first time, while she was waiting for Granville to finish up with Constable McCall.

Trent had been there too, but she suspected he'd missed the bit of information that had caught her attention. And to be fair, she'd probably have missed it too, if she hadn't heard so much of Belle's story, in her own words. And started to like her.

There was no sign of Granville, so she'd hurried up to their room to splash water on her face and straighten her hair. And if she hadn't seen him coming up behind her in the mirror, she'd have jumped a foot.

"You look deep in thought," he said, placing his hands on her shoulders in a subtle caress. "Why so serious?"

"I hate this," she said, hearing how upset she was in the words as she spoke them. "Right now, I just want to go home. And be done with it."

"What's happened?" he said, leading her to the bed and sitting down beside her. He took her hand in his.

"It's this whole investigation. We never should have come this far, chasing a thirty-two year old case."

His hand tightened on hers, support and understanding in one. She gave him a half-smile. "I'm sorry, but that's how I feel. Right now, anyway."

"I can see that," he said, giving her a concerned look. "Though you were more positive this morning. What changed for you?"

"I guess I never wanted to know what lived underneath the myth and the glamour of the gold rush days," she said, her breath hitching a little. "I grew up on those stories."

"Stories told you by a man who never had a chance to follow that dream himself," Granville said softly. "And newspapers enthralled with tales of hardship and riches."

She nodded, and clutched his hand harder. "I suppose that's true. But you lived it. Did you ever regret it? Going to the Klondike, seeking gold, I mean?"

"Never," he began.

"And don't just tell me that's because if you hadn't gone, you wouldn't have met me, either," she said.

He laughed. "I wasn't planning on it. Although it's true."

She made a face at him. "Tell me the rest of it. The truth."

"I went to find gold," he said. "Along with so many others. And came back broke. Like so many others."

"Go on."

"But the journey itself, everything from the hardships we survived to the camaraderie to the beauty and challenge of the country up there. Alaska and the Yukon—I can't describe them to someone who hasn't been there."

"I'd like to see it," she said at once.

"Then we'll go," he said. "Though this area has something of the same feel—and likely had more of it thirty-some years ago."

She thought about the journey back from Cottonwood in the snow and blowing winds. She'd been afraid, but there had been an exhilaration in it too. "I can see it, a little bit."

He nodded. "Part of that is because you've lived on the edge of a wilderness your entire life. For me, coming from England— the isolation and the ruggedness of everything here? It's nothing I could have imagined. And living through the hardships and challenges of a gold rush, having that be your life for more than a year and a half—it changes you."

Listening to him as he talked of that time, she could see it in his eyes, the impact it had on him. "I wouldn't recognize the man you were when you first arrived from England, would I?" she asked.

He grinned at that. "If such a thing were even possible? Probably not."

"So what do you think about the men who came here, to the Cariboo, chasing gold. Would they have similar experiences?"

"Some of them, probably. Even many of them. Others discovered a life they wanted in pursuit of the next gold rush."

"Like the men who followed the gold rush to the Omenica?"

He nodded. "And then on to the Australia gold rush, for some."

"What about those who stayed here?"

"Many seem to have found a home here, and were content to mine just enough gold to live on."

"Oh." She thought about that, and the conversation she'd had. "Many. But not all?"

"Not all," he agreed. "There are more stories in a gold camp than you can imagine. But what upset you so badly? Or should that be who?"

She wasn't quite ready to answer that. "What would make someone so desperate for gold that they'd murder for it?"

"You've worked enough cases to know it isn't just the gold. It's what it stands for."

Yes, that made sense. "Wealth, you mean. Or an easy life?"

"Or whatever is most important to them, that they think money can give them. Yes."

"It isn't really about gold mining, then, is it?"

"Yes and no. Because the newspaper stories are about those who strike it rich. That dream of unbelievable wealth is what draws most. For some, though, it's the grand adventure of it all."

"So if the gold rush dream is striking it rich, then most would-be miners, like Mr. Thompson, share that desire for money. So which part isn't about mining for gold?"

"The part where human nature comes in. A mining town can be a pressure cooker, a mining camp is worse. People spend a lot of time in close quarters with other people, and in the depth of winter there is nowhere to go, to get away. Petty grievances, personality clashes—things that would be quickly forgotten anywhere else can blow up here. "

Emily nodded as she listened. She could almost feel it. A small smoky cabin, the bitter cold and endless wind outside. The disappointment of working endlessly on a claim that wasn't paying out. Men who lived, slept, ate and worked shoulder to shoulder in cramped quarters.

"What about jealousy? If there arc only a few women with so many men…"

"Yes," he said. "Jealousy, envy, greed. Even fear. All can be deadly." He paused, considered her expression. "This is about Belle, isn't it?"

"Yes."

"What did she say?"

He looked concerned, and she hurried to re-assure him. "It wasn't her. It was Mr. Curtin. Also O'Grady and McKillip.

"The one who hangs around with Dunham? What did he say?"

"That he wasn't surprised Dunham had tried to shoot her. Just that it had taken him so many years to do so."

Granville gave her a thoughtful look. "That's not all he said, was it? That isn't enough to make you regret this journey."

She tried to smile, gave it up. "No. He said… He didn't even think about it, just threw it off. He said she's the reason Beau is dead."

CHAPTER 56

IT WAS HARD TO SEE EMILY SO DISTRAUGHT. AND GRANVILLE hadn't yet heard what had upset her so. The words she'd repeated weren't enough to make her want to just give up and go home.

Which wasn't like her at all.

He covered her hand with his. "I know it's hard."

"No, you don't understand."

"Then tell me."

He watched her in concern as she drew in a sharp breath.

"It's hard to say. " she said, so fast the words ran together. "How can men be so awful?"

She blushed as she said it, and he began to get an inkling as to why she might be so upset. And what Curtin must have been talking about.

"Why did he say Dunham might want to kill her?" he asked gently. "Jealousy?"

"You could call it that, I suppose," she said, looking away. "If you're feeling kind. But it seemed more like one of the big cats, marking their territory. And hissing at any male who comes too close."

He'd wondered if Belle had made her living doing more than

just dancing with the men who thronged the region. As had so many others, in those early days. A rough and ready gold town wasn't an easy place for a woman.

It seemed likely that the she had, at least for a time. And that Emily hadn't even considered the possibility before whatever Curtin had said. Which could explain her shock and her disgust with the case now.

Especially since she seemed to like Belle, even admire her survival skills. It must be hard to realize what the real cost of that survival had been for her.

"Then Dunham had an… understanding… with Belle before she met Beau?" he said, wording it carefully.

"He wasn't the only one," she burst out. "They all did. And once she met Beau, she wouldn't even look at anyone else. And they hated her for it. Hated him, too. That's what's so awful."

He winced at that, thinking about the reaction of men chasing gold in a rugged land with very few women. In the Klondike, many of the women who survived that horrendous journey north were treated like gold. As they should be. But sometimes, that very scarcity of women brought out the worst in the men.

Especially in a situation like Emily was describing.

"And they hated her enough to kill her? To kill him?"

"It sounded like it. On Dunham's part at least. And Mr. Curtin—he sounded so matter of fact. As if it were inevitable."

She drew in a deep breath. Then exploded. "What's wrong with them? And if that's not bad enough… It's been thirty-two years! And they haven't let go of their injured pride? Over something that wasn't theirs in the first place."

What could he say? She was right. "It doesn't sound like enough to trigger a shootout. But it's information we didn't have before. Maybe knowing the truth will make the difference in solving this case."

She glared at him. "You aren't surprised by this?"

"No, unfortunately I'm not. I wish I could tell you different."

She swallowed hard, blinked back tears, and looked down.

"Well," she said after a moment. "I suppose if I'm going to be an investigator, I have to deal with the ugly side of people. And murder can only come from ugliness."

"Which is another truth I wish I didn't have to agree with you on."

She gave him a watery smile. Along with a determined look. "And at least Belle isn't dead, no matter what Dunham intended. And this does give us new information."

"And there's no proof that anyone here murdered Beau. Or even that he's dead at all."

"Is that supposed to help?" she demanded, fighting back a real smile.

"It depends whether you want to give up on the case or not."

"This isn't a case. It's a… I can't think of a word confusing enough for what this is."

"Soul sucking mud pool, as Trent would say?"

Now she did smile. "I like that. Yes, this soul sucking mud pool of a case. And no, I refuse to give up. I just don't have to like it."

"Now you're talking like a real detective."

She made a face at him, and he grinned. Relieved to see her bouncing back.

"Did Belle tell you anything when you went to see her in hospital that might cast some light on this mud-sunk case of ours?"

"Not really. Mostly she seems to have decided Beau was abandoning her, and was too distraught to make much sense," she said, and he could hear the strain of that experience in her voice. "Unless…"

"Unless?"

"She was making sense, and I lacked some piece of information that would let me follow what she said. Did she or Mr. Dunham say anything after the shooting?"

"They were busy accusing each other. So yes, they said quite a bit. But perhaps we should join the others before we discuss it. If you're up to it?"

"I am now," she said firmly. "And it would help to share all our information and perspectives. Even Trent's. I'm sorry I was being silly before."

"Never silly," he said equally firmly. "Investigations that expose the evils in our world are always tough. I've never met a woman who handles them as well as you do. Except perhaps my elder sister Louisa, now Lady Waybourne.

Emily cocked her head a little and considered him. "Thank you. And I think I'd like your sister. Despite her title."

"You'll have a chance to meet her when we go to England on our honeymoon," he said. And then cursed himself for an idiot when she lost the little color she'd regained. "In the meantime, you'll have to make do with feuding with Trent."

She grinned at him, accepting the distraction, and he took her hand. Then they went looking for the others.

Before he made matters worse again.

GRANVILLE AND EMILY tracked Scott and Trent to their "office" —as they'd begun to call the private dining room they'd been using—where they seemed to be arguing about one of the charts.

"It is too important," Trent said furiously as Granville held the door open for Emily.

Hearing Trent's tone, she glanced back over her shoulder at Granville, and rolled her eyes.

He grinned at her, relieved that she seemed to have bounced back. Again. Having traveled under less challenging circumstances with his sisters, he was beginning to think his wife was something of a miracle.

But then he'd already known that.

The other two looked up as they walked into the room, and Scott winked at him. Not serious then. Good.

"What do we know about the fight between Dunham and Belle?" Granville asked as he pulled out a chair. "And what it tells us about Beau's disappearance?"

"You should know. You were there," Trent muttered.

Granville shot him a glance. What had got into him lately? Before he could say anything, Emily spoke up.

"I still think I might have caused it," she said in a small voice, casting him an apologetic look. And surprising them all into silence.

"That trouble's been brewin' between those two for longer than you've been alive," Scott said gruffly. "You didn't cause anything."

"But what did you say?" Trent asked. "And what were they fighting over, anyway?"

"Beau. And who killed him," Emily said.

"Something set Belle off," Trent insisted.

"I asked her about something Dunham had said. And I think she worked out that we considered him a possible suspect in Beau's death."

"And that was enough to send her after Dunham with a gun? After all this time?" Trent said. "I don't get it."

Emily looked a little sick, and Granville decided it was time he spoke up.

"She really loved Beau," Emily said before he could say anything.

"Sounds hokey to me. It's been thirty-two years, and she hadn't done a thing. She must not have loved Beau much in the first place."

Emily bristled. "And what would you know about love?" Then stared to see Trent turn bright red.

Granville hid a grin. So that's what was wrong with the lad. He was in love. But with whom? Someone he'd met here?

He'd been as cantankerous as a wild boar since they'd left Quesnel. Had he met someone there? Or was there someone he'd had to leave behind in Vancouver?

Either way, at least the rest of them could focus on the case, now that they knew why he'd been so belligerent lately. Which was a relief. They needed that focus if they were to have any hope of getting back to Vancouver before Christmas. And he'd promised Emily.

Not that she seemed too worried about it. She was focused on Trent. Who was still bright red. Time to intervene, take the focus off the poor lad.

"Scott, what made you conclude that there's been enmity between Belle and Dunham for a long time?"

His partner looked startled. "Isn't it obvious?"

"Humor me."

"They're wary of each other. You can see it in how they act when the other one's around."

"I think this was the first time I'd seen them together," Granville said, thinking back.

"She was at one of the pubs when we first got here," Scott said. "I didn't know who she was at the time. Or Dunham either. But I know how enemies watch each other, and I saw that wariness in them."

Forgetting about Trent, Emily was now staring at Scott. "That would explain why she reacted so fast to my question."

Scott nodded. "She already didn't trust him. Your question was like striking a lucifer to tinder."

"That fits," Granville said, glad to see a little of the tension draining out of Emily's face at the realization she wasn't the reason for Belle's behavior. "But does it get us any closer to what really happened to Beau?"

"Enmity or not, they both say Beau left town on the same day, don't they?" Trent said, apparently putting his embarrassment behind him.

Good for him.

"And Belle said he was going searching for gold again. So does Dunham," Emily said.

"Not quite," Scott put in. "Dunham said Beau had been blackmailing him, and he finally paid him off using money from his big strike. That's when Beau left town."

"How come we never heard this before?" Trent asked.

"Because it came out when the two of them were yelling at each other this morning," Granville said.

Emily looked back and forth between them, a stunned look on her face. "But this changes everything," she said.

What?

CHAPTER 57

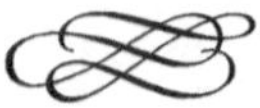

"It changes everything," Emily repeated into the stunned silence, glancing around the table. "Don't you see it? If Beau— our missing miner—knew about Dunham, and was brazen enough to blackmail him in a place like Barkerville, where everyone knows everyone else's business? Then we've been looking at this backwards from the beginning."

She leaned forward, intent on making them see. It was so obvious to her now. "Our client's view of his long lost father skewed what little information he gave us. And our entire perspective of what was going on."

None of them were nodding.

Granville was watching her closely. "Go on. Tell us what you've seen," he invited.

It wasn't clear to them? She blinked, then doubled down on explaining it to them as clearly as possible.

"We all thought we were looking for a missing gold seeker," she said. "Instead, we were looking for a crook. And now we have *proof* that Mr. Robertson didn't change when he left Seattle. This new persona of his? Beau Brody was still the same criminal that Thomas Robertson had been. He just hid it better."

She caught Granville's arrested look, and winked at him. "Which is how we ended up in the midst of this soul sucking mud pool of a case in the first place."

Her new husband grinned back, while Trent looked taken aback and Scott roared with laughter at her choice of words.

"But I'm serious here," Emily said. "If we'd looked at Robertson as a hardened, successful criminal from the beginning, we'd have asked different questions. Starting with what a man like that would be up to in a gold rush town like this one."

"He came here to hide," Trent said, but there was a question in his voice.

"Maybe. But he must have found a reason to stay for so long."

Granville looked across at Scott. "Like Soapy Smith," he said. And Scott nodded.

"Smith was a crook who had his fingers into everything, built himself a crime empire back in Colorado," Scott explained. "When he got to Skagway during the Klondike gold rush, he ended up running the place. If there was illegal money to be made, he was raking it in."

Emily nodded. "Just like that. Only Robertson, as Brody, took another path. On the surface he was a good guy, one that everyone loved."

"Not Dunham," Trent muttered.

"So what was Robertson really up to here?" Granville said, ignoring Trent. "When he wasn't playing Beau to Mrs. Darrow's Belle. Or laying tracks suggesting he was searching for pay dirt?"

"Exactly," Emily said. "Whatever it was, it wasn't obvious. Or we'd have heard *something* by now. Even after thirty-two years."

Scott looked thoughtful. And Trent, shaking his head, just rolled his eyes at her.

"To start with, if he blackmailed Dunham so easily, Robertson probably had other victims," Granville said.

"Here?" Emily asked.

"Or elsewhere. But since we're here—something tied him to Barkerville for all those years. What was he up to?"

"Some kind of scheme. Something that no-one would suspect from Beau Brady," Scott said nodding. "What if he had another identity, ready to take on as soon as he left Barkerville?"

"Which, given what we know so far, is likely," Granville said. "But to what end? And why all the traveling in the area for so long?"

"He was looking for something," Emily suggested. "But if not gold, then what?"

"Easy money of some kind," Scott said. "Had to be. He's a thief, after all. Hiding out here, looking for his next big haul."

"Out here?" Trent said. "There's nothing here but…"

"Gold," Granville and Scott said together.

"The lucky ones that struck it big sent their riches south by stagecoach," Scott said. "Were any of them robbed while he was here?"

"Would all those little drawings in his letters home tell us anything?" Emily said. "If he wasn't looking for gold, he must have drawn them for some other reason?"

"Misdirection, probably. In case the law was still looking for him, and intercepted his letters," Granville said.

That sounded right. Emily felt a pang of pity for the woman and the boy that had received those letters, and found meaning in those little drawings, much as she and Clara had tried to do on the train.

She was beginning to get a sense of who Thomas Robertson had really been, and she didn't like him at all. But at least understanding him meant they had a better chance of solving his disappearance.

And going home.

She'd had enough of Barkerville and it's dead dreams. If not of her honeymoon journey. She glanced at him, and smiled a private smile. She was looking forward to the long journey home with Granville.

"What would it matter if our missing miner did have a new name?" Trent said suddenly. "So what if he did?"

They all stared at him. Emily couldn't figure out where he

was going with the question. It seemed to have come out of nowhere.

"Doesn't help us find him. Not if he's dead, or was killed, or whatever," Trent said, his voice defensive now. "If he wasn't either Robertson or Brody when he died, his trail dies with him. There's no records for a made up guy. Who would know he'd even died?"

It was true. And a very good point.

"They didn't even have fingerprints back then," Granville said slowly. "If he is dead, and he died too far from here for anyone to recognize the body…"

"Or he died nearby, but the wildlife had been at him," Trent put in.

Emily winced at the mental picture.

"Then they'd have only the ID to go by. And there would be no missing person report, no next of kin, nothing. Not for a new identity. Good catch, Trent."

Emily smiled to see Trent beaming at the compliment, then hurriedly hiding it.

"Then how do we find him?" she asked. "If Thomas Robertson really has been dead for so long?"

"We need to check death reports. Espccially ones where the body was never claimed," Granville said.

"For thirty-two years? And he could've gone anywhere in the province. Or back across the border. It's impossible," Trent protested.

"Not quite. We can narrow it down some," Scott said. "If he was more interested in swindling people for their gold than digging for it himself, that limits where he might go."

"How?"

"He'd need a town big enough, with cnough money flowing in that people don't work out what he's up to," Granville said.

"Like a gold rush town, or a big city," Emily suggested.

"Unless he takes up cattle rustling again," Trent said.

"Too obvious," Scott said. "It was still only five years after he fled Seattle that he left Barkerville. Some of the bigger cities probably still had wanted posters up for him."

"Exactly. So we identify the most likely places he'd go, then check death reports on the applicable routes leaving Barkerville."

"That's still a lot of deaths," Trent said. "And a bunch of 'em wouldn't even have been reported. He could be buried under some avalanche somewhere and no-one would ever find him."

"Possible. But unlikely," Granville said. "Given what we've recently learned of the fellow, I suggest we'd be best to start with any deaths on our chosen routes that are related to a crime, or a murder."

"That's a long shot, even if he is dead. But what if the fella's alive after all?" Trent said. "Then what?"

"It still works," Granville said with a wink. "Hardened criminal, remember. One who ran a successful gang. And had been pretending to be a good guy for five years."

"You think he'd link up with other criminals as soon as he left Barkerville?" Emily said.

"I think it's a reasonable bet."

Scott was nodding. "Playing Beau had probably worn thin. I wonder what his new identity was."

"And what made it worth giving up his life in Barkerville after all that time?" Emily said.

"Interesting question, that," Scott said.

"Isn't it? Because the man we're talking about now doesn't seem one who'd leave a good thing with nothing better in sight," she said.

And grinned at herself for talking like one of her penny dreadfuls. And feeling a sudden rush of excitement that *she* was involved in a case like this. Instead of reading about it.

Even if it was a soul sucking mud pool of a case.

"That is a very good point," Granville said. "Maybe with a little luck we'll find out."

Trent said. "How much longer are we going to have to stay here, chasing this guy?"

"We'll be back in Vancouver before Christmas," Granville said.

"That's only a month away. How can you even say that when we've been chasing our tails for the last two weeks?"

"Because I promised Emily that we'd be home for Christmas," Granville said.

Trent shrugged, looking ready to argue that, too.

"And I promised my mother," Emily put in.

Trent looked from her to Granville, and grimaced. "I get it. So we'll be back by Christmas. What if we haven't found our missing miner by then?"

The name grated on Emily's nerves. She couldn't keep thinking about him that way—not now they knew what kind of man he really was.

"We can't keep calling him our missing miner," Emily said. "Not now we know he's a rustler and a blackmailer."

"That's a mouthful," Trent said with a nasty tone in his voice. She frowned at him. Before she could think of an appropriate reply, Scott did so.

"We call him what he is," he said. "A missing crook."

"Yes, that works," Emily said.

Trent scowled, but didn't argue. "I still need an answer," he said. "What happens if we haven't found our missing crook before Christmas?"

"Then we go back home. And tell our client the truth, that we were unable to track his father past Barkerville."

"Will we tell him what we uncovered about his father's background, and what he was up to in Barkerville?" Emily asked.

Granville nodded. "He deserves to know. No matter how painful it may be to hear, it's better than never knowing the truth about his father. And then it's up to him what, if anything, he tells his son."

CHAPTER 58

WEDNESDAY, NOVEMBER 21, 1900

The following morning, Emily stood in their room, sheer curtains drawn just enough that she could watch the shoppers making their careful way up and down the snow-covered steps to various shops. Granville had noted earlier that most of the ladies and a few of the men kept a careful hand on the railings. Ice. It must have frozen overnight, after yesterday's sunshine.

As he watched her, Emily shivered, just a little, as if at the thought of venturing out in that brisk cold. Or was she thinking about their case?

After the trauma of yesterday, he was still worried about her. "Are you alright?" he asked, and she turned to smile at him.

"Of course. Why wouldn't I be? I'm just thankful to be inside with a fire rather than out in that cold."

"I believe the mercury is well below zero. We'll need a hearty breakfast. Shall we go down?"

"I'd love to. And I hope they have pancakes this morning. I could eat a mountain of them, with a river of that wonderful syrup. And lashings of hot tea."

"You must be hungry."

"Ravenous. And I can't wait to dig into the criminal world of the Cariboo from thirty years ago."

She sounded like herself again. Relieved, he offered her his arm. "Then shall we?"

"We shall," she said, placing dainty fingers on his arm with exaggerated daintiness, and shooting him a teasing look. "After all, if we plan to be home before Mama goes on the Christmas warpath, we have no time to waste."

He laughed, as no doubt she'd meant him to, then held her a little away from him. Considered her expression. It seemed a good time to ask.

"I'm curious. Now that we're married… Don't you think you can call me John? At least when we're alone? We are married, you know."

She leaned into him, wrapped her arms around him. "I'll try. But it isn't about being formal, you know."

"No?"

"No," she said, shaking her head decidedly. "I've always thought of you as Granville. That's who you are."

"That's true."

"Besides, if I were being formal, I'd call you Mr. Granville," she said with a grin.

"Well, I'm glad of that, at least," he quipped, leaning down to kiss her.

"Though come to think of it," she said slowly, leaning even further into him as he lifted his head. "There may be certain times—very private ones—when I might prefer to call you John."

"I will look forward to those times," he said as she blushed. "Greatly," he added, leaning down to kiss her again.

~

BREAKFAST TURNED out to be a hurried affair, though Emily got her pancakes, as well as several cups of tea. They all ate well, and conversation flew around the table, but no-one wanted to dawdle.

After the emotional trauma of the previous day, and their

realization that their missing quarry was more of a crook than he was a miner, they each had their assignments for the day. And all of them were eager to move this case forward.

Granville and Scott planned to meet with the Constable again. Emily was going to see if she could track down back issues of the Cariboo Sentinel, the local newspaper which had covered the gold rush, then ceased operations twenty-five years earlier. Trent was planning to re-interview previous sources.

There was a new sense of purpose in the room. All of them seemed to share a sense that they were finally getting somewhere. It was a good feeling.

The walk to the Gold Commissioner's office was a short one, and the biting wind made it a fast one, since neither Granville nor Scott were interested in freezing. Stepping into the welcome warmth of the narrow room, they found George McCall behind his heavy pine desk, glaring at the stack of paperwork in front of him.

Looking up at the sound of the door opening, he grinned broadly. "Good to see you two. Though I doubt I'll have any answers for whatever you're here to ask."

"You might be surprised," Granville said as the young constable stood up and came forward to greet them, his hand outstretched.

"Why's that?" McCall asked as they shook hands.

"Because this twisty case has taken another turn," Scott said with an equally broad grin. "Might get you away from that paperwork for an hour or so. You interested?"

"You bet I am!" McCall said, looking from him to Scott and back. "What do you need to know?"

"First, did you get anything more out of either Mrs. Darrow or Dunham?" Granville asked.

"I'm afraid not. I think you got most of what answers there are before I even arrived on scene."

"You fixin' to charge them?" Scott asked.

"At their ages? No," McCall said. "Neither of them are pressing charges, and to be honest? They don't shoot well enough to be lethal. They've been feuding for years, and I think this was as close as they'll ever get to killing each other. Unless Dunham's wound turns septic—which the doc says is unlikely."

"Good call," Granville said. "If the missing Mr. Brody ever came back to town, you might want to rethink that position. But since I sincerely doubt that'll happen, pretending the recent "gun fight" never happened is probably your best option. I suspect the two of them will do the same."

"I hope you're right," McCall said wryly. "And that the commissioner sees it the same way when he gets back."

"Any idea when that might be?"

"I heard from him this morning. Sounds like it will be a while, as he's got some business to sort out in Quesnel now. Might be as much as a week."

At this, Granville and Scott exchanged glances.

"Then I hope you can help us," Granville said. "We're hoping to be home in time for Christmas, and the way this case is going, we're going to need a few answers pretty quickly to make that happen."

"So how can I help?"

"We're still looking for what happened to our missing crook after he left here in late April of 1868."

"Brody, wasn't it? I didn't find much on him in the records. "

"And that's our main problem. However, we've recently learned the fellow had an ugly record under another name back in Seattle. Now we're interested in criminal activity in the Barkerville area in 1868 and early 1869."

McCall considered him thoughtfully. "I'm guessing you're not looking for petty crimes."

He grinned. "You'd be right about that. No, this fellow would be going after big money. And hiring thugs to help him get it."

"It doesn't sound like he'd bother with robbing stores, or individual claims, then?"

"No."

"So around here, it would be gold thefts, in one form or

another. A stagecoach robbery, a bank robbery... something of that nature."

"That's our thinking on it."

The constable nodded. "There wasn't a lot of that in the early days, surprisingly. Not for bank or stagecoach robberies, anyway. But there were individuals leaving the gold fields murdered for their gold, probably more than we ever heard about. And it was a long time ago."

"Yes it was. Which is making our job harder. But in his previous life, Brody was a ruthless man, one used to leading a gang of cattle thieves. Judging by Dunham's story of being black-mailed by him, Brody hadn't reformed, just kept a low profile. Once he left Barkerville, our guess is that he'd go back to his old ways. And where there's a gang of criminals, there's going to be violence."

"So you're wanting to look at episodes of violence, as well as robberies?"

"As you say, it was a long time ago. We'll need to follow any hints we can find in the records, even the faintest trails, if we're going to track this quarry."

McCall nodded. "I think you might be onto something. Let me see what I can do."

~

Several hours later, Granville and Scott returned to the Gold Commissioner's office. McCall met them with a broad grin and an outstretched hand.

"Good timing," he said as he gestured them towards the visi-tors' chairs in front of his desk. "I have some answers for you, but I'm afraid the news is both bad and good."

"Start with the good," Scott said. "We've had enough bad news on this case already."

McCall chuckled. "I'll just bet you have. Though I'd point out this all happened thirty or more years ago."

"Don't remind us," Scott said. "What d'you have?"

"Well most of the courthouse records and documents from the Gold Commissioner's office as well as the sheriff's office were kept in Richfield. They weren't affected by the fire that devastated Barkerville a few months after Brody's disappearance, and are remarkably complete. The records of the sheriff's office are still there. Our office moved here a few years ago, so our records are here."

"And the bad news?" Granville asked.

"We can access most reports of death or major violence during your time frame—which means there are a lot of records to wade through, I'm afraid."

"Any way of narrowing it down?"

"Well, using Brody's departure to set your timeframe will help, especially if you worked a month at a time. With luck, you might find your lead in the first few boxes."

Scott rolled his eyes at Granville, who grinned.

"There is one other thing," the constable said. "I'm afraid that most of the records of those constables who answered criminal calls outside our immediate region were kept in Quesnel."

"Just our luck," Scott said.

Granville ignored him. "What's the best route to Quesnel in this weather?"

"With the turn the weather's taken, riding overland would be a long and dangerous journey, especially with your wife along. No, you'd be better to take the new Wagon Road."

"Which means waiting for the stage?"

"I'm afraid so," McCall said.

"Any other good news?" Scott asked.

"Only that I've got permission for you to search the relevant files for your timeframe. And arranged to have the files brought here, so you can work in some degree of comfort. They should be here just after lunch."

"Thank you. We appreciate that," Granville said, though the idea of going through boxes of undoubtedly dusty files didn't appeal to him in the least.

Scott nodded his own thanks, but his dark expression spoke louder.

Seeing it, McCall grinned. "I'd feel the same. But with the files in this office, I'll be able to help you work through the relevant information more quickly," he added.

Scott's thundercloud face immediately lightened into a broad smile. "Then lunch is on me," he said, shaking the constable's hand.

"On us," Granville said.

"As long as there isn't another shooting," McCall said wryly.

CHAPTER 59

Hairbrush in hand, Emily stared into the mirror in the room she and Granville shared, not even seeing the image reflected there. Her mind was firmly fixed on one question.

What would make anyone choose to leave a life they'd spent years building? What if Granville had wanted her to move to England with him? It hurt to think of everyone and everything she'd have to leave behind. To realize just how hard it would be. And it was unsettling to realize she'd go with him, without hesitation.

But for a man like Thomas Robertson? Who left a wife and family behind. And left the life he'd spent five years building, here. What would make him leave Barkerville?

She had been pondering the question since she'd learned that their missing crook had *not* abandoned his criminal ways while looking for gold. Quite the opposite—he'd found a new source of income in blackmailing his fellow miners. And then one day he'd just left town for good.

Why?

He had to have found something more lucrative. Maybe something that suited his criminal nature better than pretending to be Beau Brody. Another scam of some kind, like the black-mail? Or something more violent, like his earlier gig running a gang of rustlers?

Maybe he wanted to lead a gang again.

Belle would likely have been a very unlikely sidekick in any of those possible lives. Emily grinned to herself, picturing it.

Maybe he'd left Barkerville because it was the easiest way to leave Belle and her dreams behind? And he'd done so without giving her so much as a hint. The cad.

Or was it the role of Beau Brody, whom everyone loved, that he was leaving behind?

Except not everyone loved him. Dunham hadn't been a fan. And there would have been other victims who felt the same, wouldn't there? Could it be as simple as one of them having killed him when he left town for the last time?

No. They hadn't found anyone who hated him enough to actually kill him. Not so far, anyway. They'd need to still keep track of it as a possibility, though.

Which left the probability Robertson had left town on his own.

From what little she knew, Emily suspected that it was Beau Brody he'd left behind, and that his feelings for Belle had been barely skin deep. If he'd cared for her at all.

She made a face.

So where did that leave them?

Wouldn't finding a new life for himself have taken some time? Surely he'd have needed forged papers to become someone else. And she'd heard Granville talk about just how complicated that could be.

She wished Granville were here to talk this over with. Or even better, Clara. Who understood people better than she ever let on. And could read social interactions much better than Emily herself did. Making Clara a very valuable confidante in a case like this one.

Anyone but Trent. Who seemed to be angry with the world at the moment, and ready to pick a fight with anyone. Especially her.

But with Granville and Scott off talking to the constable, it was Trent she was stuck with until lunchtime. So she needed to figure out what was next before she went back downstairs and declared herself ready to go out.

It was all well and good to feel like she was inside her very own version of a penny dreadful, and that Mr. Robertson's motives for leaving were what mattered most. And it was rather exciting to sit here and decide what that motive might have been. But then what?

At some point she and Trent would need to find something to prove—or disprove—that motive. And preferably, that same something would be the clue they were looking for.

Suddenly she wondered if it was just a coincidence that Mr. Robertson had left town for good right after Mr. Dunham's mine had paid out? When his victim finally had the money to pay him off all at once? Or had the blackmail demands been steadily increasing over the years?

Emily frowned as she considered the notion. She hadn't thought of it until just this minute. But it made sense.

She'd first thought Robertson had found a new, more lucrative scam, somewhere away from Barkerville. And perhaps he had. But what if it was something that needed a bit of funding? Perhaps as seed money?

What kind of criminal activity might need money to start? Her frown deepened and she pictured Trent's response to that question. Probably most of them would.

But what kinds of criminal activity would be available to him? After all, he'd spent the months before his departure in Barkerville. And she knew he hadn't spent more than usual on his supplies before he left town. Belle had told her that much.

So what kind of bigger-than-blackmail opportunity— requiring some funding—could a criminal uncover in Barkerville, in 1868?

Now that was a question she knew how to answer. Emily straightened her back, smiled and reached for her reticule and her coat. It was time to collect Trent.

~

"So where are we going?" Trent asked as they walked as briskly as the icy sidewalks would allow towards the other end of town. "I mean, I know you said that stuff about finding Brody's motives, and him being a bigger crook and all. But it was thirty-two years ago. It's not like there's a sign or something."

But he sounded intrigued despite himself.

Emily just smiled.

Trent watched her warily, until she crossed the street towards the Post Office. Then he groaned. "Not her again. Isn't she still in hospital? And didn't you talk to her enough yesterday?"

"No. And yes. But we're not going to see Mrs. Darrow."

"We're not? Then where…" And his voice trailed off when he saw the other sign. "Not the Literary Institute? How is talking about books going to help anything?"

"You'll see," she said, and led the way up the stairs to the second floor, ignoring Trent's protests. "Think of it as finding the next piece of this puzzle. Even the one that makes sense of all the others."

"Huh?"

Maybe Trent hadn't spent much time doing puzzles. Given what little she knew of his childhood, he probably hadn't had much chance to play boardgames. She'd made an assumption without even thinking about it, one that could have hurt his feelings. If…

Emily suddenly stopped on the narrow staircase, and Trent, who was climbing right behind her, nearly ran into her.

"Trent, can you read?"

"Of course I can. What do you take me for?"

Oops. Realizing she'd just insulted him, she scrambled to fix it. "Newspapers. I meant, do you read newspapers? The print is always small and a bit fuzzy, and I'd imagine the copies of *The Cariboo Sentinel* we're going to look at are worse, given how old they are."

"Why would we want to read old newspapers?"

Grateful that he'd focused on their purpose here and not on her nonsensical explanation, she hurried to explain. "Our missing crook had been in Barkerville for months before he left town and disappeared. If he was looking for an easy way to make a lot of money, how would he find it?"

Trent stared at her as the dust motes drifted by in the thin light from the tiny window above their heads.

"Dunno," he said after a moment. "Gold is the most obvious thing to steal. Talking to other crooks, I guess. But maybe not in Barkerville." He grinned, beginning to catch her excitement.

"Maybe not. But if he knew where the money was…"

"Then he could plan the job, and go hire some crooks to help him pull it off."

"Exactly."

"So where do the newspapers come in?"

"The newspapers would have reported miners leaving the area to go back to the coast, the boats that were arriving and departing from Quesnel. Even how much gold various mines had dug out that year."

"All that?"

She nodded. "But if it's going to be useful, we have to think like he would."

"We have to be crooks?"

"No, just think like them," she said with a grin.

As he grinned back, she started back up the stairs, enjoying the feeling that they were in harmony. For a change.

ONCE SHE EXPLAINED that she was here on her honeymoon, and since her husband had business that morning, she and her cousin —that was Trent—wished to learn more of the history of the gold rush days, they were welcomed enthusiastically at the Cariboo Literary Institute. The two ladies who were running things that day waived the reading fee, and even offered them a fresh cup of tea. Which Emily gratefully accepted, and was happy to answer questions about her recent marriage while the four of them sipped tea. Trent managed to retain a polite facade, but when he caught her gaze he rolled his eyes impatiently.

Still, the ladies, long term Barkerville residents, were interesting to talk to, and knew a great deal of the town's history. And their cooperation and help in finding what they needed, and then setting them up at a reading table in a corner by the windows—with good light—was more than worth a brief delay.

Half an hour later, Trent looked up from the issue of the Sentinel he was reading. "How many more of these are there?"

"It depends what we find," she said. "We know which months Thomas Robertson spent here in town. So I thought we'd start with the day he left here, and work backwards. Probably for a year, to March or April of 1867."

He shot her a sideways look. "How many issues is that?"

"Well, they published on Mondays and Thursdays, so probably a hundred issues, give or take. Less the months he was off hunting gold. So maybe eighty.

His eyes widened. "Eighty issues? I'm only halfway through the first one."

"Well, we might find something obvious in the months around his departure, and stop sooner."

"And if we don't? We'll be here forever."

"It'll get faster, you'll see. There's a lot of repetition, and we only care about large sums of money. Just make a quick note of anything that catches your eye."

He looked so baffled that she couldn't help laughing. "Think of it as talking to your old timers, and picking out the bits that matter."

His face cleared for a moment, though he didn't look very certain as he turned back to the brittle, yellowed page of newsprint.

Let me show you," she said, moving her chair so she could see over his shoulder. "Now, this notice gives us the schedule for the BX Express back to Vancouver and Victoria. By itself, that doesn't mean much, but there's a column called "Mining News" over here, and it runs every week with a summary of how much gold is being pulled out of mines on each creek, and how each of the companies are doing."

Trent's gaze followed her finger as she pointed out these gems. Then he looked back at her. His eyes were sparkling.

"So if one of the gold companies struck it rich, the individual miners might be ready to head back to the coast. On the Express. Taking their bags of gold dust back to the coast with them."

"That's it," she said. "I haven't found an article that specific yet…"

"But there's plenty to interest a crook who likes stealing other people's money," he said.

"Granville couldn't have put it better."

He looked pleased, then turned back to the thick volume of newspapers in front of him, as if to hide his reaction. "Is there anything else I can look for?"

Emily nodded. "Unfortunately, I can't tell you exactly what that might be. I find the information from the Gold Commissioner's Court interesting, though so far I've only found disputes over claim boundaries, or unpaid wages. But they seem to report everything, so you might find something useful."

"How will I know if an article could be useful?"

"Use your own judgement," she said. "Try thinking like a criminal, someone who is looking to steal large sums of money someone else worked for."

He shrugged and stared at the page in front of him.

"If something captures your eye as interesting, or an odd thing to find in a newspaper, then stop and think how a crook might use that information," she said, trying to convey how she found things when she did research.

Trent stared at her, then back at the page. "That makes sense," he said slowly, sounding so surprised she had to bite back a laugh for fear of offending him again. "I think it might work. But why am I looking at 1867 instead of the actual year he disappeared?"

"Because our missing crook stayed in Barkerville too long,"

she told him. And laughed at his puzzled look. "We don't know yet how complex his plan was for his next venture, whatever it might have been. He could easily have been planning it for more than a year by the time he left. And if he was, something he'd read or heard somewhere might have triggered the idea that led to the plan."

"I get it. And if he was in Barkerville, he likely either talked to somebody. Or read an article. Or something."

"Or saw an ad," she added. "Yes, that's it exactly."

"Then why aren't we out talking to people, see what they know?" he asked.

"If this were thirty years ago, we would be. Or if everyone who knew him back then didn't seem to still hate him."

"Yeah, he burnt some bridges, didn't he?" Trent said with something that sounded almost like respect.

Emily hoped she was wrong. Bad enough Trent's father had been a not very successful thief himself, without the boy finding a more competent criminal to admire. Even a dead one.

She gritted her teeth at the thought, determined not to say anything and make it worse. Even knowing Robertson was likely dead didn't help any.

"I'm hoping we'll find something in these papers that will help us narrow down what he might have got involved with. That way, when we do go ask everyone more questions, we'll know what to ask."

"Oh. Well that makes sense too," Trent said. And turned back to his current issue as if she wasn't even in the room.

Well, that was one way to deal with an awkward situation.

Moving her chair back into place, she decided it was a good thing she wasn't still mad at the boy. And at least he was enthusiastic about their search now. Maybe he'd be the one to find the information they needed.

She glanced across at the scowl he now wore. Then again, maybe not.

CHAPTER 60

AFTER NEARLY AN HOUR OF PLOWING THROUGH THE 1868 ISSUES of the Cariboo Sentinel, Emily was fighting off frustration. There were the quirky articles, the inside jokes, the arguments about British Columbia becoming part of Canada or not, the comings and goings of the town. All things she'd normally be interested in.

But she hadn't found a single tidbit that got them any closer to finding out what had happened to their missing rustler and blackmailer. Not one.

Then she heard Trent draw in a sharp breath.

"What is it?" she asked, holding her breath as she turned quickly to face him.

"I think I found something."

She leaped up from her chair and peered over his shoulder. "What is it?"

"There," he said, pointing to a small article, then leaning back a bit so she could read it.

Listed under the "In the Region" heading, the piece was very brief. Apparently a young man and his cousin had been diving in the Fraser just south of Quesnel, and barely escaped drowning in the rapids there. The piece she found interesting was their story of lost treasure.

When asked why they'd do such a dangerous thing, they said they were treasure hunters. They'd heard stories that in the early days of the gold rush, a boat full of miners and their gold had capsized and sunk on that very spot. And they were determined to retrieve the gold. Both boys were taken to hospital as a precaution, and released that same day.

"Do you think retrieving that gold would count as easy money?" Trent asked before Emily had even finished reading. "For a crook, I mean?"

"If there was a lot of gold lost, it might. It had already been mined, after all," she said, hiding her smile at his enthusiasm. "But I've heard that the Fraser can be deadly. Would our missing crook see it as worth the risk?"

"Depends if he had to do the diving," Trent said practically. "And some parts of the Fraser aren't so bad."

Clearly he liked the idea of this being the clue they'd been looking for. She did too, just to finish this case. But sometimes the easy answer was the wrong one.

"They say this happened in the early days of the gold rush. That would be '63 or '64, wouldn't it?" Emily said. "Why don't you start with 1863, and see if you can find anything that confirms whether this lost gold story actually happened? And if it did, maybe they'll include more details than this article did."

"Good idea." Trent carefully marked the page he'd been reading, and reached for the volume holding the newspapers from 1863. There was no sign of his earlier frown, just an intent look.

Emily grinned as she turned back to her readings in 1868. It was good to see Trent caught up in this case again.

And if he was the one to find the clue they'd been looking for, she'd celebrate right along with the rest of them.

~

HE FOUND IT, too! They'd been reading old news papers for several hours, and Emily was beginning to feel hungry when a gargling sound from Trent made her turn and stare at him.

He was pointing at the page in front of him, eyes wide, and he seemed to be trying—and failing—to get words out.

For a moment she thought he was having some kind of fit. "Are you all right?" she asked, jumping up and going around the table to him.

He nodded, and pointed again. Oh. He'd found something. And judging by his expression, it was something good.

The headline screamed 'Six Dead And Gold Fortune Lost As Boat Sinks.'

"Trent! You found the proof."

He quit trying to talk and beamed at her, his finger still stabbing towards the article. She got it, and turned back.

Quickly scanning the article, Emily began to smile.

Back in 1863, that first summer of discovery on the creeks of the Cariboo, it seemed many of the mines on William's Creek were raking in the gold. Including the Prince of Wales and Tinker mines, both of which had struck a rich seam of gold. That fall, partners and investors from those two mines had booked passage down the Fraser River to Vancouver for the winter. Taking with them a fortune in gold dust and nuggets, all neatly bundled in leather bags.

Two boats had made the challenging run downstream from Quesnel. One hugged the west shore. The other crossed the river and steered between a small island and the far shore. That latter boat, steered by an inexperienced pilot, overturned in the rapids. Seven of the twelve passengers were lost. And all of their gold. Over two thousand troy ounces.

And the Sentinel had reported every detail in September of 1863.

"Wait until Granville hears about this," she said. "Let me make some quick notes, then we can head back to meet up with them."

Trent's smile stretched impossibly wider.

~

OVER LUNCH in their makeshift office, the four of them shared their information. But it was Trent's discovery of the shipwreck article that fired everyone's imagination. Emily smiled to see the spark in Granville's eyes, which had been missing the last few days.

Except when he looked at her, a little voice inside her head pointed out. And she promptly had to fight back the blush that stray thought inspired.

But it wasn't just Granville. A buzz of excitement seemed to electrify the air in the crowded little room.

"Do you think Brady saw the article when he first got here, and was looking for the shipwreck site ever since?" Trent was asking intently, sitting forward in his seat. There was no trace of his former sullenness.

Emily had been thinking about that as they walked back from the Literary Institute. "That doesn't quite fit with what we know about his various travels," she said. "Unless those were just a distraction."

"From this guy, that's possible," Scott said.

None of them had developed much appreciation for their quarry over the course of the investigation, it seemed. Quite the opposite.

If he were alive, she'd cross the street rather than meet him. And that wasn't true of many people. In fact, she couldn't think of anyone that was true of. Not even gossipy and critical Mrs. Smythe, the bane of her existence.

"He could have seen the article about the treasure hunters near drowning, and it intrigued him enough he went looking for the original report. Just as Trent did," she said.

Trent beamed.

"That would have given him nearly a year to plan his departure?" Granville asked. "If I have the dates right?"

Emily nodded. "You do."

All four of them turned to look at the maps where they'd overlapped Brody's various journeys.

"In that last year, Brody was in the Quesnel area a lot," Trent said. "That's why I thought we needed to check out the Antler Creek. It's the easiest to get to from Quesnel." He walked up to look at the map they'd posted on the wall more closely.

"But it also fits if he was looking for the location of the wreck," Granville said, standing up and joining him in front of the map.

"Especially if you take into account that the island is only visible at low water. Which is in the fall," Trent agreed, his finger now tracing a path on the map. "And Brody, I mean Robertson, seems to have spent some time in Quesnel in the fall of '67."

"Then why he'd leave Barkerville in the spring?" Scott asked, moving to join them. "They'd be crazy to try diving when the river's high."

"Maybe not," Emily said from where she sat, watching them. "I've heard Papa talk over the years about the currents in the Fraser. And when they've occasionally lost freight in the river, they have to hire the locals to look for it, because it never ends up where you'd expect it to be."

"So the gold could be buried where it fell," Granville said. "Or it could have washed up somewhere you wouldn't want to dive in the fall."

"But gold is heavy," Trent protested. "It would sink to the bottom."

"And the currents in that river are really strong," Scott countered. "Especially along the bottom, in some parts."

"Robertson wasn't from here. He must've talked to people to find out those things," Trent said. "I bet we can find out if he did. And what he might have been told."

"I bet you can too," Granville said as he and Scott exchanged glances.

Scott nodded. "Trent and I will take that on. You get to join the constable reading old files."

"And I'll go shopping," Emily said.

Three sets of eyes turned to her. Trent was the first to speak. "You've been asked to tea at the Literary Institute," he said accusingly. "And I'll bet you're going to talk to that crazy postmistress, too. And you'll probably come back with answers before we do."

"I'll do my best," Emily said, trying not to blush at the look Granville sent her. "But as long as we solve this case, I don't care who finds the answers we need."

CHAPTER 61

AN HOUR AND A HALF LATER, GRANVILLE WAS BACK IN THEIR increasingly chaotic office, waiting for the other three to return. Notes covered every surface, with more scribbles and arrows going every which way on the maps and sheets of information tacked to the walls. Trying to narrow any of this down seemed impossible.

And the records he and Constable McCall had gone through didn't help. They had confirmed that there had been a lot of deaths, just as Trent had suspected. And more than a few robberies, of banks and gold shipments, especially during the early '60's. Though none of those incidents seemed to fit with their missing crook's activities.

There had also been a surprising number of missing miners, often with missing stashes of gold dust and nuggets. Too many to work through easily or quickly. And that was still just the tip of the information iceberg.

For a moment, he regretted that they hadn't been able to bring Miss Kent on the journey with them. Even though it would have been ridiculous when she was needed back at the office, she would have this room and the bits of information in it organized in no time, their notes neatly typed. And she'd have neatly set up a number of appointments he hadn't even realized they needed.

Not to mention what she could do with a set of financial reports.

The thought had him frowning for a moment. The one facet of an investigation that seemed not to have come up yet in this investigation was financial records. And yet, those records often proved to be key to unravelling some very difficult cases.

How would finances play out here?

He pulled out his notebook and scanned through it, looking for any mentions he'd made about Robertson's finances.

Their client believed his father was short of funds, and had taken the job driving cattle to Barkerville to save their small ranch.

According to the Pinkertons, the reality was that the poor fellow's father, Thomas Robertson, aka Robert Brody, had been a ruthless crook and the boss of a team of cattle rustlers. He'd left town ahead of the law.

There was no suggestion Robertson had been broke, quite the opposite. According to the Pinkertons, the success of Robertson's gang was the reason he had to flee. So where had that money gone?

Had the fellow hidden it before he left town? And if so, where?

He didn't seem to have left anything with his wife and child. Their client's story had been one of suffering, barely surviving on the little money the ranch made. Then eventually losing the ranch, and being forced to move to town, as they called Seattle.

They had been assuming Robertson—who changed his name to Brody when he reached Barkerville—had been broke. But had he?

They'd also been assuming Robertson as Brody had made little money in Barkerville, just enough for he and Belle to live on between his explorations. But that was before they found out about his blackmail schemes.

So where did he keep that money?

There were several banks in town—as was common in a booming gold rush town. But even thirty years ago, it was difficult to bank money you hadn't earned. The town was too small, and someone would start asking questions.

Unless Robertson had yet another identity, one with the identification papers—real or forged—that he'd need in a larger town. And he'd opened an account somewhere else under that name.

Granville stared at the note he'd made. It suggested a long term plan, something he hadn't contemplated when they'd been discussing Robertson taking on a third identity when he left Barkerville. What if the fellow had set up that identity, along with a bank account, long before he left town? It would have to be in a town where he wasn't known as either Brady or Robertson.

In itself that wasn't an answer, or even a partial one. But as they looked for where Robertson might have chosen to relocate, a decent sized bank would likely be one of the amenities he'd be looking for. It was another factor to narrow down their search.

And the more they could narrow it down, the better.

For a mad moment he considered sending for Miss Kent and Mac Mackenzie, their accountant and sometime investigator, along with her. They really could use all the help they could get.

The logistics of doing so changed his mind, and he considered what local options might be available.

A noise in the corridor interrupted his thought, and Scott strode into the room, brushing snow from his beard. "Brrr. It's getting colder out there."

Which was another reason summoning help from Vancouver was a bad idea. It was difficult enough planning a journey that would see Emily back safely to Vancouver in this cold, without adding Miss Kent to the mix.

"You have any luck?" Granville asked him.

"Some. Nothing that looks too promising, though. You?"

"A lot of deaths. A surprising number of missing miners. So far nothing particularly helpful."

"What about criminal activity?"

"Not in these records. According to McCall, there were more incidents on the trails back towards the Fraser, which would have been handled by the constables stationed in Quesnel."

"So not much help, then."

"No."

"Any word on the sheriff and Gold Commissioner?"

"Nothing new there, either. But I did find some documents that seem to fit with my latest theory."

"A theory, is it?"

"I've been thinking about the articles Trent and Emily found, about the boat overturned in the Fraser."

"Funny you should say that."

"Oh?"

His partner grinned at him. "We heard a few more versions of that particular story, Trent and me."

"Go on."

"Seems there's not much to do in the winter, around here. So they talk about the old days: the big strikes, the failures, the miners and the criminals. Over and over. Lost gold is always a popular topic, as are missing miners, and robberies. The really popular ones are stories about catastrophes that involve large sums of money, and result in multiple deaths."

"Like our overturned boat?"

"Exactly like it."

"How accurate are these stories?"

"They're tall tales by now, so they're pretty exaggerated. Most of 'em, there weren't enough details left to link to a real time or place. But there were some, like that overturned boat, that seemed worth looking into. Trent thought so, anyway."

"Where is Trent?" Granville asked. He'd been expecting the lad to return with Scott.

"He went back to the Literary Institute, to find Emily."

"He what?"

Scott grinned. "I guess he liked finding that key bit of information. He mumbled something about digging into the records, and headed off before I could ask questions."

That was unexpected. And oddly impressive. He hadn't thought the lad had it in him—his strengths lay in other directions.

"Good for him," Granville said, wondering if Emily would be as surprised as he was. Somehow, he suspected she would not.

"Were there any additional details on our overturned boat story that might be helpful?" he asked Scott.

"Depends what you call helpful," Scott said slowly, then winked at the glare he received. "I gather that the bodies of the lost passengers were never found. The gold wasn't, either. Despite everyone's best efforts on both fronts."

"Interesting."

"And over the years, there've been rumors about a map that showed the exact spot where the poor saps and their stash went down."

"Not unusual, whenever gold is lost," Granville said as he thought about it. "But I'm not sure a map would be helpful, anyway."

"Why's that?"

"It turns out that the Fraser hereabouts is full of unpredictable currents, causing major shifts in the gravel on the riverbed. Which means nothing that came to rest at the bottom of that river would stay where it landed."

"So a map of the original location…"

"Would be a starting point at best. Even a few years later, those bags of gold would have been well buried in the shifting bottom of that cold, muddy river. Finding them would be almost as risky as getting them out."

"You figure it would worry our missing crook?"

"From what I now know of the fellow? No. He'd see the possibility of a fortune someone else had done the slow, painful work of digging out, already bagged and ready for plucking. And as for sorting out the tides, charting the likely areas that gold would have settled, and then getting it out of the river? A man like Robertson would hire men for that, let them take on whatever risk was involved."

"Yeah, that's how I see him, too."

"Problem is, even if we're right, we still need to find the fellow. And for that, we'll need more information on what he, and any henchlings he may have acquired, actually did. And when."

"Oh, is that all?"

He grinned. "And that information is probably somewhere at the police station in Quesnel, 60 miles and a mountain range away. And I hear there's another storm on the way."

"So, if I got this right, we're now looking for a live missing crook. And a sunken treasure. In a blizzard," his partner said. "You kidding me?"

"I'm afraid not," he said. "Though I'm not at all sure Robertson survived all of this."

"Let's see what we're up against," Granville said, reaching for the larger of their maps and unrolling it on the table in front of them. Scott grabbed the paperweights they had collected for just this purpose, setting them along the edges of the large map. Together they pored over it.

"Here's Quesnel, and this is approximately where the accident occurred," Granville said.

Scott traced the very steep route from Barkerville to the site, then followed the river back along the much easier route to Cottonwood. "If we'd listened to Trent earlier, we'd have ended up in Quesnel long before now."

"Without what we've learned here in the meantime, including confirmation that Robert Brody is Robertson's newest identity and the information about the wreck, we'd have got nowhere. I'm more concerned about the weather we'll face getting to Quesnel now."

"Well, it is on our way back home. More or less," Scott pointed out. "And let's face it, if you're intending to be back to Vancouver before Christmas, we'll be facing worse weather than this gettin' there."

His partner was right, unfortunately. He knew it, and hated that the case was dragging out so long. And that the weather had turned early this year.

"With a little luck, this will see us heading home within the week," Granville said. "Assuming whatever we find in Quesnel doesn't point straight back to Barkerville. And you know it could, no matter how thorough we are."

Scott shook his head. "You're the one wanted to be a detective."

"Right. Because I should have let you rot in jail, or be hanged for murder because you were being stubborn and wouldn't answer the sheriff's questions."

"Hey! I was protecting my sister."

"Who wasn't guilty."

"Well, how was I supposed to know that?" Scott said, giving him an injured look.

He grinned, knowing his partner could go on like this for hours.

"Exciting as this discussion is," he said in his most refined accent. Which Scott had broken him of using in the first six months they'd spent on the Klondike goldfields. "We do have a missing crook to catch."

Scott grinned back, but gave in. "You really think he's alive? And if he is, you planning on turning him in?"

"I have no idea if he's alive," Granville said. "I don't think anyone in Barkerville killed him, though."

"Not even Dunham?"

"Dunham is a coward," Granville said flatly. "And a poor shot. I suspect he'd have killed Brody, as he knew him, back then if he'd been able to."

"Didn't have the backbone, huh?"

"He paid Brody's blackmail, thinking that would get rid of him," Granville said. Although they only had Dunham's word for that. Which might be worth factoring into the mess they already had.

Scott just looked at him. "And if it didn't?"

"I doubt Dunham is capable of acting alone. And shared secrets are hard to keep. None of us uncovered even a whisper that Brody never left town alive. Or that he returned here after May of '68."

"And if someone from here killed him elsewhere," Scott said slowly. "Then any evidence of that would be elsewhere."

He nodded. "I really doubt there's anything more to find here. If we haven't found it by now…"

"It's not here to find."

"That's it."

"Makes sense," Scott said after frowning over it for a moment. "Did anyone find any confirmation in the newspapers about what happened to the bags of gold on the river bottom? Or the existence of a map?"

"Emily is still looking. Possibly with Trent's help. The map might just be a word-of-mouth story, not something that ended up in the papers, though."

"Yeah, that figgers. Nothing tying it to Robertson's letters?"

"Not that we could spot. I suspect he kept anything important out of those letters, while giving his family the opposite impression."

"Nasty fellow, our missing crook."

"He was at that. Which isn't information I look forward to sharing with his son."

"Yeah. Still, our client is older than his father was when he disappeared, so maybe that helps."

"You think so?"

"Wish I did. But learning his dad was a crook and a cheater? Who'd want to hear that kind of news."

"Unless the fellow's still alive."

"That'd be worse."

"Yes, I suspect so. Unfortunately, we still have to find out what happened to him. And soon. What do you think of our odds for leaving for Quesnel within the week?"

Scott glanced out the window at the snow swirling against a rapidly darkening sky. "I think we need to consult one of the locals. And start gathering what we might need for a difficult journey. You really see this as the start of our journey back to Vancouver?"

"Unless Emily or Trent uncover some information that suggests otherwise, yes, I do."

Scott groaned theatrically, then winked. "Guess we're getting a bit too comfortable here, anyway. But you think Emily's up to it? We'll probably hit real winter weather, and she hasn't seen that yet."

"I think my new wife is up for anything," Granville said. "I also think we're going to double check the weather predictions and pack for any eventuality."

"I'll second that," Scott said. "Which direction were you thinking? North or South?"

"The easiest route, for all of us," he said, knowing Scott would understand that he meant for Emily. "Would be to take the stage back to Cottonwood and then on to Quesnel.

Scott grinned at him. "Are you going to tell Trent that we're backtracking to Cottonwood, or am I?"

"You are."

"And he'll rant at me for it. Then spend the entire journey crowing that he was right all along."

"That's why you get to tell him."

"That's what I thought. You know I'll make you pay for this, don't you?"

Granville just laughed.

CHAPTER 62

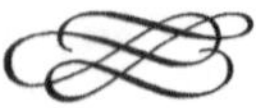

The following day, Granville and Scott paid another visit to McCall. If the constable was surprised to see him again so soon, he didn't let on. Just smiled at them both, and asked how he could help.

"Two things," Granville said. "Did you find anything else that might be related to our missing crook?"

"Not so far, I'm afraid," McCall said. "I'm still sifting through files as time allows. But finding anything more is getting less likely."

Granville nodded. "I'm not surprised. Most of our efforts are proving futile as well. And we appreciate your efforts, in any case."

"*Most* of your efforts? Does that mean you found something?" McCall was quick to ask?

He grinned. "I wondered if you'd catch that one. Which brings me to our second question. There was a tragedy back in the fall of '63 that resulted in an overturned boat, seven missing men, presumed drowned, and a great deal of lost gold dust and nuggets. Are you familiar with the incident?"

"I wasn't here at the time, but I know of it," McCall said. "You're thinking the missing gold might have been of interest to Brody, some five years later?"

"It's a possibility we're looking into. Perhaps our strongest one so far. Unless you can tell us the gold had already been found by then?"

"To my knowledge, it's never been found."

"The gold came from the "Prince of Wales" and "Tinker" sites, didn't it?" Scott asked then.

McCall nodded. "It did. I believe they were two of the richest sites on William's Creek that year."

"Interesting. And the others?"

McCall smiled, and held up a hand. "Wait here just a moment." And he disappeared into the back room. When he emerged, he was carrying a large map that he unrolled on the worktable in the back of the room.

It was large, hand-drawn and lettered in a dark sepia ink. "Is that William's Creek?" Granville asked.

"It is indeed. It lists all of the placer mines on William's Creek. Cranston created it, and keeps it current, too. You can see the various mining companies, their lot number, and the total amount of gold that company has pulled out of the Creek to date."

Granville and Scott both crowded closer to the table so they could see the details of the meticulously drawn map.

"This is impressive," Granville said, and Scott nodded his agreement.

"You can see the Prince of Wales company here, at #16, and Tinker just down the Creek a bit at #25."

Granville studied the map for a long moment. "Basically they were neighbors. So it isn't surprising that the men from the two companies would choose to travel together."

"We saw the same in the Klondike," Scott said.

"True. And over the years, those two companies each brought out hundreds of thousands worth of gold," Granville noted. "It rather puts the amount of gold lost in that sinking into perspective."

"I could live quite nicely for the rest of my life on the gold lost to the Fraser that day," Scott said quietly.

"Good point. But don't forget Brody would have needed to hire a crew. He had to have something more planned than that one job. Assuming that we guessed right about why he wanted to leave Barkerville."

Scott rolled his eyes and McCall grinned at both of them.

He grinned back, amused that he couldn't tell if the constable actually liked them, or simply found them a relief from his normal routine. "What can you tell me about about the rumors of a map that shows the exact site that boat overturned?"

McCall sighed. "There are probably several of those in existence. There usually are. Though even if the map is accurate—which is doubtful—it will probably be no help in finding that gold. The river will make sure if that."

"Because it's buried deep where it fell? Or because the currents carried it downstream. And then buried it?"

"Take your pick. I know enough about the river to know that either is possible, but not enough to know which is probable. You'd need a local riverman for that."

"Know anyone?"

"In Quesnel. And if Brody was looking into that gold, he would have had to talk to people there as well."

"Makes sense. A lot of the answers we need now seem to be in Quesnel. Which is why we're probably headed there in the next few days. I'd appreciate those names, if you have them."

"I'll get them for you. And if you're going to Quesnel, you might just cross paths with Cranston. He's now due to arrive there in a couple of days, weather permitting. And he'd be the man to talk to about Brody's disappearance. And the overturned boat incident. He was here for both of them, you know?"

"I didn't think he'd been gold commissioner that long?"

"He hasn't. But he's lived in this area from 1862, and been the Gold Commissioner since 1883."

"Then he's the man to talk to about Brody's disappearance, as well as this whole incident. We will definitely look him up. And one of us will check in with you before we leave town, in case there are updates on his schedule or your research into the files."

"Good idea. I'll see you then," McCall said, and they shook hands all around.

~

IT WAS mid-afternoon by the time Granville and Scott got back to their "office". They had barely been back long enough to discuss their meeting when they heard footsteps in the hall outside. There was no mistaking those steps, either of them. Moments later Emily walked into the room, brushing snow from her hair, with Trent striding right behind her. Neither of them had taken the time to take off their coats and boots, so there was chaos for a moment while they shed their outdoor garments.

Then Emily looked from him to Scott, her eyes dancing. "We did even better than yesterday," she said. "Wait 'til you hear what we found."

"I thought you and me did pretty good getting answers, talking to the old-timers," Trent told Scott. "And maybe we did. But me and Emily? You aren't going to believe this!"

Granville and Scott exchanged glances but managed to keep straight faces.. "In a library?" Scott asked them.

"Yes, in a library," said Emily.

"I wouldn't have believed it, either," Trent added.

"Then tell us," Granville said as he pulled out a chair for Emily.

Trent collapsed into his own chair, all gangly arms and legs. Granville suddenly realized the boy was growing fast, and likely going to mature into a tall, strong man. It was an unsettling realization, somehow, when he felt responsible for the lad.

"Go on," Scott said. "Out with it."

It was Emily and Trent's turn to exchange glances. They didn't even bother to hide their grins.

They were enjoying drawing out the suspense, the pair of them.

"This had better be good," he threatened. "After making us wait like this."

Trent chortled, and Emily grinned at him. "I'm considering whether we should share at all. Or just go and solve this on our own. Since we seem to be finding all of the answers."

Scott chuckled. "She's got you there."

"Oh? I haven't heard any answers yet," he said.

"You have too," Trent said. "Why, only yesterda…" He caught on, and stopped cold, his wide grin spreading across his face. "Oh no. That isn't going to work."

"Oh, just stop, all of you," Emily said suddenly. "This is too good to waste. Trent?"

He shook his head. "You start. This time it's more your find than mine."

"I was talking to the two ladies who run the Literary Institute. And we got to talking about lost gold, and crime, and the rough days of the frontier. At first they pointed me to several first person accounts from the early days. When I said I was particularly interested in a miner who left Barkerville for the creeks in the spring of '68, they talked about the fire, and all the books and letters that were lost to the flames.

Somehow it came up that it was Beau Brody I was looking for. And Mrs. Swinton—she's the one who grew up here—started to say she'd heard of him, then stopped, as if she'd thought of something. Then she asked if I'd talked to Mrs. Darrow. When I assured her I had, and that the postmistress had shared a number of stories with me, she looked relieved.

Then she asked if I'd heard about the town registry. I hadn't, of course."

Emily looked around the table. "Have any of you?"

None of them had.

She smiled. "I thought not. Well, Mrs. Swinton asked me to wait, and disappeared into a back room. Mrs. Gunderson looked just as confused as I felt. And Mrs. Swinton came back with an old, rather warped and rather blackened and singed ledger, half-full of signatures, and dates, and occupations, and addresses. Dated 1868.

It seems this was the only official document saved from the fire that August. The City Clerk of the time used to take this ledger home with him every night, just in case. They used it to confirm the names of those lost in the fire. Since this one was damaged, they started a new one the next day, and donated this one to the Institute. I doubt anyone remembers it even exists. Other than Mrs. Swinton. And she only knows because the City Clerk in 1868 was her uncle."

She paused, and took a sip of water.

"Just tell them," Trent burst out as the silence stretched.

"Mr. Brody registered his departure when he left that Spring. He listed his occupation as mining. And he left a forwarding address."

"From your expression, I'm assuming that address is not for his ranch?" Granville said.

She shook her head.

"Seattle?"

"Not even close. He gave 'care of' Jake Greer at the Post Office in 150 Mile House as his forwarding address..

"I did not see that coming," he said slowly. "Did Belle know he'd given a forwarding address?"

"I asked, and she said he'd never left one," Emily said.

"Did she ever report him missing?"

"No. I don't think it even occurred to her. His schedule was too unpredictable, and she never knew exactly where he'd gone."

"So since he'd left before the fire, and Mrs. Darrow never reported him missing, no one ever had a reason to check the old Registry to find out if Brody had left a way to contact him."

"No. And Belle doesn't know of any connection Mr. Brody might have had to 150 Mile House, either. As far as she knows, he'd never been there."

"Did you ask her about the Registry?"

"After the stunt she pulled with Mr. Dunham? Of course not.

And I was careful to ask about his connection with several towns along the old Cariboo Road, not just 150 Mile. And I might have hinted that we'd reached the point of looking at even the most remote possibility. She can't go and check all of them. Not in this weather."

"Nicely done."

She grinned at him. "No-one is going to fool me twice. Even if I do feel sorry for them."

He grinned back. "Well done, then. To both of you." And he nodded at Trent.

"But we haven't even got to my part yet," Trent protested.

"I'm going to ring for afternoon tea," he said. "Between your article yesterday and Emily's Registry now, I think we have enough information to allow us to re-examine everything we've learned so far. Dinner will be late."

As Granville spoke, he watched his team. Emily looked pleased, Scott just nodded, and Trent's face fell as his eyes took in all of the information that now surrounded them.

"I'm assuming everyone is hungry?" he added.

"Can we order roast beef sandwiches for tea?" Trent asked.

At his nod, Trent looked much happier, and Scott held up two fingers to double the order.

"I know cream cakes are unlikely, but pastries, perhaps?" Emily said, as if she'd just realized she was hungry.

The innkeeper was very happy to receive the generous order, and promised delivery within the half hour.

Then the real work began.

THEY STARTED with Trent's news. Much to the lad's obvious relief. Except he surprised all of them by passing the first bit to Scott. Who winked at Trent, and began.

"Talking to those old-timers who had known Brody," Scott said. "We got confirmation that he was part of several casual conversations speculating about the fate of all that gold that ended up at the bottom of the Fraser."

"Casual conversations?" Granville repeated. "It wasn't something he started?"

"That wasn't anyone's recollection of it, anyway," Scott said.

"Not surprising, since the fellow seems to be a con artist," he retorted.

Emily laughed. "True. But Trent still hasn't conveyed his news. Go ahead, Trent."

"Well, the conversation with the old-timers told us that Brody knew about the lost gold incident, and probably was interested enough to ask about it. So I went looking for anything that said that gold map really existed. I found it, too."

And wasn't that interesting? "Tell us," Granville said.

Trent beamed. "Someone was advertising to sell a copy of the map. Can you believe it? They put an ad in the Sentinel in 1867, not long before the 'treasure hunters' nearly drowned."

"And you suspect Brody saw it and bought a copy?"

"Wouldn't you?"

He and Scott exchanged glances, and laughed. "It was probably a fraud. As Brody would have known. But, yes indeed, we'd at least look into it. Even buy a copy if the price wasn't too dear."

"Well, there you are. I can't prove Brody bought it…"

"But you proved at least one version existed. Good work, Trent."

"Aw, it was nothing."

"It was solid investigating."

"Thanks," Trent said, not meeting his gaze.

There was an awkward silence, which Emily hastened to fill. "Well, if there was a map of where the boat overturned. Then perhaps that's why our missing crook needed the extra blackmail money from Mr. Dunham."

She seemed to take great satisfaction in naming him a crook. Granville wondered if she realized that her lips turned up every time she used the phrase. Or how appealing he found it.

As a distraction from Trent's embarrassment, it was very effective.

"That could fit," he said, a little more briskly than he'd intended. "Or it could be that he'd found his new crooked associates, and needed money to pay them."

"I might have found something on that," she said. There were a number of thefts early in 1868, and there were a number of letters to the editor complaining about failed miners drifting south from the gold fields of the Omenica, and causing trouble. They seemed to be in the area for a few months. Then the "crime wave" suddenly stopped. But there were no arrests reported. Maybe they just kept going south, but…"

"But maybe Brody hired at least some of 'em," Trent said. "It all fits together, see?"

"It does," Granville said. "But as professional investigators, we have to be careful of assumptions. Especially with a case as frustrating as this one has been. It can be too easy to see connections that aren't truly there."

"And sometimes they are there," Emily said, smiling at Trent.

"And sometimes they are," Granville agreed. "Which is why we're going to take all of the information we have, and work it backwards, to see if it still makes sense."

"Huh?" Trent said.

"When Emily found a forwarding address for Brody at 150 Mile House, it tied in with the information Scott and I have been gathering," he said. And filled them in on what they'd found to date.

Both Emily and Trent listened intently, then exchanged glances. But it was Emily who spoke.

"If you take what you two learned and what we learned, it feels like we now have a lot of pieces in a jigsaw puzzle, but there are some pretty big gaps."

He smiled at her analogy. "And we're going to need a different approach to fill those gaps. What if we started with Brody's giving a forwarding address at 150 Mile House, and try to backtrack his actions to when he left Barkerville? Where does that take us?"

"Oh, I get it," Trent said. "Like giving that address was nearly the last thing he did before he left here. So maybe it was just a lie, like a distraction to hide where he was really going."

"Except he didn't tell Belle about it," Emily said.

"Well, he didn't want her to know he was leaving her behind, did he?" Trent said.

It amused Granville to see the lad had the bit firmly between his teeth now.

"If he had set up another identity, and especially if he had a gang who needed to contact him, then "care of Jake Greer at 150 Mile House" could have been a real contact point. It should have been safe enough," Emily said spiritedly.

"Well, that depends," Granville said. "Is Jake Greer an associate? Or is that Brody's new identity?"

"If it's his new identity, why leave a trail straight to it?" Scott said. "That makes no sense. In fact, why leave an address at all."

"And yet he did," Emily said. "Deliberately. And in an official registry. He must have had a reason. But what was it?"

She paused, then sat up straight. "What if it's a red herring?"

"A what?" Trent asked.

"A false trail. If Granville is right that Brody was setting up a new identity, including bank accounts and a mailing address, then maybe he set up two."

"Two identities?" It was an intriguing idea.

"Why not? 150 Mile House seems too small to be the kind of place a con artist would settle, even temporarily. He'd do better with Quesnel or 100 Mile House."

"150 Mile House is on the stagecoach line. But it's also known as the Back Road to Barkerville, because it's on the original Cariboo Wagon Road, rather than the new one." Scott said. "If someone wanted to avoid Quesnel, then 150 Mile House is their next closest choice.

Emily nodded. "What if our missing crook was collecting mail at 150 Mile house using the name Jake Greer. But he also had another identity—let's call him Mr. X. And as Mr. X, he maybe he had identification cards, a bank account and a place to stay in Quesnel?"

"It sounds awfully complicated," Trent said.

"It is," Granville said slowly. "But our missing crook is a complicated man. And if the Jake Greer identity is his, it could create a protective layer between his Brody identity and the possible Mr. X one. While still allowing him to communicate with someone from his Barkerville life."

"Why do that, when he doesn't seem to have kept in touch with anyone?" Trent asked.

"Man doesn't seem to do much without a reason," Scott said. "He's too careful. But he put the "care of" Jake Greer in writing, in a public document. Which means we missed something. Or someone."

"That's it," Granville said. "So what, exactly, have we, all of us, missed?"

"And how do we find it?" Trent asked.

"That's easy. We're going to Quesnel to ask a few questions. And then probably on to 150 Mile House."

His statement was met with complete silence.

"Which means we have a lot to do before Tuesday," he added with an easy grin.

CHAPTER 63

Tuesday, November 27, 1900

On Tuesday morning all four of them were up at five a.m. to catch the BX stage—which Emily was delighted to find was a sleigh, due to all the snow that had collected over the last few days—and en route to Cottonwood. Trent was so excited by the turn the case had finally taken, that he didn't even complain about retracing their steps.

They drove through a world that was familiar, but transformed by heavy snow and the quick fingers of frost into a magical place she didn't quite recognize. If it hadn't been so cold, Emily would have been asking to stop every few yards, to take another photograph. As it was, she kept her hands in the hand warmer cuddled into the blankets that were bundled around each of them.

They were treated as returning friends at every stop, and plied with questions about their time in Barkerville. It was good to see people they'd met on their earlier journey, and it was special to feel so welcomed. But for her it made for an exhausting, if exciting day.

By late afternoon, they were disembarking in front of the

Occidental Hotel in Quesnel. Emily was delighted to be there—she had fond memories of the place and the people there. Plus she was anxious to start finding answers to some of the questions they'd brought with them from Barkerville.

And it would be nice to have some private time, just her and her husband. But first she needed to lie down for a few moments.

It had been a long day in the cold, with a lot of hard traveling. Plus the previous two days had been impossibly busy, with people to talk to, questions to ask and bags to pack for a long journey, since they had no plans to return to Barkerville. In a day or two, they might well be on their way home to Vancouver.

Which didn't feel quite real. Yet at the same time, she suddenly felt homesick. For her family and friends, for all that was familiar. And for their new home, hers and Granville's, which she would finally get to live in. And for the life they had begun on this journey, and would deepen as they built a home together.

Then she laughed silently and berated herself for being a sentimental sap. How could you be homesick for a life you hadn't built yet? Get on with it, she told herself. There was no time for this. Unless she wanted to spend a month in Quesnel, rather than the two or three days they hoped for.

Besides, there were all those questions they might find answers for here.

"Is something wrong?" Granville had asked, coming up behind her. "You have an odd look on your face."

"Oh, no. It's quite all right," she hurried to say, feeling a little guilty and a little silly at being caught. "I was just thinking too much."

"Will you want to change before dinner?" he asked prosaically.

She was grateful for the reminder. "Yes, I'll go up now. You?"

"I'll bring the bags," he said, and followed her up the steep steps to the same room they'd had before.

CHAPTER 64

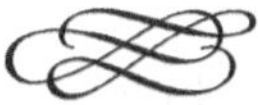

WEDNESDAY, NOVEMBER 28, 1900

The following morning, all four of them met for breakfast in the main dining room. It was still early, but Emily couldn't wait to start this new phase of their investigation. Over Granville's protests, she had insisted that they get an early start this morning.

The BX sleigh had already left, but it was still too early for the locals, so they had the room to themselves. Sipping coffee, they talked about the questions that might possibly be answered in Quesnel. And which of them would take on each assignment. By the time a huge breakfast of flapjacks, steak and eggs had been devoured, they had the day planned.

Emily and Granville would go to the banks, while Scott and Trent would see what they could find out about any search for or maps of the overturned boat with it's missing gold. They'd be surprised if any of them found answers so easily, given that all of it happened more than thirty years ago.

They discussed how much to divulge about their case, in looking for answers about what had become of their missing crook.

"Why worry about it? The guy's probably long dead," Trent said.

"But our client is very much alive," Granville said. "And the things we're learning about his father are not details any son would be proud to learn. Or have people gossiping about."

"Oh," Trent said softly. "Yeah, I get that."

The look in his eyes made Emily look away. Some hurts were too raw to be shared.

Trent's own father was a thief, if not a particularly good one, which was why Trent hadn't seen him in over a year. And why Granville had practically adopted him, though neither of them would ever admit it.

"We can't name our missing crook as Robertson, then," Scott said to distract everyone. "It links straight back to our client."

Granville nodded. "Which is tricky, since it was the fellow's original name."

"Unless it wasn't," Emily said. "We have no idea what his birth name was. He may not have started out as Thomas Robertson, after all."

Even Trent stared at her.

"Well?" she said, a little defensively. "We don't know, do we?"

Granville laughed at that. "She's right. If the fellow can disappear under two separate names, he might well have done it before under a third. Or fourth."

She grinned at him. "Exactly. But we'll have to call him something. Why not stick with Robert Brody. Since it was his "last known" name. Isn't that how they say it?"

"It is," Granville said. "And it's a good idea. That name isn't connected with his son in any way. And he may have actually used it here, if he spent time nearby looking into the missing gold."

"So we use Brody?" she said.

"Makes sense to me," Scott said. "But what about the Jake Greer name. Is it worth trying that?"

"Why don't we ask about Brody first. If no-one recognizes the name, then we try the Greer one," Granville said.

Trent nodded wisely. "We can say we've learned he knew a man called Jake Greer," he said.

It was a good point, but something about Trent's tone nearly set Emily off. She didn't dare look at Granville because if his eyes were dancing, she wouldn't be able to hold her own laughter back.

"Then we have a plan," Granville said, and they all agreed quickly.

It wasn't ideal, but it would do. They'd find out what they could, and meet back at the hotel dining room at six for dinner. The cook had even promised a hearty stew and fresh rolls.

Trent made a face at the menu, and this time Emily didn't hide her laugh. She'd be quite happy not to be offered another steak. And a hearty bowl of stew would be welcome on such a snowy day.

THE DAY FLEW BY, as Granville and Emily found their way around the bustling little town. They started with the post office, where Emily asked after her missing uncle, one Robert Brody.

She even showed them the sketch of Thomas Robertson that Laura had done for them, what seemed like a lifetime ago.

"Since our missing crook seems to be something of a chameleon, he probably would have changed his appearance enough that casual acquaintances wouldn't have recognized him," she had said to Granville as they walked through a quiet section of town. Their steps squeaked loudly on the packed snow.

It was a good place to talk, because while the shops were busy, the sidewalks were empty. Probably because of the wind that was whipping loose snow everywhere.

"That's true. And?" he said.

She smiled at that, pleased that he waited for her to explain her thought, rather than rushing in with his opinion. And that he always noticed when she had more to say.

"I'd thought of saying the sketch was of his brother, so they'd look for similarities rather than differences. But I can't seem to come up with a reasonable excuse as to why we'd have the brother's photograph from thirty years ago and not our missing crook's."

"It's a good approach," he said. "It's too bad we don't have Miss Kent with us, to simply create another sketch."

"Yes, it really is. And Laura would have sorted out our mess of information days ago," Emily said.

"I was thinking that myself. But we need her and Mac there to keep our other cases running."

"True," Emily said. "I wonder if there are ways to work with those still in the office when we're away?"

"There's always the telephone. And the telegraph," he said thoughtfully. "And I suppose, if we'd thought of it, we could have asked her to send a sketch with the BX Express while we were still in Barkerville."

"Is it worth phoning and asking her now?" Emily said, half thinking aloud. "It would take what? Four or five days, sent express mail."

"Yes, weather permitting. And that is a very interesting thought. It might be something we need to consider as part of our preparations for any out of town case."

"We'd want to think whose abilities we'd need for each particular case, and which things can be done while they are still in the office?" Emily said. "Yes, I can see that being important for complex out-of-town cases.

"Because we can't take everyone out of the office. And our revenues are good, but we can't keep hiring more people, just to have someone in the office at all times."

He grinned. "No, we can't do that. Still, with a little planning, we might be able to use everyone's skills effectively, even if they are still back in the office. Like your asking Miss Kent for a drawing now. If we think we'll be here for the next four or five days, it might be worthwhile. Even if the original photograph is thirty-two years or more out of date"

"How can we possibly know if we'll be here that long?"

"We can't. All we can do is see how we make out today. And decide from there."

"I still don't have a good explanation as to why we'd have the brother's photograph."

"Tell whoever you're asking that both men are your uncles. Twins. And that the family is estranged from our missing crook, and so don't have any photos, but only this sketch of your other uncle."

Emily scuffed her boots a little on the thick snow covering the sidewalk as she ran that scenario in her head. Then she beamed at him.

"Yes, I think that will work quite nicely," she said. "Why don't I try it at the post office? I'm more likely to get answers there. And perhaps you can try it at the banks? They tend not to want to deal with women, even now."

"No, they don't. But the strategy works. I can tell them I'm looking for my uncle-in-law. All quite believable."

And so it proved, once she explained that she'd heard her estranged uncle was in the area, perhaps even under an assumed name. And that she was hoping to get in touch with him if he'd left arrangements to collect his mail here. Hearing this, the postmaster was quite willing to check his old records for her, but found nothing for Brody in 1868.

Emily then asked him to try using Greer instead. Finding no Jake Greer, either, the postmaster suggested she consult the old-timers. "You'll find them at the Quesnel's Best bakery this time of day," he added.

Emily slid a sideways glance at Granville, who had laughed and nodded in answer to her unspoken question.

So they both had coffee and she had a butter rich pastry with blackberry jam while three old miners considered her sketch carefully, two of them squinting a little as if trying to see someone they would recognize in the lines and shading of the little portrait. The drawing moved from hand to hand, each time with a shake of the head. Eventually the third old-timer handed it back to Emily with an apology.

"Not someone I knew, or recollect ever seeing," he said. "Not even close."

The others nodded agreement.

"Well thank you, anyway," she said, accepting the sketch back with a warm smile. "It was a long time ago, after all. I do appreciate your time."

"Good luck with your search. I hope you find your uncle," the first man said, and nodded at Granville standing beside her.

That afternoon, they repeated a similar scenario at each of the town's three banks, with Granville taking the lead, and enquiring after his uncle-in-law. They had no luck at the first two banks, but the third one was different.

"He said he didn't recognize him," Emily said, turning to Granville as the wind caught the heavy wooden door and slammed it behind them. "But I think he saw something when he looked at the sketch. Something he didn't want to tell us. He flinched, just a little, and tried to cover it up. Which is odd, because he's too young to have known our missing crook back in 1868."

"Unless he met him later. Or had seen a photograph of him from that time."

"If that's the case, why try so hard to cover up something from so long ago?" she said. "He explained too much, as well, did you notice? Though I don't think he reacted to the Brody name. Maybe it was the Jake Greer name? Or just the sketch?"

"It wasn't clear. And given how young he is, his reaction doesn't make much sense, on the face of it," Granville said. "It seemed too personal. I wonder if he had a family member that was involved with our missing crook?"

"So it might be shame that he was hiding? Or fear of exposure for his relative? Of his family?"

"Something like that," Granville said. "And I'm not sure he recognized either name. My money would be on the sketch."

"That's possible," she said, picturing the interaction in her mind's eye. "But then, I wonder what name our missing crook was using? How many names can one man have, anyway?"

"It depends how smart he is. And how careful. With too many aliases, it's easy to trip up on some detail."

"I can see that," she said thoughtfully. "And so far, we haven't found any sign that Robertson, aka Brody, did trip up, have we?"

"No, unfortunately. But he will have. Even the smartest of them trip up somewhere. We just have to find it."

"We've all been saying that since we left Vancouver," Emily pointed out. "And it's like that final clue we need keeps moving ahead of us, keeping the same distance away."

"Just a soul sucking mud pool of a case," he said.

And she burst out laughing. "Yes, exactly that. And right now I'd rather think about dinner," she said. "I'm hungry."

WHEN THEY MET for dinner in their hotel dining room, Trent had given up complaining that steak wasn't on tonight's menu. Which was a good thing. Emily was so hungry, and so glad to be sitting in the warmth after the day they'd spent trudging about in the heavy snow, she didn't much care what she ate. Or have patience for listening to him go on about it.

At least from their expressions, Trent and Scott's day appeared to have gone better than hers had. Feeling grumpy after her own frustrating day, Emily found the suppressed excitement that was all but bubbling out of Trent a little hard to take. On the other hand, if she could listen to their adventures rather than have to revisit her own, she'd enjoy her dinner more.

And as long as they solved this case, did it really matter where the solution came from? With that thought firmly in mind, she settled back to enjoy the flavor rich stew.

"We found something," Trent said as soon as they were served. "Maybe something big. You'll never guess what it was."

"Why don't I tell it," Scott said, grinning at Trent's crestfallen look at having his guessing game usurped.

"Long story short, we started with the local constable, told him what we needed. He got someone to pull the files out of storage, and we spent a chunk of the afternoon going through them. There were quite a few boxes of files, so it took most of the afternoon to go through 'em."

"But that's not the good part," Trent said. Then met Scott's gaze and made a "buttoning my lips" gesture.

Scott grinned and continued. "We didn't find much we didn't already know. Then we found a guy who's really interested in lost, missing and stolen gold stories from the early Barkerville days."

"He's talkin' about setting up a museum, and you should see the stuff he's got out back," Trent burst in again.

This time Scott simply carried on. "As Trent says, this guy's in his twenties, but he's collected an unbelievable amount of stuff dating from 1862 right up through last year. He's got newspaper stories, first person accounts, maps, you name it."

"Maps?" Granville said.

Scott nodded. "Four different versions of the map for the lost gold we're interested in, the one from the overturned boat. We took a quick look, and all of them show roughly the same area."

"That should help."

"Yes, but he's got something even better."

Granville laughed. "You're worse than Trent, but I'll bite. What is it?"

"He's got a series of file boxes, broken out by year, that deal entirely with major crimes throughout the Cariboo."

"Does that include 1868 and '69?"

"It does."

"Then I eat my words. You're not worse than Trent," Granville said.

"Hey!" Trent said as Emily gave in to a fit of the giggles.

She tried to resist it, but after the day she'd had, she just couldn't. And it felt so good to laugh.

Trent glaring at her just made it worse, until she was nearly hiccuping. Still focused on his conversation with Scott, Granville reached over and gently rubbed her back to help her get her breath back.

"And was there anything in those boxes that might help us find Robertson?" he asked.

"We didn't have time to do more than skim the file labels in those five boxes, but from what I saw, it's every bit of information we hoped we'd be able to track down. If we can't use this hoard to figure out what happened to Robertson after he left Barkerville, then we might as well give up and go home from here."

Wow. Emily stared at Scott's calm face. She'd never heard him so resolute about a case. And she'd never heard him talk about giving up before, either.

It was official. Cases more than thirty years old truly were soul suckingly awful.

But if this collection really did have answers for them…? She swallowed hard. They might be going home even sooner than she'd hoped. And with a solved case.

She glanced at the softly gleaming gold wedding band that now held her emerald engagement ring firmly in place. She'd be going back as a married woman. One who'd traveled, in winter, to Barkerville and back. And helped solve a terrible case.

She wanted to beam just like Trent was doing now.

Except that this case wasn't solved yet. Until it was, she'd try to remember she was supposed to be a dignified married lady now. Well, somewhat dignified, at least.

"So how do we approach this?" she asked.

CHAPTER 65

The following day, all four of them descended on the poor fellow who had collected the treasure trove of Cariboo crime. As Scott had told them, Malcolm "call me Mal" Hissop was in his mid-twenties, medium height, medium build, with brown hair and gray eyes. And brimming over with enthusiasm for his hobby, and anyone who shared his interests.

Hissop—whom Granville couldn't bring himself to call Mal, no matter how comfortable the others were doing so—apparently never stopped talking. He showed them around the back of his house to a large building that had likely once been a stable. Quite a bit of work had been done to insulate the building and water-proof it, from the look of it. Then the entire area had been sectioned into one large room and what appeared to be a series of smaller rooms, all filled with shelving. It was impressive.

Had Hissop done the work himself, or had he had help? Either way, he was clearly fascinated by gold rush history, and justifiably proud of what he'd accomplished.

Scott hadn't mentioned that Hissop was equally fascinated with detectives. While happy to share every bit of information he'd gathered, he peppered them with questions as they tried to work. Especially about their case, and how the information he'd collected might help them solve it.

Chatting about a case to anyone except his client and his team wasn't Granville's preferred way to work, but as he saw it, Hissop deserved something in return for the information he was so freely sharing. And he knew his collection better than they ever could. Perhaps he could find a connection they might have missed.

So he explained the highlights of the search for Robert Brody as they'd unravelled it so far, deliberately leaving out their quarry's original surname, occupation, and any details that could lead back to their client.

"This Brody guy," Hissop said when he'd finished. "How sure are you he'd have been looking to hire a few other criminals?"

"He'd worked with a gang before, so I'd say the odds are good. Which is as sure as we can be without any proof. Why?"

"Huh," Hissop said, glancing around the crowded shelves that lined every wall of the smallish room that he'd led them to. "And he left Barkerville in May of 1868?"

"That's right."

"And no-one has seen or heard from him since?"

"Correct."

"But you suspect he could have taken on another false name."

"At least one."

"And that he was interested in the gold lost to the Fraser when that boat overturned back in '63?"

"So far, it's the only 'easy money' we've found that fits what we know of our quarry."

Hissop nodded. "So far, you say. But you haven't had access to all of the information I have here." And he swept his arm in an expansive gesture towards the loaded shelves in the room.

"No, despite our efforts, too much has been lost over thirty-two years," Granville said. "Where would you suggest we start, given everything?"

"Nothing I have here is going to help you identify your man's new name, or names. So I'd suggest you start with the criminals he might have associated with. See if you can spot a crime that might fit your missing crook."

Granville nodded, showing no sign that he'd laid out the same plan to the team a few days before.

"Show him the boxes you showed us earlier," Trent broke in. "Granville, you won't believe this."

Hissop smiled at them, and hurried towards a stack of boxes near the door. "Give me a hand with these, will you?"

He indicated five boxes. Each was clearly labeled with a date, and it looked like they covered 1867 and 1868. Perfect. It was short work to lift the boxes from the shelves, carry them out into the larger space outside, and lift them onto what had once been a door, now resting on two wooden trestles in the middle of the outer room. The re-purposed door was clearly meant to be used as a long sorting table.

"I don't think it matters which box you look at first," Hissop said. "But they're in date order, so please try to keep them that way."

"We'll do that," Granville promised. To get access to this information? He was willing to promise anything. Well, almost anything.

Each of the team took a box, seated themselves on one of the stools that ringed the table, and began sifting through documents. Their host watched them for a moment, then nodded at Granville and began to go through the fifth box himself.

They worked in silence for nearly an hour. At which point their host packed up his box and stood up. "Nothing in this one of interest to your case, I'm afraid. And I have to be somewhere. So carry on, and I'll be back in a few hours. If you finish first, just lock the door behind you."

"Thank you," Granville said, and watched as the fellow replaced the box he'd gone through, and departed.

Scott looked over at him. "That was odd."

"He didn't do that yesterday?"

"No. Showed us around and helped us find relevant documents for hours."

Granville nodded acknowledgment. It was odd indeed, but some inner sense kept him from commenting.

"No matter," he said. "We have the most relevant documents. Our work is cut out for us here for at least a couple of hours." And he made a mental note to keep track of their host's reactions.

Scott met his eyes, and nodded back. Message received.

They worked in silence for another half hour. Granville made a point of retrieving the box Hissop had been working on, and flipping quickly through it's contents. He found nothing, either. But it was good to be sure, he decided as he turned back to the file he'd been working on before. Hissop's actions and potential motives still worried him.

Scott was the first one to speak up. "I have what looks like a small crime wave here."

Granville stood up, held up one hand in a "just a minute" gesture. He went outside, and walked slowly around the building, scanning it for anything that didn't belong. Finding nothing, he went back it."

"Now, about that crime wave...," he said with a grin. Enjoying Trent's puzzled look, and the laugh in Emily's eyes.

"Half a dozen bank thefts in three weeks," Scott said.

"When?" Granville asked.

"Spring of '68. They seem to start in April and run through May."

"Our missing crook hadn't left town yet," Emily said. "It might not be connected.

"Or maybe this is his gang, raising their share of the investment they're about to make," he said.

"Doesn't sound like Brody," Trent put in. "Didn't he like to be the one in charge?"

"Maybe he was the mastermind behind the robberies," Granville said. "Staying behind the scenes with a solid alibi, in case anything had gone wrong."

"Still. Why would these guys go along with being dictated to by a failed gold miner?" Scott said. "One who wasn't even riding with them."

"Brody may have been using his "failed gold miner" story as a cover. For all we know, he could have been highly successful as a blackmailer. As Brody, he didn't have the reputation to pull that off. But any criminal or law enforcement officer from Seattle to San Francisco who recognized him would know otherwise. That reputation would have made it easy for him to intimidate his victims. Certainly Dunham knew exactly who he was."

"And if the bank robbers knew his reputation, they might have been willing to rob a few banks to prove themselves to him," Emily said. "Like a job interview. Or an actor, auditioning for a part."

Scott gave them both a skeptical look. "He must have had a pretty good gift of the gab to convince these guys."

"Or he had a map and a good story of missing gold," Trent said. "If the payoff sounded good enough, maybe they wanted in."

"We may never know for sure, but that's a plausible answer," Granville said. "Scott, can you mark that article as a possibility, please."

"Will do. And we may be able to get more information on anything we find here when we meet with the constables later."

"Good thinking," Granville said. "Anyone else got anything?"

No one did.

"Then let's keep looking," he said.

~

BEFORE ANOTHER HOUR HAD PASSED, they had half a dozen flagged files. Robberies, claim jumpers, shootings, a couple of murders, a larger number of missing people. Each of which suggested a possible path that their missing crook could have taken. None of which were obvious connections to Brody.

At some point Hissop had returned, chosen another box, and

resumed his seat at the table. Granville noted the fellow watching their progress with interest, while slowly, very slowly, turning the pages in his own box. Was he spying on them? And to what end?

The fellow could easily have refused to let them near his precious files. Or simply avoided Scott and Trent. Instead, he seemed to have gone out of his way to meet them and help them. All the while watching them with a badly hidden intensity.

Was it Brody he was interested in? One of them? Or did their investigation somehow implicate someone he cared about?

It was close to impossible to tell, given what little information they had. Good. He did love a challenge.

And despite all that, it was Emily who found the key.

She didn't make a sound, but Granville noticed how quiet she'd suddenly become, and looked up to find her staring, her eyes wide and her face stark, at the page in front of her.

"What is it?" he asked. "What did you find?"

"A murder," she said softly. "Just outside Quesnel."

"When?"

"Early October. 1868. Not quite six months after Brody's disappearance."

"You think he was part of it?"

"I think he was murdered. Horribly," she said, swallowing hard. "And here we've been thinking terrible things of him."

"Which he'd earned," Granville pointed out. "If it is Brody. Tell us what you've found."

He noted Hissop now had pale lines of stress around his mouth, and the fellow was staring at Emily with an unreadable expression. What was that about?

Granville was finding Hissop's behavior increasingly concerning, but right now, most of his attention was on Emily.

Who cleared her throat and began to read. "Police were called to the scene of a grisly murder late last night. The corpse was found draped across the trail leading from downtown to a group of rented cabins on the Quesnel River. He had been shot and then mutilated, his broken body left lying in the middle of the trail."

She swallowed hard. "Who would do such a thing?"

"Nasty way to go," Trent commented. "But what makes you think it was our guy?"

Emily thrust the file at him. "Here. You read it. Out loud," she added as he began scanning the article.

"Fine," he said, and began to read. "The facial features were too damaged for recognition, but the deceased had dark brown hair and hazel eyes. He is estimated to have stood just under six feet, with a lean but muscled build."

He rolled his eyes at Emily. "Sure, that much matches Brody. But that could be anyone."

"Keep going."

Granville nearly snapped at Trent to quit badgering Emily, when he realized her color had improved with their interaction. The lad was distracting her. Good for him.

"There was no identification on the body, but a well-worn wallet was found further up the trail. The wallet contained no money, only a closed account book showing a zero balance in the name of Jake Greer." Trent stopped reading and looked at Emily. "That's Brody's contact person. And you think it means Brody's dead?"

She nodded.

"They're just as likely to be two different people," Trent argued. "Sure, Greer could be one of Brody's other names, but what if he wasn't? He could be an accomplice, someone Brody was working with here in town. Brody did leave Greer's name as his contact, after all."

He noted Emily's frown, Scott's amused look, Hissop's narrowed eyes.

"But he looks like Brody," Emily was saying.

"He has the same coloring and build," Trent pointed out. "So do a lot of people. We don't know what this Greer actually looked like."

Emily frowned a little. "I suppose it would be in character for Brody to choose someone who resembled him as an accomplice."

"Handy if he needed a scapegoat," Scott said.

"That does sound like what we've learned of our missing crook," Emily said. Then turned back to Trent. "Read the rest of it."

He ran his finger down the article to find his spot, then began to read again. "Further up the same trail was found a battered and empty carry bag that still contained traces of gold dust." He stopped reading. "Whose gold dust? Greer's? If he was a real person, could he have been a miner? Or maybe they found the gold from the overturned boat?"

"Keep reading," Emily said.

"Police remain baffled by the brutal killing. No trace of the killers has been found, and no-one has been able to identify Greer, what he was doing in the area, or even where the gold dust might have come from."

"What about the bank book? Which bank?" Granville asked.

"It doesn't say," Emily said.

"Is there a follow up article?"

"Not in the week following," she said. "I'll keep looking, but this may take some time."

"There's no point us speculating until we have all the details these papers can give us, then," he said. "Unless anyone has come across anything that might relate to this?"

No one did.

"Then carry on, Emily, and let us know what you find," he said, glancing at Hissop, who was studiously bent over the file he was working on. And he wondered again what the fellow knew. And how best to get him talking.

IN THE END, Granville was the one who found the details. It took nearly an hour, with all of them finding and flagging articles on crimes that seemed to be related. But Greer's murder wasn't mentioned again until nearly a month after the article Emily had found. He scanned it quickly, and bit back a curse.

"Listen to this," he said, and something of what he was

feeling must have come through in his voice, because every eye in the room was suddenly glued to him. "It was written nearly a month after Greer's body was found, and there's only a couple of paragraphs."

"Read it," Trent said.

Granville ignored the unnecessary request. "Police yesterday gave a statement on the discovery of the body of Jake Greer, found early this month. The murdered man has not been formally identified, and his bank records confirm only his name and his temporary lodging at the cabin he was presumably returning to on the night of his murder.

It is assumed he was robbed, since he'd closed his account and emptied out his safe deposit box at the Bank of North America earlier that day. Police have uncovered no information on what might have been stolen, or if indeed theft was the reason for the killing. The investigation is ongoing but will no longer be a priority, as every lead has gone dead."

"That's it?" Emily asked.

"I'm afraid so."

"So we still don't know who was killed, Greer or Brody," she said.

"Assuming Greer is an actual person, rather than Brody in disguise," Trent said.

"I'm afraid it gets worse," Granville said. "All we have is a superficial likeness to our missing crook, and Brody's mention of Greer's name. This fellow might not even be a crook, just some unfortunate who encountered either Brody or Greer, and paid for it with his life."

"He might not even be related to our case at all," Scott said quietly.

"I hate this case," Emily said with feeling.

He grinned. "At least it's not boring."

It took nearly the rest of the day to go through the five boxes, with the four of them working until their eyes crossed from the tiny, blurred type of yellowed newspapers. Hissop had vanished for most of the afternoon, just as he'd done in the morning.

When he reappeared at the end of the day, Scott thanked him for his assistance and willingness to let them review his files.

"Any way we can leave these boxes as they are until morning?" he asked. "It might help to take another look, with fresh eyes."

"I'd agree," Granville said to Hissop. "And I also want to convey how truly grateful we are to you for everything you've done for us. You've provided us with more information than we'd managed to find since we started this case."

Their host stammered a bit as he said he was happy to have helped. "And please, feel free to come back in the morning. I have other appointments, but I'll leave a key for you at the general store. And I'll give you a hand later if I can."

They all shook hands with him, and Granville invited him to join them for dinner. Which the fellow turned down, to everyone's relief.

"Something is wrong with him," Emily said quietly to Granville as they walked arm in arm back to their end of town. She'd waited until they were well out of Hissop's earshot, then the words burst out of her. "It's like he was trying to act like he thought someone interested in history and just happy to help us out would act."

"I agree," Granville said. "He knows something, but I can't for the life of me figure out what the connection might be. Not when Brody has been missing longer than that one has been alive."

"So how do we find out?" she asked. "And then what do we do about it?"

"I'd suggest dinner," he said.

At which she poked him in the ribs. "I'm hungry, but that's no answer."

"It wasn't meant to be," he said with a grin. "We need a distraction, and a break from thinking about all the articles we looked at today. Dinner seemed like just the thing."

"So we just forget about it for the night?"

"Well, perhaps we can stop in at the local branch of the Bank of British North America first, since that's the bank the gold came from. We can check if they have any decent records, while Scott and Trent go and talk to the local constables again. Now that we have new information."

"And they might even have a record showing that Greer banked there."

He smiled. "They might indeed."

She shook her head at him. "You could have just said that in the first place."

"Now, where would be the fun in that?"

"Answers are what will be fun," she told him. "So we can solve…

"This soul sucking mud pool of a case," he finished for her.

And they both laughed.

"What's so funny?" Trent wanted to know, looking back over his shoulder from where he and Scott were walking ahead.

"It's nothing," Emily said. "Just a married joke."

Trent made a face at that, and went back to his conversation with Scott.

Emily smiled at Granville, looking pleased with herself. "Dinner might be fun after all," she said. "Especially if some of us get a few answers."

CHAPTER 66

The following morning found all four of them back in Mal's repurposed carriage stable, working their way through the same files they'd looked at the day before. Only this time, they had swapped files, so that each tagged article was reviewed by a second set of cyes. And then the surrounding articles were scanned for connections that might have been missed.

It was tedious work, and Emily could tell that the others were feeling as exhausted as she did. It was hard to sit and re-read documents for hours. Especially when so far, nothing seemed to give them the answers they needed.

After the treasure trove they'd found in Mal's files, their attempts to verify or expand on any of it had been frustrating. Greer's bank, the Bank of British North America, was only able to confirm the bare information that had been in the newspaper. The police records had nothing further on Greer or his murder. Which was still unsolved.

Thirty years on, who the man was, where he'd come from, and why he'd been killed was as much a mystery as it had been the day his corpse was found.

Even the case notes in the constable's files hadn't added anything to the information they'd found in the yellowed documents in Mal's files. Which made no sense to her.

And no-one seemed to know of any connection between Mal himself and Jake Greer.

"He's a local, grew up here," the constable had said. "Fascinated by the gold rush and anything in it. Soft-hearted about that history stuff, happy to share information with anyone who's interested."

Harmless, if a little odd, his tone implied.

Emily understood fascination with history, and especially gold rush history. It was why she was here, after all. That fascination with gold rushes just didn't dim.

And if he'd been born here, as she suspected, he'd grown up in a town the gold rush built. He'd have listened to the old-timers, fascinated. Heard the stories first hand.

And as people cleared out attics of old newspapers, memorabilia that no longer mattered to them, he'd have been right there to collect it.

Part of her envied him. To have access to all that information, to learn so much about the gold rush days. It was almost as good as living it. And his willingness to share that information, and to help them look?

Without that, they'd still be nowhere.

Which didn't mean Malcolm Hissop was soft-hearted though. Or soft-headed, which is what the constable seemed to have thought him. And it didn't necessarily tell her why Mal had collected all that information.

There was still his odd reaction when they'd talked about the connection between their case and Greer. In fact, now she thought about it, it was odd he hadn't mentioned Greer's murder in the first place. It was the grisliest murder they'd come across. And it was less than six months after Brody's disappearance.

Wouldn't the timing have triggered his memory of that unsolved murder?

But he hadn't said a word. Just watched closely to see their reactions when they eventually found it.

Yes, that was what had been odd about it. He'd been watching and listening to them all very carefully, while seemingly engaged in going through his own box of files. That's what she'd picked up, but it was only thinking about it now that she could see it for what it was.

Maybe it was nothing, and she was just bored with their lack of progress on their real case. But if he'd been born here, grown up here? What connections might he have to their case?

"It's been awhile since breakfast," she said, glancing around the table. "Can I interest anyone in a coffee break? I'm sure the bakery will have fresh pastries by now."

The mention of coffee was enough to convince Granville, as she knew it would be. Trent was always hungry. And Scott? Winked at her. "I could get out of here," he said.

Leaving her wondering if he'd guessed what she was thinking. And just how much Granville's partner saw.

ONCE THEY WERE SETTLED in a back corner of Quesnel's Best Bakery, she looked directly across the table at Scott. "How did you meet Mal?"

He looked up from the sugar he'd been stirring into his coffee, and his gaze sharpened. "After we talked to the constables, we stopped for a beer," he said. "Mal came up to us, said he'd heard we were interested in the gold rush days."

He hadn't asked why she wanted to know, she noted. "Did he mention who he'd heard about us from?"

"No, he didn't. Just seemed thrilled to have found someone else interested in what he called "the early days.""

"Was he born here?"

"Didn't say. But it sounded like he grew up here."

"I think the house was his parents'," Trent added.

It made sense. But she needed to know more. "Did he say anything else about himself?"

"Nope. Mostly it was all about the history, and what he'd collected," Scott said.

"Did he ask what we were looking for? Or why?"

"He already seemed to know most of it," Trent said. "Small towns, y'know?"

It all sounded so innocent. So why would Mal care about Greer enough to watch their reactions so closely? Almost as if he had something to hide?

She glanced at Granville sitting beside her, then asked, "Did anyone else find Mal's reaction to our focus on Greer's murder odd?"

All three of them nodded.

"Like he knows something he's not saying," Trent said.

"And is worrying we'll figure it out anyway," Scott added.

She nodded. Yes, that was it. "So far, he seems to be the only one who is reacting to our search for Brody at all," she said.

"We need to know why. And what the connection is to our case," Granville agreed.

"So how do we find out?"

They were interrupted as a tall, solidly built man in his late fifties walked towards them, stopping by their table. Right in front of Granville.

"Excuse me, but are you the Granville party?" he asked in a resonant voice.

Granville stood up and held out his hand. "John Granville," he said. "How can we help you?"

"David Cranston," was the answer as they shook hands. "Gold Commissioner for the region. I understand you have some questions about the old days?"

Emily watched the interchange with interest. Commissioner Cranston had a weathered face that spoke to as much time out on the creeks, settling disputes for the miners as he spent in the office. He had a calm demeanor that appealed to her, and a deep resonant voice.

"Indeed we do, and I thank you for searching us out."

"Wasn't hard," the commissioner said. "When you ask questions in a town the size of this one, people know who you are."

"And where you are, apparently," Trent muttered.

Emily wasn't sure if he'd meant to be heard or not. With Trent it was hard to tell, these days. But instead of being offended, Commissioner Cranston winked at Trent. "I see you understand the dynamic well," he said.

"Please, join us," Granville said. "Would you care for coffee?"

"Sorry, just on my way to another appointment. But I have some time available on my schedule at half-past twelve, if that suits."

"Indeed it does. Name the place," Granville said.

And it was set.

"That might help," Emily said once the commissioner had left.

"We can only hope," Granville said. "But yes, it may. Especially as we now have a better feel for the area and what was going on. And even Brody's role in it."

"We just need someone to arrange the pieces a bit for us," Emily said, thinking of a jigsaw puzzle she'd once spent weeks putting together.

Granville must have caught the reference, because he grinned. "Or maybe toss out the pieces that don't belong in this puzzle," he said. "We seemed to have jumped straight from the "too little information" problem to the "too much information" one."

Trent snorted and started to say something, then wilted under Granville's look.

"Good thing Cranston has a sense of humor," Scott put in. "Or we might have lost a man who could be our most valuable information source."

Under Scott's glare, poor Trent looked ready to melt under the table.

Just when he'd been really pulling his weight, too. And

Granville had been impressed, she could tell. Now Trent had some ground to make up. Looked like he knew it, too.

"No harm done," Granville said. "This is a frustrating case, and a little humor lets off steam. Why don't we all meet for a late lunch after Scott and I meet with Cranston. It'll give us a chance to plan our strategy, and decide whether to get back to Hissop's files. Be careful around him, though. And if the fellow does or says something that doesn't feel right, let me know right away."

Emily smiled to herself, proud of her new husband. And still a little astonished that he really was hers.

CHAPTER 67

At noon, Granville and Scott presented themselves at the Quesnel police station. They had arrived early, hoping the constable on duty could to answer a few questions before their meeting with Cranston. Their timing was rewarded—they were able to ask their questions, then shown directly into the inner office where Gold Commissioner Cranston was reading through a file he'd spread on the desk before him.

When the constable announced them, David Cranston looked up with a smile. He struck Granville as a very calm man. "Right on time," he said, closing the file and striding forward to shake hands. "Granville, good to see you again. And…?"

"My partner, Sam Scott," Granville said as Cranston turned to shake Scott's hand.

"Please, have a seat. Now, what can I do for you gentlemen? I gather you are searching for a miner who left Barkerville in '68?"

"And hasn't been heard from since. That is exactly right," Granville said as he and Scott settled themselves in the straight backed chairs in front of the desk. "And since you were actually working in the area at the time…"

"You're hoping I can help," Cranston finished for him. "I'm

happy to, though I'm afraid he won't be the only miner who left Barkerville and was never heard of again. But I confess I'm intrigued that you're looking for him now."

There was a question in there that Granville made the split second decision to answer. "We were hired by the man's son, whose own son is now about the age our client was when his father vanished."

"Ah, I see," Cranston said.

And Granville could see that he did. "Your constables have been very helpful, which we appreciate," he said. "But thirty-two years is a long time."

"It is," Cranston said. "And for these parts, it's a time that's seen a lot of change."

Granville nodded. "We've discovered a few things since we began the search. One fact that our client seemingly didn't know, is that his father had a criminal history in Seattle before he headed north."

"He wouldn't be the first," Cranston said.

"No. And in Barkerville, he seems to have gone by the name Robert Brody."

"Not Beau Brody?"

"The same."

"I remember him," Cranston said. "He was a charismatic man, and seemingly an honest one. I liked him, enough that I wondered a few times what had become of him after he left town that last time. And you think he may have gone back to his criminal ways?"

"To some extent, at least. He was blackmailing Silas Dunham, who also had a criminal past, I gather."

"Well, well. I thought my judgement better than that. Go on. What do you want to know?"

"You've already shared your impression of the fellow, so, anything else you remember about him, his business and his relationships would be helpful."

"I'm afraid I can't help you much there. I remember he came and went from Barkerville, like most miners who hadn't yet found their big strike. It surprised me a little that he didn't move on after several years of finding little gold. But then there was Belle."

He paused for a moment, a distant look in his eye as if seeing a memory, then shook his head. "She was a beauty, in her day. Have you talked to her?"

"Yes, at some length. She is still devastated at his loss, and was even more so to learn that she hadn't known his true identity. She believes him dead, and blames Dunham for it."

"Dunham, eh? No, I can't see it. He might once have been a petty criminal, but he's too much of a coward to kill anyone."

Granville smiled at that. It matched his opinion exactly.

"And do you think he's still alive?" Cranston asked.

"If he is, he's proving devilishly difficult to find. But he left permanently by his own choice, I suspect he had at least one new identity ready when he did so."

Cranston considered that. "I don't envy you the case," he said. "Are you making any progress?"

"We spent too much time looking for Robertson before we realized he'd been known as Brody," Granville said.

Cranston's brows went up. "Robertson? Not Thomas Robertson?"

"Yes. You knew him?"

"No, never met the man. Well, not as Robertson, anyway. But I remember the wanted poster. There was a lot of interest in breaking up his gang of rustlers at the time, since they were a particularly violent bunch." Cranston looked almost shaken. "Are you sure he and Beau Brody are the same man?"

"Belle is sure."

"She should know. And I suppose if Dunham was being blackmailed by Brody, he'd know Brody was Robertson as well."

"I'm not certain of that. Brody seems to have had some ability with disguises. Given Dunham's initial reaction, he might not have realized who was blackmailing him until we showed him a sketch of Robertson and called him Brody. Although he may have recognized the fellow and chosen not to admit it."

"In any case, you're hunting a hardened criminal with few, if any, moral values. One who is something of a chameleon, and who draws people to him. Finding a man like that after this long is as close to impossible as makes no difference."

"So we've been discovering."

"And the son, your client? Knows nothing of this?"

"No. So I'd appreciate it if you could keep the information quiet, at least until we have a chance to break it to him."

"Of course. No-one else ever needs to know, as far as I"m concerned," Cranston said. Then shook his head. "Poor man. That will be quite a shock, hearing such news about his father after so long."

Granville nodded. "It isn't a conversation I'm looking forward to."

"I can imagine. Have you uncovered any other links to Brody?"

Granville quickly went through the connections they'd made so far. None of which sparked any recognition from Cranston. Then he brought up Jake Greer's murder.

"Jake Greer," Commissioner Cranston said leaning back in his chair. "Now there's a name I remember, and quite clearly, too. Still one of the ugliest murders we've seen in these parts. But we were never able to learn much about Greer, let alone who killed him. Remind me when that was?"

"Early October of '68."

"Nearly six months after Brody left Barkerville, then?"

"Yes."

"I don't believe in coincidences."

"Neither do I. Especially when Brody left a forwarding address care of Jake Greer at the 150 Mile House post office."

"What? I never heard a word of that!"

"It was in a city hall ledger that was archived at the Cariboo Literary Institute not long after the big fire. From the looks of it, the ledger was forgotten in that chaos, since the reference to Greer was never followed up when the fellow was murdered.

"Likely the connection was never made," Cranston said. "Pity. We might have actually solved it if we'd had that."

He paused, glanced at them. "Or not. There was never even a rumor about Brody after he left town. If he'd still been in the area in October, he was really good at hiding his tracks."

"Indeed. Unless Brody was murdered or left the region entirely within the first month, he was a genius at vanishing."

"What are the chances he was murdered?"

"That was one of the questions we'd hoped to ask you. I believe you were the postmaster and based in Richfield at the time? So you'd have heard all the news."

"And probably most of the gossip, too," Scott added.

Cranston grinned. "You have that right. But it was a long time ago, and the Brody I remember wasn't a man anyone took seriously. Except his Belle, of course."

"Which is a pretty amazing feat for a man who'd been running a ruthless gang of rustlers only a few months before," Granville said.

"I still find it hard to believe that Brody and Thomas Robertson were the same person," Cranston said. "Especially given the rumors that I do remember about Brody. All related to his trysts with Belle, and how perfectly they danced together."

Here the gold commissioner closed his eyes for a moment, as if looking inward, back into the past. "Brody never found much gold that I ever heard of, though he spent as much time at it as most. Mediocre card player, handled his whiskey fairly well. A charming smile, and pretty much everyone spoke well of him. That's about it."

"Sounds like the ideal guy to vanish into another identity," Scott said.

"When you put it like that, you're right," Cranston said. "If that was an act, it took me in completely. And even back then, I was considered a pretty good judge of character."

"It's a long shot," Granville said. "But do you remember

anything unusual happening that spring and summer? An unsolved murder, or an uptick in crime? Anything that, if he was alive, Brody might have been connected to?"

"If you've been going through Malcolm Hissop's collection from those years, I suspect you'd have better information on that than anything I can remember."

"Possibly. But given the work you've done all these years, you know that region and those miners better than almost anyone. Anything that stuck in your mind? Or struck you as odd enough that you still remember it?"

"Hmmm. Interesting question." He picked up a pencil, tapped it on the file in front of him while he thought. "When you put it like that, there is one thing."

"Oh?"

"Not long after Brody left town, there was an increase in the number of known criminals in the area. Mostly clustered around Quesnel, though a few showed up briefly in Barkerville. They kept a low profile, but they were there. It never seemed to come to anything, but I remember it made Commissioner Ball and his constables nervous for a few months there."

"Anyone ever figure out what they were up to?" Scott asked.

"No. And they all just seemed to vanish around the same time."

"When was this?" Granville said.

"It's hard to remember exactly. Near the time of the fire, and maybe just after."

"Around the time Jake Greer was killed?" Scott said.

"Yes, I suppose so. The impact of the complete destruction of the fire and the chaos following it was so strong, it's hard to keep the timeline straight. But probably they were around before the fire, then vanished not long after."

Another coincidence? "Was there ever any suspicion that the fire was arson?" Granville asked suddenly.

Cranston stared at him, speechless. "The town was a tinderbox," he said after a long pause.

The Commissioner's voice was distant, as if he was drawing

on an old memory. "Bone dry weather that had dragged on all summer. All the buildings were built snugged up against each other, back then. All wood framed, many with canvas walls. And everyone had wood stoves, with chimney pipes that vented through the roof, and sparks flying everywhere.

Our stage driver called the fire "inevitable", afterwards. One visitor, a photographer, was up on the town hall roof a few nights before the fire, taking photos of the Northern Lights. Seeing the sparks flying up from the stovepipes on every building, and into the night air, he called the town doomed.

And he tried to get the city council to take action the following day, too. But they laughed in his face, said they'd handled fires before.

So no, as far as I know arson wasn't even considered. Just an accident that got out of control."

"An accident?" Granville pounced on the word. "Whose accident? I don't think I ever heard the official story on the fire."

Cranston smiled at that. "Barkerville was a typical mining town, so the fire started in the back of a saloon."

"Makes sense to me," Scott said with a grin.

"Grease fire?" Granville asked. It was just a feeling, but he wanted details.

"Nothing so mundane," Cranston said with a wink. "One of the dance hall girls was ironing her costume in a back room, had built up the fire in the wood stove to keep her iron hot."

Scott chuckled. "Stove got too hot?"

"No. She wasn't the problem. It was the miner who'd had one too many and tried to steal a kiss. She shoved him back, he fell against the stovepipe, dislodged it, and the sparks ignited the canvas walls. Then the roof went. Within five minutes, the saloon was engulfed, and the flames had spread to the bank across the street."

"Which saloon was it?" Granville asked.

"Adler and Barry's."

He mentally pictured his hard-won map of 1868 Barkerville.

"So it was the Bank of British North America that caught fire next?"

"Yes. With the wind up, it went fast."

The same bank Greer had used in Quesnel. And he'd had a safety deposit box there. Interesting.

"What if it wasn't an accident?" he asked Cranston. "Other than the buildings, what was lost in that fire?"

Cranston's face tightened. "Surely you can't think...Arson?"

"Is it possible?" Granville asked.

Cranston paused for a long moment. "I suppose it might be," he said at last. "It was probably the accident we've always assumed it to be. But given the dry conditions, arson could easily have been made to look like an accident."

As they left the police station, Scott was quiet, frowning slightly. Thinking. They hadn't yet had time to discuss what the constables had told them about Malcolm Hissop's history. Nor about Granville's new arson theory and Cranston's response.

Scott's size and strength were deceptive. He was happiest in action, but he also liked to ponder things before commenting.

Granville waited until they had turned down the main street and were well out of earshot. Then grinned at his partner. "What question are you chewing on now.?"

"You really think the Great Fire was deliberately set?" Scott said. "So that... what? The crooks could steal something from the bank?"

"Why not? If it was arson, they set it for a reason. Meaning they must have wanted something. And from the way Cranston talked about the criminals hanging around, they either knew about something of value that they wanted, or were looking for it. And for a way to steal it. A fire made a perfect distraction."

"A pretty risky one, Scott said. "Didn't you hear the man? The entire town was engulfed in flames in less than half an hour.

One wrong move and they'd have been trapped in that. What's worth that?"

"Gold, most likely. Dust or nuggets. A lot of them"

"You aren't talking about the overturned boat, are you?"

"No. The bag the constable found near Greer's body, the one with the traces of gold dust?"

"The one they showed us yesterday?"

"Yes. It had been stenciled. Very faintly. BBNA."

"Bank of British North America?"

"That would be my guess."

"You thinking some of the safety deposit boxes in the Barkerville branch held gold? Wouldn't the miners have entrusted it to the bank, like we did in the Yukon?"

"I think we have too many overlaps, too many coincidences. I can't see the plan behind this yet, but now I'm sure there is one."

"Arson?"

"Is part of it. Yes."

"Brody?"

"I'm beginning to think so."

"He'd left town months before that."

"We only have Belle's word for that. And she used to dance at Adler and Barry's."

"Where the fire started."

"Yes. An accident caused by an altercation between a dance hall girl and a miner."

"Like Belle and Beau."

"Exactly like the two of them. Or like Belle and one of Brody's new gang members."

Scott stopped walking to stare at him. "So you think the post-mistress has been lying to you all this time?"

"I don't know. I hope not, for Emily's sake. But, too many coincidences make me doubt everyone and everything.

His partner groaned. "I hate it when you're right. It makes you insufferable. But this is way too many coincidences. Why did no-one see this thirty-two years ago?"

"They weren't looking for it. Their focus was on surviving first, and then rebuilding their town."

"We still haven't found our missing crook, though."

"Not unless Emily is right about Greer being Brody. In which case, our missing crook is a pile of bones buried in an unmarked grave somewhere in the cemetery. Under a false name."

Scott winced. "That's a pretty ugly end. It doesn't feel like a fitting end to this case."

"No, it doesn't. So let's go finish it properly," Granville said, meeting Scott's wide grin with one of his own.

CHAPTER 68

"I think it's time we checked out 150 Mile House," Granville said as the four of them sat down for a late lunch. "If we pack up and rent a carriage after lunch, we could be there by dinnertime."

They were meeting in the small private dining room at the Gold Rush Grill, the only place in town that could offer them the privacy this conversation would need on such short notice. He'd pre-ordered the meal, so covered platters of steak with baked potatoes and root vegetables as well as a large apple pie sat steaming on the sideboard, along with a jug of water, and a carafe of coffee and a pot of tea.

"All of us?" Emily asked.

He paused, glanced around the table. It was a good question, one he wasn't sure he had the answer to. "That was my first thought," he told them all. "But why don't we decide what makes sense after we've shared what we've learned this morning."

She nodded, and they all turned their attention to the sideboard. Once they all had food, and full glasses of water and coffee or tea, Granville turned to Scott. "Since we have new information, why don't you start with our conversation with Constable Ackwell?"

"You mean about Mal?" Scott asked.

"Stop teasing us," Emily ordered. "Did you get an explanation for his odd behavior?"

"You could call it that," Scott drawled. Then he grinned. "Seems Mal has deep roots in the area. "Not only has he lived here all his life, he was born here, as were four of his uncles. His mother very nearly was too."

"So a pioneering family? Were they miners too?"

"Not exactly," Scott said, exchanging glances with Granville. His partner was struggling to hold back a grin, he could tell.

"Oh, just tell us," Trent said, apparently out of patience.

Granville had wondered who would break first, his wife or Trent. He glanced beside him to see Emily looking at both of them with a measuring eye.

Before Scott could say anything, she stole his thunder. "They were crooks, weren't they?" she said. "Robbers and thieves."

"How did you figure that out?" Scott demanded, leaning forward and studying her face.

"It was the obvious answer," she said airily. "Once I realized he was watching us, I guessed he was protecting someone. Family is the logical answer, but his parents are gone, and there are no other Hissops in town. And his lack of reaction to Greer's murder? Especially given Greer's connection to our case?"

She shrugged as if to say there could be no other answer.

Emily wasn't wrong. It was the logical answer. But she'd put it together faster than the rest of them.

Trent's eyes were twinkling as he watched them. Obviously he was enjoying seeing Emily turn the tables on Scott. And himself, probably. He grinned.

"Well done. But there's more."

Emily grinned back. "Like the other constable is Mal Hissop's cousin? On his mother's side?"

"I'm impressed." He had to ask. "How did you figure that one out?"

"Trent and I figured it out. We weren't getting enough information, even for a thirty-two year old case that had gone ice cold. And when Scott and Trent initially made inquiries, they got more information from Constable Ackroyd than they did from Constable Burton." She paused. "I gather it was Constable Ackroyd you talked to today?"

Scott chuckled.

Granville shook his head. "Got it in one. Nicely played."

"Maybe you should marry her. Keep her on the team," Trent said with a cocky grin. "Oh wait. You already did that, didn't you?"

"You can be replaced," he threatened. Trent's grin widened. The lad had enough confidence now to recognize when his leg was being pulled.

"Besides, I couldn't have figured it out without Trent recognizing what Constable Burton was up to," Emily said.

"Do you want to hear the rest of it?" Scott asked.

Emily and Trent exchanged glances.

"Of course," Emily said. "We weren't able to work out which relative—or was there more than one?—had been involved, or how? And is Mal protecting someone, or just trying to protect the family name?"

"Hissop's mother had a sister, as well as two older brothers and three younger, so it was a big family. Constable Burton and his twin are her sister's only sons. And one of her brothers is in jail, one is dead, and the last three are very much alive."

"Burton's twin is the bank clerk, isn't he? The one who wasn't giving us straight answers," Emily said.

"Right again," Granville said. "They're fraternal twins, not identical. And they must take after different sides of the family."

"Do the last three of Mal's uncles live in town?" Trent asked, seemingly not interested in a bank clerk over a couple of possible crooks. Granville couldn't blame him, though they'd have a chat later about not overlooking even the least likely potential suspect.

"One inherited the family farm, a few miles out of town," Granville said. "Another returns home occasionally, but from what Constable Ackroyd didn't quite say, he's a more successful crook than his brothers."

"And the third?"

"Ackroyd didn't seem to know what happened to him. The only thing he could tell us for sure is that he hasn't been back to town in at least fifteen years."

"What about the next generation?" Emily said. "Cousins?"

"The farmer had two daughters, both married with young children. One of the daughters lives and works on the family farm, the other lives in town with her husband, a local lawyer. Other than that, it's only the two Burtons and Hissop. All of whom seem to be protecting the family name. And perhaps the remaining brothers."

"I don't get why Mal showed us all the files," Trent said. "We might never have put any of this together without those."

"It's what we all recognized yesterday," Granville said. "Hissop was keeping an eye on us. Which was smart, because we clearly weren't giving up our hunt for our missing crook, and we'd already made the connection to Greer. Whoever he's protecting over Greer's death, Hissop wants to keep ahead of us."

"What is his mother's maiden name?" Emily suddenly asked.

"Partridge. Why?"

Emily and Trent looked at each other. Both groaned.

"What's wrong?"

"If we'd known that, we could have saved a couple of hours of searching," Emily said.

"What did you find?" Granville asked.

"There are all kinds of articles and mentions of the Partridges in those files," she told him. "We need to take another look at those."

"I don't recall seeing them."

"That's because they are never the focus of anything. Except the occasional farm article," Emily said. "But this afternoon, as we went through more files, for some reason we started to see them. And once you've noticed, well, we made a game of counting them. We got up to 72 Partridge mentions before we stopped for dinner."

Granville and Scott exchanged glances. The whole family was hiding in plain sight. Another coincidence?

"That has to mean something. What were the names of the married cousins, again?" he asked his partner.

"Koslowski. And Jurgen," Scott said.

"Wait. Which one lives in town?" Emily asked.

"E. Jurgen."

"The editor of the paper is named Jurgen," Emily said.

"So there are four cousins actively protecting the family name," Granville said.

"Seems so," Scott said. "But does that get us anywhere?"

"Not yet. But it ties into the rest of it somehow," Granville said. "It has to."

"Yeah, yeah. No coincidences," Scott said.

Emily was laughing. "Well, we may not be able to find our missing crook," she said when she got her breath back. "But we certainly will have unearthed every detail related to him."

At her words, Granville's grin faded. This next part might be hard on her. "We may have missed a few things."

She glanced at him, her expression turned serious. "What's up?" she asked softly.

He filled both of them in on the conversation with Commissioner Cranston.

"Arson," she said when he finished.

He nodded.

"You know, it fits. It's almost unbelievable that in searching out our missing crook, we find out that Barkerville's Great Fire might actually have been arson. Which no-one else noticed for thirty-two years.

But it fits right into place. The problem is we now have even more pieces of this puzzle. And too few connecting pieces."

"And those missing pieces are the reason we're heading for 150 Mile House this afternoon."

"So what's in 150 Mile House?" Trent asked.

"With a little luck, a few answers about who Jake Greer really was. So far, no-one's been able to confirm his name really was Jake Greer."

"Sounds made-up to me," Trent said.

"I agree with you. And the original investigators had the same thought. They just couldn't get anywhere with it. So he was buried in a temporary grave, until he could be identified.

"I thought at first that Greer was our missing crook. But could he be the missing Partridge brother? That could be what the cousins are protecting," Emily said.

"At this point, anything is possible."

"So why not stay here and try to find answers?" Trent asked. "This is where the Partridges live, after all. So far, they seem to be the only ones who have any idea what really happened."

"Not quite. And we can always come back to here to take another look at the files if we feel we need to. And if Mal will allow it," Emily said softly. "But if Granville's theory about the arson is right, it's possible that Belle was involved all along. She may know Brody is dead, and is still covering up her own role in the arson."

"If she is, she's a far better actress than I gave her credit for," Granville said. "Though you could be right. Burning down an entire town is not something that can be explained away, even after thirty-two years."

"I hate that she might be lying that well. And that we may need to go back to Barkerville and talk to her again," she said. "But are we placing too much importance on Brody's writing in "c/o Jake Greer" as his forwarding address? It could have been simple misdirection, couldn't it?"

"Possibly. But it seems too clumsy, given what we've learned of the fellow's ability to stay ahead of the law. Especially when that ledger could easily have been destroyed in the fire," Granville said.

"And there's no-one left to tell us," Trent said.

"Except Belle," Emily said.

"Who is either telling the truth, which means she can't help us. Or she's lying, which means she won't help us," Granville said. "Do you really want to talk to her again, and start by accusing her of lying?"

"No. I really, really don't," Emily said. "But I will, if it would solve this."

"It's simple," Scott said. "We hit a dead end in Barkerville. We've hit another here. The only place we haven't checked is 150 Mile. I say we pack up, all of us, as soon as we've eaten, and head for 150 Mile. We can stay at the roadhouse there."

They all nodded, and Granville raised his coffee cup. "Here's to finding the answers we need in 150 Mile House," he said with a grin. "And when we solve this thing, the champagne is on me."

And they all raised their cups with a heartfelt, "Cheers."

He savored the moment of optimism. They were almost out of options. Again.

150 Mile House had to hold the missing piece they needed. And all of them knew it.

CHAPTER 69

On Saturday morning, Emily opened her eyes to the blue-gray light of dawn, filtering through a snowfall. She considered the unfamiliar room, then blinked at Granville, already dressed and having pulled back the curtains, looking out at a lace-edged landscape.

"What are you doing up so early?"

He turned to smile at her. "I couldn't sleep."

"Is something wrong?"

He lifted one shoulder a little. "It's this case. We're gambling on what may be our last chance to truly solve it."

She understood the feeling. "This one hurts," she said. "And we all seem to be feeling it. Why?"

"Some cases are like that. Perhaps it's seems harder to give up because it happened so long ago, and there has never been an answer."

"Especially for the ten year old boy who watched his father ride away. And never return."

He smiled at her. "Trust you to find the heart of it. Yes, that's the pull. And we may have no choice but to accept that boy will never have an answer."

"Which seems impossible," she said. "I know. I can't seem to shake the feeling that we left something essential behind in Quesnel," she said. "A clue, a direction, maybe even an answer. Despite how much time we spent going through every source we could find. Including ten years of Mal's extensive files, while he stared at us."

"He did do that, didn't he?"

"He did. But we found nothing that said our missing crook had ever been in Quesnel."

"Unless your first thought was right, and Jake Greer was really Brody in yet another disguise," he said. "In which case he had definitely been in Quesnel."

"And he never left it," Emily said, shaking her head. "It isn't a happy thought. And we can't even prove it."

Her new husband grimaced. "I've been picturing myself debriefing our client, once we get home."

"And?"

"At the moment, all I have to tell him is that we think we found his father. Who may have been trying to find lost gold in the Fraser."

"That sounds all right so far."

"It gets worse. Based on the only viable theory we have so far —that Jake Greer is actually our missing crook—I'd have to tell him that while we don't know where his father obtained his gold, what we do know suggests he was killed for that gold."

"Not good news," she said. "But at least it's an answer. Which is more than he has now."

"A very speculative answer, with a lot of holes in it. And not one he might want to tell his son."

"The facts you've mentioned so far are sad, but he could share them with his son."

"Only because I left out all of the criminal elements."

"Well, yes. I suppose that's true."

"That aside, giving him a report based on so few facts just doesn't sit right."

"It was thirty-two years ago," she pointed out. "There were always going to be pieces missing from whatever personal history we could piece together on Thomas Robertson."

"True enough. But I'm questioning my conviction that this was the next logical step," he said. "Like you, I have this niggling sense that we're missing something that we should have seen."

She smiled at him. "But as both you and Scott said, we ran out of places to ask about Brody and Greer in Quesnel. If Greer actually lived in 150 Mile House for a time, we may have better luck here. We need a thread to unravel. Just the beginning of a hint of a clue."

He grinned at her, as she'd meant him to. "Something that strong? I can tell your hopes are high."

"Maybe not. But our missing crook left an address in 150 Mile House for a reason. I have to believe it will lead us somewhere." She paused, winked at him. "Besides, I'm quite curious to see if Mal will follow us."

"You think us being here unsettled him enough for him to actually follow us here?"

"Don't you?"

"I would have thought it too obvious, myself."

"Not if he's desperate."

"It's a thirty-two year old case that has long gone cold. How can it make anyone desperate?"

"Did you see how Mal was watching us?"

This time he laughed. "I did. That may be too much to expect after so long. Still, not knowing might be a blessing in this case. Given what we've learned about Robertson Senior."

"I still believe knowing is better than not knowing," Emily said. "If it was me, I'd want to know. Even if the truth is painful."

"Of course you would. I've yet to see you flinch at anything," he said.

"Except Mama's idea of a proper wedding," she said with a grin. To hide how much his words had touched her.

"I think your mother's plans for our wedding would have terrified anyone," he said.

She considered it. "That's probably true. Which reminds me, there's something I've been meaning to tell you about Mama's plans."

He shook his head. "Probably not a conversation we want to have on an empty stomach. I suggest we go down for breakfast, then get a start on finding out why our missing crook set up a forwarding address here. We'll have plenty of time to talk about her plans on our homeward journey."

OVER BREAKFAST, the four of them were welcomed with expansive hospitality and a full meal, just as they had been at dinner the night before. They chatted with the innkeeper and his wife, with their fellow passengers, and with another traveler who was staying there. None of whom recognized the name Jake Greer, or the sketch of Robertson. Which was hardly a surprise.

But it wasn't an opportunity they could ignore, no matter how remote it seemed. Because you never knew where the answers might hide. Emily smiled a little, remembering the first time she'd realized that. It was the first time she'd ever felt like a real investigator.

By nine, the snow had let up, and the four of them set off to explore the town. Which proved to be little more than a wide main street that stretched for several blocks, with back alleys running behind it on both sides. The most obvious features included the blacksmith shop, several drinking establishments, and the general store.

Emily had already learned from Mrs. Darrow that while Barkerville had been the official Post Office for the region during the gold rush, the 150 Mile House general store had served as a satellite post office. So she and Granville would start there, while Scott and Trent took on the blacksmith shop and the bars.

She just hoped that the store and post office was run by

someone who valued the history of the place. And kept good records. Even though she knew it was unlikely.

And it grew less likely as she stood on the sidewalk looking at the reality of the compact building housing the store. Typical of the area with clapboard siding, a small porch and a steeply peaked roof, it was hard to believe such a small building served so many functions for the town. The building had been kept up, and recently painted, but she suspected every inch of the place had to bring in money for the place to survive.

Why would anyone bother keeping records of post office box rentals for three decades in a place that small?

Feeling resigned, she pushed through the bright red door and into the crowded interior. To find she'd been right. Merchandise of all sorts arranged in colorful stacks on every flat surface. And some that weren't. She couldn't see a clear spot anywhere.

"May I help you?" came a pleasant male voice from somewhere to her right."

With so much to look at, it took her a moment to register the man standing behind a sturdy pine sales counter.

"I hope so," she said as she carefully made her way around a truly impressive selection of goods, Granville at her side. "But I won't be surprised if you can't. We're looking for any information you might have on someone who collected their mail here in the late 1860's."

He gave a bark of laughter, quickly choked off. She had the impression she'd startled him.

"We've always kept good records for the post office as well as the store, but thirty years or more? I'm glad you realize it's unlikely we'll have anything."

Something in his phrasing gave her hope, but Emily just nodded. Leaving it to him to fill the gap.

And the owner didn't disappoint her. "The late sixties, was it? That would have been when the original owner ran the store. And he had an... unusual...form of bookkeeping."

"Oh?" Emily said, trying to sound encouraging.

The fellow grinned. "He filed everything. Straight into a box.

When that box was full, he stuffed it up in the attic, and started a new one."

"With separate boxes for the post office business?" she asked.

His grin broadened. "Nope. Same box, no matter what it was."

Emily pictured trying to find anything in that kind of system, and swallowed hard. It would be next to useless. No-one would have saved records that badly kept. Resigned to the answer, she still had to ask. "I don't suppose you know what happened to those boxes?"

His grin widened. "The next owner—I'm the fourth—was a conscientious sort, so I hear. He believed in keeping five years of good records. So that's what he did."

"I see," she said. Well, it had been a long shot.

The current owner chuckled. "Except he never found the time to go through the previous owner's records. I suspect he couldn't face the chaos, myself. In any case, he lasted four years, so…"

"So some of the old records might still be available?" Emily held her breath.

"Hard to say. After owner number two's first attempt at sorting, he shoved those old boxes into the furthest back corner of the attic and ignored them. And neither of us that followed him ever quite got around to changing that."

She blinked at him. "You mean they're still there?"

He nodded.

Granville's chuckle joined the owner's.

Feeling her face warming, Emily ignored both of them, thinking furiously. An unnamed quantity of file boxes. Kept in an unheated attic, that probably had mice, for over thirty years. Anything that had survived would likely be in dreadful shape. Especially if the rain or melting snow had got in. Still, it wasn't like they had any better options. She had to ask.

"Can we look through them, then?"

The current owner gave her a sly look. "On one condition."

"And what condition is that?" She tried not to sound too

eager, but she knew it was too late. She wanted those records, and he knew it. Which left her in no condition to argue.

"Simple. You get those old boxes down. And you take them away with you."

She stared at him. "You don't want them?"

He was laughing too hard to speak. "The only reason they're still there is no-one would take the job of removing them at a price I was willing to pay."

She looked up, calculating the probable height of the attic, with its peaked roof. It wasn't something she could do. Not alone. She glanced at Granville, who nodded.

"You'll need help. Even with two of you," the fellow said, observing their interaction.

"I have it," Granville told him. "When can we get access to that attic? And we'll need somewhere with light where we can go through the boxes. Probably a wagon to transport them. And the name of whoever deals with junk removal here."

The owner had stopped laughing. "You're serious?"

Emily and Granville exchanged a glance and a smile.

"Oh, you have no idea," Granville told the general store's current owner.

IT TOOK THEM THREE DAYS.

While Scott and Trent explored the town, looking for anyone who might have known Greer, she and Granville spent most of that first day in the slope-roofed, cramped attic, sorting dusty, cobwebbed boxes.

They couldn't take the boxes out until the store closed at five. So Granville had cleared a space near the trap door that was the only access, while Emily started going through the boxes to find out how old they were. Then Granville stacked the boxes that seemed useful in the cleared space. By the end of the first hour, both of them were sneezing badly.

At least the store had been well-built. There was no trace of damp, except in two of the boxes from 1865, which had been on the bottom of the stack in the furthest corner. The mice had been active, though, and here and there insects scuttled away from the light into the dark corners. Emily shuddered and pulled her skirts more closely around her ankles. She was glad she'd thought to bring an old pair of gloves, which she wouldn't hesitate to throw out after this was done.

By the time the store closed, they were covered in dust, but they had two groups of stacked boxes. The first group they would take with them to an empty warehouse that Scott had hired. The second group were either too old or too new to be relevant. The cart driver that Scott had also hired would load those up tomorrow night and take them away for burning.

Emily noted that it had at least stopped snowing, though the air was so cold she thought she'd freeze just from the air coming in from the open doors as the three men, with some help from the driver, ferried out box after box to the waiting cart. By the time they finished, the store owner was ecstatic, Emily was exhausted and Trent was muttering to himself.

Granville and Scott were imperturbable through the whole thing, slinging the boxes around like they were nothing. Which made Emily truly understand for the first time just how utterly exhausting digging for gold in the frozen Klondike must have been.

It gave her an unexpected insight into their missing miner. Brody wasn't willing to work that hard, in such an unforgiving land. He'd grown used to easy money, and as soon as he'd found an opportunity, he'd gone back to a life of crime.

Maybe he'd never left it.

It shook her, a little, that anyone would think of that as an easy choice. And made her think even less of their client's father than she had. If that was possible.

Cheating, stealing, killing. It took a particular kind of person to see that as easier than hard physical work. Didn't it?

Emily shivered a little, told herself it was too many hours in an unheated attic, and now the frigid air whipping in through the open doors. But in truth, moving and sorting through boxes had kept her warm enough. It was this case, and the ugly things she'd learned that felt for a moment as if the warmth had drained out of her world.

Then Scott made some comment, and Granville laughed that deep laugh of his and suddenly her world was right side up again.

Which was a good thing, because it was nearly midnight by the time they had loaded and unloaded all the boxes. Granville had tried to convince her to turn in earlier, but she'd insisted. It felt important, somehow, not to miss any of this. Even if it didn't turn up anything, at least they were doing something.

CHAPTER 70

Sunday, December 2, 1900

The next day was mostly tedious. The only bright spot was that it gave Scott and Trent time to fill Granville and herself in about an old timer they'd tracked down the day before. One who actually remembered Greer.

"Or says he does," Trent muttered.

Emily hid a grin. This trip seemed to be testing Trent in unpredictable ways. She was going to get to the bottom of it, she decided. He wasn't usually this annoying for this long.

Unless something was really wrong? That wouldn't do.

Scott simply ignored Trent's comment. "The old guy said Greer was a bruiser, and none too bright. No idea what year he'd arrived, or what had happened to him. But he said he remembers him being here in '67 because they had a bet over how high the river would flood, and he lost."

"The others said that flood wasn't '67, it was '68. Or maybe '69. And none of them remembered Greer," Trent put in.

"In any case," Scott said. "None of them had heard about the murder, or made the connection to Greer."

It was the only gleam of hope Emily could see as the four of them worked their way through box after box of paper of all sizes and shapes. And they had to look at every scrap of it. Just in case.

Some of it had faded to near illegibility, some looked as crisp as the day it had been printed. And they'd brought big kerosene heaters into the warehouse, so at least it was warmer while they worked. Outside it was snowing lightly, and a wind had risen from the north, whipping around corners and sneaking through scarves and under coats. By contrast, the warehouse felt almost cosy.

They'd also brought in two long folding wooden tables, and set them up so that Scott and Trent worked on one, and she and Granville had the other. It gave them a lot of room to spread out the contents of each box. And a line of oil lanterns hung over each table gave them a clear pool of light to work under.

For herself, Emily preferred to leave everything in its box, and remove one document at a time, putting it into a second, empty box when she was done. She also had a small stack of documents off to one side that either mentioned Greer or seemed relevant. Very few of those documents were obviously useful, but something stopped her from throwing them out. Just a feeling, but what could it hurt?

By late afternoon of a day that had turned up nothing helpful at all, Emily was tired, and feeling slightly nauseous from the smell of the kerosene, as well as headachy from trying to read tiny smudged print and illegible handwriting.

"Hang on," Scott's voice came from the table behind her. "I think this might be something."

They all turned to look at him. He was holding a dusty brown ledger, opened to the middle. It looked to be in surprisingly good shape. All three of them clustered around Scott and tried to look over his shoulder to see the entry his finger was resting on.

"Is that a post office ledger? Where did you find that?" Emily asked. She'd been looking for anything post office related, and especially ledgers, the whole time she'd been sorting through boxes.

Scott grinned and pointed to the unlabeled cardboard box he'd been going through. "It is. And there."

The box itself told her nothing. How annoying. "What year?"

"1867."

That was a surprise. "That's earlier than we'd expected. What does it say?"

"This looks like Jake Greer to me," Scott said. Then held up a hand as they all crowded closer.

"It's hard to read," he cautioned, and handed the volume to Emily."

Who peered at it.

"Really bad handwriting," she muttered. "And yes, it looks like his name to me, too. And I think it's dated November of 1867."

"Almost a year before Brody vanished," Granville commented as she passed him the ledger. Then he passed it to Trent.

Who squinted at it for a moment, then grimaced. "Great. A day and a half of this and we have a barely legible line that just tells us he was here. Maybe. So what's next?"

Emily reached for the ledger again and he handed it over. She looked closely at the entry. "A name, a date, an amount and he seems to have paid in full. Plus a speck of dirt in an unlabeled column. Or maybe it's a symbol of some kind. Can someone bring me a lantern?"

Granville obliged, and looked over her shoulder as she squinted at the mark. Gently she brushed at it with her fingertips. It didn't move.

"I don't think it's dirt. A small notation, maybe? She ran a gentle finger up the column, finding nothing similar. "Or maybe it's an age spot."

Placing the ledger on the table, she flipped back a page, and repeated the motion. Then stilled. "No, here's a similar notation, in the same column. But I don't think it's the same."

"I agree," Granville said. "It may mean nothing. Or.."

"It may be important," she finished for him. And flipped forward two pages. "Two more notations. One new, and the other the same as the Greer one. And that column isn't labeled anywhere."

"Perhaps he labeled the first pages?" Granville suggested.

She flipped back to the beginning of the book, scanned the page. "No. That would be too easy. But this book starts in January of 1867." She flipped to the end. "And ends in December of the same year. So we need to see the books from 1866, 1868 and especially 1869."

Granville nodded. "When was the account set up, and was it active after the murder? Smart thinking."

"We really need Laura for this," Emily said. "But since she's not here, if it's all right with everyone, I'm going to spend some time with this book, and see if I can figure out that notation. Can you please keep an eye out for the ledgers for other years?"

"We can," Scott said, and even Trent agreed.

But that first ledger seemed to turn their luck. Or perhaps they'd finally hit the motherlode of boxes from the post office. The one the current owner hadn't believed existed.

In the next several hours, all three of the ledgers she'd needed turned up. Emily smiled to herself at the notion of a motherlode as she worked through them. Less than a month in Barkerville and she'd even begun to think in gold mining terms.

After that, she found a jotting on a paper napkin so brittle she'd made a hasty copy of it before it disintegrated. Then a letter that mentioned Greer. It wasn't enough to tell them who Greer had been, or why he was here. And certainly not enough to say if Greer had been a real person, or just another cover name for Brody.

But these signs of progress made all the difference. Emily could feel the change in the energy of the room. Everyone was more focused, and moving faster. The little stack of Greer related items they'd created on the far end of her table slowly grew.

Every so often she looked up, and blinked slowly to rest her tired eyes. Then she'd look at that slowly growing stack of information. And smile. Then get back to work.

They stopped for dinner, but only long enough to eat the

sandwiches that had been packed for them. They were too tired to talk much, and too determined to finally finish what had seemed a monumentally impossible task only this morning.

By midnight, Emily closed the last ledger, put down her pencil, and closed the notebook she'd been using to keep track of tiny bits of information. Stretching out her neck and shoulders, which felt on the edge of cramping, she looked around her.

The stack of "finished" boxes had grown huge. There were only a handful left to go. Granville had noticed when she stopped working, and looked up to smile at her.

"Tired?"

She nodded. "We're almost done, though." And she swept an arm from one pile to the other.

He grinned. Raising his voice a little, he told the others to wrap it up.

Scott and Trent looked up, blinking a little to focus on something that wasn't paper, and then glanced around the room.

"We're nearly done. Why don't we just keep going?" Trent said.

Emily had to hide her smile. He'd quit complaining the moment they'd started to see progress. Thankfully.

"It's been a long day. We'll finish this faster in the morning," Granville said. "And with fewer errors."

Trent looked about to protest, then straightened and stretched out his shoulders. "You might be right, at that."

Emily gathered their stack of "Greer items" into two carrying bags she'd brought with her, strangely unwilling to leave them behind. Granville and Scott carried them back to the hotel for her, and she was tired enough not to protest that she could carry at least one.

CHAPTER 71

Monday, December 3, 1900

On the third day, they breakfasted early and took Emily's carry bags back to the warehouse. And Granville had been right. They did finish faster. Just before eleven, Trent closed the last box with a snap.

Emily looked up, to see the other three moving the last few boxes to the front of the warehouse, to be carted away later. To her surprise, their stack of Greer papers had grown by nearly a third since yesterday. Finally, they had something to work with.

If there was something useful in that stack.

She glanced back at the ledger she'd been working through, and wished Laura were here. It felt like the answer was right in front of her, but she couldn't see it.

"Granville, is there a way we can call Laura?"

"She'll be in the office this morning, so I'm sure we can arrange a long distance call. It won't be very private, though."

"It doesn't need to be. I think I've sorted out the symbols, but I can't quite see what they mean. I think she could. I hope."

"Well since we can't bring her here, it's worth trying. The general store is the closest, and they should have a telephone."

Emily stared at him for a moment. "I'm an idiot."

He grinned. "I sincerely doubt that."

"The post office. Why didn't I think of that? I can ask the current owner if the symbols make any sense to him."

"It's worth a try. Though given the state of the original owner's files, I doubt his symbols will mean much to anyone else."

"If not, then I'll call Laura," Emily said.

"What do you want us to do in the meantime?" Trent asked, glancing at the Greer papers. Though it wasn't clear if he was asking her or Granville.

In any case, it was Scott who answered. "We'll be stacking boxes," he told Trent.

Emily had to hide a grin as she gathered up the ledger and her notes. Clearly Trent was more interested in what those papers held than he was willing to admit.

"We won't be long," she told them both as she and Granville headed out.

The current owner was again behind the counter at the general store, and he looked intensely curious when he saw them enter. "It's only been two days," he said with a wink. "Don't tell me you found something useful."

"Too early to say for sure," Granville said. "But my wife has a question for you."

"Happy to help."

"Thank you," Emily said. And she pulled the ledger from 1867 and her notebook out of her carry bag. "I'm wondering if you know what these notations mean?"

The owner leaned forward on the counter. "Old Jim kept ledgers?" he said, running a finger down the page she'd opened to. "And you actually found Greer. Good going."

He sounded surprised, Emily thought. And maybe a little guilty? These ledgers were records that should have been kept. It wasn't like they took up much space.

But maybe that was her love of the history of the Cariboo Gold Rush speaking. It wasn't like anyone else had come looking for this information, after all. Not in thirty-two years.

"We're still using a system rather like this," the fellow said after running a finger down the page. "But I don't see too many of these symbols. Do you have a list of any others that Old Jim used?"

Did that mean he might recognize them? "I have," Emily said, and held her breath as she placed her notebook, open to the page of symbols she'd compiled, in front of him.

Now he was nodding. "We use a simpler system now, but there used to be a list of these old symbols. I think I can remember them well enough."

It took a moment that seemed forever to Emily, but then he picked up a pencil and looked to her for permission. At her nod, he jotted down the meaning for each symbol, then passed the notebook back to her.

Unlike the files they'd spent the last few days reviewing, his handwriting was clear and legible. Even if some of the terms weren't.

"Can you explain them to me?" she asked.

"Of course. This one for Greer, means it's a new account, and he can receive packages," he began, and worked his way through the list. "Was there anything else I can help with?"

"Not at the moment. I may have more questions, depending on what we find," she said. Then thanked him calmly and gathered up her materials. Only when they were heading back to the warehouse did she let her excitement show.

Granville gave her a sideways look. "I gather this is important."

"Yes. I found more symbols in the other ledgers. And now that I know what they mean…"

"You know what happened to Greer?"

"I need to check something first," she said. Then pressed her lips together, and made a gesture as if she were throwing away a key.

He laughed. "Fine. I'll wait until we're back."

∾

HALF AN HOUR later she was ready. And so were the three of them, she noted. Rows of battered old boxes, sorted by year, stood neatly in front of one of the big doors. Bits of paper had been swept up and checked for relevance, then discarded in an empty box. The only things remaining on the table were five ledgers and the stack of Greer papers.

"I think I have a rough timeline on Jake Greer," she said.

"That's it?" Trent said. "After three days?"

"I'm hoping we can fit the Greer documents we've found into that timeline."

"And find our answers," Granville said before Trent could argue with her.

Frustration was a funny thing, Emily decided. She'd felt like giving up a few times, but in the end it made her more determined to find answers.

Granville seemed to take delays and setbacks in stride, as he did everything else. But he never backed down either. Scott seemed the same, and she wondered if it was their shared hardships in the Klondike that had shaped them so.

Trent, on the other hand, simmered with frustration until it boiled over. He wasn't mean with it. Just annoying. Maybe it was something working with Granville and Scott would cure him of?

"Go on," Granville urged her.

"A man named Jake Greer opened a post office box at the general store on November 2 of 1866," she said. "He renewed that account in November of 1867 and 1868. It was not renewed in November of 1869 or at any time in 1870.

Trent blinked at her. "But… Jake Greer was murdered in October of 1868. Who renewed his box in November?"

"According to the records, Jake Greer," Emily said.

"That makes no sense," Trent argued.

"It makes all kinds of sense if someone else made the payment," Granville said. "Was the account ever closed?"

"Not officially, no. It would have been closed for non-payment in 1870."

"And were there changes made to the account after that last renewal? Of any kind?"

"Only one," she said. "See this symbol here, on November 7th?" And she pointed at a line item on the ledger while they all peered over her shoulder. "It means there was a request to forward any mail sent to this box."

"Why does it say Barkerville D? And what's the date?" Trent asked.

"Barkerville D means the mail is forwarded to the General Delivery at the District Post Office in Barkerville."

"Of course it was," Granville said with a wry smile.

Emily returned the smile, then continued. "And December 1 is the date the forwarding took effect. Which leaves us with two options, as I see it. The first is that Jake Greer was a colleague of Mr. Brody's, and was murdered in 1868. And that it was his murderer—possibly Brody or one of his new gang—who renewed the account in November.

"Makes sense," Granville said. "And the second option?"

"That Mr. Brody had been using the name Greer as an alias, and that it was Brody himself who was murdered outside of Quesnel," Emily said. "Again, the account could have been renewed by the murderer. Though it may be more likely it was renewed by someone in Brody's gang that we haven't identified yet. They might have been using it as a message drop of some kind."

"There's a third option," Scott said. "Even if Greer *was* Brody's alias, he may not have been the murdered man. It could have been an unidentified crook that was killed. The body was found with no identity papers, after all. But that option gets us no closer to finding Brody."

"So where does the forwarded address fit?" Trent asked.

"If there was a third associate, maybe he lived in Barkerville," Scott said.

"On the other hand, if Jake Greer actually lived here, it's possible our murderer thought the police would eventually track Greer this far after his murder," Granville said. "Forwarding the box may have been intended to dead end the investigation in Barkerville."

"Sending them in circles?" Emily asked. "Or might it instead point them at a scapegoat? Someone like Belle, just because she's the postmistress?"

"She wasn't then," Granville said.

"No," Emily said. "But she worked in the post office a day or two a week. From little things she let drop, I think she had trouble making ends meet after her Robby left."

"Maybe her, maybe not," Scott said. "But could be there's something in Barkerville that we missed. Maybe one of Brody's accomplices—maybe even the murderer—lived there. Or still does."

"And maybe the crook who renewed the mailbox forwarded it to Barkerville to set up the other crook, who still lived there," Trent said gleefully.

Emily stared from one to the other. Both suggestions seemed possible, if you looked at them sideways long enough.

"We have too many options," she said slowly, picking her words as she worked it out. "And *we* know that the police didn't come to 150 Mile. Or go to Barkerville. But back then, no-one knew how the investigation would unfold."

"You're probably right. So?" Trent prompted her.

"So it makes it hard to see things the way Brady's accomplices might have, thirty-two years ago. We need to eliminate some of our possibilities."

"Then let's have a look at that timeline, and see what we can fit into it, shall we?" Granville said.

With the four of them working, it took no time to sort the "Greer" documents by year, and then re-sort them by month within that year. Lacking the system they'd set up in Quesnel, Emily pulled several miscellaneous pages from the discard box and wrote a timeline event on the back of each. Then they included each event in the timeline by its date. When they were done, they'd used both of the long tables.

"Very pretty," Scott said, looking at the result. "What do we do with it?"

Only the twinkle in his eyes gave him away.

"This is going to take all of us," she said. "We have a few facts, and a tiny bit of information. Which is part of a larger picture, one we've been gathering a lot of information about. We don't have much time. It's already December. Every day that passes gets us closer to Christmas. And none of our usual methods are going to work on a case this old."

"Yeah, you got that right," Scott said, and this time there was no twinkle.

Trent looked a bit shocked.

"What we do have is we all look at things a little differently. And we're going to use that to put this story together. And solve this case." Emily said firmly.

"How?" This time it was Trent, and he sounded… subdued? That was new.

"We're going to talk about every single Greer document, one by one," Emily said. "And each of us needs to think about it in the context of this case, and everything we've learned about Thomas Robertson, aka Robby 'Beau' Brody. And where that particular document might fit in. Or what it might tell us about Jake Greer and where he fits in."

Trent opened his mouth and she shot him a look. He closed it again. Emily hid a grin.

CHAPTER 72

GRANVILLE STOOD UP AND WALKED THE LENGTH OF THE TABLE
and back. "These events," he said, thinking out loud. "We have
Brody leaving Barkerville, and the murdered man, possibly Jake
Greer, found half a year later. Shouldn't we include the date
when the article on lost gold in the Fraser ran? As well as the date
of the Barkerville Fire."

Emily nodded and quickly created a page for each. "Anything
else?" she asked him, then glanced at the others when he shook
his head.

"Good," she said, picking up her notebook. "Now, each of
you gets a year, starting with 1866. And you're going to read out
every document we have, month by month, one at a time. And
we'll talk about each one. I'll be the note taker."

So they did.

Granville smiled to see Emily confident enough to take
control like this. She knew exactly what she was doing, and how
to use this odd collection of documents to pull together everything else they'd learned on this convoluted case. She did it well,
too. Much better than he would have.

And her growing ability to keep all three of them in line and focused on the case continued to amuse him.

Most of the documents didn't relate directly to Greer's mail, though each gave them a better sense of what had been happening at the time. There were a few pages detailing items the fellow had bought at the general store, which was enough to suggest he had lived in town.

"He's mostly buying food. Enough for a month. Nothing for mining, or rescuing a sunken treasure," Trent concluded after reading out a list from November of 1867.

"So Greer probably did live here," Emily said. "And Brody was still living in Barkerville then. Which suggests they probably are not the same person."

"Was Brody actually in Barkerville in November of '67?" Granville asked.

Emily flipped a few pages in her notebook. "Yes. Belle was worried when he didn't come back until the last week of October that year. I wondered later if he was late because he was checking out the site where the gold was lost into the Fraser when the boat overturned. Since that tragedy occurred in the fall, when the river was at its lowest."

"What about in '66, when Greer opened this account?"

She flipped a page. "Brody was in Barkerville all of that November. And December, too."

"Which eliminates several options, right there. Including Brody actually being Greer," Granville said. "Presumably at some point in 1866, Brody hired Greer. Making him the second man in the gang. The timing is right if they were going after that lost gold."

"I wonder if Brody considered that they looked something alike when he hired Greer?" Scott said.

"Given what we've learned of Brody, he probably did," Granville said. "Though it's possible Greer had worked for him in the past."

"Now all we need is the clue that unlocks everything," Emily said with a laugh.

Trent frowned at her. "So where does the fire fit in?" he asked.

They all looked at each other.

"How could we have missed that?" Emily said. "It was a miner and a dance hall girl that started it, wasn't it?"

"That's one of the stories."

"Then let's talk about that story. What if the dance hall girl was Belle?" she said. "And the miner was Brody? He might have sneaked back into town in disguise."

"Pretty high risk of him being recognized," Scott said. "And just because they said the miner was trying to steal a kiss, doesn't mean he was."

"Good point," Granville said. "If the dancer was Belle, that miner could be our third man, the one in Barkerville. Dunham would fit for that, especially since Brody was already blackmailing him. Though I wonder what Belle's role is in this?"

"She was probably threatened," Emily said. "Or maybe Brody managed to convince her that he needed her help. From the way she talks about him, I think she'd have done anything for him."

"Everyone I talked to said there was a lot of miners and dance hall girls in Barkerville back then. Could have been anyone," Trent said. "And I still don't get it. How does someone setting the Great Fire fit in with all this?" And he waved a hand at their makeshift timeline.

"That is a very good question," Granville said. "Where do we see connections?"

"The second building to burn was a bank," Scott said. "The one right across the street from the dance hall, where the fire started. And it was a branch of the same bank Greer used in Quesnel."

"That's an interesting coincidence. And it seems odd that one of the buildings right beside the dance hall didn't go up before the bank across the street," Granville said. "I wonder which way the wind was blowing?"

"We know it was windy, and the town was tinder dry. If

sparks were flying from that wood stove, it wouldn't take much for gusts of wind to blow them in more than one direction," Scott said. "Fire is unpredictable. But…"

Granville nodded. "Exactly. And Greer—or the body thought to be Greer—was found with an empty bankers bag with traces of gold dust from that same bank."

"That's a pretty big coincidence," Scott said.

"I agree," he said. "So. What if we assume that the fire was arson, designed to cover up a bank robbery. The Barkerville branch would likely have been holding bags of gold dust and nuggets, with the same design as Greer's empty bank bag."

"And when everyone was distracted by the fire, the thieves stole those bags of gold dust from the bank. In the confusion, they somehow got the gold from Barkerville to Greer's account at the Quesnel branch," Emily said. "Except… how would they manage that? The gold would have been in a safe, wouldn't it?"

"Undoubtedly," Granville said. "Probably a fireproof one. Far too heavy for the bank to move during the fire, even if they'd had time before the fire got too hot." He paused. "Was any of their gold reported lost after the fire?"

"The stories about the fire don't mention it," Scott said. "But even if it was arson? And if the thieves managed to break into the bank and set a second fire? How would they get away with any gold? Even gold dust is heavy, and that fire spread too fast."

"The thieves couldn't have broken into the safe in the time they had, either," Granville said. "They'd have found themselves in a burning building with no way to steal the gold in time."

"There may have been a way," Emily said slowly. "The CPR station in Vancouver sometimes has gold and other valuables in their main safe overnight, or for several days. And the gold always has transfer papers, verified and carefully guarded, that state where the gold is going, and if it's going to a bank, to which account.

Usually a designated senior manager takes a briefcase full of the current transfer papers home each night. So even if the safe is burgled, they have a record of the lost valuables, for insurance purposes. What if something like that happened here?"

"If so, and if Brody's gang could change the recipient account on those transfer papers, it would be the perfect theft," Granville said. "They could steal gold without even having to actually move it."

Emily nodded. "And Brody could have set up a fake identity or two for either himself or Greer, or even for the third gang member. Then the first fake identity could open a safety deposit box for the gold transfer, and a second identity could set up another box at a the same bank.

If they were fast and stealthy enough to change the paper-work that transferred the gold from the bank in Barkerville to a safe deposit box at the Quesnel branch of the same bank? Then they could easily use another identity to move the gold dust again to a different box at the same branch, where it could sit until things cooled down.

If that was all done within days of the fire, it would be close to impossible for the bank to trace. The fake names would have vanished, and the gold with them. Neatly eliminating the risk of being caught."

"If they were smart, they might change the transfer date, too. Make it earlier."

Emily nodded. "That way the gold would be gone before the real owner even thinks to ask about it. Especially in the chaos after the fire."

"If similar safety procedures for transfers were used here," he said, thinking aloud for the benefit of the team. "The bank manager is the logical person to have taken the transfer papers home. When he fled his home and sought shelter along the river-banks, like everyone else in town, it created an opportunity for our thieves. It's possible that in the confusion, one of the thieves could have gained access to those papers, and changed the account information on the transfer forms for the bags of gold dust in the safe."

"Which normally would have been taken by stage to their

Quesnel branch on the transfer date," Emily said. "Whoever this is, they'd need quite a bit of insider knowledge. Maybe one of the gang worked at that bank? Or knows a gullible bank clerk."

Her eyes met his. "Like that bank clerk in Quesnel. Hissop's cousin."

"Partridges, both of them," she added in an aside to Trent and Scott. "Only this bank clerk's too young to have anything to do with the Barkerville fire. But in a family with a lot of crooks, like the Partridges, a bank clerk or two could be very useful."

"They could indeed," he said. "I wonder if that fifth Partridge brother, the one that no-one is willing to talk about, has ever been to Barkerville. Or knew Brody?"

"You think there's another member of Brody's gang?" Trent guessed. "That would make it five, right? If Belle's part of Brody's gang, I mean."

Right now, Granville was feeling pretty impressed with his own gang. "It would. And if Emily is right about how they managed to steal the gold, a fifth member might have been involved in those transfers."

"If they even did that," Emily said in wry tones.

He grinned. "Oh, I'm getting a strong feeling that's exactly what happened."

"Good luck proving it," Scott said.

"It's all about the questions you ask," he said calmly, knowing that would rile his partner. "Where were we?"

It was Emily who answered. He'd counted on that. "If the bank transfers worked the way we suspect, when they decided enough time had passed, Greer took the gold out of his second box, and was on his way back to the cabin he'd rented, and then to…where?… when he was murdered."

"In that scenario, either Greer was trying to run off with the gold and got killed by Brody or his gang," Granville said. "Or he was taking the gold to meet up with Brody and the gang, and someone else killed him."

"Or maybe he was going to meet them, but Brody and the third man—or maybe that fifth man we wondered about—killed him. Because Greer was the only one who could tie all of them to the actual stolen gold," Scott said heavily. "From what little we know about Greer yesterday, he was the muscle, not the brains."

"Not likely to plot against Brody, then?" Granville said. And frowned. Something wrong there. If Greer's murder was just convenient for Brody, why all the violence?

"The way Greer died? Looks like someone lost their temper," Trent said, apparently not noticing Granville's reaction.

"Or wanted it to look that way," he said. "It could be about sending a message, too." But what kind of message? And to whom? "Scott, did we ever hear what killed Greer?"

"No. We got the graphic description of the mess they made of his body, but not what killed him."

They exchanged a look. "If he was shot, then the violence was just for show. We'll have to find out," he said. "And we still have no idea what happened to Brody. If indeed it was Greer who was murdered."

"But wait. Why was Greer's body found with only one empty bank bag?" Trent asked. "Where's the rest of it? Who ended up with the gold?"

"That is a very good question," Granville said. "When Greer closed his account, if he took all of the gold with him, whoever murdered him has the lot. But if Brody moved most of the gold, perhaps to a different bank, and Greer was paid out only his own share, then the murderer got away with only the gold Greer was carrying. Which likely only partly filled that bank bag."

"Except who would even know Greer had closed his account and was carrying gold?" Emily said. "Given the timeline, this was likely the only time Greer was carrying any of the gold on his person, other than in the safety deposit box room."

"With odds like that, Greer was either very unlucky, or he was betrayed," Scott said.

"The only ones who knew were Brody, and Brody's gang," Granville said. "Even the bank manager doesn't know what's in a safety deposit box."

"So it had to be Brody or another member of his gang, then? It only took one," Trent said disgustedly. "But which one?"

"In every detective story I've ever read, they always ask *qui bono*? Who benefits?" Emily smiled at Granville. "Granville speculated earlier that Brody might have worked with Greer before. If so, he must have trusted him. Once Brody had the gold, Greer's part was done and he needed to vanish.

The easiest thing would be to pay Greer out, and send him away, breaking the only link between the gold and Brody. My guess is Brody did exactly that, leaving him with one less gang member to worry about, and holding most of the gold."

"Huh," Trent said. "So you're saying Brody wouldn't benefit when Greer was murdered."

"When that murder is a gruesome one, drawing attention to Greer and his banking history? No, Brody wouldn't benefit," Granville said.

"Leaving one of the gang," Scott agreed.

"But all of this is still speculation, even though it fits everything we *do* know," Emily said. "How can we be sure we're not just forcing things together that really don't have a thing to do with each other?"

Granville nodded. "We really need that clue you talked about earlier. Something that links Greer and his role firmly into all of this."

CHAPTER 73

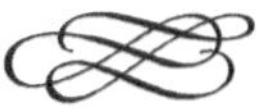

Granville picked up the next document in his stack, a pale yellow flimsy, and stared at it for a moment. Instead of reading it out, he turned to Emily. "What date did you say Greer's post office account was renewed after his death?"

"On November 2. Of 1868," Emily said. "Why? What did you find?"

"Bear with me for a moment. And when did the request go through to forward that mail to Barkerville?"

"November 7. It was to take effect on December 1, 1868."

"Why does that even matter?" Trent asked.

"Because I'm looking at a copy of a telegram sent from the 150 Mile House Post Office to the Barkerville Post Office, advising them of the change," he said. "And the date sent stamp reads November 8, 1868."

Trent looked puzzled, but Emily's eyes widened and her face drained of all color. "It must have been standard practice to notify the other Post Office involved when a mailbox address was to be forwarded," she said, half to herself.

"And if Brody was the one using Greer's account, he likely wouldn't have known that," Granville said.

"No. There was no reason for him to know," Emily said. "But Belle would have known."

"Tell Trent why that matters."

"If we're right that Belle was in on this, Brody probably promised her that if she played her role, he'd take her away from it all, and they'd live a better life together somewhere else. Once they had the gold."

"If she was part of the gang, she must have known Greer was dead by then?" Trent said.

"Most likely. So seeing that notice would tell her in blunt terms that her Robby was planning to leave the area. And he wasn't including her in his plans," Emily said softly.

"Maybe he'd already paid out her share, and the Belle and Beau story was just a cover," Scott said.

"Even if it started that way, she loved him by the end," Emily said. "I saw it in her eyes. She probably expected for Brady to keep her share of the gold until they could both leave town. Together."

"He might have blackmailed Dunham into accepting a similar arrangement," Granville said.

"Sounds like his style," Scott agreed.

"And Belle's reaction when she saw this notice?" Granville asked Emily.

"She would have known immediately that Brody planned to disappear without her. And without paying out her share," Emily said.

"Leaving her deserted and broke?" Scott gave a low whistle. "That's a low blow."

"But, we said earlier that Brody wanted the link with Greer broken. So why would he be using Greer's mail account, anyway? I still don't get it," Trent complained.

"Hard to say," Granville said. "Keeping Greer's accounts active must have played some role in either his alibi or in whatever scheme he was running at the time."

"But why forward the account to Barkerville if he was planning on ditching Belle," Scott asked.

"There was probably a risk the police would keep digging into Greer's death," Granville said. "If someone ever came asking questions in 150 Mile House, by forwarding the mail account like he did, Brody was pointing the investigation back to Barkerville. And possibly setting up Belle or the third man, both of whom probably still lived there."

"I wonder if Belle recognized that?" Emily said. "At the very least, she'd already understood that she was no longer included in Brody's plans. That alone must have been a horrible shock."

"And she found out three weeks sooner than Brody would have expected her to," Scott said. "While he was still living here."

"In the wrong hands, that was dangerous information," Granville said. He turned to Emily, watching her with concern. "Given what you know of her, how would Belle react to seeing all of this?"

His new wife had seen all of the implications even more quickly than he had. And she'd realized that the moment Belle saw that telegram, she'd have understood that the man she loved was betraying her. And in the worst possible way.

Emily drew in a harsh breath. "From what I know of Belle, I think she'd be shocked. And deeply hurt. And then angry. Very, very angry."

"How would she handle that anger?" Granville asked.

"It's hard to say," Emily said, picturing Belle as she'd looked talking about her Robby. "Her anger might turn inward, until she drowned in it. Or it might turn outward, and she'd decide to get even."

"That's how I see it, too. We need to talk to Belle again," Granville said heavily, staring at the tattered notice in front of him.

"Wait. I still don't get it. If this is Brody, all he's doing is forwarding the mail, because he's going back to Barkerville," Trent said. "How do you get all this "pointing fingers" stuff? And why would Belle think any differently?"

"Because after the fire, Belle knew that Brody couldn't afford to let anyone know he was still in the area. He'd lose the alibi his disappearance gave him," Emily said. "And at this point, Brody was probably the one holding most of the stolen gold. Maybe all of it, if he killed Greer. None of which he could spend in Barkerville without raising suspicions."

"Oh," Trent said. "So going back to Barkerville would trap him there. And her too. I guess she wouldn't be too happy about that."

"No, she wouldn't be," Emily said. "But not for the reason you're thinking. She'd know Brody would never put himself in that kind of trap. Not for anyone. If he was leaving, Barkerville was the last place he'd go."

Trent thought about that for a moment. "So she'd guess what he was up to," he said. "She must have been stinking mad."

"That's one way of putting it," Granville said, hiding his grin. The lad was developing a gift for understatement.

"I get it," Trent said. "But what if she wasn't involved? The name Greer would mean nothing to her. Going back to Barkerville to talk to her could be a giant waste of time."

Granville shook his head. Trent was also developing a habit of asking blunt questions that poked holes in their theories. Which was starting to annoy him. But the lad's contrarian perspective meant they wouldn't take anything for granted. Which was good for the case. And therefore good for the team.

No matter how annoying he was.

"Even if she wasn't involved," Granville told the lad. "Belle probably has a better shot at identifying the other team members —one or both of whom is likely a murderer—than we do. And in turn, that murderer is still our best chance of finding Brody. Dead or alive."

No-one had any further arguments.

And though it took another four hours to go through them, the rest of the Greer documents yielded no further clues. It was time to go.

~

Late that afternoon, all four of them were warmly bundled in a hired coach heading back to their hotel in Quesnel.

Where Granville and Scott had a long chat with Constable Ackerman, who had a few things to say about bodies turning up in the area between Quesnel and 150 Mile House in 1868 and 1869.

Ackerman had pulled all of the relevant files, and spread them out on his desk. Granville was particularly interested in the one found a few miles downstream of 150 Mile House in 1869.

The victim had washed up on the bank of the Fraser, during the fall low waters. There wasn't much left but bones, but even bones could tell a story. And these did.

Ackerman got quite excited in the telling, because the victim had been shot twice in the heart. "The shooter, he was good. Both shots were so precise, the bullets lodged in his ribs. Within inches of each other, too."

"I don't suppose you found those bullets?" Granville said.

"Sure did. They were still lodged in his ribs when we dragged him out of the river. Same rib, too."

"Not something you'd see every day," Scott said.

"Well, not usually. But in this case? We might not know who the victim was, but we sure knew the killer."

"Let me guess. This killer had a pattern?" Granville said.

Ackerman beamed. "He did. There was nothing linking the victims, but he killed them all exactly the same way. Two bullets to the heart, fired at a downward angle, bullets lodged in the ribs."

"A shooter, then?"

Ackerman nodded. "Prided himself on it."

"A pattern like that's a good way to get caught," Granville said.

Ackerman grinned. "By the time that body washed up, we'd already arrested Partridge for three other murders."

"Partridge." Why did he know that name? Then it came to him. "Hissop's uncle?"

"He sure is."

"You ever identify the victim?"

"No. The case went cold years ago. Nobody ever reported missing in the area, either."

Brody. It had to be. "So Partridge never talked?"

"Nope. Even when he was charged with shooting whoever it was."

"So no idea why he'd have shot this particular victim?"

"He was a hired killer. Someone must've wanted this guy dead," Ackerman said.

Granville nodded, thinking hard. If it was Brody, with Greer dead, the most likely suspects were Belle or maybe Dunham. But how would they have known Partridge? He wouldn't have been cheap to hire, either.

Unless Partridge was that fifth member of the gang that Emily had speculated about. Which would automatically link him to Belle and Dunham. And to Brody.

"Got any names for us?" Scott was asking.

"We tried. Partridge wouldn't give up his clients."

"Where is Partridge now?" Granville asked.

"Still in jail," Ackerman said. "I checked. With this case, it made four murders, so he's serving consecutive time, no parole."

"So Partridge was convicted for this murder, too?"

"He was."

Interesting. "Did the victim's bones tell you anything about who he was?"

"Not much left of him but bones and teeth, I'm afraid. And Partridge wasn't talking. Still hasn't. Judging by the bones, though, the doc said the victim was male. His approximate height and weight match your missing crook. And it looks like he was dark haired, as well. But that's all we got, I'm afraid. Nothing to confirm he's your man."

"What about dental records?"

"Might help, if they still exist."

Granville and Scott exchanged glances. It was a long shot, but their client might know where to look. Though after so many years, it was unlikely.

But there was one person that knew for sure whose body that was. And who had hired the killer, too.

It was time for yet another long shot.

"Any chance you could arrange a meeting with Partridge?" Granville said. "We'd like to ask him a few questions about this case."

"Maybe. Depends what you want to know. You'd have to talk to his lawyer and the judge."

"If you can give me the names, I'll have our lawyer talk to his lawyer," Granville said. "Randall will take care of it."

He would, too. Granville was pretty much convinced that there was no part of the legal system that Josiah Randall couldn't make sit up and beg.

"I can do that. Anything else I can help you with?"

"Which prison?" Scott asked. "New Westminster?"

Ackerman nodded.

"And Partridge's first name?" Granville asked.

"Ned," Ackerman said. "He's the oldest of that family."

Which didn't quite explain why Hissop was keeping such a close eye on them. Unless Ned had help from one of his brothers, perhaps the youngest brother who seemed to have vanished.

It might be worth having a conversation with Hissop before they left town, after all. He was protecting something. Or some-one. And Granville wanted to know what, or who, Hissop and his cousins were so worried about.

He had a feeling that Hissop's Uncle Ned might just share that concern, if he knew about it. It was always easier to get a suspect to talk when you had something meaningful to bargain with. And that went double when the suspect was a convicted murderer.

"What about Greer's murder," he asked. "Were there any similarities between that and this one?"

Ackerman smiled. "I had a feeling you'd ask that, so I went

through that file again. And no, there weren't. Greer was shot from behind, and that shooter wasn't particularly accurate. Took him three bullets, then he tried to hide them with all the slicing he did. Nasty piece of work, but not a professional killer."

"Sounds like a coward to me," Scott said.

"Going by the files, it looked like one, too. A coward who hated his victim," the constable said. "Sorry, I know that's not much help."

"Quite the opposite. We'd be nowhere without the information you've given us," Granville said.

And nothing Ackerman told them disproved their theory about the third man. And he still liked Dunham as the killer on that one. 'Coward' was a title that fit him to a "T".

He stood and shook the constable's hand, then Scott did the same.

"We'll be heading back to Barkerville tomorrow, to see if we can shake loose a bit more information. Anything we can verify, we'll send your way," Granville said.

"Though with Partridge already in jail for what's likely to be Brody's murder, I doubt we'll see more arrests. Not in a case this old. But at least we'll have an answer for our client."

"Good luck on that," Constable Ackerman said.

"I suspect we'll need it," Granville said wryly.

As the door closed behind them, Scott rolled his eyes. "You know our chances of getting back home before Christmas are getting worse with every conversation you have, right?"

"I promised Emily," Granville said. "We'll make it in time."

CHAPTER 74

Tuesday, December 4, 1900

The following day was a long one, starting with an enormous breakfast at the Occidental Hotel, and ending with an even more enormous dinner at the Barkerville Inn, where they were welcomed with surprise and pleasure. The stagecoach journey was mostly by sleigh, given the amount of snow that had accumulated everywhere.

It took them two more days to find the answers to the questions they now knew to ask. They re-interviewed everyone, including Commissioner Cranston, who was back in Barkerville, and who added some details to what Constable Ackerman had told them. Including the information that he remembered having seen Ned Partridge in Barkerville from time to time, around the time Beau Brody lived there.

That information strengthened the likelihood that Partridge had a connection of some kind with Brody's gang. Though why the fellow would have taken the risk of being seen with any of them was a mystery.

They then set Constable McCall to digging into any piece of evidence they could find. Which wasn't much.

Re-interviewing the old-timers with the right questions didn't get them far, either. Even Dunham dodged almost every question. According to him, he'd never seen Ned Partridge in Barkerville.

And when asked who had killed Greer—whom he'd finally admitted knowing—Dunham blamed Brody. Though he dropped a few hints, he still danced around admitting that the eviscerated body found near Quesnel in '68 had indeed been Greer.

Since they had no proof, there was no shaking the fellow's story. Not yet.

It wasn't until late on the second day that Granville and Emily arranged to meet with Belle Darrow, in private.

They had worked out most of her role by then. But despite the vitriol that Dunham didn't even try to hide, he'd done no more than fling a few accusations Belle's way. He had no proof. And not many details, either.

Granville suspected Brody hadn't trusted Dunham with his plans. Or Greer. If he'd relied on anyone, it likely would have been Belle. The dancehall girl who'd told Emily that she'd do anything for "her Robby".

In the end, though, Brody hadn't trusted Belle with his plans either.

Which might well have killed him.

Unless Belle was innocent of anything except loving the wrong man.

And one way or another, they were going to find out.

It took every bit of knowledge they'd gained, every bit of strategy and guile, to get the answers and confirmation they needed from Belle Darrow. And every bit of patience. And still it wasn't enough.

They started, carefully, with Greer's death. Belle didn't seem to know, or care, who had killed the fellow. Though she was happy to point a finger at Dunham.

"He knew Greer and Brody were meeting, didn't trust either

of them. And then he went out of town, suddenly," she told them. "Acted odd when he came back. And he suddenly had money again. A mine that finally paid off, he told us. Hah. The fool couldn't find a mine on his own if he tripped over it. No, Dunham's sudden wealth is the reason Greer's dead."

"What about the rest of the stolen gold?" Granville had asked her. "Was Greer carrying all of it?"

"Hardly," she said. "But you'd have needed to ask my Robby about that. I never saw a penny of it."

Emily swallowed hard as Belle's mask slipped, hatred mixing with pain and the long years of lies on that once beautiful face. It was an ugly glimpse into what hardship had done to someone who'd once fought to believe in love.

Granville glanced at Emily, and was quick to change the subject, asking Belle about the telegram that had pointed them to her. Testing Belle's reaction.

"Yes, I saw that telegram," she'd said. "And I knew then. My Robby intended to vanish into a new identity, taking the gold that meant too much to him, and leaving me behind."

"What happened to Brody after that?"

Her tears were his only answer.

Emily asked the questions then, keeping her voice quiet and her comments supportive. It was enough to get past the tears. Once Belle realized what they had learned, she quickly understood how little they could prove. It was a golden opportunity for her.

And she grabbed it.

Finally, after thirty-two years, she could tell the whole story, her way. To what she believed to be a sympathetic audience. That was when she opened up.

She told them everything, but from her perspective. How she'd been betrayed, and used, by the man she'd loved for so long. How she'd finally got even with him. All of it accompanied by floods of tears. Some of which were probably genuine.

The reality was, they had nothing on her. Nothing they could prove, at least. And Belle knew it. Which made them an audience who couldn't do a thing about anything she told them.

She was right about that, too. It was extremely frustrating. But Belle Darrow knew exactly what she was doing. She'd won.

Or so she thought. There was one thing Belle hadn't anticipated.

Josiah Randall had come through for them yet again. And they had one card left to play.

Ned Partridge, the man they suspected of killing Robert "Beau" Brody, aka Thomas Robertson, had agreed to talk to them when they returned to Vancouver. He was already serving a life sentence for a number of murders. He had very little to lose by talking to them. Or so they hoped.

They boarded the BX Express sleigh the following morning, in a snowstorm. Headed home.

CHAPTER 75

Monday, December 10, 1900

It was early evening when the four of them stepped down from the train at the station in Vancouver. Emily had never been so happy to see that familiar sight in her life. As they stood waiting for their luggage to be brought out, she wanted to hug the engine that had brought them all this way, embrace a lamp post or two.

And kiss Granville silly. Though that would have to wait until they arrived home.

Home. To Granville's house. Which would be her house too. She'd never again sleep under her parents' roof. She had her own roof now. A husband. A life.

She felt like pinching herself, but Granville would want to know why, and she'd feel foolish telling him she was so happy it scared her.

Except that he'd understand. He'd proved that to her, day after day, as they worked to solve their terrible, awful, almost finished case.

She felt a little nervous, too, at the idea of going home with him. Which was truly ridiculous. They had been living together as husband and wife for six weeks now. There was nothing to be nervous about.

Still. They'd sleep in their own house tonight. Wake up there, together, in the morning.

And Bertie would have the breakfast ready. She smiled, thinking of the day she'd asked him to come work for them, she had offered to call him by his Chinese name, but he was adamant he didn't want to give up Bertie.

"You chose it for me, Miss Emily," he said.

It felt like an honor, and she'd been so glad he was going to work for them, to take care of the house and… Wait. He would have got in groceries for them, but could he even cook? Or would she be expected to do so?

Were there enough sheets? Would he know to make up the beds? What about heating the house? Getting in firewood. Had she asked too much of him?

Her brilliant notion of hiring Bertie to get the house set up ready for their return now seemed filled with problems.

Then she remembered the night she and Granville had camped in the snow in the intimacy of that small tent, and smiled. If the house was cold, or they had to hunt for clean sheets, they would do so. The two of them, together. They could even make coffee and cook eggs for breakfast. Probably.

And after breakfast, she would be Mrs. Granville, but she would still go into the office with him, just as she had when she was Miss Turner. And she'd do her job, while he did his.

While she was lost in thought, their luggage had arrived, and Scott had hailed a couple of hackney carriages. Luggage had been loaded, destinations sorted out, then Granville gave her a hand as she stepped up into the cab.

As their hack drove through the quiet streets, Emily squeezed Granville's arm, and thought how lucky she was to be his wife.

And then the doubt crept back. She was Mrs. Granville now, with all that meant, in a town where people knew her. Knew she had eloped. Would be watching and questioning.

To say nothing of Mama's questions. And plans.

Suddenly Emily felt very young. And a little queasy.

Then she reminded herself that in the morning Granville and Scott would be asking questions of the killer, while she and Trent put together their report on the case. Then all four of them would meet with the client. To finally close this impossible case.

She felt a beat of pride at the knowledge. Somehow, they had pulled out the answers to questions that should have been asked thirty-two years ago, and made sense of their quagmire of a case. And she'd been a part of the team, every step of the way.

No-one judged her or asked impossible questions when she was working.

And society with its questions could go hang. Which was rude, but it amused her. And gave her perspective.

This was her life now. The life she'd chosen. And the ring on her finger gave her a kind of social power that she'd never have been allowed as an unmarried girl. A power she could ignore or make use of, as she chose.

The more confident she felt that her life was hers to shape, the fewer people would question it.

The idea nearly stopped her in her tracks. Was that how Mama managed to get away with the things she did?

Oh, this was going to be fun.

CHAPTER 76

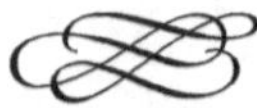

On Tuesday morning, Granville walked Emily to the office at eight, then he and Scott caught the trolley to New Westminster. By 9:30, they were sitting in the penitentiary's dismal little waiting room, waiting for a killer.

Granville wasn't sure what strings Randall had pulled to make this happen, but he didn't care. Once Partridge had agreed to speak with them, the sheriff and both sets of lawyers had agreed, so the warden had gone along with it.

He just hoped they'd learn a few key answers, before their meeting with Stephen Robertson that afternoon. Especially since their client was traveling from San Francisco to hear that report in person.

No matter what Partridge did or didn't tell him, they would be closing the Robertson case this afternoon. Their client had hired them to find out what had happened to his missing father, thirty-two years before. And they had done that.

They now knew that Thomas Robertson was dead. They knew where, when and how he'd died. And who had killed him. Though they couldn't prove it.

They still didn't know why he'd died, though. Not for sure.

Though they had strong suspicions. Strong enough that Granville was prepared to share them with their client. If Stephen Robertson wanted to hear them.

Which was a big if, given the poor light those suspicions cast on his late father.

Whether Robertson wanted the full truth or not, Granville would feel less than satisfied with this case if they didn't have all of those answers to give him. Even though the case was thirty-two years cold. And he knew the others felt the same way.

Regardless of whether their client chose to hear them, their team of four would prefer to have uncovered all of the answers about Thomas Robertson's death.

He didn't trust anything either Dunham or Mrs. Darrow had told them. Not without some kind of verification.

He was hoping Partridge would be able to give them that, at least.

It was a long shot. But it was worth the risk. If the killer was willing to answer their questions.

Granville and Scott waited nearly half an hour for Ned Partridge to be brought in, handcuffed and chained. He was seated opposite them, and his chains attached to a heavy steel loop driven into the cement floor. Then the two heavily armed guards left the room and took up their post just outside the door.

Granville considered the multiple murderer across the table with interest. So this was Brody's killer. Which made him the man who had killed Stephen Robertson's father. And maybe he was also the one who could give them the answers they needed.

Ned Partridge's resemblance to Mal Hissop was marked. Partridge was the same height and coloring, and his facial features were similar. He was thicker through the shoulders and body than his nephew, and his face bore the marks of time.

For all his suspicious behavior, though, Hissop was no killer. And the man in front of them was.

Granville could see it in Partridge's eyes, in the way he assessed them at a glance. He'd seen it before. Even though this fellow had been locked up for more than thirty years, he still looked like a killer.

Despite the fact that he was watching them with curiosity.

Which was interesting. That interest could serve them well.

"I don't get a lot of visitors wanting to talk about a thirty year old case when I'm already doing a life sentence," Partridge said. "And my memory's not so good these days."

A flash of humor in his eyes told Granville that was a lie. Partridge would play them if he could.

But he might also tell them at least some of what they needed to know. Especially if he was interested in what they had to say.

He'd take those odds.

It turned out Partridge was happy to talk about part of the case. With nothing to lose, the convicted killer had been quite forthcoming. He confirmed it was Brody's body they'd dragged from the river, complete with his own signature two shots to the heart.

"Too bad, that. I didn't expect anyone to make the connection, if they found him at all. After I tossed his body in the river, that current would've taken it a long way downstream from where I shot him." Partridge said with a grin. "Brody was going by Thompson at the time, too. Jeremiah Thompson. The fool. Like no-one could find him just 'cause he changed his name."

But when it came to questions about Belle, Partridge changed the subject, wouldn't say a word against her.

Dunham, however, was given no such consideration. Apparently Partridge didn't much like the fellow, either. "Yellow-bellied little weasel" was the nicest term he used as he confirmed that Dunham had killed Greer.

"Shot him in the back. Then cut him up. Pure greed. The fool was afraid he'd get cut out of the gold," he'd said. "Stupid, too. Brody was the one he should have worried about, not Greer."

"And who should Brody have been worried about?" Granville asked him. "You? Or Belle Darrow?"

That earned him nothing but a shrug.

Granville considered the man sitting across the table, seemingly nonchalant despite the chains he wore.

If you are a poker player, and serious about it, you learn to read your opponents. Beginners think it's the cards that matters. The ones who win, though? They know it's all about your opponents.

What cards was Partridge holding close?

And what might be more important to him than avenging Belle's supposed betrayal at another man's hands?

Everything Granville had learned on this case ran through his mind; all the players, all their connections. And he knew.

Deadpan, he played the card that Partridge would never expect. And waited, watching the convict's weathered face freeze.

Got him.

CHAPTER 77

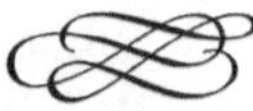

AT 3:30 THAT AFTERNOON, MISS RIZZO USHERED STEPHEN Robertson into their nicely appointed meeting room. Granville met their client with a smile and an outstretched hand.

"Robertson. Glad to see you made it," he said. "I'd like to introduce the others who worked on your case with me. My partner, Sam Scott. My wife and key investigator, Emily Granville. And our junior detective, Trent Davis."

Then he hid a smile as Trent beamed at his new title, one he'd earned on this case. Despite his attitude, he had the making of a good detective.

Their client nodded acknowledgement of each name, politely said, "Ma'am. Scott. Davis," but Granville could see he was struggling with unexpectedly being faced by all four of them. It was news Robertson would undoubtedly have preferred to receive in private, but Granville had his reasons for including them.

"You found him?" Robertson demanded before Granville had a chance to explain. "You found my father?"

"We did. Though I'm sorry to say it isn't the news that any of us hoped we'd find."

"He's dead, then." Robertson sounded as if he'd taken a

sudden blow. He must have still hoped, despite everything, that his boy could get to know his grandfather.

"I'm afraid so," Granville said.

"You're sure it was my father?"

"Very." Granville waited a moment to let their client absorb the impact. "We tracked him down beyond any doubt, under the false name he was using at the time. I'd be pleased to give you all of the details, if you decide you want to hear them. It's why I've included the entire investigative team in this meeting."

"All four of you journeyed to Barkerville?" Robertson sounded surprised.

"We did. And all four of us followed your father's trail, both during his time in Barkerville, and after he left there, until his death in November of 1868."

"He died not long after the last letter we received from him, then?"

"He did."

"Why do I feel I won't like what you uncovered about how he died?"

"Because no man would want to hear such news of his own father."

"Not just dead, then. And not a hero, either, I'm guessing."

"No." Granville said, and waited for the fellow's answer.

Robertson clearly wrestled with the decision for a moment or two. Then his lips thinning and his jaw firming, he leaned forward.

"I want to know. I've spent too many year missing my father, wondering about him, and why he never returned. Now that there are answers, I need to hear them. All of them."

"Very well," Granville said. And proceeded to tell Robertson what they'd learned about his father.

"He changed his name to Brody? And was nicknamed Beau?"

"He did, and he was. He presented himself as a much younger man, and was accepted as such."

Their client shook his head. "I find that hard to reconcile with the man I remember my father to be."

"So did we," Scott said. "In fact, we followed the trails from his letters and drawings for nearly a week before we first heard of Brody. None of the old timers recognized the photo you'd given us. Even the ones we later found out had known Brody swore they didn't recognize him from the photograph."

"But… how?"

"Your father seems to have been something of a chameleon," Granville told him. "He changed a great deal more than his name when he left your farm, seeming to become a different person."

"How is that possible?"

"He started with the obvious changes. Your father was heavily bearded, Brody was clean-shaven. Your father stood and walked stiffly, Brody had an easy stance and gait. Most of the differences seem to have been in his personality and mannerisms, though.

Your father was a serious man. People turned to him as a leader. Brody was accepted as a good fellow, an addition to any gathering. But a lightweight."

Robertson frowned and sat back in his chair, visibly struggling to accept this version of the man his ten-year-old self remembered his father to have been.

"And your father re-invented himself again when he left Barkerville," Granville added.

"Another name? But why change it then? He was coming home." A glance. "Wasn't he?"

There was a hint of resignation in his voice now.

"I'm afraid not. He already had a new identity in place."

"I see. Where exactly was he killed?"

"Just outside of 150 Mile House, on the Cariboo Wagon Road."

"That's quite a way from Barkerville.

Yes. It's a journey of at least a day. Longer, if the weather is bad."

"And my father wasn't using the name Brody when he was killed? Or his own name?"

"No, he wasn't. He took another name for a short time, but mostly he was Jeremiah Thompson."

Thanks to Partridge stalking Brody for a few days before ambushing him, they now had a name for Emily's theorized Mr. X.

Robertson's jaw grew harder still. "What was my father doing there? Tell me all of it," he said, his voice flat.

"I'll need to start back a bit," Granville said. "And I'm afraid I have more difficult news for you. Before he left Washington State, your father was not exactly a failed rancher."

"Not? What was he then?" Robertson asked sharply.

Granville explained briefly about what they'd learned about Thomas Robertson from the Pinkerton's, once they realized they were not simply looking for a missing miner.

"Foster from Pinkerton's Seattle office said to tell you he'd be happy to review their file on your father with you. If you wish."

Robertson, still looking stunned, just nodded. "So my father was a crook. One with a price on his head. And he was hiding out in Barkerville?" he asked after a moment.

"It seems so. Once in Barkerville, he took a new name, a new profession and a new love interest. A dancehall girl known as Belle. Who is still in Barkerville. Mrs. Darrow, as she is now known, is the region's postmistress."

Their client swallowed hard. "I see. This is the first time I've ever been glad my mother has passed on."

Since he didn't seem to have any more questions, Granville continued, briefly explaining how they'd uncovered the connection between Robertson, Senior and Robert "Beau" Brody.

"At that point we still thought of your father as a miner. Which was confirmed by those we spoke to who had known him. Including Mrs. Darrow.

However, we came to realize that Beau Brody had no interest in mining gold from underground. It was far easier to acquire that gold from those who had already done the hard work of bringing it to the surface."

Their client's face was rigid, every muscle held under tight control. "Go on," he said.

"He seemed to have pursued a number of possible sources of easy money. Including blackmail. But he eventually came up with a complex plan to steal gold dust and nuggets from a local bank, using arson as a cover."

"Arson?" Stephen Robertson shook his head slowly, as if in disbelief. Then suddenly his face changed.

"1868 was the year that Barkerville burnt to the ground. We even heard about it in Seattle. But my father had left Barkerville by then. Surely he wasn't involved…?"

"I'm afraid he was the man behind it," Granville said. "And he put together a gang of four to carry it out. Including Belle."

Robertson appeared to have gone beyond shock by now. "Tell me," was all he said.

Granville did so, as succinctly as possible.

At one point Stephen Robertson stared at him. "My father did all that to burn the town to the ground? But why?"

"Gold," Granville said. "Though he may not have expected the whole town to burn. The bank across from the dancehall was the target. It was the second building to burn. The manager and his staff had just enough time to move most of their paperwork to a place of safety near the river.

In the confusion, Brody's accomplice managed to change the recipient name on the destination documents for a shipment of gold dust and nuggets. The change went undiscovered in the chaos after the fire, and the gold was shipped to the banks' Quesnel branch the following day."

"Who was this accomplice?

Thanks to Partridge's information, Granville was able to answer that without hesitation. "A miner and former thief named Dunham. Like your father, he was hiding out in Barkerville. And looking for the easy way out."

Robertson just nodded. "Go on."

"Another member of the gang, a fellow named Greer, was the recipient of the shipment. He moved the gold into a safety deposit box in Quesnel. Then a week later Greer moved moved the gold again to a box owned by one Jeremiah Thompson."

"My father?" their client asked.

Granville nodded. "Greer gave your father the key to Thompson's box, and five days later closed out his own deposit box. Thus confusing any possible trail even further.

Due to the chaos caused by the fire, no one seems to have realized that so many bags of gold dust were missing for quite some time. When the cry was finally raised, they only name they had was Greer's. That search had barely begun when a man carrying Greer's card was brutally murdered just outside of Quesnel."

"My father," Robertson said in a flat voice.

"That was our first thought, as well. But no, it really was Greer. And he'd been murdered in a uniquely ugly way by Dunham, the gang member from Barkerville."

"Did Dunham confess?"

"Quite the opposite, I'm afraid. He accused your father of doing the foul deed. Apparently because your father ended up with most of the gold."

"Then how do you know Dunham's the murderer?"

"Because Mrs. Darrow…"

"The girlfriend."

"Yes, your father's former girlfriend. She identified Dunham as Greer's murderer.

"And you trust her statement?"

"Not on its own, no. But this morning Scott and I were able to speak with another member of your father's gang, one serving a life sentence for multiple murders. With nothing to lose, he confirmed that Dunham had killed Greer."

"I see. Which left my father in possession of a fortune in gold dust, I gather?"

"It did."

"Whatever happened to that gold?"

"No-one knows. Our best guess is that your father hid it somewhere near 150 Mile House, where he was staying at the time. Most likely buried it. There is still a lot of desolate country in that area. That gold could be anywhere."

CHAPTER 78

JUST THEN MISS RIZZO BROUGHT IN A TRAY OF TEA AND gingersnaps. It was a welcome break for all of them, but particularly their client. Robertson's eyes looked tired and sad. It had to be hard for him, hearing about his father's life and death. And in such a complicated case, too. Nothing was straightforward.

His team was tired, too. They'd only got in last night, and all of them had been working on the report while on the train from Ashcroft for most of the previous day. And they brought only hard news for their client.

Once the tea had been poured and doctored and the cookies passed around, Miss Rizzo left, closing the door softly behind her. Before Granville could speak up, Robertson did so.

"So who killed my father? And when? This Dunham?" their client demanded. Apparently he had grown impatient with the convoluted tale, and he wanted answers. Now.

It was understandable. Granville decided he'd probably feel the same way, if he hadn't spent so much time chasing nearly invisible clues. At least Robertson looked a little better for the tea.

"Your father was killed less than two weeks after the murder of Greer," Granville said. " Shot twice in the heart and dumped in the nearest river."

"It was November. Wasn't the river frozen?"

"Not yet. It had been a mild fall. In any case, I'm afraid your father's body washed downstream and ended up along the bank, where ice was just beginning to form. His bones were only found after the river receded a bit the following summer. And his remains were never identified."

"How do you know any of this, then? If no-one identified the body."

"We built the case detail by detail. When we realized that your father had likely been killed somewhere near 150 Mile House…"

"How did you know that?" their client asked skeptically.

Granville explained about the post office box, and what they had pieced together. "At that point we didn't know for sure who had killed him."

"But someone from Barkerville?"

"His death was triggered by that telegram to Barkerville. Yes. And we talked with the local constables in Quesnel. There was only one unsolved murder in the 150 Mile area at that time, that matched your father's height and weight."

"They kept the bones from a thirty-two year old murder?"

"They did. And the two bullets that were found with them as well."

"Is that enough to identify him for sure?"

"Only checking his dental records will do that. If they still exist. And I wanted your permission first."

"Then do it. I'll get you the name of his doctor from back then," Robertson said. "But who shot him?"

"A local gun for hire. And the fourth member of your father's gang. Name of Partridge. Ned Partridge. He's currently doing several lifetimes in maximum security in New Westminster for a string of murders. And his pattern was to shoot his victims in the heart. Twice. Using the same caliber of gun as killed your father."

"So he's already paying for what he did," Robertson said. "Good. But who hired him?"

"Belle Darrow hired him, I'm sorry to say."

"His girlfriend had him killed? Why?" Robertson demanded.

"She was in love with him, or so she says. She was a key part of his whole arson scheme, as well. And by her own admission, she would do anything for him.

In return, she anticipated that once he had his new identity set up, she would join him and they'd begin a new life together. One where she lived like a queen on the gold they'd stolen."

"It was the post office cancellation, wasn't it?" Robertson said heavily. "That tipped her off, I mean."

Their client was a quick one, Granville noted. As his father had probably been.

Though without his father's influence, the son had gone into business—and made a success of it—rather than crime. But the cost of losing his father so young, and never really being sure he was dead? Might have been higher still.

"It was," Granville said. "When Belle, as she was then, got that telegram, she guessed immediately that he intended to vanish into a new identity, taking the gold and leaving her behind. Broke and miserable."

"If she was so broke, how did she manage a hired gun?"

Robertson would have made a good investigator, as well, Granville decided. He could see why the fellow was successful in his businesses—he asked the right questions.

"She was sleeping with him," he said bluntly, with an apologetic glance at his wife. Who looked amused.

It was one of the nuggets Belle Darrow had dropped when they questioned her. Though she'd dismissed him as unimportant compared to her passion for "her Robby".

A detail that had horrified Emily at the time. "That she could be so uncaring," she'd raged to him that evening. That detail had also proved immensely useful in their conversation with Ned Partridge.

"I thought she was supposed to be in love with my father," their client said harshly.

"She still swears that she was. And she certainly mourned him as if that were true. But she'd been quietly 'entertaining' Partridge for the odd weekend when Beau was out of town. Which was often."

And it had been going on for at least a couple of years before Brody's murder. But Granville saw no reason to mention that.

"Some love," Robertson said bitterly. "Betrayed him with a hired killer whenever his back was turned."

"It gets worse, I'm afraid. Partridge was living with her when that telegram came in. And he left for 150 Mile House the following day. Early."

"So her reaction to that telegram was white hot rage."

"Ice cold fury would be my read on her."

"Same difference."

"Possibly. Though in my experience, cold fury doesn't burn off. This woman kept up a charade of having lost her only love for thirty-two years."

"Ah. Though if it was such a good front, how were you able to verify all of this?"

"She told us everything. In floods of tears, I might add. Called it a moment of madness, said that when she eventually "came to her senses", as she put it, Partridge had already left, gun in hand."

"She implicated herself? But why? What did you have on her?"

"Nothing we could prove. Not at that point. And she knew it. Delighted in it, I think, despite her fake tears.

After all this time, she finally could explain her cleverness to an interested audience. One who couldn't do a thing about anything she told them. Us.

It was extremely frustrating, let me tell you. But she knew exactly what she was doing."

"Wait. You said you couldn't prove anything "at that point.""

Do you mean you have something now?" Robertson frowned at him. Then his eyes widened. "Partridge talked, didn't he?"

"He did."

"I'm surprised he didn't defend the dancehall girl that seemed to have everyone wrapped around her finger."

"He did. Swore nothing would make him turn on her."

"How did you convince him?

"Since Partridge is in jail for life, there wasn't much we could use to get him to talk. And though Belle's dismissal of their liaison as unimportant clearly upset Partridge, it wasn't quite enough to break thirty years of silence.

But we had learned in Quesnel that he's part of a close knit family. Half of whom have had run-ins with the law. It seems his youngest brother has a major legal problem to face. I offered to take care of it."

"And he agreed? Just on your word?"

Granville smiled. "I offered him the assistance of my lawyer, Josiah Randall. Who is the one who had arranged for us to meet with Partridge this morning.

Apparently Partridge was impressed with Randall's ability to deal with the various and conflicting interests that normally make arranging such a meeting in anything less than ten months impossible."

"Josiah Randall? Oh, well no wonder Partridge agreed, with Randall in the bargain."

While their client reached for another biscuit, eating it slowly as though to buy himself some thinking time, Granville wondered exactly how far their lawyer's well-earned reputation had spread.

"And Partridge confirmed that Belle Darrow, my father's girl-friend, ordered his murder?" Robertson said after a moment.

"He did. She didn't pay him for it, though, which could prove an issue if you want to pursue the matter in court. We would also need to get a confirmation that the bones are indeed your father's."

"Is Partridge willing to testify to it? In court?"

"Surprisingly, yes," Granville said. "Randall's legal skills made an amazingly effective bribe."

For a fleeting moment, a smile touched Robertson's eyes. "I hope you cleared that with Randall first. It would be... unfortunate to lose such a lawyer over this."

"Of course," Granville said, not betraying his own amusement. Robertson would have been surprised to hear Randall's reaction. And even more surprised by Granville's suspicion that their lawyer would be a little disappointed if they didn't send odd legal entanglements his way from time to time.

Then Robertson was all business again. "So I now know when my father died. And who killed him.

And that Mrs. Darrow had her lover murder my father, because my father didn't keep his bargain with her. He was leaving, and taking the life he'd promised her with him. Is that right?"

"That sums it up."

"Ice cold indeed," Robertson said. He paused. "Which I suppose also applied to my father. They were well-matched."

"I liked her," Emily said unexpectedly. "Belle Darrow, I mean. When I met her, and she told me about your father, whom she called "her Robby", I felt sorry for her. And even admired her a little. I still think that love she described to me was real. And that she gave him as much love as she was capable of.

Perhaps the same as your father did with you.

They neither of them were capable of giving more. And they were both very good at appearing to be more than they were."

Robertson nodded slowly. "From what I remember of my father, I think you might be right. Thank you. It helps to think that the father I looked up to did love me. In his way."

The meeting ended shortly after that. Granville gave him the report he'd prepared, Robertson handed Granville a check. Then he shook hands all around.

"If I decide to pursue the matter of Mrs. Darrow, I will want to hire you again. In any case I would recommend your firm to anyone," their client said. "And my thanks to all of you for finding my father for me. And for answering the questions that had plagued me for years. Even though and he wasn't the man I thought he was, he was my father. "

And once his identity is confirmed, I'll be bringing his remains home for burial beside my mother. Who also loved him, despite everything, and who would have wanted that."

CHAPTER 79

As they left the meeting, Granville invited them all to join him for dinner. A celebration for the Barkerville team, as he put it. And he'd scheduled a dinner for the entire team on Thursday, to celebrate the completion of a challenging case. And to thank the home team, as he insisted on calling them, for all the work they too had done.

Emily had laughed at his calling them teams, as if they were lacrosse players or some such thing. But she had a feeling the terms would stick. They were useful, for one thing. And there was a sense of belonging that left her with a warm feeling inside.

None of the others said anything, though Scott rolled his eyes. But she suspected they felt the same way.

As she strolled with Granville towards Garrity's Steak House —because of course the men thought that more steak was called for—she tucked her hand in the crook of his arm. "It feels odd to be back home, doesn't it?"

"I suspect more so for you than for me," he said. "I came back to the same house, while you live with me now, instead of with your parents. A huge improvement in my book."

And he smiled at her while her knees threatened to melt.

"I quite like it, myself," she said, giving him a teasing look. "This bed is much more comfortable."

"Well, I'm glad the bed pleases you," he said, his emphasis transforming her words into something else entirely.

Emily fought back her blush at his suggestive tone. and was pleased with herself when she managed it.

"You say that now," she said. "But tomorrow we are dining with my parents. And Mama will have a few comments. Not to mention questions. For both of us."

He gave her a knowing look and that grin she couldn't resist. "I look forward to it. After all, we're married, so she won't have a wedding to arrange."

"It was my wedding," Emily muttered.

"Of course it was," he told her.

"And you don't believe a word of that."

"Of course I don't. I have met your mother, you know."

She tried for a scowl and somehow it dissolved into a joyous smile that matched how she felt inside.

"Besides, our case is now finished.

"Our soul sucking mud pool of a case?" she offered.

"That's the one. Our client is satisfied."

"He didn't look all that satisfied."

"Who could blame him? It wasn't easy news that we brought him. Still, now he knows what really happened to his father. A question that haunted him so strongly he hired us to answer it, thirty-two years later."

"And he learned more than he'd expected about who his father really was," she said soberly.

"I suspect he still prefers that to the ghosts that were all he had before. Or at least he will prefer it, in time. And I wanted to thank you for finding the right words, earlier."

Since she knew which words he referred to, she simply held his arm a little more tightly. "I'm glad you suggested this dinner. It wasn't an easy case. It will be good to talk over every detail again, now that we know how they all fit together."

She paused. "And that they actually do fit together, and we're not just chasing will-o'-the-wisps."

"Soul sucking mud pool…" he said softly, and grinned when she lightly punched his arm.

"We'll have fun, you wait and see," she said.

"I can see we'll end being there until they turn out the lights."

She nodded. "Maybe even longer. But can you believe it's only two weeks until Christmas Day?"

"I can. I made you a promise we'd be back in time, and for a few days there I thought we weren't going to make it."

"Really? I couldn't tell."

"Believe me. We had your mother to account to, after all."

She laughed at that, and then they reached the restaurant, and joined Scott and Trent inside. It was a good evening, sharing laughter along with stories of their frustrating case. Granville offered champagne, but Scott and Trent were happy with beer, while she and Granville enjoyed a particularly nice Cabernet.

It was fascinating to discuss "the Barkerville murders" as the case had become, now that they knew what really happened. In fact, they started back at the beginning and discussed each clue as it had arisen. Turning it into a contest to see if any of them could identify a way to get an answer to that specific clue earlier than they had done at the time.

By the end of the evening, they had all agreed that Brody had been an unscrupulous crook who treated women horribly, but he had a complex mind and might have been an interesting addition to a dinner party.

"As long as you never believed a word he said," Emily added.

At which the other three burst out laughing. She felt a little miffed for a moment, but it wasn't really aimed at her. And they hadn't spent time with Belle like she had.

The postmistress might not have much in the way of morals, and the fact that she'd had "her Robby" killed made Emily feel sick to her stomach every time she thought about it. Especially because of that hint of smugness, even thirty-two years later, when Belle had told them the full story.

But Brody, with his smooth dancing and smoother lies, had really hurt her. For a moment Emily wondered who Belle might have become if she'd never met the man. Then she let it go.

The case was over, they had solved it, if not exactly resolved it. Belle still went unpunished for Brody's murder, after all.

Or maybe not, Emily thought as she pictured the pain on the woman's face as she told the story of her life with "her Robby". Long gone now, and as much her doing as his.

Whatever. It was time to move on. There would be another case to challenge them tomorrow.

And tonight, she'd go home with Granville. To their home, and the life they were building together.

Except for the part where they were having dinner with her parents, and she'd have to explain, in person, why she'd chosen to elope. And then there was the wedding party Mama had decided Emily and Granville needed to hold. The Friday before Christmas, thank you very much. It would be a disaster. She reached for her wine.

Then Trent said something about the night they'd camped along Lightning Creek, and Granville made a crack that had Scott guffawing. And Emily could clearly see them all around that campfire, trading jokes and cooking over the coals and drinking beer in the snow. And knew the memory of the trip to Barkerville would never leave her.

If she could do that, if she and Granville could survive that sludge pool of a case on their honeymoon? And if the four of them, the Barkerville team, could find the answers to a case that was so cold it had frozen solid? Then they, all of them, could survive anything.

Even Mama's ideas for a combined engagement and wedding dinner party. One that Emily and Granville were supposed to host. To Mama's plan, of course.

She grinned, and raised her glass. Across the table Granville caught the motion, and raised his glass to her in return. And Emily winked at him.

Mama hadn't seen either of them since before their wedding,

she realized. Before they'd spent so many days and nights together, in what Clara's eighty year old Grandmama would call "somewhat trying circumstances."

Mama didn't know what she was letting herself in for.